Nonverbal Communications

Codes

Written by
Nigel Nelson

Illustrated by
Tony De Saulles

Thomson Learning

New York

Books in the series

Body Talk
Codes
Signs and Symbols
Writing and Numbers

Picture acknowledgments
British Telecommunications 14; C.M. Dixon 6 (left); Eye Ubiquitous 10; Daniel
Pangbourne *cover*, 6 (right), 8, 27 (all), 28; Tony Stone Worldwide 20 (Lester
Lerkowitz), 23 (Stacy Pickerell), 29 (top, Andrew Sacks), 29 (bottom,
Poulides/Thatcher); Topham Picture Library 9 (bottom), 19, 22; Wayland Picture
Library 13; Zefa 4, 9 (top), 16, 18 (top); Zul: Chapel Studios 5, 18 (bottom), 21.

First published in the
United States by
Thomson Learning
115 Fifth Avenue
New York, NY 10003

First published in 1993 by
Wayland (Publishers) Ltd.

Library of Congress Cataloging-in-Publication Data applied for

ISBN 1-56847-157-2

Printed in Italy

Contents

Words that are printed in **bold** are explained in the glossary.

What is a code?

A code is any set of words, letters, colors, numbers, or signs that has a special meaning. Codes are useful for keeping things secret. If you want to send a secret message to a friend, you can use a code that only the two of you understand.

But not all codes are secret codes. Codes are used every day as a quick and easy way of sending messages. Traffic signs are a type of code. Drivers can understand this traffic sign even if they cannot understand the written message.

A zip code uses letters and numbers to stand for the town and the street where the letter is being sent.

Mr. P. Wilson
525 Blacksmith Lane
Apartment 13B
Staten Island, NY 10319

Zip codes make the task of sorting letters much easier.

The first codes

Long ago, people who went on trips to unknown areas would leave marks, or tracks, along the way. These tracks warned of dangers or showed which way to go. They were a sort of code for the people who later walked along the same path.

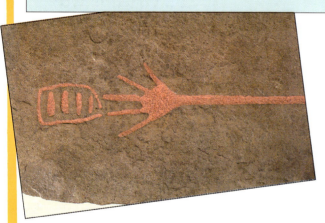

Tracks may have been simple signs scratched into rocks. This sign was made thousands of years ago.

Sometimes tracks were made by using things found in nature, such as sticks and rocks. These children are making a track from branches and flowers.

Activity

Leave a trail around your house or yard. You can make your tracks with pieces of paper, twigs, or small stones. Use the signs shown here to leave a trail leading to a little gift or a secret message.

 = go straight on

 = turn right

 = turn left

 = don't go this way

 = end of trail

In the fairy tale of Hansel and Gretel, what tracks did Hansel leave behind as they went into the forest? What was his mistake?

Color codes

Colors are sometimes used as a quick sorting code. Many school libraries use a color code to show where books on a certain subject can be found. A number code then helps you to find the exact book you want.

The colored shirt and cap that a **jockey** wears is a sort of code. They tell people at a glance who owns the horse the jockey is riding.

Traffic lights use a simple color code. Red means stop; green means go; and yellow means that the lights are about to change.

Say it with flags

Flags are a good way of sending messages over a short distance. The international flag code is used on ships all around the world. Each flag has a pattern that stands for a different letter or number. Some flags have special meanings. The flag for "P," which is called Blue Peter, means a ship is about to leave the harbor.

A code book explains the flag code in many different languages. This means that ship captains who speak different languages can still send messages to each other using the flag code.

Activity

This ship is showing the Blue Peter flag as it leaves the harbor. Use the international flag code shown here to make up your own message.

Semaphore

Semaphore is another way of using flags to send messages. But with semaphore, only two flags are used. The flags are held in a certain position for each letter of the alphabet.

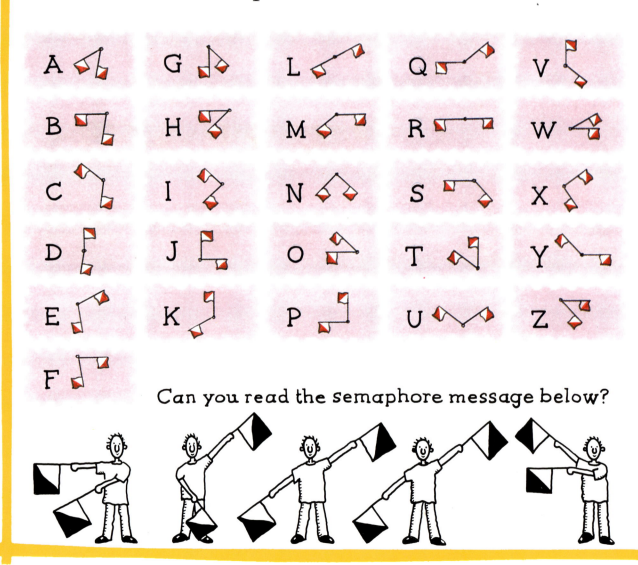

Can you read the semaphore message below?

Semaphore was first used in France about 200 years ago. A line of semaphore towers, each with large moving wooden arms, was built on hilltops. The position of the wooden arms was changed to spell out a message. These semaphore signals could be seen from a long distance. The message was then passed on from tower to tower.

Morse code

The Morse code is made up of dots and dashes. These two signs are combined in different ways to stand for each letter of the alphabet. The first Morse code messages were sent by using telegraph wires. Today, Morse code is usually sent as a radio signal using long and short buzzes. This man is sending a Morse code message by radio.

A • —	H • • • •	O — — —	V • • • —
B — • • •	I • •	P • — — •	W • — —
C — • — •	J • — — —	Q — — • —	X — • • —
D — • •	K — • —	R • — •	Y — • — —
E •	L • — • •	S • • •	Z — — • •
F • • — •	M — —	T —	
G — — •	N — •	U • • —	

The most famous Morse code message is SOS. Ships or planes send this message if they need help. These letters were chosen as the help signal because they are easy to understand. Try tapping out the SOS signal on a table.

Activity

Morse code signals can also be sent by using long and short flashes of light. Send a Morse code message to a friend using flashlights in a dark room.

Map codes

Maps can show a lot of information by using **symbols**. But you have to know what the symbols mean. A map usually has a **key** to tell you what the symbols stand for.

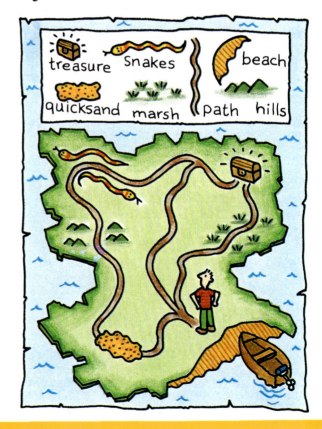

Here is a map of an island with a buried treasure. Use the key to decide which is the safest way to get to the treasure.

Activity

This weather map of the treasure island has no key to tell you what the symbols mean. Try to work out from looking at the symbols what sort of weather you can expect.

heavy rain

showers

cloudy

sunny periods

rough seas

sunshine

Here is a key to explain the symbols used on the weather map. Make up your own symbols for other types of weather.

Letters and numbers

Letters and numbers are special codes used to describe things. Different languages use different words and letters. These Arabic letters are very different from the letters used in the English language.

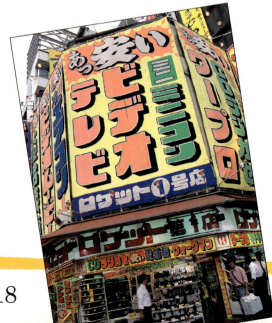

To someone who reads and writes in English, these Japanese words look like a very hard code to **break**.

The words used to describe numbers are different in every language. The French word for the number seven is *sept*; the German word for seven is *sieben*. But when you write the numeral "7," you are using a code to stand for the word "seven." Numerals are symbols, or codes, that everyone can understand, even when they use different words to describe the same number.

The speed limit on this highway is understood by all drivers, even if they do not speak the same language.

Talking to computers

Computers do many smart things. But they do not "think" the way we do and they do not understand our language. In order to "talk" to a computer, the information has to be put into a special code that the computer can understand. This code is called a binary code, and it is made up of just two signals: "on" and "off." The millions of **electronic signals** that pass through the computer are switched either "on" or "off." This picture shows the inside of a computer.

The on-and-off binary code is used to describe words, numbers, and even pictures to the computer. When the computer has finished its tasks, it turns the information back into words and numbers these children can understand.

Bar codes

Many of the things you buy have bar codes on them. A bar code is a row of thick and thin black lines. All the food in this picture is marked with bar codes. Find the bar code on this book.

The computer at the supermarket checkout counter can "read" bar codes. Each line of the bar code tells the computer something about the item. When the item is passed through the checkout, the bar code tells the computer what it is and what it costs. The computer sends this information to the **cash register**, where the price of the item is shown. If the price of something is changed, the computer is told the new price for things with that bar code.

Spies and secrets

Sometimes it is important that messages are kept secret. In times of war, sending secret messages can be a matter of life and death. Spies pass on information about the enemy by using codes that are very difficult to break.

A code book shows the **spy** how to change his or her message into a code. The person who is being sent the message has a copy of the same book. The code book is then used to **decode** the message and find out what it says.

Activity

Here is a simple code. A sign is used to stand for each letter of the alphabet.

A	B	C	D	E	F	G	H	I	J	K	L	M

N	O	P	Q	R	S	T	U	V	W	X	Y	Z

Use the code to decode this secret message.

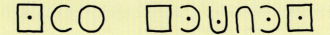

A secret code of the past

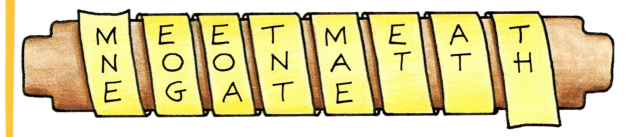

A long time ago, the **ancient Greeks** used a scytale to send secret messages. A scytale was a stick of a certain shape and size. A piece of **parchment** was wound around the scytale. The message was then written on the parchment along the length of the stick.

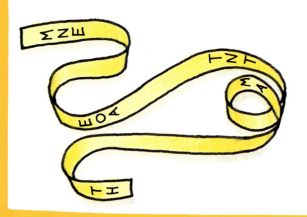

The parchment was unwound and sent to someone else. The message on the unwound parchment did not make sense.

To read the message, the parchment had to be wrapped around a scytale of exactly the same size and shape as the one used to write the message. So, the only person who could read the message was someone with exactly the same scytale.

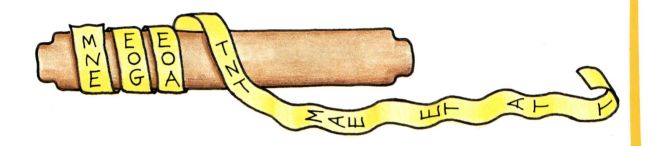

Activity Make your own scytale and send a secret message to a friend.

Making it safe

Codes are very useful for keeping things safe. Some locks can be opened only if you know a secret code number. This girl knows from memory the only numbers that will open her bicycle lock.

This bicycle lock is called a combination lock because it can be opened only if the correct series, or combination, of numbers is moved into the right place in the lock.

Safes also use combination locks. You can turn the dials to make thousands of different combinations of numbers, but only one combination of numbers will open the safe.

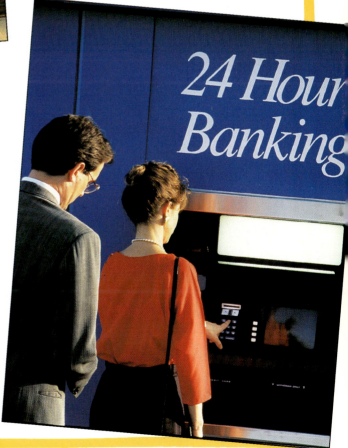

This woman is using her own secret code number to get money out of this automated teller machine. The code number tells the machine that this card belongs to this person. The machine then gives her money from her bank account.

Glossary

Ancient Belonging to times long past.

Break To work out, or solve, a code.

Cash Register A machine behind store counters where money is kept. A cash register also shows the price of a thing that is being sold.

Decode To work out what a coded message means.

Electronic signal A signal made by using electricity.

Greeks The people who live in Greece.

Jockey A person who rides a horse in a horse race.

Key A chart that explains the symbols on a map.

Parchment The skin of an animal, usually a sheep or a goat, that has been dried and stretched. Parchment was used in the past as a sort of paper.

Safe A strong locked box or room used to store valuable things.

Spy A person who secretly watches other people to gather information.

Symbol A mark or a sign that stands for something else.

Books to read

Albert, Burton, Jr. *Code Busters!* Morton Grove, Ill.: Albert Whitman & Co., 1985.

Albert, Burton, Jr. *Top Secret! Codes to Crack.* Morton Grove, Ill.: Albert Whitman & Co., 1987.

Broekel, Ray. *Maps and Globes.* New True Books. Chicago: Childrens Press, 1983.

Janecko, Paul B. *Loads of Codes and Secret Ciphers.* New York: Macmillan Children's Book Group, 1984.

Kerby, Mona. *Samuel Morse.* First Books. New York: Franklin Watts, 1991.

Nelson, Nigel. *Signs and Symbols.* Nonverbal Communications. New York: Thomson Learning, 1993.

Nelson, Nigel. *Writing and Numbers.* Nonverbal Communications. New York: Thomson Learning, 1994.

Travis, F. *Spy's Guidebook.* Tulsa, Okla: EDC Publishing, 1978.

Index

Becoming a Nurse

Making the Transition to Practice

Becoming a Nurse

Making the Transition to Practice

maria fedoruk | anne hofmeyer

OXFORD
UNIVERSITY PRESS

Oxford University Press is a department of the University of Oxford.
It furthers the University's objective of excellence in research,
scholarship, and education by publishing worldwide. Oxford is a registered
trademark of Oxford University Press in the UK and in certain other
countries.

Published in Australia by
Oxford University Press
253 Normanby Road, South Melbourne, Victoria 3205, Australia

National Library of Australia Cataloguing-in-Publication data

Author: Fedoruk, Maria.
Title: Becoming a nurse: making the transition to practice/Maria Fedoruk.

ISBN: 9780195569292 (pbk.)

Notes: Includes bibliographical references and index.
Subjects: Nurses–Training of.
Nursing–Study and teaching.
Medical care–Employees–Training of.
Dewey Number: 610.73

Reproduction and communication for educational purposes

Cover design by Canvas
Typeset by Diacritech, Chennai, India
Edited by Kirstie Innes-Will
Proofread by Venetia Somerset
Indexed by Jeanne Rudd
Printed by Sheck Wah Tong

Foreword

Dr. Rosemary Bryant
Commonwealth Chief Nurse
and Midwifery Officer

I am very pleased to have been asked to write the foreword of this timely and much needed resource.

For too long, graduating from university and beginning work as a registered nurse has been a period of uncertainty and apprehension for new nurses. The first year after graduation is very often a trial by fire, with very rapid assimilation into the working role. These pressures mean that many nurses choose to leave the nursing profession completely after only two years. This is a most unfortunate and avoidable waste for the individual nurse, the profession and the community.

I firmly believe it to be the responsibility of senior nurses to nurture, encourage and teach our junior colleagues. We need to support them in as many ways as possible to ensure that they have the most rewarding, effective and successful career they can. This handing down of knowledge and experience can take many forms. This book will be a very valuable resource, as it fills a gap in current nursing literature gap.

The publication of the book is very timely, considering the current moves to national registration and accreditation of the health professions. Increasingly, nurses are being seen as a national resource.

As well as providing advice and information about nursing practice in current work environments, *Becoming a Nurse* contains valuable chapters on professional career development. With increasingly stretched undergraduate curricula, these vital learning areas are often overlooked or squeezed to the margins of nursing courses. This book provides clear guidance for new graduates on how professional development is essential to remaining competent. Given that many nurses today change their career orientation several times over their working life, the career advice offered is also very welcome.

With significant workforce shortages both in Australia and internationally, it is more important than ever to find ways to support junior nurses. Nursing is a wonderful profession and for those who choose to make it their livelihood, nursing provides deep satisfaction as well as the privilege of working with others at critical times in their lives. I see my career in nursing as the most incredible privilege and one which gives me the opportunity to continually improve and develop, both personally and professionally.

Because of my commitment to nursing and my confidence in the profession's ability to offer the most rewarding of careers, it saddens me that the transition from student to registered nurse is a difficult one for many new graduates. Through its practical advice, quiet reassurance and realistic information on what to expect in the workplace, *Becoming a Nurse* will prove to be a most valuable resource for those embarking on the challenging shift from student to practitioner.

I thoroughly recommend the book to all new graduates.

Rosemary Bryant
Commonwealth Chief Nurse and Midwifery Officer

Contents

List of Abbreviations

ACHS	Australian Council on Healthcare Standards
ACSQH	Australian Commission on Safety and Quality in Healthcare
AHPRA	Australian Health Practitioner Regulation Agency
AIHW	Australian Institute of Health and Welfare
AIMS	Advanced Incident Managing System
AIN	assistant in nursing
ANF	Australian Nursing Federation
ANMC	Australian Nursing and Midwifery Council
ATNA	Australasian Trained Nurses Association
CNS	Clinical Nurse Support
CoP	community of practice
CPD	continuing professional development
EI	emotional intelligence
EAP	employee assistance program
HWA	Health Workforce Australia
ICN	International Council of Nurses
IELTS	International English Language Testing System
ISO	International Organization for Standardization
KPI	key performance indicator
NHA	National Healthcare Agreement
NHHI	National Hand Hygiene Initiative
NHHRC	National Health and Hospitals Reform Commission
NHMRC	National Health and Medical Research Council
NMBA	Nursing and Midwifery Board of Australia
NRA	Nurse Regulatory Authority
OET	Occupational English Test
OHS&W	occupational health, safety and welfare
PCA	personal care attendant
PR&OD	performance review and organisational development
RCNA	Royal College of Nursing Australia
RVTNA	Royal Victorian Trained Nurses Association
SMARTTA	specific, measurable, achievable, realistic, time, trackable, agreed
TPPP	Transition to Professional Practice Program
VET	vocational education and training
WHO	World Health Organization

Contributors

Dr Marion Eckert completed undergraduate training at Flinders University (South Australia). Following graduation Marion completed a number of postgraduate qualifications including a doctoral degree. Marion worked for a period of time in the Joanna Briggs Institute to complete further research and then returned to pursue her passion in direct nursing care at the Royal Adelaide Hospital (SA), becoming the first clinician at the RAH to have the Doctorate of Nursing and be actively working in patient care. Currently Marion is the Director, Nursing and Midwifery Education at Flinders Medical Centre, Southern Adelaide Local Health Network.

Dr Maria Fedoruk RN, PhD has been with the School of Nursing & Midwifery, University of South Australia since 2000 as a lecturer and project officer. Prior to coming to the university she worked in senior management positions in the acute community and aged care sectors. Since 2005 Maria has developed curricula, and been course coordinator/lecturer in the postgraduate and international programs as well as teaching in the undergraduate Bachelor of Nursing program. Maria is an external examiner for the International Medical University (Malaysia). Maria chairs the School of Nursing & Midwifery's OHSW&IM group. Maria also works with the Australian Council on Healthcare standards as an accreditation surveyor.

Ms Elizabeth Grinter holds a Master of Nursing degree and is an experienced nurse and midwife. Currently, Beth is the Program Director for the Bachelor of Midwifery Program at the University of South Australia. In this role, Beth not only administers the Bachelor of Midwifery Program but teaches and coordinates various courses within the program. This year Beth has been directly involved in developing a new curriculum for the Bachelor of Midwifery program to be accredited in 2012. Research interests include E'portfolio development for midwifery undergraduate students.

Dr Anne Hofmeyer holds a PhD and Masters Degree (Primary Health Care) from Flinders University, Adelaide, Australia. In 2004, she completed an Intensive Bioethics Course at the Joseph & Rose Kennedy Institute of Ethics, Georgetown University, Washington DC. In 2005 she was awarded a prestigious Postdoctoral Fellowship funded by the Canadian Health Services Research Foundation (CHSRF) and Canadian Institutes of Health Research (CIHR) CADRE Program and the Knowledge Utilization Studies Program, University of Alberta, Canada. Prior to her academic career, Anne had extensive experience in administration, teaching and clinical environments including community nursing, aged care, radiation oncology and over 15 years in palliative care. Dr Hofmeyer teaches in both the undergraduate and graduate programs and coordinates six courses. She is an active peer reviewer for Australian and international journals, has examined postgraduate masters and doctoral dissertations for Australian and international universities, published widely, and presented papers at state/provincial, national and international conferences.

Lucy Hope graduated from the University of South Australia in 2009 after completing the Bachelor of Nursing program. Following graduation and registration Lucy has worked in both the private and public sectors and has had nursing experience within a broad range of specialties including cardiology, orthopaedic and surgical specialties, and oncology. Currently Lucy is employed at the Royal Adelaide Hospital within the Medical Specialties Unit which includes specialties in immunology, infectious diseases, endocrinology and geriatrics. Her current position affords her a leadership role and allows her to coordinate shifts and mentor and preceptor junior staff members and students on the ward. Lucy's career goals include undertaking further study to specialise in Acute Nursing Science and Infection Control.

Dr Angela Kucia is a Senior Lecturer at the University of South Australia and a Clinical Practice Consultant in acute cardiac assessment at the Lyell McEwin Hospital in South Australia. Angela has worked in clinical, academic and research environments for a number of years and was a clinical nurse manager in a coronary care unit for ten years, working closely with student and graduate nurses in the mentor and preceptor role. Angela works with multidisciplinary research teams in the area of cardiology and presents scientific papers at international cardiac society conferences as well as publishing extensively in this area.

Dr Barbara Parker has worked extensively in the clinical environment, specifically in the areas of anaesthetics and recovery and orthopaedic and urological surgical nursing. She has published in the area of obesity and diabetes and has expertise in gastrointestinal and nutritional physiology as well as expertise in programs in obesity, impaired glucose tolerance and diabetes in both pharmacological and lifestyle interventions. Dr Parker is currently a Program Director in the School of Nursing and Midwifery and teaches within the undergraduate nursing program at the University of South Australia.

Alice Wickett completed her undergraduate studies at the University of South Australia in 2009 and has had clinical placements in the country, acute, teaching and aged care sectors. In 2010, Alice completed her Graduate Nurse Program at St Andrew's Hospital, a private hospital in Adelaide. Currently, Alice is employed in the Head, Neck and Lung Unit, Peter MacCallum Cancer Centre Melbourne, Victoria. In this role Alice manages patient care across the continuum of care. This position provides her with opportunities to develop clinical leadership skills.

Dr Di Wickett RN,RM, PhD was recently appointed Professional Officer of the Australian Nursing and Midwifery Federation (SA Branch). Prior to this appointment, Dr Wickett spent several years in nursing and midwifery regulation employed at the Nurse Board of South Australia. During this time, Dr Wickett worked in national working parties on the development and review of the regulatory framework for nursing and midwifery practice. It became evident that a significant number of nurses and midwives had little knowledge of the benchmarks of their practice, and this, therefore, has been a driving force for Dr Wickett to provide a greater understanding of the regulatory framework in which nurses and midwives practice. Dr Wickett gained a PhD at the University of Adelaide on 'A Critical Analysis of the Assessment of Overseas Qualified Nurses'. Dr Wickett had a nine year appointment as a Board Member of Resthaven Inc., a large aged care provider in South Australia, and was previously a SA Chapter Chair of the Royal College of Nursing where she spent many hours lobbying a number of bodies on professional issues for nurses. Dr Wickett is currently a member of the South Australian Health Performance Council, an advisory council to the Minister for Health in South Australia.

Preface

Graduate registered nurses and midwives are entering health care systems and organisations that are fast paced, dynamic and in a state of constant change. This state of constant change emerges from changes in the political, socio-cultural, economic and technological environments. Significant health workforce shortages in Australia and elsewhere have also impacted on the practice of registered nurses and midwives which you will have observed during your clinical placements.

Other changes that will impact on the registered nurse/midwife role and function are the internal organisational changes that are focused on ensuring quality and safety in the healthcare workplace while managing increased demands for healthcare services and achieving efficiencies. Other broader systemic changes include the move to national registration for nurses and midwives and the requirements for maintaining that registration.

In the past twenty years in Australia, there have been significant changes to nursing/midwifery practice as a result of whole-of-system changes designed to meet increasing demand for healthcare services and expectations of the healthcare consumers. These changes may be seen in the development of the Nurse Practitioner role and Midwifery-led clinics offering graduates career pathways into the future. While these expanded roles for nurses and midwives recognise the capacity, capabilities and intellectual rigour required to work in these complex and diverse roles there are also expectations from the community, employers and regulators that practitioners will accept and demonstrate responsibility and accountability for what they do.

The aim of this book is to assist undergraduate student nurses and midwives to make a seamless transition from the student nurse/midwife role into the registered nurse/midwife role. The book deals with the everyday issues student nurses/midwives encounter while on clinical placements. The exercises and case studies in each chapter provide opportunities for the student nurse to fast-forward into the registered nurse role and integrate theory with practice while developing, monitoring and evaluating nursing interventions identified in the exercises and case studies from the registered nurse perspective. There is a chapter written specifically for student midwives that provides an overview of midwifery practice in Australia.

The exercises and case studies introduce the student nurse/midwife to the dynamics of working in teams. In today's healthcare organisations there is an emphasis on multidisciplinary teamwork and registered nurses/midwives are an integral element in these teams. The current health workforce shortages have made working in multidisciplinary teams more important than ever, requiring team members to have higher-order critical thinking, communication and interpersonal competencies.

Registered nurses and midwives play a significant role in retrieving, analysing, interpreting and managing information used by clinicians and non-clinicians to ensure safe delivery of health services to patients. As student nurses/midwives you were introduced to the concepts and principles of evidence-based practice—that is using good-quality research outcomes to inform and improve nursing practice. Other data or information you will collect, analyse and interpret daily will include physiological, socio-cultural and psychological information that will inform your clinical decision-making and care planning and delivery.

This book will be invaluable to student nurses/midwives at the beginning of their undergraduate programs and to those student nurses/midwives making the transition into their new professional roles. It will help student nurses/midwives develop an understanding of the complexities of their professional roles and their place in a contemporary healthcare system. The complexities and ambiguities of these roles are discussed in detail, integrating theoretical concepts with practice and providing direction on how to make a successful transition from student to professional practitioner. Academic and others will find this book useful in preparing students for their transition into the registered nurse/midwife roles. The contributing authors to this book are experienced clinicians, educators and managers who have drawn on their experience, knowledge and expertise. Contributors to this book also include two recently graduated registered nurses who have shared their experience as student nurses and as new registered nurses adding their unique perspectives to this book.

Acknowledgments

The author and the publisher wish to thank the following copyright holders for reproduction of their material.

Australian Health Practitioner Regulation Agency (AHPRA) for extracts from (2010) *Continuing professional development registration standard,* <www.nursingmidwiferyboard.gov.au/Registration-Standards.aspx>, Nursing and Midwifery Board of Australia, from (2010) *Recency of practice registration standard,* <www.nursingmidwiferyboard.gov.au/Registration-Standards.aspx, Nursing and Midwifery Board of Australia, from (2006) *National competency standards for the registered nurse,* 4th edn, Australian Nursing and Midwifery Council, from (2007) *Midwifery practice decisions summary guide, national framework for the development of decision making tools,* Australian Nursing and Midwifery Council, from (2008) *Code of ethics for nurses in Australia,* Australian Nursing and Midwifery Council & Royal College of Nursing & Australian Nursing Federation, from (2008) *Code of professional conduct for nurses in Australia,* Australian Nursing and Midwifery Council; Stephen Duckett and Sharon Willcox for extracts from Duckett, S & Willcox, S (2011) *The Australian health care system, 4th edn,* Oxford University Press, Melbourne; Elsevier Australia for extracts from Staunton, P & Chiarella, M (2007) *Nursing & the law, 6th edn,* Elsevier, Sydney; Elsevier for extracts from Pappas, AB (2009) 'Ethical issues' and Zerwekh J (2009) 'Effective communication and team building' in JA Zwerkeh & JC Claborn, *Nursing today, transition and trends, 6th edition,* Saunders Elsevier, St. Louis, Missouri, Copyright Elsevier 2009; National Health & Hospital Reform Commission for extract from (2009) *A healthier future for all Australians: final report,* June 2009, used by permission of the Australian Government; National Health & Medical Research Council for extracts from (2009) *NHMRC levels of evidence and grades for recommendations for developers of guidelines,* Australian Government, National Health and Medical Research Council; Pearson Education Australia for extracts from Madsen, W (2009), 'Historical and contemporary nursing practice' in B Kozier & G Erb (eds), *Fundamentals of nursing practice,* Pearson, Sydney; Pearson Education US for extracts from Sullivan, E & Garland, G (2010) *Practical leadership and management in nursing,* Pearson Education, UK; World Health Organization

for extract from (2009), *Safe surgery saves lives*, www.who.int/patientsafety/safesurgery/en/.

Every effort has been made to trace the original source of copyright material contained in this book. The publisher will be pleased to hear from copyright holders to rectify any errors or omissions.

The authors of this text book would like to thank Dr. Rosemary Bryant, Commonwealth Chief Nurse and Midwifery Officer for writing the foreword to this book. Dr. Bryant is also the current President of the International Council of Nurses (ICN).

Thanks also go to the contributing authors of the book, especially the newly registered nurses, Lucy Hope and Alice Wickett who gave the student nurse and recently qualified nurse perspective. Thanks also go to Debra James, Publishing Manager, who kept us on track throughout the process.

Finally, but not least, to the wonderfully patient and talented editorial team at Oxford University Press, Australia, who have taken a rough draft and made it into a very readable text book. A publishing take on 'spinning straw into gold'.

A very big thank you to you all.

Introduction

This textbook is intended for final year undergraduate nursing and midwifery students who on completion of their studies will enter the healthcare system as beginning registered nurses. This book should provide you with insights on the complexities of the registered nurse role and how this role is pivotal to the functioning of the health care system in this country. There is a chapter on the development of professional nursing in this country resulting from legal and professional regulation. This should raise your awareness of your legal responsibilities as a nurse, making you reflect on your personal values and views as you begin to engage with the principles, practices and expectations of nurses and midwives.

You will be introduced to the practical aspects of nursing and your role in promoting health as well as providing nursing care to the sick person. There are case studies and exercises throughout the book which are real life examples of situations nurses face on a day-to-day basis. A theme that runs through the book is that of the nurses' role in managing safety in the workplace. As student nurses you will have been taught the principles of safe nursing practice and how to apply these in your everyday work. Those already working in a healthcare or aged care organisation will be very aware of how important the issues of safety in the workplace is.

The book deals with the everyday issues the student nurse encounters while on clinical placement and which as a registered nurse you will be expected to deal with and manage to ensure the achievement of positive outcomes. The book introduces the student to the complexities of the healthcare system; the demands placed on all healthcare workers working in a multidisciplinary environment. Critical thinking and analysis as core competencies are emphasised as integral components of the registered nurse role required for informed decision making. The book integrates the theoretical and practical learning of the student nurse curriculum, focusing on the transitioning process from student nurse to registered nurse.

The book also takes into account the fact that new graduate nurses in the twenty-first century are entering a workforce where there may be up to four generations of nurses working. Thus, a part of becoming a registered nurse is learning how to work as a team member of a multigenerational workforce.

The book is written in everyday language and where possible is jargon-free. The first chapter provides the theroretical framework for the rest of the book and this too is expressed in a jargon-free language. The book provides transitioning student nurses with the knowledge and skills/competencies required to move effortlessly into the registered nurse role.

Contributors to this book are experienced clinicians and academics as well as two recent graduate registered nurses, both of whom are completing their TPPP this year. Topics covered address the changes to legislation from 1 July 2010 which will nationalise nursing practice through registration and the imperative for each nurse and midwife to provide evidence of fitness for continuing registration.

Nurse and midwife registration

From 1 July 2010, national registration for nurses and midwives has come into effect, replacing the current system of state and territory registration managed by Nurses' Boards. Flow-on changes from this include having each nurse and midwife provide evidence of competency in practice in a professional portfolio and evidence of continuing professional development (20 hours per annum), which will be monitored using an audit process with the Australian Nursing and Midwifery Council.

One positive outcome of national registration will be that you will be able to move for work to other states/territories without having to reregister. But if in the future you do plan to move out of your home state/territory to work elsewhere then find out what the responsibilities of the registered nurse are in the organisation you are planning to move to. There may be some variations in clinical practice and you should become aware of these differences.

Also, from 1 July 2010, the *Health Practitioner Regulation National Law* has for the first time 'made mandatory reporting requirements apply nationally for the ten health professions (doctors, nurses, dentists, ptometrists,osteopaths, pharmacists, physiotherapists, chiropractors, podiatrists and psychologists) regulated under the new legislation' (Gorton 2010, p. 1). Notifiable conduct is the trigger for reporting and this is where a registered health professional:

- practises while under the influence of alcohol and drugs
- engages in sexual misconduct in connection with their practice
- places the the community at risk of substantial harm while working under the influence of drugs and alcohol

- places the public at risk by practising ouside of accepted professional standards(p.1)

It is also worth noting that members of the community and other health professionals can make voluntary notifications if they believe that a health professional has acted inappropriately or acted without due care and/or illegally. So you can see how important it will be for you to practise within the Australian Nursing and Midwifery suite of standards which have been used to to underpin the content in this book

Being a registered nurse is multifaceted. All nurses and midwives work in complex and dynamic environments subject to continuous change and reform that is politically and economically driven. While in this early part of your nursing career you do not have to know the detail of reforms in the healthcare sectors you should have an awareness of the potential impact these reforms may have on your practice.

The sequence of chapters and information in the book begins with the processes of transition from student nurse to registered nurse, providing you with the theoretical frameworks that explain these processes. The next chapters discuss the regulatory frameworks that regulate registered nurse and midwifery practice in Australia. It is important that you are familiar with the nurse registration requirements because breaching these may result in penalties that are clearly documented. Also, be aware of the requirements for continuing registration and providing evidence that you meet these requirements. The chapter on regulation should raise your awareness of the administrative factors around nurse registration.

This is followed by a chapter on Australia's healthcare system, contextualising nursing practice and the practice of other health professionals. This chapter has been written to give you some insights into how the Australian healthcare system works and where you as a new registered nurse fit into it. Having some insight into how the healthcare system works will enable you to better understand how decisions are made and why they are made around health priorities.

The next group of chapters focus on registered nurse practice beginning with competencies you will be need to demonstrate in the workplace; all of which you will have begun to develop in your undergraduate program. The ability to apply competencies to the clinical workplace is essential if you are to develop/evolve into a safe clinical practitioner. It is important that you understand the significance of this form of knowledge transfer because this is precisely what you will be doing. You engage in knowledge transfer while on clinical placement as a student nurse, and as a registered nurse you will be assuming accountability and responsibility for this.

Assuming responsibility and accountability for your actions as a health care practitioner is a key factor in your ongoing development as a registered nurse. These are reflected in your everyday work and the outcomes of your nursing interventions or the nursing interventions you may delegate to others. To delegate safely as a registered nurse you will need a strong and current knowledge base but importantly you will have to be able to communicate this effectively and accurately to others. These chapters should give you some strategies on how this should be done in the clinical workplace.

By now, you should have realised that underpinning the information in this book is the notion of 'joining the dots'. Joining the dots in the context of registered nurse practice refers to the fact that nothing really happens in isolation and that everything you do is interrelated. A simple example relates to critcal thinking. You will not wake up one day and say 'today I am going to be a critical thinker'. What you will do, however, is go to work and use your critical thinking skills to provide the best possible care for your patients. And as you become more experienced as a registered nurse these abilities and competencies will enable you to provide seamless nursing care to patients.

The final chapters in this book focus on the ethical frameworks that shape and support nursing practice. In the appendices you will find the ANMC ethical framework for nurses and midwives and you should be able to relate this to your registration requirements. Other contemporary issues that are touched upon include quality improvement, safety and the registered nurse, and clinical governance, which are designed to ensure that the care given to all patients is safe, current, and based on quality research. Your role in this is to ensure that the nursing care you give is evidence-based and meets the needs of your patients. To do this, you will have to be able to source information, evaluate its relevance to a clinical situation and then incorporate it in the care plan and delivery.

As well as clinical competencies you will be expected to develop good communication skills with a diverse range of health practitioners/service providers and your patients their families; learn to work in multidisciplinary healthcare teams and work with patients and their families and/or carers. You will begin this in your undergraduate program and continue it once you have graduated and entered the workplace.

Each of the previous chapters discusses the role of the registered nurse from a number of perspectives. The information in each chapter focuses on the role of the registered nurse and while you are now a student nurse it will be helpful for you to fast-forward into the future and visualise yourself in the registered nurse role. Some questions you may begin asking yourself:

- What sort of competencies will I need to focus on in my TPPP?
- How will I begin to build on the knowledge I already have?

- How will I apply the knowledge learned in the classroom to the clinical setting?
- What do I need to do to be a safe clinician?
- What will the expectations of the organisation be? The expectations of my future colleagues?
- What are my expectations of myself as a registered nurse?

Reflecting on these questions will give some insights into what the role of a registered nurse may look like and perhaps give you ideas on how you will develop your own unique role. You may wish to look at these questions in conjunction with the information on professional development for some ideas on how to develop the registered nurse role.

The authors of this book wish you every success in your career as a registered nurse.

Below are some references and web links you may find useful

References

Black, B.P. (2011) Critical thinking, the nursing process and clinical judgement. In Chitty, K.K. & Black, B.P. *Professional nursing, concepts and challenges.* Saunders Elsevier, MI, Chapter 8.

Ellis, J.R. & Hartley, C.L. (2009) *Nursing in today's world: Trends, issues and management.* Wolters Kluwer/ Lippincott Williams & Wilkins, Philadelphia.

Gorton, M. (2010) *Mandatory reporting client bulletin.* Russell Kennedy. Kennedy Strang, Legal Group, Melbourne.

Homer, C.S.E., Griffiths, M., Ellwood, D., Kildea, S., Brodie, P.M., Curtin, A. (2010). *Core competencies and educational framework for primary maternity services in Australia. Final report.* Centre for Midwifery, Child and Family Health, University of Technology, Sydney.

Kane, R.L., Shamliyan, T., Mueller, C., Duval, S. & Wilt, T.J. (2007) The Association of Registered Nurse Staffing Levels and Partient Outcomes. *Medical Care.* vol. 45, no. 12, pp. 1195–204.

Zwerkekh, J. & Claborn, J. (2009) *Nursing today. Transition and trends.* 6th edn. Saunders Elsevier, St Louis, MI.

Useful Websites

Australian Council on Healthcare Standards (2006). **www.achs.org.au.**

Australian Commission onSafety and Quality in Healthcare (ACSQHC). **www. safetyandquality.gov.au/internet/safety/publishing.nsf/Content/home.**

Australian Commission on Safety & Quality in Healthcare—Safe medication management. **www.safetyandquality.gov.au/internet/safety/publishing.nsf/ Content/com-pubs_NIMC-34210-MedSafetyUpdateAug2010.**

Australian Commission on Safety & Quality in Healthcare—National Adult Inpatient Medication Chart. **http://www.safetyandquality.gov.au/internet/ safety/publishing.nsf/Content/61DB2FF338077BF0CA2577850028AD5F/ $File/34210-MedSafetyUpdate-Aug2010.PDF.**

Australian Commission on Safety & Quality in Healthcare—Centre for Research Excellence in Patient Safety. **www.crepatientsafety.org.au.**

Part 1

Becoming a health professional

Core competencies

As a registered nurse or registered midwife, you will:

- practise within the legislative, ethical and administrative frameworks underpinning professional nursing or midwifery practice
- practise within your own scope of practice
- integrate relevant healthcare knowledge, skills, behaviours and attitudes to deliver safe and effective nursing or midwifery care
- practise within the boundaries of organisational policies, clinical protocols, guidelines and professional standards
- demonstrate understanding of the differences in accountabilities and responsibiliites among registered nurses, enrolled nurses and other healthcare workers.

Chapter 1

Transition from student nurse to registered nurse

Maria Fedoruk

Learning objectives

After reading this chapter, you will be able to:

- understand the process of transition from student nurse to registered nurse
- discuss the professional responsibilities of the registered nurse in relation to other categories of nurse

Key terms

Belongingness
SMARTTA model
Transition
Transition to Professional Practice Program (TPPP)

Transition

The Oxford Australian Dictionary (2005) defines **transition** as 'the process of changing from one condition, style, etc., to another'. Becoming a registered nurse is a complex and stressful process of transition (Newton & McKenna 2007). Transition is a process of complex change, as individuals move from a familiar way of living to a new way, because of life events. The life events that prompt transition may be disruptive or even catastrophic. Kralik, Visenttin and van Loon (2006) describe the process of transition as a redefinition of the sense of self and the redevelopment of self-image in response to changes and life events. Transition is about endings and beginnings.

In this case, the ending is the successful completion of a university undergraduate nursing program. Your student days end and you enter a new role—a beginning—as a registered nurse. The transition process of becoming a registered nurse has four phases: familiar life, ending, limbo, and becoming ordinary (Kralik, Visenttin & van Loon 2006, p. 116). These are shown in Table 1.1.

Table 1.1: Four phases of transition

Familiar life	Ending	Limbo	Becoming ordinary
The life of a student nurse is predictable, and situations are taken for granted.	Being a student nurse ends.	Becoming a registered nurse may be disorientating and disempowering, as you develop a new identity.	In the new role and identity you begin to incorporate new patterns of working into a new life. Life and work occur in a way that is coherent.
As a student nurse, you experience patterns of living and being that: • are predictable and structured • give you a recognised identity • give you status • give you a sense of security • give you a range of acquaintances in similar situations and states of being • are socio-culturally acceptable.	Following the completion of your undergraduate studies you may experience: • disruption • ambiguity and a loss of identity • a sense of loss of or disconnection from the familiar • disempowerment and inadequacy • insecurity • vulnerability • marginalisation.	During this phase you may experience: • confusion • alienation • disruption • powerlessness • isolation • loneliness • self-pity • insecurity.	During the phase of becoming ordinary you may experience: • renewal • transformation • a sense of returning to 'normal' • a return to familiarity • a sense of 'I'm good now' • reconnection with work colleagues.

Adapted from Kralik, Visenttin & van Loon (2006, p. 116)

In Table 1.1, the four phases of the transition process are represented in a linear manner. However, transition is not always linear. The phases can occur simultaneously as individuals try and make sense of their lives and situations and return to an ordinary way of being. For Bridges (2004), transition is not a fixed event, but rather a continuing reorientation and redefinition of an indvidual's sense of self and way of thinking about oneself and one's social and professional roles. Transition is multifaceted and the process of transition occurs over time, with individuals moving back and forth through the phases depending on what is occurring in their lives.

Your attitudes, values, beliefs and socio-cultural background all play an important part in the way you experience the transition process. Transition processes are very individual and the move from student nurse to registered nurse will not be exactly the same for everyone. You as an individual bring to this transition process your personal beliefs, attitudes and values. During the course of your undergraduate program, you have also been exposed to the culture and values of your school or faculty of nursing. As a student nurse, you may have found that these differed somewhat from the culture and values of your **clinical placement**. This can make starting in a new role in a new healthcare organisation a little daunting, but you will find all healthcare organisations have well-established support programs for new registered nurses. These include the Transition to Professional Practice Program (TPPP), mentoring and **preceptorships**.

Point to ponder

You have already made many transitions in your life to get you to this point. Reflect on how you managed these earlier transitions.

The transition to becoming a registered nurse is also a social process. The ending of the student nurse life is represented in the graduation ceremony, which is very formal and public. Through this ceremony, you begin a new phase of being and take on a new social role.

Once you are a registered nurse, you enter the 'ordinary' phase of transition, having left the student nurse identity behind. You have a new way of living and thinking—as a registered nurse. Becoming a registered nurse requires that you change the way you think. One area where this is particularly noticeable is in clinical decision-making. Etheridge (2007) observes that for many new graduate nurses clinical **decision-making** is troublesome because they have not moved from thinking as a student to thinking as a registered nurse. The social and professional expectations of a registered nurse are very different to that of a student nurse, and your behaviours, thinking, attitudes and actions need to reflect your new role and responsibilities.

Point to ponder

Becoming a registered nurse requires you to change the way you think, because registered nurses must use a higher order of decision-making than student nurses.

Maria Fedoruk

The responsibilities of a student nurse are very different from those of a registered nurse. A student nurse is a learner and works under the direction and supervision of a registered nurse. A registered nurse assumes responsibility for the care of **patients**, and directs student nurses in the planning and delivery of this care. Registered nurses use high-order decision-making skills in the planning and delivery of safe and appropriate nursing care. This decision-making is based on a high level of clinical knowledge, which is a synthesis of theoretical and practical knowledge gained in the undergraduate program. As well as clinical knowledge, registered nurses have to have corporate knowledge, which is embedded in organisational policies and procedures. Registered nurses are also expected to demonstrate **clinical leadership**. Clinical leadership means developing advanced clinical knowledge and competencies, and being able to apply these in your practice.

WORKING IN GROUPS

In your study group, discuss the transitions that have already occurred during your undergraduate program:

- your first day as a university nursing student
- receiving the results of your first assignment
- your first clinical placement
- moving from first year to second year to third year
- clinical placements in second year and third year.

What were the high and low points at these times?

Transition to Professional Practice Program

To facilitate the transition from student nurse to registered nurse, hospitals in Australia offer a Transition to Professional Practice Program. This was formerly known as the Graduate Nurse Program. Ideally, the TPPP is a consolidation year that enables new registered nurses to become familiar with their roles and responsibilities. The TPPP year is central in helping registered nurses develop a sense of **belongingness**, which helps them move through the four phases of transition. TPPPs are designed to introduce new graduates to the organisation's policies and procedures, as well as reinforce clinical knowledge and learning.

We discuss the TPPP further in Chapters 4 and 5, which explain in more detail the transition from student nurse to registered nurse or midwife, with Chapter 4 providing a student nurse perspective. For now, read through Box 1.1, which gives you a model of the first five days in an ideal TPPP.

BOX 1.1: A MODEL TPPP ORIENTATION

Below is an outline of an ideal **orientation** program for the TPPP. You will find that orientation programs are specific to each hospital or healthcare organisation, and they vary between each state and territory. Therefore, you need to be very clear about what your objectives and learning requirements are.

DAY 1

You arrive with other new registered nurses at the hospital or healthcare organisation where you will work. You are greeted by nursing staff from the education or staff development department.

After the administrative formalities (signing contracts, etc.) are completed, the formal orientation to the organisation begins. In the orientation, you learn about the policies, procedures and expectations of the employer. You may be asked to express your expectations. For instance, you may be asked 'why did you choose to come to this hospital/organisation?' Your response is important— remember that the hospital or healthcare organisation is expecting you to be professional in your outlook and behaviour.

DAY 2

Further opportunities are provided for you to learn more about your new organisation and place of work. Do not be afraid to ask questions about issues that concern you. This may be daunting because you are nervous and want to make a good impression, but it is better to clarify issues at the beginning. Remember there is no such thing as a 'dumb' question. In order to ask the most appropriate questions, you should have done some homework about the TPPP in the hospital or healthcare organisation you are going to work in. The more you find out about the organisation at this stage, the less stressful your first few days on the clinical unit will be.

DAY 3

This day may be taken up with assessing your mandatory competencies (as determined by the organisation and, in some states or territories, the registering authority) including:

- medication calculations
- managing intravenous therapies and other clinically related functions

---

- fire and evacuation procedures
- **basic life support** or **advanced life support** training
- occupational health, welfare and safety—for example, organisational policies and procedures, mandatory competencies (manual handling), interprofessional relationships (workplace **bullying**), maintaining a safe work environment
- managing **critical incidents**.

You will also have the chance to familiarise yourself with:

- the documentation used in the organisation
- how to manage workloads on a shift
- how to use the nursing **information systems** to measure workloads and to allocate staff per shift
- human resource management processes, such as how to apply for leave
- details such as your leave entitlements, salary and industrial relations.

You should also ask about professional development opportunities that will support and enhance your own professional and career development.

The industrial body representing nursing and nurses will provide you with information. In Australia, the principal industrial agency for nurses is the Australian Nursing Federation (ANF). The relevant registering authority may also make a presentation that covers the role of the Nurses Board in your state or territory. Other professional nursing organisations, such as the Royal College of Nursing, may also provide information about their role and the professional opportunities now open to you as a registered nurse.

DAY 4

On this day you go to your clinical unit and meet the clinical nurse consultant or nurse in charge (titles of senior nurses may vary in the different states and territories). You are also introduced to other staff who are part of the multidisciplinary team working in the unit. At this point, you may be introduced to your clinical facilitator, who will be your mentor for the first three months of the program.

DAY 5

Day 5 is a supernumerary day in the clinical unit, where you have time to familiarise yourself with the geographical layout of the unit (it is always important to know where equipment, especially emergency equipment, is located) and the policies and procedures that apply to the unit. It is also an opportunity to familiarise yourself with the emergency contact details for the unit and the organisation.

Your clinical facilitator may also provide an orientation program to the clinical unit—this will include the clinical skills, knowledge and competencies you are expected to develop while working in the clinical unit.

You may be asked to develop learning objectives around the clinical skills and competencies you wish to develop or improve while you are working in the unit. You should be familiar with the process of setting objectives, as you will have done this throughout your undergraduate program. The **SMARTTA** framework (Dwyer & Hopwood 2010) can be used to develop effective learning objectives. SMARTTA stands for:

S = Specific
M = Measurable
A = Achievable
R = Realistic
T = Time
T = Trackable
A = Agreed

It is important to set yourself achievable learning objectives that will contribute to your professional development. Your objectives should be achieved during your time in the clinical units.

Remember your clinical facilitator is there to support your socialisation and integration into the clinical unit. While you may feel a little uncomfortable that at first you always seem to be asking questions, this is the only way you will learn. Your clinical faciliator will respect and understand this.

After this five-day period is over, you will be included on the normal roster for the unit. In the first few days of the roster, you may be supernumerary: that is, not included in the staffing establishment. If this is the case, use the time wisely by becoming really familiar with the activities of the clinical unit.

In some organisations, the orientation period continues throughout the TPPP year. New staff meet with their clinical facilitators and the staff development team every three months to discuss the clinical and non-clinical issues graduate nurses have experienced, and to monitor and update clinical skills. These sessions help you resolve issues during your first year of practice as a registered nurse.

Point to ponder

The SMARTTA model is an extension of the SMART model, which you will probably be familiar with from your undergraduate studies.

Maria Fedoruk

As a new registered nurse, once the initial period of orientation is over you will work as a team member and be responsible for the clinical care of a group of patients. Ideally, you will have received a thorough orientation, as outlined in the box above. However, this does not always happen, due to shortage of registered nurses. New graduates are often expected to 'hit the ground running' (Greenwood 2000). This means that you may find yourself in charge of shifts—usually after hours shifts—in the early part of your TPPP. While organisations try and minimise this occurring, staff sick leave or emergency leave can make it unavoidable. So, one of your learning objectives could revolve around organising staff on a shift.

FOR REFLECTION

Imagine that you have begun work as a registered nurse. Use the SMARTTA framework to develop some learning objectives for yourself. These could include some specific clinical aspects of nursing practice, and also some non-clinical aspects of your practice, such as organising staff on a shift.

In your study group and with your lecturer, discuss these objectives and how you might evaluate them. What criteria might you consider using?

The TPPP is the formal orientation to the healthcare organisation. Alongside it, there is also an informal process of orientation to the socio-cultural norms of the organisation. These norms will be reflected in the culture of individual clinical units, and in the organisational mission and values statements. Once you enter the clinical unit where you will work as a registered nurse, you will be socialised into the culture and norms of that unit. By observing the behaviours and values demonstrated by the people already working in the unit, you will learn 'how we do things here'. You will also hear staff talking in clinical shorthand specific to the clinical speciality. In order to fit into this workgroup, one of the first things you need to learn is the language of that particular unit. For instance, if you go into an orthopaedics unit, you need to learn the language of orthopaedics; in a cardiac unit, cardiac language, and so on. Learning the language of the clinical unit is the first step in becoming a member of the group. You will already have experienced and observed this in your clinical placements and in your current place of work.

Point to ponder

Learning the socio-cultural aspects of a clinical unit will help you become a member of the team.

FOR REFLECTION

Reflect on your clinical placement experiences.

- When you went to your first placement area, did you take note of the language being used to describe clinical conditions?
- Did you understand what was being said to you?
- How did understanding or not understanding the language being used affect your ability to plan and deliver nursing care?
- Did you have to ask for clarification of terminology?

Maria Fedoruk

SUMMARY

This chapter focused on the process of transition and identified the stages of transition you will go through as you enter the workforce as a registered nurse. You were introduced to the SMARTTA model for developing learning objectives. Using this model during the TPPP will help you navigate the transition process.

DISCUSSION QUESTIONS

1   What were the critical points in your undergraduate program?
2   What were some highlights and lowlights of your program?
3   How did you deal with these different situations?
4   Did you learn from these experiences?
5   Did you notice a difference in yourself and your approach to nursing between the first clinical placement and the final placement?

REFERENCES

Bridges, W (2004) *Transitions: Making sense of life's changes*, Da Capo Press, Cambridge, MA.

Dwyer, J & Hopwood, N (2010) *Management strategies and skills*, McGraw-Hill, Australia.

Etheridge, SA (2007) 'Learning to think like a nurse: Stories from new nurse graduates'. *The Journal of Continuing Education*, vol. 38, no. 1, pp. 24–30.

Greenwood, J (2000) 'Critique of the graduate nurse: an international perspective', *Nurse Education Today*, vol. 20, pp. 17–23.

Kralik, D, Visenttin, K & van Loon, A (2006) 'Transition: A literature review', *Journal of Advanced Nursing*, vol. 55, no. 3, pp. 320–9.

Newton, JM & McKenna, L (2007) 'The transitional journey through the graduate tear: A focus group study', *International Journal of Nursing Studies*, 44, pp. 1231–7.

Chapter 2

Belongingness and teamwork

Maria Fedoruk

Learning objectives

After reading this chapter, you will be able to:
- understand the importance of belongingness to new nurses
- describe the socialisation processes new nurses undergo in order to belong
- discuss the complexities of these socialisation processes
- discuss the concepts of professional boundaries and therapeutic relationships.

Key terms

Belongingness
Multigenerational workforce diversity
Professional boundaries
Therapeutic relationship

Belongingness

In Chapter 1, we discussed the transition process that new graduates go through in becoming registered nurses. The socialisation processes of belongingness are an integral component of this transition process.

As social beings, we belong to many groups, beginning with our family units. We also belong to communities and work groups. Historically, human beings have belonged to groups defined by ethnicity, social status and religion. We also usually belong to groups that reflect our personal interests, beliefs and value systems.

Belongingness is defined by Levett-Jones and others (2007, p. 104) as a very personal and 'contextually mediated experience', which is an evolutionary response unique to each individual, relating to their feelings of security and acceptance in a group. As a new registered nurse you will want to be accepted into a new work group where the personal values of all members of the group are complementary and 'in synch'.

Research in psychology indicates that belongingness is necessary for the development of self-esteem and confidence. For the new registered nurse this translates into being valued for clinical knowledge and competencies in the workplace. The concept of belongingness also adds to the development of social capital in the workplace. Social capital in nursing is about developing **communities of practice** by connecting with others through teamwork to achieve common goals. At the heart of social capital theory is the notion that social networks have value and result in personal and collective benefits (Levett-Jones & Lathlean 2006, p. 213). Returning to the new graduate nurse, this means that belonging to a group increases personal and professional value which is seen in positive health outcomes for patients. Thus, the socialisation process for the new registered nurse must incorporate strategies that enhance the individual's process of belongingness.

Where there is a low level of belongingness, the individual feels devalued and has low self-esteem and confidence, which then leads to poor performance in nursing practice. Belongingness is about social inclusion, a characteristic of human socialisation. Where graduate nurses are socially excluded, this then impacts on their behaviours, which can be negative and lead to poor outcomes for patients.

Human beings are social beings, and as such all human beings have a need to be accepted into their social and professional groups. In order to be included, some will engage in negative behaviours that fall outside of corporate policies and procedures, for instance taking shortcuts to 'get the job done'. While the need to be accepted is a strong driver and motivator, negative behaviours can have long-range negative implications for individuals in terms of continuing employment.

Understanding the concept of belongingness and its operationalisation in the workplace through the TPPP in hospitals and other healthcare organisations is important for all key stakeholders working with student nurses and later with graduate registered nurses.

Nursing is a practice-based discipline, and since the shift of nurse education from hospitals to the university sector, clinical practice experiences for students occur on clinical placement in hospitals and other health- and aged-care agencies. The clinical placement experience varies for students from extremely positive to extremely negative. Anecdotal evidence from students returning from clinical placement indicates that the level of belongingness felt by the individual student while on clinical placement determines the quality of the clinical placement experience for individual students. Research reported by Levett-Jones and Lathlean (2006, 2009) and others (2007) supports the idea that variability in clinical experiences for student nurses is related to their level of acceptance and belongingness while on clinical placement. This is significant because often the clinical placement venues are also the future employers of the graduate registered nurse and so clinical placement venues have a vested interest in ensuring that the student clinical experience is a positive one.

A low level of belongingness in the clinical setting often results in the new registered nurse being marginalised or excluded from the work groups. Marginalised people are viewed as being different and view themselves as being different (Boychuk & Cowin 2004a). Marginalisation is evident in the labelling of new graduates as 'new nurses', who are seen as being distinctly different from more experienced registered nurses (Boychuk & Cowin 2004a, p. 291). This stigmatisation of new graduate registered nurses through labelling leads to the perception that 'new nurses' have limited knowledge and competencies. Sustained marginalisation of new graduates is a factor in the high turnover of nurses (Boychuk & Myrick 2008).

FOR REFLECTION

Remember a time when you wanted to belong to a particular group and reflect on this experience.

- Why did you want to join this group?
- What did you do to become accepted?
- How did you feel about this?
- How long did the process of becoming accepted take?

In contemporary healthcare organisations, you will find yourself belonging to a workgroup that is multidisciplinary and multigenerational, working together to provide appropriate and relevant health services to patients. The process of belongingness is complicated because work groups are multigenerational. This means that the members of a work group will have different values, beliefs and attitudes to do with work and the role of the registered nurse. They will also have had very different educational preparation, ranging from hospital training to university. Even among university graduates, nurses may have had varied educational experiences, having come to nursing from other disciplines or occupations.

Nurse education curricula vary from university to university and from state to state or territory, but essentially they need to incorporate and be responsive to the increasing demands on health services due to population and demographic changes, community expectations, political and economic changes, biomedical technology and information technology developments, as well as the expectations of the twenty-first century health professional. Governments control the numbers of nurses entering the nursing profession by funding places in universities and nursing positions in healthcare organisations. For instance, in response to a shortage of nurses in Australia, federal and state governments have responded by funding more places in universities and more nursing positions in healthcare organisations (National Health Workforce Taskforce 2009).

The contemporary **healthcare workforce** is multigenerational, adding to the complexities of your workforce socialisation becoming a member of a new workgroup. One of the things you will have to understand as a new registered nurse is that entering a new group is challenging because you have to learn to understand what makes this group work together and what you will have to do to become a member of this group. There are times when this is relatively easy because the group welcomes new members, but there may be times when this process is more difficult and you will have to develop strategies to deal with this: for example, developing interpersonal competencies and positive professional relationships.

Point to ponder

It is a truism but worth remembering: you will not like all the people you meet and neither will all the people who meet you like you.

Becoming a member of a workgroup in healthcare is an integral component of your socialisation as a professional into a profession that is highly regarded. How you manage this is a measure of your professionalism. There will be people in the healthcare facility that you can go to for advice, and during the TPPP you should take every opportunity to help you transition into your new role successfully.

We now look at some of the issues that you will encounter as you move through the belongingness process.

Multigenerational workforce diversity

In contemporary healthcare organisations, four generations of nurses work side by side (Sherman 2006). There are four different and discrete cohorts of nurses. Each of the four generations of nurses brings to the workplace the work and life experiences of their generation (Stuenkely, Cohen & de la Cuesta 2005). This generational diversity includes differences in work habits, attitudes, beliefs and expectations, and also the way they perceive themselves as registered nurses. The four generations are represented in Table 2.1.

Table 2.1: Multigenerational nursing workforce

The Veterans (born 1922–1945)	The Baby Boomers (born 1946–1963)	Generation X (born 1963–1980)	The Millenials (born 1980–2000)
Few in number	Largest cohort	University trained	University trained
Hospital trained	Hospital and university trained	Technologically savvy	Technologically sophisticated
Exemplify Nightingale's 'good nurse'	Technologically adept	Work–life balance important	Use technology—for example, social media—to communicate
	Exemplify the 'me' generation	May have had more than one career	Tend to 'talk with their thumbs' (use SMS or text messaging a lot)
			Will have more than one career in their working life
			Career mobility and flexibility important

For hospital-trained nurses, the focus of their educational experiences was on mastering tasks. Hospital-based nurse training programs were functionally oriented, and student nurses were taught *how* to do things, but not necessarily *why* these tasks or functions were done. A cornerstone of hospital-based programs for student nurses was obedience to authority. This stands in strong contrast to the focus on **critical thinking** and analysis in contemporary nurse education programs. In your undergraduate studies, you would have been encouraged to think independently and to ask questions about the 'whys' of nursing practice. As a **clinician**, you will be expected to make decisions on behalf of others and you can only make effective decisions once you understand *why* you are making them and what the consequences are going to be. However, you will be working with nurses and other professionals who have very different educational backgrounds. Working with them will add to your professional development.

Point to ponder

Remember that all decisions result in consequences — even not making a decision will have consequences.

For the transition process to be effective you need to be aware of multigenerational diversity and how this can influence your transition process. However, as long as you understand *why* some problems arise within a **multigenerational workforce**, you can deal with these problems. Multigenerational diversity exists in other health professional workforces as well.

Having four generations of nurses working together is a contemporary phenomenon. In the past, nurses retired or reduced their working hours as they neared retirement age. In Australia, the retirement age has been removed, enabling people to continue working beyond the previous retirement age of sixty-five years. Increased life expectancy, changing lifestyles and global financial crises have resulted in a more mature and experienced workforce remaining in the healthcare industry. The median age of registered nurses in Australia is fast approaching more than fifty years (National Health Workforce Taskforce 2009).

The maturing of the nursing workforce in Australia is in part due to re-entry into the workforce of older registered nurses in response to the global nursing workforce shortage and in part to the financial incentives offered by the Federal Government. The maturing of the nursing workforce is also evident in the United States (Sherman 2006). Some writers indicate that this maturing of the nursing workforce will continue for some time, as healthcare organisations struggle to staff their organisations and meet the expectations of the public for high-quality, safe healthcare. However, nurses remain the backbone of healthcare systems around the world.

Different generations of nurses working in the one clinical unit can make the transition process for the new graduate registered nurse quite complex, because you will need to learn how to work with the different values, attitudes, educational experiences and work habits of these older nurses. One way of dealing with this generational diversity is to learn from these older nurses.

For example, they could teach you the routines of the clinical units and how to relate to patients, because this is something they have been doing for many years and they have developed expertise in these areas. You should also remember that while your knowledge may be more current, their knowledge is experiential and has been gained over many years. In some instances, it may even appear to be intuitive.

So, having different generations of nurses working together can contribute to the learning and professional development of new graduate registered nurses. While the nursing workforce in the twenty-first century is multigenerational and diverse, what is common to all registered nurse is their responsibilities to be safe, competent practitioners.

Nursing as a profession

Before we discuss the professional responsibilities of the registered nurse, we need to understand what is meant by the term 'profession'. Historically, nursing has been viewed as a vocation (Peate 2006), with nurses providing a service to others (Cutcliffe & Weick 2008). Nursing has strived for professional status, especially in the latter half of the twentieth century, as evident in the nursing literature of the time (Cutcliffe & Weick 2008). The Oxford Australian Dictionary (2005) defines a profession as 'an occupation that needs special education and training' and specifically mentions nursing: 'Recognised professions include being a doctor, nurse or lawyer'. Bilton and others (in Cutcliffe & Weick 2008, p. 501) provided the following criteria to define a profession:

- skill based on theoretical knowledge
- an extensive period of education
- a focus on public service and altruism
- the existence of a code of conduct and ethics
- the insistence upon professional freedom to self-regulate
- the testing of competencies of members before admission to the professions.

WORKING IN GROUPS

In your study group, reflect on the criteria for a profession given above.

- In your opinion, is nursing a profession?
- How do you, as a new registered nurse, become a professional? Is it by demonstrating professional competencies in the workplace and by integrating theoretical knowledge with practice-based knowledge?
- How have your responsibilities changed from when you were a student nurse and/ or an enrolled nurse?

Maria Fedoruk

It has been argued that nursing fails to meet some of the traditional criteria used to define a professional. Nurses work under the direction of others, so it has been argued that they don't possess a distinct body of knowledge and are not autonomous practitioners. A counterargument is that nursing is developing 'a well defined body of knowledge' (Madsen 2009, p. 14), using conceptual models developed over the twentieth century. The development of nursing theories in the twentieth century has been described as an indicator that nursing is maturing as a clinical profession.

In the twenty-first century, the scope of nursing practice is increasing. The nurse practitioner role is an example of registered nurses working autonomously, and in some states and territories nurse practitioners have prescribing rights.

As you near the end of your nursing program, reflect on the various theories and theorists you were introduced to and how this knowledge was applied to what you were being taught Did you think that this part of your education program was worthwhile? What do you think now? Theories provide a framework for practice, and nursing theories 'provide new possibilities for understanding the discipline's practice' (Walker 2009, p.39). Towards the end of the twentieth century, the focus for nurse theory development was the understanding of the relationships between person, health, environment and nursing (Walker 2009, p. 40). In this meta-paradigm of nursing:

- **Person** refers to the patient, with whom you as the nurse have to develop a professional relationship in order to plan and deliver care.
- **Environment** refers to the internal and external surroundings you and the patient find yourselves in. This can also include the different groups of people you interact with as individuals and collectively.
- **Health** refers to the level of health being experienced by the patient at a particular point in time.
- **Nursing** refers to the process of delivering care to a patient, using the nursing process.

FOR REFLECTION

Reflect on your undergraduate program and consider how many times you came across this meta-paradigm of person, environment, health and nursing. It may not have been presented in quite this way, but it should be familiar to you. Does this meta-paradigm describe nursing practice as you understand it? Do you believe a case has been made for nursing to be called a profession?

Professional responsibilities of the registered nurse

Inherent in the definition of professional responsibility are the concepts of responsibility and accountability. Responsibility means accepting the consequences of your decisions. In nursing terms, being responsible means that you accept the outcomes of decisions and any actions you have made on behalf of your patients. **Accountability** means accounting for your decision-making and actions that result from this. Since professional nursing practice is legislatively controlled, it is important that you have some knowledge of the legal dimensions around nursing practice. This is necessary for the following reasons (Zetler 2010, p. 56):

- to ensure your decision-making and actions are consistent with current legal principles
- to protect you from liability
- to practise nursing with understanding and confidence.

The responsibilities of the registered nurse are very different from other categories of nurse. These responsibilities are clearly articulated in the Nurses Act that governs your practice. Prior to July 2010, each state and territory had its own legislation and you had to register with your state or territory Nurses Board annually to legitimately practise as a registered nurse. Since July 2010, the responsibilities and accountabilities of registered nurses and midwives are articulated in *The Health Practitioner Regulation National Law.*

Point to ponder

It is worthwhile to take the time to understand your legislative responsibilities.

These legislative responsibilities are then translated into organisational 'Job and person specifications' for registered nurses. During the induction for your TPPP, you will be given a 'Job and person specification'. You may have already obtained one in order to prepare your application for the TPPP position. This document clearly details the responsibilities of the registered nurse in a particular organisation. It is in your best interests to familiarise yourself with the specifications, to help you work safely in the registered nurse role.

You may find that specialist clinical units have 'Job and person specifications' that detail the registered nurse responsibilities for that particular clinical specialty. For example, if you were working in an orthopaedic unit, then the 'Job and person specification' would have competencies relating to orthopaedic nursing. If it is an area you wish to work in following your TPPP, then the 'Job and person specification' is a starting point for finding out about the responsibilities and competencies required of the registered nurse to work in that particular clinical speciality.

The legislative responsibilities of the registered nurse work in tandem with the Australian Nursing and Midwifery Council (ANMC)'s national competency standards for registered nurses and midwives and the codes of professional conduct and ethics for nurses and midwives. The ANMC national competencies for registered nurses and midwives are organised into domains (ANMC 2006):

- professional practice
- critical thinking and analysis
- provision and coordination of care
- collaborative and therapeutic practice.

Appendix E sets out the ANMC competency standards in detail. The competency standards are broad but cover all the dimensions of the registered nurse and midwife. These competency standards may be adapted to individual workplaces and sites, but in all instances these competency standards frame nursing practice. From these standards you can see the complexity of the registered nurse role.

As a registered nurse, you incorporate the following functions in your day-to-day work. At any given time during your shift, you may be:

- *a teacher*—the teaching role may include teaching patients and their carers about ongoing care (for instance, managing wounds or medications) once thay are discharged from hospital.
- *a patient advocate*—in this role, you act on behalf of the patient and/or their carers when they feel unable to do so. This includes relaying concerns to other health professionals involved in the care of the patient.
- *a patient/family counsellor*—as a counsellor, you support the patient and/or their carer to deal with social and psychological issues that may have arisen as a result of their health problem. This could involve helping people change behaviours or attitudes by encouraging them to look at alternative ways of achieving and maintaining positive health outcomes. By providing emotional, intellectual and psychological support, you enable patients to make the right choices for health.
- *a clinical leader*—in this role, you provide leadership to other members of the healthcare team by demonstrating a high level of clinical knowledge and by translating this knowledge into good clinical practice. It is also about supporting other members of the healthcare team to develop their clinical competencies and knowledge.
- *a clinical practitioner*—to be effective as a clinical practitioner, you need to apply the clinical competencies and knowledge you learnt in university to your workplace.

- *a change agent*—a change agent by definition changes things. In this role, you are prepared to help patients change their behaviours to achieve positive health outcomes and then to maintain these. As a change agent, you are prepared to use literature-based evidence to suggest changes to clinical practice. Even during your TPPP, you may have opportunites to act as a change agent, and you should consider this to be part of your professional development.

- *a manager*—during your TPPP, your non-clinical management responsibilities may revolve around managing a shift, for instance allocating staff to patients, managing resources, and so on. Other non-clinical managerial responsibilities are concerned with ensuring a safe working environment for staff, patients and visitors. As a clinical manager, you will be responsible for managing the clinical care of patients by supervising the work of others, including ensuring that all health workers function in a safe and competent manner.

- *a user of research*—all nurses need to be able to use the findings of quality research to inform their practice. If you are working in an area or areas that engage in clinical research with patients as subjects, then you have a responsibility to ensure that their human rights and dignity are not compromised during the research project.

- *a communicator*—this perhaps is the most important competency and function of the registered nurse. As a registered nurse, you need to be able to communicate using a variety of media (verbal, non-verbal, electronic, written) and with diverse groups of people, including other health professionals and non-health professionals, patients and their carers. Your abilities as a communicator are a significant factor in the delivery of care to a patient or groups of patients in your care. Your communication capabilities are also important for your roles as an effective teacher, patient advocate and patient counsellor.

- *a negotiator*—in this role, you will negotiate with other health professionals how best to plan and deliver care to patients. You will involve the patient and/or carer in developing a plan of care. You may find yourself negotiating for resources to ensure care to patients is not compromised. On a pragmatic level, you will at some point negotiate shift changes with team members.

- *a care giver*—in this role, you plan and implement processes of care using the framework of the nursing process for your patient or group of patients. Care giving in this instance involves not only the physical aspects of nursing—'doing nursing'—but also the psychological and spiritual dimensions: the holistic model of nursing.

(Adapted from Madsen 2010)

Maria Fedoruk

So, you can see that the role of the registered nurse is quite complex, and while you most probably became aware of these complexities during your undergraduate days and while on clinical placement the reality of the registered nurse role may be quite daunting and overwhelming at first. Below are some suggestions to help you manage the process of becoming a registered nurse:

- Develop learning objectives, using the SMARTTA framework.
- Set some priority areas for learning in the first few weeks of your TPPP—develop these with your clinical facilitator.
- Familiarise yourself with the policies and procedures of your clinical unit.
- Do not be afraid to ask questions if you are unsure of things.

Professional boundaries

Within contemporary health practice, **professional boundaries** between health professionals are becoming increasingly blurred. In the past, there were quite clear delineations between health professionals. Traditionally, medicine was the top profession, followed by allied health groups, and then nursing. Nurses came from hospital-based training programs that were medically controlled, and they worked under the direction of medical practitioners (Walker 2009). These lines are becoming blurred, especially where the scope of nursing practice is expanding.

Benner (2001) described a 'novice to expert' model, for understanding various levels of experience and competency among registered nurses:

- *novice*: a nursing student with limited experience in nursing practice
- *advanced beginner*: a new registered nurse beginning to develop and apply clinical practice skills
- *competent*: a registered nurse with two or three years' experience, a nurse who is able to organise, set priorities and plan care for patients
- *proficient*: a registered nurse with up to five years of experience who is able to engage in effective **clinical reasoning** and decision-making
- *expert*: a registered nurse highly skilled and competent in all aspects of clinical practice.

As a new graduate, it is advisable that you work within your scope of practice and begin developing your clinical expertise.

In contemporary health and nursing practice the concept of professional boundaries also describes the professional relationship between nurse and patients or carers. Competency standard nine in the *National Competency Standards for the Registered Nurse* (ANMC 2006, Appendix E) states that a registered nurse 'demonstrates an understanding of standards and practices of professional boundaries and therapeutic relationships'.

Therapeutic relationships have been described as being perceived by patients to be caring, non-judgmental and supportive and to provide safety from potentially threatening events during the recovery period from illness (Moltram 2009). Effective therapeutic relationships are an outcome of effective professional relationships (between health professionals) in which individual health professionals use expert knowledge to deliver appropriate and relevant care to patients (Jacobson 2002). These therapeutic and professional relationships are limited and regulated by the professional boundaries described in the ANMC codes of conduct and codes of ethics (Appendices A–D) and the Australian Health Practitioner Regulation Agency (AHPRA) legislation.

Point to ponder

Do not place unrealistic expectations on yourself, as this only leads to burnout. Becoming an expert takes time, patience, persistence and lifelong learning.

Professional boundaries may also become blurred with the introduction of interdisciplinary models of health services delivery (Peate 2006). Interprofessional practice has the potential to enhance service delivery to patients but for this model of service delivery to be effective all healthcare workers must be willing and able to work within a team-based environment, though other groups may not be comfortable working in this way. Mutual respect is needed and understanding of how other healthcare groups work and their contribution to developing the care processes for patients. Integrated care pathways, clinical pathways or critical pathways may facilitate interprofessional practice and these you would have seen while on clinical placement as a student nurse. Effective interprofessional practice is dependent on team members communicating well with other team members and with the patients they are caring for. However, professional boundaries in this model of service delivery may become blurred through inappropriate **delegation** between the different health professions. Outcomes of inappropriate delegation are discussed above and will be discussed in more detail later in the book.

Another area where the blurring of professional boundaries may be problematic for you as a new registered nurse is in the area of the therapeutic relationship, which is the relationship that develops between you as the nurse and the patient(s) you are caring for (Peate 2006). It is very easy to blur professional and personal relationships when working as a registered nurse. Professional relationships are defined by the use of expert knowledge by an individual to provide care to a patient or group of patients.

Maria Fedoruk

Personal relationships or social relationships are not dependent on the use of expert knowledge (Jacobson 2002).

You must always be aware that the therapeutic relationship between you and your patient(s) is based on the fact that the patients in your care depend on your professional skills and knowledge to help return them to their optimal state of health. The focus of the therapeutic relationship is the patient(s)—not you. It is normal at times to develop an affinity for some patients over others, but your role as a registered nurse is to ensure that all patients receive the most appropriate care.

Point to ponder

It might be timely at this stage of your nursing career to begin thinking as a registered nurse.

Case study: An overlooked patient

While working a shift on clinical placement, you notice one particular patient, Mrs M, is being continually ignored by nursing staff working in that area. Mrs M is an elderly lady of 87 years, who lives alone but was admitted earlier in the day because of severe dehydration following a recent spell of extreme heat. Mrs M was found by a neighbour, who called an ambulance. Normally, Mrs M would have been rehydrated in the emergency department (ED) and sent home, but while in ED Mrs M experienced an episode of chest pain and so was admitted for further investigations. Mrs M is anxious to go home, and wants to talk with someone about this, but is being ignored by nursing staff. As a student, you are reluctant to intervene—the nurses looking after Mrs M are all older than you and have worked in the area for many years, and you sometimes feel intimidated by them.

Questions

- What strategies would you use to deal with this situation?
- Would you discuss this with a more senior nurse on duty, for example a nurse manager?
- Would you discuss this with your clinical facilitator?
- Now, what would you do if you were a registered nurse in the same situation?

The only appropriate therapeutic relationship between you as a nurse and your patients is one that is focused on the patient's care needs. In this relationship, there is the potential for a power imbalance, because patients need your care, support and guidance (Peate 2006). Effective therapeutic relationships (Peate 2006, p. 120) are based on:

- trust
- respect
- the appropriate use of power.

Point to ponder

The principles of a therapeutic relationship are the same for nurses at all levels, and you should already be aware of them. These principles are found in the ANMC competency standards for registered nurses and midwives.

An abuse of power in the patient–nurse relationship occurs when the focus of the relationship moves from the patient's needs to the nurse's needs. A simple example of this is when a nurse does not respond to a patient's calls for support, or when a nurse 'forgets' a patient in the bathroom, because they went on a break. You may have observed such behaviour during your clinical placements, or when you have visited friends or relatives in hospitals.

More extreme forms of abuse in the patient–nurse relationship include (Peate 2006, p. 126):

- physical abuse
- psychological abuse
- sexual abuse
- financial or material abuse
- neglect—not giving patients medications on time; not ensuring that patients are well nourished; not reporting changes in a patient's clinical condition.

FOR REFLECTION

What would you do if you observed another nurse or health professional engaging in an abuse of power with patients? Remember your legal obligations regarding mandatory reporting of unprofessional behaviour. What are your responsibilities as a professional registered nurse?

The ANMC and the Nursing Council of New Zealand (2010) have produced the document 'A nurse's guide to professional boundaries' where

Maria Fedoruk

the professional boundaries are defined as 'limits which protect the space between the professional's power and the client's vulnerability' (p. 3). How does this definition compare with the information above? As a registered nurse you enter the therapeutic relationship with competencies, skills and knowledge and you have the authority to plan and implement care for the individual. This professional relationship is maintained if you as the nurse focus on the goals of care for the patient. This document provides guiding principles for maintaining safe therapeutic relationships:

- The priority for nurses is to plan care around meeting the assessed care needs of the patient.
- Nurses should not withhold care from patients as a form of punishment and should note that any intent to cause pain or suffering as a retaliatory measure in response to the behaviour of a patient in their care is unprofessional.
- Nurses are aware of their own needs, behaviours, attitudes, values and beliefs and are conscious of their potential to affect the therapeutic relationships.
- Nurses are aware of the inherent power imbalance in therapeutic and care relationships, knowing that coercing power compliance may be an abuse of power.
- Nurses are aware of and have the ability to validate the therapeutic or care purpose of their actions and take into consideration the person's preferences and responses to those actions.
- Nurses are aware of the potential for personal discomfort for both the person receiving care and themselves when care involves touching, holding, other personal contact or invasion of personal space and they should respond appropriately.

(Adapted from ANMC & Nursing Council of New Zealand 2010, p. 21)

Professional nursing organisations

Like other professions in the healthcare sector, nursing has its own professional organisations. The Royal College of Nursing Australia (RCNA) and the Australian Nursing Federation cater for the concerns of all nurses. Nursing also has many specialisations and each specialisation has its own professional organisation. For example, there is a specific professional organisation for critical care nurses: the Australian College of Critical Care Nurses. These professional organisations are linked to international professional nursing organisations, providing you with a global network of nurse colleagues with similar interests to your own. While it may be a little early in your career to consider specialising in a particular area of nursing practice, it is not too early to begin looking into what these professional nursing organisations offer in terms of professional support and resources as you move forward in your nursing career.

The benefits of belonging to a professional nursing organisation include access to:

- **continuing professional education** programs
- research grants for clinically based research
- education seminars (including online seminars, which count towards your continuing professional development points)
- professional nursing journals, which provide you with opportunities to publish and to read published research
- information relating to workforce development issues
- information relating to **policy** changes at the national level
- opportunities to comment on policy changes as these relate to nursing practice and patient care
- information on position vacancies around the country
- information on how to apply for positions
- virtual mentoring services.

The websites of nursing organisations are valuable resources for you, and with today's technology you can access these from any location using a networked mobile device.

Royal College of Nursing, Australia

The first professional nursing organisation you should consider joining is the Royal College of Nursing, Australia. The RCNA is Australia's peak professional nursing organisation and is the Australian member of the International Council of Nurses (ICN). RCNA is a national membership organisation, open to nurses and nursing students in all areas of the profession. Established in 1949, the RCNA initially provided formal ongoing education for nurses who wished to gain higher qualifications in nursing. However, following the transfer completion of nursing to the higher education sector in 1993, the focus of the RCNA shifted to professional development and policy analysis and development. The RCNA continues to provide professional development opportunities for nurses. These include research scholarships for nurses wishing to engage in research in a clinical area of interest.

As you progress in your career and begin to specialise, you may consider membership in a specific specialist professional nursing organisation.

Membership in such an organisation enables you to network with other professional nurses in your clinical specialty, and provides you with ongoing education opportunities. Perhaps most importantly, it exposes you to current best practices in your area of expertise.

The Australian Nursing Federation

Another professional nursing organisation which you might consider joining is the Australian Nursing Federation. Established in 1924, the Australian Nursing Federation is the national union for nurses, midwives, assistants in nursing, and nursing students. The ANF represents the industrial and professional interests of nurses and midwives through the activities of a federal office and branches in each state and territory.

The ANF's 170 000 members are employed in healthcare and other settings in urban, rural and remote locations in both the public and private sectors. ANF members work in hospitals, health and community services, schools, universities, the armed forces, statutory authorities, local government, professional organisations, offshore territories and in industry. ANF members have the opportunity to contribute to and influence nursing issues by becoming involved in ANF special interest groups, committees and events, or by becoming a job representative in the workplace. In the current rather volatile job environment, membership of the ANF may be particularly worthwhile. While there is an ongoing nurse workforce shortage, healthcare organisations also continue to be reformed and restructured to meet efficiency goals and targets, and a quick way of doing this is by replacing registered nurses with less qualified staff. There has been an increase in ancillary nursing staff in healthcare organisations, despite the findings that registered nurses make a positive difference to health outcomes for patients (Needleman & Hassmiller 2009). Ancillary staff in this context refers to assistants in nursing and physician assistants. You may need industrial support in cases of workplace bullying and **harassment** at some point so the ANF has a range of national policies, **guidelines** and position statements. These can be accessed from your state/territory branch office.

All ANF branches have a network of job representatives in workplaces where there are members. Job representatives often provide the first point of contact with the ANF in the workplace and are the vital link between the ANF and its members. ANF branches also represent the profession by lobbying state and territory governments on issues affecting nursing and midwifery legislation, **regulation,** education and employment and the healthcare generally.

The ANF has run successful campaigns to increase nurses' wages and improve their working conditions across Australia. Provisions now enshrined in nursing awards and enterprise bargaining agreements include mandated nurse-to-patient ratios in Victoria and workload management arrangements in other states, professional development leave, qualifications allowances, revised career structures and paid leave for trade union training.

WORKING IN GROUPS

In your study group, discuss the following questions:

- Now that you are completing your undergraduate program, have your perceptions of the role and function of the registered nurse changed?
- Has the program made you consider how the nurse registration legislation is going to influence your practice as a registered nurse? What are some of the things you need to be very aware of?
- How different are these things from your role as a student nurse or even in the role you are currently working in?
- Do you think it is necessary to join a professional nursing organisation at the beginning of your registered nurse career?

Maria Fedoruk

SUMMARY

This chapter introduced you to the concept of belongingness and how this is reflected in the nursing workplace and related to the process of transition discussed in Chapter 1. We then discussed the complexities of the registered nurse role, which you will have already observed while on clinical placements. The case study and exercises gave you the opportunity to imagine yourself in the role of the registered nurse and consider how you would act in certain situations. The case study has ethical dimensions—ethics in nursing are discussed in more detail in Chapter 12.

The chapter gave you a brief introduction to the professionalisation of nursing. You should be beginning to be aware of your future professional responsibilities as a registered nurse. The chapter also offered you information about professional nursing organisations you may consider joining.

DISCUSSION QUESTIONS

1 What were three 'take home' messages for you from this chapter?
2 Do you believe there are any differences between your responsibilities as a student nurse and your future responsibilities as a registered nurse?
3 Why might you want to join a professional nursing organisation?

REFERENCES

Australian Nursing and Midwifery Council (2006) *National competency standards for the registered nurse*, 4th edn, Australian Nursing and Midwifery Council, ACT, <www.anmc.org.au/userfiles/file/competency_standards/Competency_standards_RN.pdf>, accessed 13 September 2011.

Australian Nursing and Midwifery Council & Nursing Council of New Zealand (2010) *A nurse's guide to professional boundaries*, Australian Nursing and Midwifery Council, ACT, <www.anmc.org.au/userfiles/file/PB%20for%20Nurses%20-%20Final%20for%20web%20+PPF%20Watermark%20-%20%20March%202010.pdf>, accessed 13 September 2011.

Benner, P (2001) *From novice to expert—excellence and power in clinical nursing practice*, Prentice-Hall, Upper Saddle River, NJ.

Boychuk, JE & Cowin, LS (2004a) 'The experience of marginalization in new nursing graduates', *Nursing Outlook*, vol. 52, pp. 289–96.

Boychuk, JE & Cowin, L (2004b) 'Multigenerational nurses in the workplace', *Journal of Nursing Administration*, vol. 34, pp. 403–501.

Boychuk, JE & Myrick, F (2008) 'The prevailing winds of oppression: Understanding the new graduate experience in acute care', *Nursing Forum*, vol. 43, no. 4, pp. 191–206.

Cutcliffe, JR & Weick, KL (2008) 'Salvation or damnation: Deconstructing nursing's aspirations to professional status', *Journal of Nursing Management*. vol. 16, no. 5, pp. 499–507.

Jacobson, GA (2002) 'Maintaining professional boundaries: Preparing student nurses for the challenge', *Journal of Nursing Education*, vol. 41, no. 6, pp. 279–82.

Levett-Jones, T & Lathlean, J (2006) 'Belongingness: A montage of nursing students' stories their clinical placement experiences, *Contemporary Nurse*, 24, pp. 162–74.

Levett-Jones, T & Lathlean, J (2009) '"Don't rock the boat": Nursing students' experiences of conformity and compliance', *Nurse Education Today*, vol. 29, pp. 342–9.

Levett-Jones, T, Lathlean, J, Maguire, J & Mcmillan, M (2007) 'Belongingness: A critique of the concept and implications for nursing education', *Nurse Education Today*, 27, pp. 210–18.

Madsen, W (2010) 'Historical and contemporary nursing practice' in B Kozier & G Erb (eds), *Fundamentals of Nursing Practice*, Pearson, Australia, pp. 56–72.

Moltram, A (2009) 'Therapeutic relationships in day surgery: A grounded theory study'. *Journal of Clinical Nursing*, vol. 18, no. 20, pp. 2830–7.

National Health Workforce Taskforce (2009) *Health workforce in Australia*, KPMG.

Needleman, J & Hassmiller, S (2009) 'The role of nurses in improving hopsital quality and effciency: Real world results, *Health Affairs*, vol. 28, no. 4, pp. w6250–w633, <http://content.healthaffairs.org/content/28/4/w625.full. html>, accessed 12 June 2009).

Peate, I (2006) *Becoming a nurse in the 21st century*, John Wiley & Sons, UK.

Sherman, R (2006) 'Leading a multigenerational nursing workforce: Issues, challenges and strategies' *Online J Issues Nurs*, vol. 11 no. 2, <www.medscape. com/viewarticle/536480_print>, accessed 22 May 2009.

Stuenkely, D, Cohen, J & de la Cuesta, K (2005) 'The multigenerational workforce: Essential differences in perceptions of work environments', *Journal of Nursing Administration*, vol. 35, no. 6, pp. 283–5.

Walker, S (2009) 'Nursing theories and conceptual frameworks' in B Kozier & G Erb (eds), *Kozier & Erb's Fundamentals of Nursing*, Volume 1, Pearson Australia, Sydney, pp. 23-40.

Zetler, J (2010) 'Legal aspects of nursing' in B Kozier & G Erb (eds), *Kozier & Erb's Fundamentals of nursing*, 1st Australasian edn, Pearson Australia, Sydney, pp. 55–85.

USEFUL WEBSITES

Australian Health Practitioner Regulation Agency (AHPRA): **www.ahpra.gov.au**

Australian Nursing and Midwifery Council (ANMC): **http://studentweb.usq. edu.au/home/w0031419/Site2/web%20links/ANMC.htm**

Australian Nursing Federation: **www.anf.org.au**

Royal College of Nursing, Australia: **www.rcna.org.au**

Chapter 3

Transition as a process for newly qualified nurses

Anne Hofmeyer

Learning objectives

After reading this chapter, you will be able to:
- understand the lifelong process of successful transition and adaptation
- understand that previous reflective learning can influence current success
- describe the ways social capital networks and norms can mediate transition disruption
- discuss the ways communities of practice can mediate isolation and foster inclusion for new graduates.

Key terms

Transition
Adaptation
Lifelong learning
Professional responsibility
Social capital
Communities of practice

Transition as a lifelong adaptative process

In Chapter 1, you were introduced to the concept of transition as a way of understanding the experiences of concluding familiar and predictable life as a university student and eagerly joining the healthcare workforce as a registered nurse. Graduating as a registered nurse is a significant achievement

(Morrow 2009) and signals the end of a familiar way of being and the need to nurture a new valued self-identity and new way of being in our world.

In this chapter, we revisit the concept of transition, and in particular look at it as an ongoing process in our life. As we do so, ask yourself:

1   what do we know about the four phases of transition?
2   why is it important to understand the experience of transition?
3   what can we learn from previous successes and setbacks to manage current transition challenges?
4   will disruption resolve over time or is transition ever present in our lives?

Then we will explore the concept of transition as an ongoing process in our professional relationships with colleagues by considering questions such as:

1   how can we foster positive transition experiences for ourselves and others in professional and interprofessional healthcare teams?
2   how can social capital networks and norms contribute to successful transition experiences?
3   how can the concept of communities of practice support the lifelong process of transition and learning?

Coping with transition

The process of facilitating transition in nursing and for patients, clients, families and communities has long been considered central to the profession (Meleis & Trangenstein 1994; Schumacher & Meleis 1994; Kralik, Visentin & van Loon 2006). Transition is an ongoing process with four phases: familiar life; ending; limbo; becoming ordinary (Kralik & van Loon 2008). The process is not linear and occurs over time, so experiences can be unpredictable, confusing, disorientating and isolating, before a sense of connection and realignment emerges (Kralik & van Loon 2008). Change in our professional and/or personal lives may be eagerly anticipated and welcomed. Conversely, change may threaten our identity, esteem, equilibrium, well-being and happiness, so transition experiences have the capacity to trigger a complex range of thoughts and emotions. Specific events such as the change from university student to registered nurse can challenge professional identity and confidence. Many undergraduate nursing students report a mix of excitement and anxiety during the final semester of their Bachelor of Nursing degree as they anticipate the transition process. Although the change from university student to newly qualified registered nurse is welcomed and is an exciting time, there can be accompanying doubts. There is an urgent need to receive affirmation, understanding and support from other registered nurses in order to moderate these feelings of disruption and vulnerability in clinical practice.

Developing lifelong skills to adapt and cope with transition is essential to professional identity, clinical excellence, safe practice and personal well-being. This is because the need to effectively adapt is an ever-present challenge in the career of the registered nurse and does not diminish at the end of the first year as a graduate nurse. For example, nurses work in many different work environments and healthcare settings, so frequent adjustments such as roster changes can present challenges that require adaption, new skill development and building relationships with new colleagues. Transition can be disruptive and stressful but can also help us create new meanings in our world (Becker 1997). So, developing skills to manage the uncomfortable feelings related to disruptive events is critical for our well-being and effectivenesss.

The transition shock experienced by new graduate nurses in the first year of practice can be acute and dramatic (Duchscher 2009; Morrow 2009; Pearson 2009; Mooney 2007; Maben, Latter & Macleod Clark 2006). **Competence** in clinical skills and confidence have been identified as issues for new graduates (Roberts & Johnson 2007). Confidence is key to learning and strategies to boost confidence have been explored for over forty years, but strategies to successfully foster the confidence of newly qualified nurses remain vague (Roberts & Johnson 2007). Later in this chapter, the concept of communities of practice is proposed as a concrete strategy to address this largely neglected issue.

You can develop resilience to manage transitions in your professional life by:

1   reflecting on personal and professional strategies that have assisted you to manage successful change in the past
2   building social capital networks with others to access information, support and other resources to perform competently in clinical practice
3   adopting a **lifelong learning** attitude and affiliating with others with similar values, including influential opinion leaders and communities of practice, on an individual and group basis.

Point to ponder

Transition is a process, not an event. It involves personal responses, and occurs over time.

Anne Hofmeyer

Reflecting on past transitions

Personal transitions

In your personal life, you have faced endings and new beginnings, but you may not have reflected on your capacity to cope with these challenges and changes. Reflecting on your personal experiences can provide cogent insights about personal and external elements that can promote or limit success. Feedback from family, friends and/or work colleagues can be influential but is only one component in the transition process. Self-reflection about supports or barriers experienced during personal transitions is invaluable.

Your willingness to engage in personal critical reflection is key to understanding successful transitioning strategies and creating a new coherent identity and confidence. By understanding how you have managed change in previous personal circumstances, you will then be able to develop adaptive strategies to cope with ever-present change in your professional circumstances. Use the following questions to guide your reflections about how you coped with a transition (change) event in your personal life.

FOR REFLECTION

Write a reflective paragraph about a transition (change) event in your personal life that went well:

- What happened?
- What did you do to secure success?
- What skills and attitudes contributed to your success?
- What other skills and attitudes could have improved your success?
- What else could have happened?

Write a reflective paragraph about a transition (change) event in your personal life that did not go so well:

- What happened?
- What did you do that did not work well?
- What skills and attitudes could have improved the outcome?
- What else could have happened to improve the outcome for you?

We can learn from successful and poor transition outcomes

- List three key messages to recall when faced with similar experiences in the future.

Transitions as a university student

It is important to recognise that your feelings during times of transition are a natural aspect of the disruption that occurs when we end familiar experiences and transition to unfamiliar roles, situations and relationships. The clinical placements during your undergraduate program provided opportunities for you to build your competence and confidence in a range of clinical skills, critical thinking and clinical reasoning. You received feedback from your clinical coaches and other registered nurses to strengthen your knowledge, skills and competence to achieve the expected level of a newly qualified registered nurse. Use the following questions to guide your professional reflection and learning.

FOR REFLECTION

Write a reflective paragraph about a transition (change) experience that went well during a clinical placement.

- What happened?
- What did you do to secure success?
- What skills, competencies, attitudes contributed to your success?
- What skills, competencies, attitudes could have improved your success?
- What else could have happened?

Write a reflective paragraph about a transition (change) experience that did not go well for you during a clinical placement.

- What happened?
- What did you do that did not result in a positive outcome?
- What skills, competencies, attitudes could have improved the situation?
- What else could have happened to improve the situation for you?

We can learn from successful and poor transition outcomes

- List three key messages to recall when faced with similar experiences in the future.

Belongingness

As you learnt in Chapter 2, the concept of belongingness is important because it underpins the socialisation processes that enable you to become a member of a multidisciplinary team. As you become more experienced in the registered nurse role, you will learn how to apply this concept of belongingness in building your own work teams.

However, there is a potential danger: a desire for belongingness can result in excessive compliance and conformity. For instance, a student nurse may observe instances of poor nursing practice but not comment on them, because to do so would jeopardise the process of belongingness (Levett-Jones & Lathlean 2009).

WORKING IN GROUPS

In your study group, reflect on your first clinical placement.

- What were your feelings?
- What did you do to become accepted into this first work group?
- What did you learn from this experience in terms of clinical placement?
- How compliant and conformist were you in this first clinical placement?
- What knowledge did you take from this first clinical placement into your subsequent clinical placements?

Another outcome of the process of belongingness is discussed in the next section.

Building social inclusive networks with others

We are connected to others in our personal and professional networks. These social relationships influence our health, well-being and ability to get on in life. Studies identifying factors influencing nurses' intentions to remain employed (Tourangeau et al. 2010; Tourangeau & Cranley 2006) and work values, attitudes and motivation of the four generations of nurses all confirm the importance of effective relationships with colleagues (Morrow 2009; Newton et al. 2009b; Rafferty & Clarke 2009; Wray et al. 2009; Carver & Candela 2008; Duchscher & Cowin 2004; Hu, Herrick & Hodgin 2004). Other studies have examined the role of **adaptation** of newly qualified nurses in relation to other generational groups (Duchscher 2009; Leiter, Jackson & Shaughnessy 2009) and inclusive strategies to increase cohesion between nurses and motivation in a multigenerational nursing workforce (Newton et al. 2009b; Rafferty & Clarke 2009; Wray et al. 2009; Carver & Candela 2008). The marginalisation of new graduates in unfriendly practice environments and the ensuing problems of alienation and turnover have been examined extensively in the literature (Morrow 2009; Duchscher & Cowin 2004). Building social capital networks and norms of trust, cooperation and inclusion is a strategy to tackle nurses' feelings of isolation and exclusion that erodes self confidence.

Given the importance of retaining newly qualified and experienced nurses, it important to build social capital in nursing teams. Capital can be understood as a form of wealth, assets, resources or investments resulting from the production and exchange of commodities. You are probably familiar with the term 'economic capital'. The concept of capital can also be applied to our social assets. Social capital is as the internal capacity for groups and teams to perform using networks and norms of trust, reciprocity and cooperation to act collectively to solve problems (Ernstmann et al. 2009; Woolcock & Narayan 2000).

As illustrated in Table 3.1, we can distinguish between bonding, bridging and linking networks:

- *Bonding* refers to links with others with similar social identity (age, class, ethnic group, etc).
- *Bridging* refers to links with others with different social identities but more or less equal in terms of status and power.
- *Linking* refers to ties with others who are dissimilar in terms of their status and power.

A social capital framework offers a critical approach to examine the exertion of power in relationships and can help us examine why some teams and groups are more successful in working together and accessing resources than others (Nyhan Jones & Woolcock 2009; Newton et al. 2009a; Sheingold 2009; Hofmeyer & Marck 2008; Scott & Hofmeyer 2007; Grootaert et al. 2004). The premise is that we can achieve more collectively than we can working alone—this is proven by cohesive nursing and interprofessional healthcare teams.

A social capital framework is relevant to the transition process in our nursing workplaces because it provides a way of talking about the necessary components of trust, confidence, cooperation, communication and knowledge exchange between newly qualified and more experienced nurses (Hofmeyer & Marck 2008; Burt 1999). Typically, knowledge and resources to do our job are exchanged (or withheld) in the context of our social networks (Newton et al. 2009a; Scott & Hofmeyer 2007). Newly qualified nurses who are able to build diverse and resource-rich network links with other nurses in their work environment and beyond are more likely to access and reap benefits and favours.

Anne Hofmeyer

Table 3.1: Social capital value in healthcare teams

Dimension	Description	Value in building social capital for clinical action
1. Networks, groups	*Bonding*—ties to others with similar demographic characteristics (age, class, ethnicity, etc.) *Bridging*—ties with others dissimilar in social identity, but similar in status and power *Linking*—ties to others with different status and power	Groups with diverse membership and linkages have better access to resources. Participating (giving and accessing resources such as information, support, favours) with different colleagues brings benefits. Characteristics most valued include trustworthiness, reciprocity, cooperation, honesty and respect.
2. Trust	There are two kinds of trust: • particularised trust (trust of familiar colleagues) • generalised trust (trust of strangers and organisations)	Trust enhances cooperation with others in difficult or changing circumstances. Trust is the extent to which we can rely on others (familiar and strangers) to either assist us or do us no harm.
3. Collective action, cooperation	Collective action and cooperation refers to whether and how effectively people work with others on common goals, or cooperate with strangers to solve a problem or crisis.	Cohesive professional and interprofessional teams. Reciprocity, cooperation and confidence in the competence of professional and interprofessional colleagues.
4. Information, communication exchange	Opinion leaders and influential nurses are critical to this dimension. It concerns the various modes of knowledge transfer and the methods by which groups receive and share research evidence, and for what outcomes.	It is important to communicate information and research knowledge to do the job within and across networks, and to consider who is excluded from information sources and the impact on them doing their job safely.
5. Social cohesion, inclusion	This dimension concerns the tenacity of ties and the capacity of a social network to include or exclude members. Inclusion promotes equitable access to group resources.	Team activities can improve communication and resource exchange and strengthen cohesion. Consider the impact of exclusion on well-being; ability to perform job; quality and safety.
6. Empowerment	Empowerment is the extent to which we have control over processes directly affecting our work life and well-being.	The perception of personal power, ability and capacity to make or influence decisions can affect everyday activities and may change one's life.

Source: adapted from Scott & Hofmeyer (2007); Grootaert et al. (2004).

Case study: Supporting a new graduate

Emma graduated as a registered nurse three months ago and was allocated to work in the same ward as you about two months ago. Judy was assigned to be a mentor for Emma but complains to anyone who will listen that this mentoring role has added to her workload. Emma avoids Judy as much as possible and asks other registered nurses for information and support to do her job, including you. Some registered nurses are willing to help Emma but a small group of older registered nurses (including Judy) laugh and refuse to answer her questions about clinical care.

You graduated as a registered nurse six months ago, so you understand Emma's plight and need for practical guidance, but you don't have sufficient clinical experience to answer all her questions. You are aware that Emma is becoming increasingly isolated and withdrawn, has made a few clinical errors, eats lunch by herself away from the ward, and struggles to complete her patient care on time.

As you leave the ward at the end of a day shift, you see Emma crying on the stairs. She tells you that she is overwhelmed with all her problems, so you both go to a quiet place to talk. She explains her current problems to you:

1   She is thinking of leaving the nursing profession because she is so unhappy. The current clinical experiences are definitely not what she expected as a university student and she does not know how she will survive coping with the pressure and disappointment.
2   She also overheard Judy and another older nurse decide not to report a drug error they had made together.

Questions

Discuss how you might draw on the ideas from this chapter to:

- support Emma personally as a newly registered nurse
- advise Emma professionally about how to handle the dilemma in the overheard conversation.

This case study is an example of professional sabotage which has been described in the literature as poor nursing role models, values conflict and the lack of genuine professional support for newly qualified nurses (Maben, Latter & Macleod Clark 2006). This serious tension between what is taught in universities and what happens in the reality of clinical practice must be addressed by nursing leaders in healthcare organisations and the academy (Duchscher & Cowin 2004). Mentorship by influential trusted nurses, improving the moral integrity of nursing workplaces and fostering communities of practice are strategies worth considering to build hope and cohesive teams.

Anne Hofmeyer

How do I learn what I don't know?

We know the spread of information and knowledge is a social process (Rogers 2003). This means that we typically prefer to access information from people we trust (such as opinion leaders) by word-of-mouth and/or face-to-face communication (Thompson, Estabrooks & Degner 2006; Burt 1999). For newly qualified nurses seeking to manage an effective transition from university to healthcare workplace, the mentoring gained from influential individuals such as opinion leaders and within groups such as communities of practice (CoPs) are critical strategies for lifelong learning, fostering confidence, building competence and enhancing well-being.

Opinion leaders

Opinion leaders are recognised by others as influential, respected, trustworthy, approachable, and willing to share credible information (Thompson, Estabrooks & Degner 2006). Individuals such as newly qualified nurses turn to opinion leaders for help in solving complex clinical problems. This social process is important because a combination of tacit knowledge (practical experience) and explicit knowledge (research evidence) is required to respond effectively to clinical complexities and inform evidence-based decision-making (Li et al. 2009).

Communities of practice

Promoting lifelong learning by fostering communities of practice is also a strategy to effectively manage tacit and explicit knowledge in nursing work environments (Li et al. 2009; White et al. 2008). Communities of practice are groups of people such as nurses and colleagues from other professions who share a concern for something they all do, and a desire to learn how to do it better as they interact with others (Wenger, McDermott & Snyder 2002). Registered nurses are well placed to support and work effectively with new graduates to facilitate their transition in communities of practice. In CoPs, people can be encouraged to share their stories and talk about what concerns them with others who are genuinely respectful and supportive. This process may create increased self-awareness and understanding of what has changed and the impact on their esteem, confidence and identity. Confidence is a critical component in successful transition but can be undermined by disruption, loss and grief, alienation and loneliness.

As Pearson (2009) highlights, newly registered nurses cannot be expected to know everything but the pressure to perform at a high standard is relentless.

So CoPs are an effective de-briefing environment to strategise how to manage successful integration in the process of transition.

Interprofessional practice

Notably, the ability to work in interprofessional teams is one of the twenty-one key competencies required for health professional practice in the twenty-first century (Pew Health Professions Commission 1998). The World Health Organization has promoted interprofessional practice since the 1970's, recognising 'interprofessional collaboration in education and practice will play an important role in mitigating the global health crisis' (WHO 2010, p 36).

> Working alone with no regular exchanges of experience for mutual improvement can no longer be considered professionally satisfactory. Working in a team enables the professions to solve complex health problems that cannot be adequately dealt with by one profession alone.

BOX 3.1: INTERPROFESSIONAL PRACTICE

Barr (1998, p. 185) argues that interprofessional education helps students develop the following essential collaborative competencies for practice as qualified professionals:

- Describe one's roles and responsibilities clearly to other professions.
- Recognise and observe the constraints of one's role, responsibilities and competence, yet perceive needs in a wider framework.
- Recognise and respect the roles, responsibilities and competence of other professions in relation to one's own.
- Work with other professions to effect change and resolve conflict in the provision of care and treatment.
- Work with others to assess, plan, provide and review care for individual patients.
- Tolerate differences, misunderstandings and shortcomings in other professions.
- Facilitate interprofessional case conferences or team meetings.
- Enter into interdependent relations with other professions.

As Boyce and others (2009, p. 433) noted: 'poor communication and teamwork practice has been implicated as a contributing source of error affecting patient safety'. Hence, it is important for newly qualified nurses to develop interprofessional team competencies and practice.

FOR REFLECTION

Newman (1994, p. xv) challenged nurses to consider the purpose of their practice through the following statement: 'The responsibility of the nurse is not to make people well, or to prevent their getting sick, but to assist them to recognise the power that is within them'. This message still resonates today. As you transition from a university student to a newly qualified nurse, connecting with your power so you feel confident is a key step in developing a new coherent identity and successful clinical practice. We connect with our power when we feel we have practised in a competent and ethical manner and have made a difference for others.

Consider the following questions:

1   Think about a situation in which you made a difference to the outcome in terms of clinical decision-making for a patient or in communication with other members of the team.
2   Write a short account of the situation and reflect on your specific actions that made a difference to the outcome of the situation.
    a   How did you feel about your actions and why?
    b   Did you take an ethical stand to ensure a good outcome for a patient or colleague?
3   What significance does *connecting with the power within you* have for you when you are trying to manage the disruption and change in your life?
4   Imagine you are a registered nurse in your second year of practice. As you look at newly qualified nurses, try to see yourself not so long ago and embrace a disposition of empathy and sensitivity towards these nurses.
    −   What three key messages would you offer these new nurses to build their self-identity and be the best they can for themselves and others they care for?
    −   What are your anchor points to foster resilience and help you understand your place in the world so you can live in the world as you want to be? (Kralik & van Loon 2008).

SUMMARY

Nursing practice is a way of being and a form of engagement and interaction with colleagues, patients and families and communities. The primary purpose of this chapter has been to explore the way of being in the process of transition from university student to a newly qualified registered nurse in clinical practice.

At a system level, we know that retention and graduate inclusion in clinical work environments is improved by high levels of cooperation, trust, communication and exchange of knowledge in cohesive teams (social capital). On an individual level, we know that our adaptability, flexibility and willingness to reflect are key factors in growth and mitigating disruption due to ever-present change in our professional relationships and work environments.

This ongoing learning, adaptation and building resilience cannot be undertaken alone or in a vacuum. It is the collective responsibility of all nurse leaders, managers and front-line nurses. Strategies such as building supportive relationships with influential nurse leaders and participating as members of vibrant communities of practice are strongly recommended.

DISCUSSION QUESTIONS

1   In what ways do the social structures and processes described in this chapter fit with how you currently practise or are taught to practise?
2   As you read this chapter, what were you able to identify about your own connecting style with other professional and interprofessional colleagues?
3   What do you need to unlearn to enhance your social capacity?
4   What three ideas from the concepts covered in this chapter could improve your practice?
5   How might you draw on the ideas from this chapter to enhance your work with professional and interprofessional colleagues?
6   How might you draw on the ideas from this chapter to support Emma in her transition towards a coherent sense of self?
7   How might you draw on the ideas from this chapter to enhance your work with patients and families?
8   Describe one 'ah ha!' moment that you experienced as you read this chapter, which prompted you to critically reflect on your taken-for-granted assumptions in clinical relationships.
9   What do you anticipate the challenges would be in building social capital in your practice?
10 How could the exchange of social resources and support contribute to better outcomes for health professionals and patients?

Anne Hofmeyer

11 What strategies could nurses use to build resilience in teams?

12 How could bonding and bridging social capital assist nurses in different healthcare units to cooperate, share ideas and work towards a common goal?

13 What do you anticipate might be the challenges for you personally and professionally as you confront poor practice in nursing?

REFERENCES

Barr, H (1998) 'Competent to collaborate: Towards a competency based model for interprofessional education', *Journal of Interprofessional Care*, vol. 12, no. 2, pp. 181–7.

Becker, G (1997) *Disrupted lives: How people create meaning in a chaotic world*, University of California Press, Berkeley.

Boyce RA, Moran MC, Nissen, LM, Chenery, HJ & Brooks, PM (2009) 'Interprofessional education in health sciences, University of Queensland Healthcare Team Challenge', *Medical Journal of* Australia, vol. 190, no. 8, pp. 433–6.

Burt, RS (1999) 'The social capital of opinion leaders', *The Annals*, American Academy of Political and Social Science, vol. 566, pp. 37–54.

Carver, L & Candela, L (2008) 'Attaining organizational commitment across different generations of nurses', *Journal of Nursing Management*, vol. 16, pp. 984–91.

Duchscher, JEB (2009) 'Transition shock: The initial stage of role adaptation for newly graduated registered nurses', *Journal of Advanced Nursing*, vol. 65, pp. 1103–13.

Duchscher, JEB & Cowin, L (2004) 'Multigenerational nurses in the workplace', *Journal of Nursing Administration*, vol. 34, no. 11, pp. 493–501.

Ernstmann, N, Ommen, O, Driller, E, Kowalski C, Neumann, N & Bartholomeyczik, S (2009). 'Social capital and risk management in nursing', *Journal of Nursing Care Quality*, vol. 24, no. 4, pp. 340–7.

Grootaert, C, Narayan, D, Nyhan Jones, V & Woolcock, M (2004) *Measuring social capital: An integrated questionnaire*, World Bank working paper no. 18. Washington, DC.

Hofmeyer, A & Marck, PB (2008) 'Building social capital in healthcare organizations: Thinking ecologically for safer care', *Nursing Outlook*, vol. 56, pp. 145–51.

Hu, J, Herrick, C. & Hodgin, K (2004). 'Managing the multigenerational nursing team', *The Healthcare Manager*, vol. 23, no. 4, pp. 334–40.

Kralik, D & van Loon, A (2008) 'Community nurses facilitating transition' in D Kralik & A van Loon (eds) *Community nursing in Australia*, Blackwell Publishing, Melbourne, pp. 109–21.

Kralik, D, Visentin, K & van Loon, A (2006) 'Transition: A literature review', *Journal of Advanced Nursing*, vol. 55, no. 3, pp. 320–9.

Levett-Jones, T & Lathlean, J (2008) 'Belongingness: A prerequisite for nursing students' clinical learning', *Nurse Education in Practice*, vol. 8, pp. 103–11.

Levett-Jones, T & Lathlean, J (2009) '"Don't rock the boat": Nursing students' experiences of conformity and compliance', *Nurse Education Today*, vol. 29, pp. 342–9.

Leiter, MP, Jackson, NJ & Shaughnessy, K (2009) 'Contrasting burnout, turnover intention, control, value congruence and knowledge sharing between Baby Boomers and Generation X', *Journal of Nursing Management*, vol. 17, pp. 100–9.

Li, LC, Grimshaw, JM, Nielsen, C, Judd, M, Coyte, PC & Graham, ID (2009) 'Evolution of Wenger's concept of community of practice', *Implementation Science*, vol. 4, p. 11.

Maben, J, Latter, S, & Macleod Clark, J (2006) 'The theory-practice gap: Impact of professional-bureaucratic work conflict on newly qualified nurses,' *Journal of Adevanced Nursing*, vol. 55, pp. 465–77.

Meleis, AI & Trangenstein, PA (1994) 'Facilitating transitions: Redefining of the nursing mission', *Nursing Outlook*, vol. 42, pp. 255–9.

Mooney, M (2007) 'Facing registration: The expectations and the unexpected', *Nurse Education Today*, vol. 27, pp. 840–7.

Morrow, S (2009) 'New graduate transitions: Leaving the nest, joining the flight', *Journal of Nursing Management*, 17, pp. 278–87.

Newman, MA (1994) *Health as expanding consciousness*, 2nd edn, National League for Nursing, publication no. 14-2626, New York.

Newton, MS, Hofmeyer, A, Scott, CS, Angus, D & Harstall, C (2009a) 'More than mingling: The potential of networks in facilitating knowledge translation in healthcare', *Journal of Continuing Education in the Health Professions*, vol. 29, pp. 192–3.

Newton, JM, Kelly, CM, Kremser, AK, Jolly, B & Billett, S (2009b) 'The motivations to nurse: An exploration of factors amongst undergraduate students, registered nurses and nurse managers', *Journal of Nursing Management*, vol. 17, pp. 392–400.

Nyhan Jones, V & Woolcock, M (2009) 'Measuring the dimensions of social capital in developing countries' in E Tucker, M Viswanathan & G Walford (eds), *The Handbook of Measurement*, Sage Publications, Thousand Oaks, CA.

Pearson, H (2009) 'Transition from nursing student to staff nurse: A personal reflection', *Paediatric Nursing*, vol. 21, pp. 30–2.

Pew Health Professions Commission (1998) 'Twenty one competencies for the twenty first century', Chapter IV of *Recreating Health Professional Practice for the New Century*, the fourth report of the Pew Health Professions Commission.

Rafferty, AM & Clarke, SP (2009) 'Editorial, nursing workforce: A special issue', *International Journal of Nursing Studies*, vol. 46, pp. 875–8.

Roberts, D & Johnson, M (2009) 'Newly qualified nurses: Competence or confidence?' *Nurse Education Today*, vol. 29, pp. 467–8.

Rogers, EM (2003) *Diffusion of innovations*, 5th edn, Free Press, New York.

Schumacher, KL & Meleis, AI (1994) 'Transitions: A central concept in nursing,' *IMAGE: Journal of Nursing Scholarship*, vol. 26, no. 2, pp. 119–27.

Scott, C & Hofmeyer, A (2007) *Networks and social capital: A relational approach to primary healthcare reform*, Health Research Policy and Systems, http://www.health-policy-systems.com/content, accessed 4 January 2010.

Sheingold, BH (2009) *Measuring the extent, distribution and outcomes of social capital in the nursing community*, ProQuest Dissertation and Theses Database.

Thompson, GN, Estabrooks, CA & Degner, LF (2006) 'Clarifying the concepts in knowledge transfer: A literature review', *Journal of Advanced Nursing*, vol. 53, no. 6, pp. 691–701.

Tourangeau, AE & Cranley, LA (2006) 'Nurse intention to remain employed: Understanding and strengthening determinants,' *Journal of Advanced Nursing*, vol. 55, no. 4, pp. 497–509.

Tourangeau, AE, Cummings, G, Cranley, LA, Ferrone, M & Harvey, S (2010) 'Determinants of hospital nurse intention to remain employed: Broadening our understanding', *Journal of Advanced Nursing*, vol. 66, no. 1, pp. 22–32.

Wenger, E, McDermott, RA & Snyder, W (2002) *Cultivating communities of practice*, Harvard Business School Press, Boston, MA.

White, D, Suter, E, Parboosingh, J & Taylor, E (2008) 'Communities of practice: Creating opportunities to enhance quality of care and safe practices', *Healthcare Quarterly*, vol. 11, pp. 80–4.

Woolcock, M & Narayan, D (2000) 'Social capital: Implications for development theory, research, and policy', *World Bank Research Observer*, vol. 15, pp. 225–50.

World Health Organization (2009) *Safe surgery save lives*, <www.who.int/patientsafety/safesurgery/en/>, accessed 11 October 2011.

World Health Organization (2010) *The framework for action on interprofessional education and collaborative practice*. WHO Department of Human Resources for Health, Geneva.

Wray, J, Aspland, J, Gibson, H, Stimpson, A & Watson, R (2009) 'A wealth of knowledge: A survey of the employment experiences of older nurses and midwives in the NHS.' *International Journal of Nursing Studies*, vol. 46, pp. 977–85.

Chapter 4

Entering clinical settings

Barbara Parker, Angela Kucia and Lucy Hope

Learning objectives

After reading this chapter, you will be able to:
- discuss the employer's expectations of the registered nurse role
- begin planning your career in nursing
- develop a professional relationship with your preceptor
- apply the principles of experiential learning to your nursing practice
- identify your ongoing learning needs as you move into the registered nurse role.

Key terms

Clinical assessment
Clinical placement
Experiential learning
Preceptorship
Transition to Professional Practice Program

Transition from university to the clinical setting

The transition from university to the clinical setting is an opportunity to put into practice new knowledge and skills. Clinical placements prepare students for the final transition to the workplace and the registered nurse role. There are many support systems available to help you navigate this transition. In this chapter, we look at these supports and consider what you need to consider before clinical placements and when you undertake the Transition to Professional Practice Program as a new graduate.

Point to ponder

Making the transition from student nurse to registered nurse can be an anxious time for you—ensure you are aware of the support systems available to you to make this transition.

Prior work experience

As a nursing student, you have already gained experience from many different sources and will be expected to bring all of this to your subsequent employment as a registered nurse. During secondary school, you may have undertaken part-time paid work, for instance in a retail or customer service environment. If you entered your nursing course straight after school, you may have continued with this part-time work during your undergraduate nursing degree program. Many young people gain experience in management roles in part-time jobs, for instance working as shift supervisors or assistant managers. Thus, part-time employment provides opportunities for you to gain valuable skills that are transferable to the healthcare sector. Many nursing students do not recognise that these skills can be used to succeed in a nursing career.

Point to ponder

Remember that you will bring to the registered nurse role all of your previous work experiences.

If you are a mature-aged student, you may be coming to nursing as your second or even third career. Often you have substantial financial commitments and established full-time or part-time careers in other employment fields. Combining this with study is challenging, as nursing demands a large commitment to study, on-campus activities and clinical placements. While existing career roles do provide you with essential skills that can be transferred to the healthcare setting, you can also benefit from shifting to a healthcare role during study.

Working in healthcare while studying

Universities recognise that students need to work to support themselves during their courses. When you are considering your employment choices, take every opportunity to immerse yourself in the nursing profession. Remember that at the end of your degree you will be working as a registered nurse and it makes sense to make the move into the field as soon as possible. Working in health will help you:

- gain **time management** skills
- hone fundamental nursing skills such as assessment, skin care and hygiene

- learn how the healthcare system works, from inpatient to community services
- increase confidence in your own practice (Alsup et al. 2006).

Working in a healthcare environment offers you plenty of opportunity for practice, and, if you pick the right workplace, you will be supported in taking time off for study, examinations and clinical placements. It is advisable to discuss this at the interview.

Major public and private hospitals offer employment positions for nursing students in the second and third years of their program. Depending on the curriculum you are studying, you may be offered an assistant in nursing (AIN) position during second year, but the majority of venues offer this position to third-year students. This is because third-year students usually have a more established knowledge and skill base and can practise at an advanced student level. At second-year level, you may be able to secure a personal care attendant (PCA) role in an acute care setting, without undertaking additional qualifications such as a Certificate III. In addition, from the first year of a program many students are employed as PCAs in aged care facilities. These positions may also require some additional training, either by the institution or in the form of a Vocational education and training (VET) qualification.

Point to ponder

Take advantage of the employment opportunities that may be offered by healthcare organisations during your student nurse program.

PCA and AIN positions are advertised in the careers sections of newspapers and on careers websites, or you could approach the nursing administration department of the organisation in which you would like to work. Treat this like any other interview process and before you apply for a position, make sure you prepare adequately by following these steps:

- Research the organisation. Get a sense of the vision and mission of the organisation, the type of clients it caters for, and the care that is provided.
- Find out the name of the director of care/nursing or the recruitment officer.
- Write or update your **curriculum vitae**. If you need help with this, your university careers department should be able to assist.
- Compile essential documentation such as police clearance, senior first aid certificate, and immunisation information.
- Gather evidence and records of your clinical practice—for instance evidence that you have completed manual handling, **infection control** or blood safe modules, and so on.

Barbara Parker, Angela Kucia and Lucy Hope

Experiential learning

Experiential learning refers to practical experience, such as that you receive in your clinical placements. It prepares you for your future role in complex and changing work environments. It enables deep and applied learning within the context of practice. Formal placements within healthcare settings are essential to learning safe practice and should provide outcomes that give you clear guidelines for staged improvement across a program and constructive feedback that will assist in learning. Clinical placements enhance lifelong learning, capability and professionalism, and provide opportunities to transfer, reorganise, apply, synthesise and evaluate knowledge.

Point to ponder

Clinical placements are opportunities for applying what you learnt in the classroom to real-life environments.

Within undergraduate nursing programs there are many formal placement opportunities to gain experience and interact with clients in the community, aged care facilities, the acute care sector and other specialty environments. Some nursing programs expose students to the clinical setting in the first semester of the program, while others delay this until students have a broad knowledge base from which to practice. This latter approach is strengthened by informal experiential learning activities that expose students to healthy people across the lifespan so that fundamental nursing skills, such as assessment, can be mastered. In addition, simulation, role play and interactive online activities are used in the learning environment. This is a non-threatening way for you to practise new skills in an environment where getting it wrong is an opportunity for learning, not a punitive experience.

Students are rigorously assessed in the clinical environment. Assessment occurs under the supervision of clinical preceptors, and a clinical facilitator employed by the university. At times it may feel that you are under a microscope and every staff member is keeping an eye on your practice, but clinical placements can be a very positive experience. Nursing staff welcome students into their work areas, and many nurses are very keen to provide you with additional support. Official support roles include those of the clinical facilitator (or clinical lecturer) and the preceptor.

The role of the clinical facilitator is to ensure that you meet the course objectives and maintain the standards of nursing practice. They are there to mentor, support and assess students on placement. They do not usually take on a teaching role, and you can expect to see them about two to three times per week. The clinical facilitator may be seconded from the venue—that is, they normally work at the venue as a nurse but are given time off to undertake the facilitation role—or they may be an external person employed by the university. Either way, the clinical facilitator's role is to advocate for you and ensure that an environment exists in which you can achieve your learning objectives. The facilitator also undertakes all of the clinical assessments and is an excellent resource if you are having difficulty with any of these.

The preceptor is a registered nurse that you are paired with, who provides additional mentorship, guidance and support at each point of the day. Nursing students will often be rostered on with the preceptor so that they can work alongside each other. In this way, the preceptor provides a teaching and support role while still attending to their usual patient workload.

Preparing for placement

In order to be ready to engage fully in the clinical placement, you need to have a broad knowledge base and have had the opportunity to undertake some skill practice, role play and simulation activities at university. It is important that you engage as much as possible with these opportunities and with the university environment. People will talk about the clinical setting as the 'real world', but students inhabit many 'real' worlds. These include home, work and recreation, which all impact on the amount of time a student spends on their university study. Students sometimes parrot the saying that 'Ps get degrees'. A 'P' is the minimum required to pass a course. However, what a 'P' really means is that instead of knowing half of what you need to know, you actually *don't know* half of what is vitally important for your safe practice. This, in turn, has a profound effect on your patients' outcomes. Your theory courses are essential learning for your clinical placements, and you should apply yourself wholeheartedly to your study. An understanding of pathophysiology, pharmacology, sociology, primary healthcare, law and ethics, quality and safety is essential to you being able to adequately assess and manage your clients' care.

Essential criteria

Make sure you are aware of your university policy regarding uniforms, name badges and essential documentation. All healthcare settings in Australia require students to produce a national police clearance, so your university will require this before they can place you in a venue. Some states require additional documentation, such as a blue card, 'Working with children' check or placement orientation checklist from the health department in your state.

In addition, your immunisation status is important, and you should consult your general practitioner or local government immunisation service to be screened and immunised for infectious diseases, as recommended in

The Australian immunisation handbook, ninth edition (Department of Health and Ageing & National Health and Medical Research Council 2008). You should also check that all other standard childhood immunisations are up to date for the state in which you are attending the healthcare venue. To assist you in this, government websites in each state provide information about immunisation guidelines for healthcare workers.

In order to be able to place you in the clinical setting, many universities also require a current senior first aid certificate with annual CPR updates. Your university will have this information online. Because some items may take some time to complete, make sure you are aware of your requirements early in the program.

Orientation

Either before placement begins or on the first day you can expect an orientation to the venue and the ward in which you will be working. Among other things, it is essential that you understand where the emergency exits are, what sounds signify danger or an emergency, and that you are very familiar with the infection control and manual handling procedures of the venue. The orientation will also outline your responsibilities as a student, including what shifts you will work, what time the shifts start and finish, who your preceptor is, how long and when you can take your breaks, the rules around when you can leave the ward, and who to call if you are going to be off sick. Some venues may require you to undertake a cardio-pulmonary resuscitation (CPR) and manual handling update, and this is an excellent opportunity for further learning and practice in these essential skills.

Point to ponder

Take every opportunity to apply what you have learnt in the classroom in the clinical setting.

Learning objectives

Be sure you understand how you will be assessed and compile relevant documentation before you start your placement. If you are unsure of where to locate any of this information, seek advice from your lecturer or course coordinator. It is expected that students will arrive at placement with some idea of what they wish to achieve during this time. Think about the skills you have studied and practised at university and are really keen to put into practice. Think not only of tasks such as 'setting up an intravenous therapy line' or 'showering a patient' but also about your time management and communication skills. In preparing these objectives, consider also how you would prove that you are performing these skills well. Your ability to devise strategies and collect evidence for your safe practice will help your clinical facilitator provide ongoing feedback and evaluation, assess your competency to practice and decide on your grade.

Point to ponder

Clinical placements are also an opportunity for you to engage your critical thinking skills to problem-solve and make decisions for the patients you are caring for.

Reflecting on practice

Working with different nurses can help you determine what sort of nurse you want to be (Bradbury-Jones, et al 2009). Critically appraise others and their work, and determine if the behaviour(s) and practice(s) you observe are what you would incorporate into your safe practice. Or are they examples of what *not* to do?

Measuring performance

Most clinical assessments are competency-based. These competencies have been accepted as the standards by which we measure safe practice. The benefits of using competencies in clinical assessment are that you can clearly identify what you should be doing and how to achieve it. You will need to know and understand the ANMC's *National competency standards for the registered nurse* (ANMC 2006, Appendix E) and/or *National competency standards for the midwife* (ANMC & Australian College of Midwives 2006). These are available on the Nursing and Midwifery regulatory board website in your state, or directly from the ANMC website, <www.anmc.org.au>.

Competency-based assessment on clinical placement:

- emphasises the importance of clinical practice, in addition to theory, in learning outcomes
- stimulates student learning
- recognises student excellence
- provides measurable outcomes
- provides evidence to support the university policies regarding assessment
- provides future employers with evidence of skills (a more effective way of communicating with employers)
- facilitates the move away from task-oriented clinical practice.

Barbara Parker, Angela Kucia and Lucy Hope

Apart from your clinical skills, professional practice requires a number of other skills. You will also be assessed on your organisation, time management, critical thinking and problem-solving abilities. Some strategies for meeting your learning needs on clinical placement include:

- Ask questions. If you don't know something—ASK. You are not expected to know everything. You are expected to have a beginner's knowledge base and to use this to ask appropriate questions.
- Consider what resources are available for you to begin to find solutions to things you don't know. These resources may include:
    - registered nurses, enrolled nurses and care workers
    - medical officers
    - policy and procedure manuals—online and hardcopy
    - journals, texts
    - other students
    - your clinical facilitator
    - websites (remember to use only official and reliable websites for healthcare information).
- Provide suggested solutions to problems you identify.
- Understand the link between theory and practice and be able to articulate this.
- Provide a rationale for nursing care—why are you doing this?
- If you have not had the opportunity to undertake an activity or skill in the clinical setting, then this is okay. Explain to your preceptor that you understand the theory that underpins the practice and have practised in the simulation environment. Ask if you can observe the preceptor undertake the task and then supervise you doing it. Request that you are notified the next time there is an opportunity to do the skill.
- Provide a list of skills and activities to your preceptor that will help you meet your learning objectives. If possible put this list in the nurses' station and ask the rest of the staff to let you know if any opportunities for these arise.

Personal considerations

Most students have a wonderful, exciting clinical experience. It is normal to feel anxious in the early days at a new clinical placement, but with support from facilitators and preceptors this soon settles. The first week of the first placement is a particularly vulnerable time, and students should try to reduce other life stressors at this time. Students want to do well and above all they want to do no harm, and this can contribute to putting enormous pressure on themselves. This stress can manifest in different ways: some students may find that they become tearful or irritable, sometimes forgetful, or vulnerable to illness (Elliott 2002; Yonge, Myrick & Haase 2002). There is no doubt that the clinical experience is tiring for students, because of both shift work and stress, and you need to ensure that you are getting adequate rest and sleep, good nutrition and exercise to sustain energy levels. For some students, the added stress at this time means that they need additional support beyond what can be provided by the venue or academic staff. Universities offer counselling services and learning advisors who can help with strategies for assessments, so familiarise yourself with these services.

Point to ponder

Make sure you take care of yourself during your clinical placements — minimise stressors in your life as much as you can.

Before you applied for your degree, you should have planned to ensure that you can meet the requirements of the program. You should know how much time you need to commit to study, how long and when your clinical placements are, and when and for how long you are expected on campus. This will help you to plan your work and family commitments to ensure that you are available for all aspects of your program. When you are planning, be sure to factor in time for rest, for family and for fun. Be realistic about what you can achieve and talk to your institution about a part-time study plan if needed. It may take a little longer but you will maximise your opportunity to gain the knowledge and experience you require to complete the degree and emerge as a safe novice practitioner.

Point to ponder

All schools and faculties of nursing have information available to potential students on their websites. Use this information to plan your undergraduate program.

When you have finished your placement, make sure that you keep all originals of your placement assessment items. Employers will request these when you apply for your TPPP. Remember that all the information you collected during your placements, such as strategies and evidence to show that you meet the competencies, can be used in your application and interview to prove that you are capable of meeting the standards of safe practice. This, together with

Barbara Parker, Angela Kucia and Lucy Hope

a high grade point average (GPA) will be important in securing the venue of your choice.

Career goals

Even before you began your program, you may have had some idea of where you wanted to finish up. If you don't, don't worry, as you have plenty of time to make these decisions. Many students are still not sure at graduation, and the transition year is a good time to look at what specialty areas are available.

One of your early goals should be to work hard to gain a high GPA and good clinical assessments. Although nurses are still in demand, employers will want to take the best graduates, and these markers of your ability to practise safely will assist you to gain the TPPP of your choice.

Point to ponder

A high GPA will support your career goals, as well entry into postgraduate programs—for example, the minimum requirement for a nurse practitioner is a Masters degree.

The third year of your program is a good time to start seriously thinking about your career goals and aspirations, and positioning yourself to meet these. Use the clinical placements as a time to seek out the knowledge and expertise of registered nurses and find out what areas are available for you to work in once you complete your degree. At university, talk with your lecturers, program directors and counselling staff, as these people have experience in the clinical area and/or in assisting students gain employment. Your university should also have a career centre that can assist in compiling curriculum vitae, applying for positions, interview skills and more.

Your longer term goals should be built around lifelong learning, and a high GPA will position you to take up further study opportunities. Some of these opportunities include specialising in your area of practice through Graduate Certificates, Graduate Diplomas, Masters or Nurse Practitioner programs. In addition, evidence-based practice requires excellent research skills, and you may consider an Honours research program leading to a PhD.

Transition to Professional Practice Program

The transition from student to registered nurse is a major milestone. You have been working towards this goal for some time, but initially being a graduate nurse may seem a bit daunting. Most newly graduated nurses will undertake TPPP. According to Levett-Jones & Fitzgerald (2005), transition programs share three primary goals:

1 to develop competent and confident registered nurses
2 to facilitate professional adjustment
3 to develop commitment to a career in nursing.

For the majority of nurses, the TPPP is a hospital-based program that takes place over a twelve-month period. During this time, the graduate nurse gets an opportunity to work in different ward environments, with the aim of applying the knowledge, theories and experiences obtained during university studies to the nursing management of particular patient populations and clinical situations. During the TPPP year, the graduate nurse also learns to deal with relationship issues with patients and their families, as well as other members of the healthcare team, including nursing colleagues. As a graduate nurse, you will have many new experiences. You will have an opportunity to apply and further develop the critical thinking skills that underpinned your nursing undergraduate studies.

Adapting to a new role and a new working environment

The TPPP year is going to be challenging, and sometimes stressful, but it is exciting too. This may be your first experience of paid employment, and the transition from student to paid employee is likely very welcome from a financial perspective. Shift work and working at weekends may take some getting used to and you will need to structure your social life around your work commitments. Fortunately, most employers are aware of the importance of retaining nurse employees and many offer flexible shift patterns.

Healthcare is constantly evolving and changing due to technological advances, increasing economic pressures and public expectations. A nursing career involves lifelong learning to keep up to date with new evidence and changes in practice. Although you are no longer a student nurse, you are entering a new stage of your education, and you must be prepared to continue to be involved in active learning.

Working in a hospital, you will become aware that there is a hierarchical administrative structure and complex social system that you will need to learn to work within. You will develop many new relationships at a number of different levels and you will need to adapt to the social aspects of your new environment. You will also need to understand what is expected of you and what resources are available to you to help you to perform effectively in your role.

Barbara Parker, Angela Kucia and Lucy Hope

Orientation programs

A comprehensive orientation program is important in preparing graduate nurses for their new role, and it is also a key factor in retaining staff (Mayer & Mayer 2000). It is therefore in the best interests of your employer to provide appropriate orientation, and in your interests to seek employment in an organisation that has a good orientation program. Orientation to the organisation usually takes place over a few days, and includes information such as the physical layout of the institution, the departmental and hierarchical structure, core business and organisational values, goals and policies. The importance of organisational values, goals and policies was discussed in Chapter 1. The orientation program may also provide an opportunity to undertake compulsory training sessions such as manual handling, fire safety, basic life support, and drug calculation tests.

Preceptorship

It is likely that when you start work in a new ward or clinical setting, a preceptor will be assigned to you. The preceptor is usually a senior nurse who has had sufficient experience in the clinical setting to be able to act as a role model and resource person for more junior nurses. When starting somewhere new, it is often reassuring to know that there is a person who has agreed to be available to you and assist you in your practice, education and socialisation to your new working environment. Some senior nurses have had educational preparation or in-service education to support their preceptor role, while others may be selected because of their clinical skills and expertise or expressed willingness to teach junior staff. Usually, the relationship with the preceptor lasts for a few weeks, and it may be that you do not often work on the same shift as your preceptor. The assignment of a preceptor to a new graduate is often somewhat arbitrary, and you may find that you identify another registered nurse on the ward who you find is an appropriate role model for you and who is willing to help and guide you.

Employers' expectations

As you begin your career as a registered nurse, you will find that expectations of you in your role are quite different from those that you encountered as a student. You need to be aware of what your employer expects of you. Some of these expectations are explicitly stated in the contract that you signed prior to commencing employment, but there may be other expectations that are implicit in the role. It is assumed that the graduate nurse is functioning at the advanced beginner level, with basic levels of competence that require support and guidance for safe practice. New graduates should be aware of their limitations and seek guidance as needed. As adult learners, new graduates are expected to identify their learning needs, and in collaboration with the preceptor, manager and clinical educator, participate in planning learning experiences and goals (Santuci 2004). Graduate nurses are expected to be accountable for their own practice and for developing their own best practice (Santuci 2004). As you have recently been a student, you may be aware of recent developments or changes in practice that may allow you to raise questions or make suggestions in your working environment when you see that practices could be improved or updated in line with current evidence. New perspectives from newcomers can offer fresh ideas for positive change (Santuci 2004). Don't be discouraged if your suggestions for change are not immediately embraced by your colleagues—resistance to change is firmly entrenched in some workplaces. It may take some time and representation of the evidence for change and the benefits to be expected to persuade people to embrace new ideas.

As a healthcare employee, there are a number of expectations regarding professional behaviour and safe practice that apply to almost all work settings, some of which may have ethical and legal aspects.

Access to electronic records and resources

During orientation, you should be provided with an overview of the computer-based systems that are in use within the organisation. To facilitate this, you should have good general computer skills. You may be expected to use a number of computer programs that are integral to activities such as:

- generating nursing care plans
- recording patient admissions, discharges, transfers and movement within the hospital
- ordering tests and services
- obtaining laboratory and investigative results
- email communication
- accessing library resources.

You will be given passwords in order to access these systems. Before accessing these systems, you will have to acknowledge that you are aware of privacy policies and that you will not access or disclose information inappropriately. Be aware that any activity you undertake in accessing these systems is monitored and can be tracked back to you. Therefore, you should ensure that you log out of the system when you complete the necessary activity. You also need to be aware that you are accountable for inputted information.

Information on the regulation of health privacy in Australia is available from the Australian Government's National Health and Medical Research Council (NHMRC) online at <www.nhmrc.gov.au/guidelines/publications/nh53>.

Occupational health and safety

An introduction to organisational expectations with regard to occupational health and safety (OH&S) is usually part of the orientation program. As an employee, you must agree to comply with the organisation's OH&S directives. This is for your own personal safety, and that of other employees and clientele of the organisation.

Most nursing orientation programs have a training session on manual handling. Historically, nurses commonly experienced back injuries as a result of lifting patients. Hospitals now have 'no lifting' policies to prevent these injuries. It is important that you are familiar with organisational manual handling policies and that you comply with them at all times. Ensure that you know how to safely use manual handling aids and equipment, and that you prepare to undertake annual manual handling updates.

You should not use equipment unless you have been shown how to do so safely. You should also be aware of issues pertaining to electrical safety, particularly in critical care areas, where patients are attached to monitors and often have several infusion pumps and various other medical devices in use. If you find a fault with any equipment, electrical or otherwise, it must be removed from use, the ward manager must be notified, and the equipment should be tagged to alert other ward staff that it is faulty.

Needlestick injuries are another common source of injury for nurses. They are preventable providing that appropriate processes are followed. Blood-borne diseases that could be transmitted by needlestick injuries include human immunodeficiency virus (HIV), hepatitis B (HBV) and hepatitis C (HCV). Information on organisational strategies to reduce the **risk** of needlestick injury should be provided during your orientation program. You should explore policies and procedures for reducing the risk of needlestick injury to yourself and others. Ensure that you know how to dispose safely of sharps, and where sharps containers are located.

Point to ponder

Safety in the healthcare workplace is your responsibility.

Infection control

Healthcare-associated infections continue to be a major problem for patient safety, and contribute to unexpected patient deaths. They also place a significant burden on healthcare resources (Pittet 2005). The evolution of multiresistant organisms makes some forms of infection difficult to manage. Preventing the spread of infection in the healthcare setting, where patients are often immuno-compromised, is essential. Nurses have an active role in reducing the spread of hospital-acquired infections. In fact, Florence Nightingale was the first person to suggest that nurses could survey hospital-acquired infections (Pittet 2005). Many hospitals have specific policy and procedure manuals for infection control, and may have an infection-control nurse or infection-control team. You should be familiar with infection-control policies and procedures and do everything that you can to prevent the spread of infection. Many healthcare organisations offer vaccination to their staff, to prevent diseases such as hepatitis, tuberculosis, tetanus and influenza. Vaccination against these diseases is in your best interests and the interests of the patients for whom you are caring. You may have been immunised during your undergraduate training, but if not you should consider this as a priority.

A good resource for you to access for more information on infection control is the Australian Government's Department of Health and Ageing infection control guidelines, available online at <www.health.gov.au/internet/main/publishing.nsf/content/icg-guidelines-index.htm>.

Responding to hospital emergencies

Various emergency situations can occur in the hospital setting, and staff must know how to manage them. During your orientation, it is likely that you will undergo some training in how to manage situations such as fire, security threats and medical emergencies. It is important that you know what is expected of you as a graduate nurse in these situations. Generally, annual updates are required, and it is your responsibility to ensure that you complete these updates when they are due. You may have had some experience of these updates during your clinical placements.

Shift work

Service industries, such as hospitals, operate over a 24-hour period, and therefore must employ shift workers. Generally, the number of staff on duty outside of business hours is kept to a minimum, but it is likely that you will be expected to do rotations of night duty during your graduate year. Shift work disrupts the synchronous relationship between the body's internal clock and the environment, which can affect your general health and feeling of well-being. Physiologic effects include changes in rhythms of core temperature, various hormonal levels, immune functioning, and activity–rest cycles. Problems such as sleep disturbances, increased accidents and injuries, and social isolation may result (Berger & Hobbs 2005). It is important that you do what you can to reduce the negative effects of shift work. Schedule six to eight hours of sleep and use power napping before work when needed. Avoid food and drinks that are likely to cause wakefulness, such as alcohol and caffeine, for at least six hours prior to scheduled sleep times.

Developing a sense of belonging

During your TPPP, it is likely that you will have three to four different ward placements. You may have had some input into your ward placements, but the overall goal is to provide you with a range of nursing experiences. Each of your placements may be quite different and it may take some time to settle in to each. You will enjoy some more than others, and this may be influenced by how supportive your co-workers are. It may help you to decide where you want to work when you complete your TPPP. If you find a ward or workplace that you really enjoy and would like to come back to when you complete your TPPP, let the nurse manager know, as they may then be in a position to advocate for you if a position becomes available.

For some years now there has been a shortage of nurses in most Western countries, which means that hospitals in particular are employing a larger number of graduate nurses. Some wards depend upon a large cohort of graduate nurses to maintain staffing requirements. Being a new graduate on a ward that has a high percentage of new graduates can have advantages and disadvantages. On the plus side, the staff are accustomed to working with graduate nurses and will understand the need for education, support and mentorship. However, constantly mentoring new staff can be quite exhausting for the permanent staff on a ward, particularly if they have a heavy workload of their own. The staff may feel that once a graduate nurse has reached some level of independence in a particular ward and the need for close supervision is lessened, the graduate nurse is moved to another area and the cycle begins again. Permanent ward staff may feel frustrated that they haven't got time to adequately support new graduate nurses. If this frustration is outwardly expressed, it may leave you feeling inadequate and inept, and this may result in you feeling hesitant about approaching certain ward staff for help. Don't be tempted to undertake a task for which you have not had sufficient experience or practice without guidance or support. If you are not getting the support that you require, you may need to address the problem with the nurse manager.

Case study: Lifting patients

During my nursing training, we were taught how to lift patients with a lifting machine. It didn't seem to be too difficult...I learnt how to operate the machine (although it was a bit technical). We (the student nurses) broke into groups of three and took turns being the patient. We lifted each other using the machine—it was fun, and as far as I was concerned (and the nurse educators, for that matter) I was competent to lift patients! During my first week on the ward, I had to use the lifter to lift a patient from his bed to the chair. He had undergone major abdominal surgery and had intravenous drips, wound drains, a urinary catheter and a huge abdominal wound. I didn't ask the other staff to help me. When I had asked for help on other matters, some of the staff had seemed irritated because they were busy, while others seemed unapproachable. I thought I should be able to do this by myself. When I tried to get the patient into the lifter, he seemed to have a lot of pain and was afraid of falling. He struggled against me, and I was afraid I would dislodge some of his drips or drains in the process of moving him. The result was that we both ended up in a tangle, and I felt very foolish when I had to go and ask the senior registered nurse for help. I found that the reality of lifting a patient in the clinical setting is a lot different from lifting a nurse in the clinical skills lab. Although I had been taught how to use a mechanical lifter, I had not had experience that helped me to anticipate problems or variations that may arise in lifting an unwell patient in the clinical setting, and the need to plan around these factors. I also learnt that the welfare of the patient was far more important than my fear of an unfavourable reaction if I asked for help.

Questions

Consider the situation above.

1   After reading this chapter and considering the issues with transition from student to graduate nurse, why do you think the nurse may have acted in this way?
2   How do you think this situation may have been prevented?
3   Are there occupational health and safety issues involved in this example?
4   Was patient safety at risk?

BOX 4.1: THE NURSING STUDENT PERSPECTIVE—LESSONS LEARNT

Whether you are at university or in the clinical environment there is much to learn, and students who have already navigated this path can provide excellent insights and strategies about everything from how to succeed in your theory courses to what types of employment can assist you during your studies and

Barbara Parker, Angela Kucia and Lucy Hope

how to secure that longed-for position after you graduate. Provided below are some tips from a high-achieving student to ensure your success.

TUTORIALS AND WORKSHOPS

Tutorial and workshop sessions are often a fun and interactive way to learn the practical and theoretical content in the course. Most tutorial and workshop sessions are based on groupwork, and include scenarios that are based closely on the theoretical content. To get the most out of your tutorial or workshop:

- Come to the workshop or tutorial session prepared, having read the online content for that week or other required readings, and consider any questions that you may have to bring up during the tutorial.
- Engage in the scenarios and groupwork, as the practical application of your theoretical knowledge will help prepare you for clinical placements or your future employment.
- Discuss issues that arise with other students in the group—you will learn a great deal if you are open to the thoughts and viewpoints of others.

Workshop scenarios are very relevant to the types of circumstances that you may come across in your future employment. Engaging in these activities will allow you to understand how to deal with challenging circumstances and the types of problem-solving skills you may need in the workforce. The emphasis on teamwork mirrors the professional working environment, as health professionals continually work collaboratively in order to provide a high level of care.

PREPARING FOR EXAMS

Exam time can be very stressful, as there is often a great deal of theoretical content covered throughout a semester. In order to be adequately prepared for exams it is important to keep up to date with the theory content throughout the semester. Attempting to learn a semester's worth of work in a few short weeks is near impossible.

Towards the end of the semester there are often revision tutorials and lectures that summarise some of the topics that will be covered in the exam. While these lectures and tutorials will not cover everything you will need to know for the exam, they are a useful reminder of what to revisit over your revision period.

It is also sometimes possible to download your lectures, as PowerPoints or podcasts, from the online university resources, so that you can revise this material easily.

After revising a topic, it is often helpful to go over the material with other students in a study group, as you can ask each other questions and hopefully get a better understanding of the course content through these discussions.

Use the textbooks to look up any concepts that you are unsure of. Do not try to read the whole textbook and memorise large sections. Instead, try to get a good understanding of the material and take notes. Refer to the text when clarifying or to obtain more information about particular topics.

Create your own practice questions and prepare answers for them; share these with other students.

Talk through questions and answers out loud to assist in remembering difficult concepts.

CLINICAL PLACEMENTS

Clinical placements are an essential part of the nursing degree. While they can be a daunting experience, they are also very rewarding. In order to make the most out of your clinical placement experience, it is important to ensure that you are adequately prepared.

- Consider what areas of nursing you are most interested in, as there are many different settings where you may have the opportunity to undertake your placement.
- Don't be afraid to choose a placement that may be outside your comfort zone, as this may be an area where you can learn a great deal and that will help you to decide if this may be an area of interest for employment in the future.
- Consider what types of skills you want to improve on throughout your placement. Consider your strengths and weaknesses, and use them to form the basis of possible learning objectives while on placement.
- Keep a journal of all your activities, as this can be used as further evidence to present to your facilitator or lecturer.
- Interact with the multidisciplinary team as much as possible—it is useful to have a good understanding of these services (for instance social work or physiotherapy) so that you can refer patients.

Take advantage of any opportunities to undertake tasks that you are not yet comfortable with, such as wound dressings or drain removal. Ask to first observe a registered nurse perform the task, and after reading the venues policy and procedure manual, request to perform the task under supervision of the registered nurse. Once you have become very comfortable with a particular task, it may be possible for you to demonstrate your accurate technique for other students while explaining the procedure. This will allow you to gain more experience and will additionally benefit other students' level of understanding.

Take note of the various roles undertaken by registered nurses within the clinical setting. Management, specialty areas, and even education are often undertaken by registered nurses. If there is an area that you are particularly interested in, it may be possible for you to spend a short period of time with a registered nurse in that area, such as a mental health nurse or breast care nurse. Ask your facilitator if there is any possibility of something being arranged so that you can learn more about some of these specialised roles.

It is important to remember that while the clinical placement experience can be overwhelming, it is a learning environment. Allow yourself some time to settle into the clinical setting. Make the most of debriefing sessions organised by your clinical facilitator. Discuss any issues with some of your fellow students, as you may find that they are having similar issues or they may be able to provide solutions to problems you are facing.

UNDERGRADUATE EMPLOYMENT OPPORTUNITIES

To maximise your learning opportunities and time within the clinical setting, a position within the field of nursing throughout your degree may be beneficial. Personal care attendant and assistant in nursing undergraduate positions are available in many acute care and aged care facilities. Within the acute care facilities undergraduate positions enable the student to undertake nursing duties under the indirect supervision of a registered nurse, depending on the venue's policies and procedures. This may include experience managing postoperative patients in consultation with a registered nurse, admissions and discharges, and preparing patients for theatre.

These employment positions can be beneficial to your future career, as your employment in the clinical setting is viewed positively by prospective employers. It is also likely that gaining employment in an acute setting may lead to a job prospect within this organisation, as they will have gained insight into your work ethic and competence in a clinical environment.

Attaining an assistant in nursing undergraduate position in an acute care setting provided us with valuable experience and insight into the role of the registered nurse. As our time management and organisational skills improved, so too did our confidence at practising in a more independent manner. It wasn't until we worked within this setting that we began to understand how the shift was structured, allowing patient care to be carried out in an orderly manner. We were also able to gain insight into the need for the registered nurse to be very flexible, as while a plan of action may be produced at the beginning of the shift this may need to be rearranged to best manage the patients within your care. We were also able to observe that while there are standard practices within nursing, some tasks can be done in various ways while still following best practice and result in the same outcome for the patient. This enabled us to develop many problem-solving strategies.

Perhaps the most beneficial attribute from this position was the effective communication techniques that we gained in speaking with staff, patients and relatives. This has enabled us to gain further confidence, as we feel that we are now able to communicate effectively with staff and patients in a professional manner. This environment has also allowed us to develop our assessment skills.

This position allowed us to become very confident in some aspects of the job, which meant that we have now been able to focus our attention more on the responsibilities that are specific to the registered nurse role. This made clinical placements easier, as we had some knowledge of the manual handling and care roles and were then able to focus more on complex procedures such as medication administration, wound care and IV therapy, and thus were offered more opportunities to practise these specialised skills.

SUMMARY

In this chapter we have looked at the processes of transition that students and new registered nurses go through in entering the clinical environment. Case studies and boxes provided in this chapter come from the experiences of new registered nurses who have been through the transition experience personally. Part-time work experience in healthcare, clinical placements and the formal TPPP were all discussed, as were experiences where nursing students move into the formal clinical environment for the first time. This chapter provided a more detailed overview of the TPPP, which you were introduced to in Chapter 1, and further explored your new responsibilities as a registered nurse. Embedded in this chapter is Benner's (2001) novice to expert model and as you read through this chapter you should begin to see how applicable this model is to your transition from student nurse to registered nurse.

Barbara Parker, Angela Kucia and Lucy Hope

DISCUSSION QUESTIONS

1　What are some key points you believe you will take with you from your student nurse experiences to your new role as a registered nurse?
2　From your perspective, how prepared are you to begin work as a registered nurse?
3　What are your expectations of the registered nurse role?
4　In your opinion, is it too soon to begin planning your career?

REFERENCES

Alsup, S, Emerson, L, Lindell, A, Bechtle, M, & Whitmer, K (2006) Nursing Cooperative Partnership: A recruitment benefit, *Journal of Nursing Administration*, vol. 36, no. 4, pp. 163–6.

Australian Nursing and Midwifery Council (2006) *National competency standards for the registered nurse*, 4th edn, Australian Nursing and Midwifery Council, ACT, <www.anmc.org.au/userfiles/file/competency_standards/Competency_standards_RN.pdf>, accessed 13 September 2011.

Australian Nursing and Midwifery Council & Australian College of Midwives (2006) *National competency standards for the midwife*, Australian Nursing and Midwifery Council, ACT, <www.anmc.org.au/userfiles/file/competency_standards/Competency%20standards%20for%20the%20Midwife.pdf>, accessed 1 October 2011.

Benner, P (2001) *From novice to expert: Excellence and power in clinical nursing practice*, Prentice-Hall, Upper Saddle River, NJ.

Berger, AM & Hobbs, BB (2005) 'Impact of shift work on the health and safety of nurses and patients', *Clinical Journal of Oncology Nursing*, vol. 10, no. 4, pp. 465–71.

Bradbury-Jones, C, Hughes, SM, Murphy, W, Parry, L, & Sutton, J (2009) A new way of reflecting in nursing: The Peshkin approach. *Journal of Advanced Nursing*, vol. 65, no.11, pp. 2485–2493.

Department of Health and Ageing & National Health and Medical Research Council (2008) *Australian immunisation handbook*, 9th edn, Australian Government, Canberra, <www.health.gov.au/internet/immunise/publishing.nsf/content/handbook-home>, accessed 1 October 2011.

Elliott, M (2002) 'The clinical environment: A source of stress for undergraduate nurses', *Australian Journal of Advanced Nursing*, vol. 20, no. 1, pp. 34–8.

Levett-Jones, T & Fitzgerald, M (2005) A review of graduate nurse transition programs in Australia. *Australian Journal of Advanced Nursing*, vol. 23, no. 2, pp. 40–5.

Mayer, RM & Mayer, C (2000) 'Utilization-focused evaluation: Evaluating the effectiveness of a hospital nursing orientation program', *Journal for Nurses in Staff Development*, vol. 16, no. 5, pp. 205–8.

Pittet, D (2005) 'Infection control and quality health care in the new millennium', *Journal of Infection Control*, vol. 33, pp. 258–67.

Santuci, J (2004) 'Facilitating the transition into nursing practice', *Journal for Nurses in Staff Development*, vol. 20, no. 6, pp. 274–84.

Yonge, O, Myrick, F & Haase, M (2002) Student nurse stress in the preceptorship experience,' *Nurse Educator*, vol. 27, no. 2, pp. 84–8.

USEFUL WEBSITES

Australian Government's OHS&W (Workplace Health and Safety) advice: **http://australia.gov.au/topics/employment-and-workplace/ohs-workplace-health-and-safety**

Department of Health and Ageing *Australian immunisation handbook*: **www.health.gov.au/internet/immunise/publishing.nsf/content/handbook-home**

Department of Health and Ageing *Infection control guidelines*: **www.health.gov.au/internet/main/publishing.nsf/content/icg-guidelines-index.htm**

National Health and Medical Research Council's information on the regulation of health privacy in Australia: **www.nhmrc.gov.au/guidelines/publications/nh53**

Workers Health Centre fact sheet on sleep and shift work: **www.workershealth.com.au/facts043.html**

Chapter 5

Making the transition to professional midwifery practice

Elizabeth Grinter

Learning objectives

After reading this chapter, you will be able to:

- discuss the principles of listening to women for accountability and professionalism
- consider ways of thinking to assist in making the transition to professional practice
- discuss sources of knowledge
- outline the principles of research and evidence-based practice.

Key terms

Accountability
Empathy
Critical assumptions
Reconnaissance

Making the transition to midwifery practice

This chapter provides you with an overview of the transition and belongingness processes you will move through from student midwife to registered midwife. Just as a student nurse goes through a transition to become a registered nurse, as a student midwife you will make a similar transition to become a registered midwife. Chapters 1 and 2 provide a theoretical overview of the processes of transition and belongingness, while Chapter 3 provides a more detailed discussion of these processes. These chapters apply to both student nurses and student midwives, whereas this chapter looks at the specific area of practice for midwives.

Professional registration

To work as a registered midwife, you will need to register with the Australian Health Practitioner Regulation Agency. Registration as a midwife brings with it the responsibility and accountability to do no harm and to provide evidence that you are a safe and competent practitioner. It is advisable to be very aware of the expectations the public and your professional colleagues will have of you once you are registered.

There are professional associations for midwives that will provide you with support and advice as you begin your career as a midwife. The Australian College of Midwives is the main professional organisation, and each state or territory has its own branch. The Australian College of Neonatal Nurses is another national association.

Point to ponder

What evidence will you have to provide to demonstrate competence as a midwife? What evidence have you collected so far?

Working as a midwife

During your undergraduate program, you will have spent time on clinical placements with registered midwives, and have become familiar with the different contexts in which midwives practise. Clinical placements provide an opportunity to observe other midwives and find out for yourself what makes a skilled midwife. Clinical placement periods are times of intense learning, and when you come back to the classroom—physical or virtual—you can reflect on what is considered to be best practice in midwifery.

WORKING IN GROUPS

In your study group, discuss your reasons for becoming a midwife.

- What motivated you to enter the midwifery program at your university?
- Has the reality of midwifery practice met your expectations so far?
- Have you found some of your assumptions about midwifery practices to be unrealistic?

Elizabeth Grinter

Qualities of a skilled midwife

Pelvin (2010, p. 299) states that 'the role of the midwife is concerned with the making of mothers'. Central to midwifery practice is the relationship that you develop with the woman you are caring for. To achieve this goal, you need to bring certain qualities to your role as a midwife. During your studies, you will have learnt the clinical skills, knowledge and competencies required for the midwifery role, but what qualities will you need to develop to accompany these?

To develop in the role of midwife, you first have to integrate your own personal values, knowledge and belief systems with the requirements of the role (Pelvin 2010). This means developing strong self-awareness and understanding how the values you hold can influence your practice.

Some of the qualities expert midwives have and demonstrate include empathy, honesty, trustworthiness, ethical behaviours, integrity, robustness and resilience, curiosity, and practicality. Having empathy means that you have the capacity to understand another's feelings. As a midwife, demonstrating empathy means you can understand the feelings and perspective of the woman you are caring for. Honesty and trustworthiness are essential if you are to successfully work with the woman throughout her pregnancy—she has to have trust in you as a professional. Ethical behaviours are important in terms of maintaining confidentiality and working within the professional boundaries between you and the woman you are caring for. All of these qualities are embedded in the *National competency standards for the midwife* (ANMC & Australian College of Midwives 2006). You should familiarise yourself with these if you have not already done so.

As well as the professional relationships you develop with those women in your care, you will also develop professional relationships with other midwives and other health professionals. As part of the transition to registered midwife, you should begin developing relationships with the health professionals and midwives you meet during the course of your undergraduate program.

Two other qualities you will need to develop are reflectiveness and self-knowledge. Inherent in reflectiveness are critical thinking and critical analysis—skills you will need throughout your career as a midwife. Reflectiveness means being able to look back on your practice and determine what is working well and which areas you may need to further develop. Critical thinking skills enable you to look at research-derived evidence to inform your practice. While at university, you will have learnt how to access information relevant to your practice.

Culturally safe practice

Point to ponder

What skills and knowledge will you need to develop to ensure the women you work with feel culturally safe with you?

As a midwife, one of your roles is to ensure women feel culturally safe with you. The following example, based on a case study from Pairman and McAra-Couper (2010, p. 323), emphasises the multicultural nature of midwifery practice. Read the scenario and then discuss it in your study group.

Case study: Cultural awareness

Jess, a student midwife, is visiting a woman she has followed as part of her midwifery student case load, to discharge her. The supervising independent midwife, Sarah, is accompanying her. Jess asks the woman being discharged what sort of contraception she used in the past and whether she intends to continue using it. The woman becomes uncomfortable and has difficulty in answering the question. Sarah quickly steps in and changes the subject. The discharge process is then completed.

Once they are out of the woman's home environment, Jess asks Sarah why she had corrected her line of questioning. Sarah replies that contraception is against the woman's values, religious and cultural beliefs, and that her family are unaware she had used contraception. Jess is then able to reflect on her critical assumptions around her practice. She has learnt a lesson about making assumptions that other people share her values and belief systems.

FOR REFLECTION

Discuss this case study in your study groups, using the following questions as starting points for your discussion. You may also think of other questions to discuss.

- What are three take-home messages for you from this case study?
- Would you have done anything differently if you were in a similar situation?
- Does this case study emphasise the importance of being culturally aware?
- How would you describe your own cultural background? How similar is it to the cultural backgrounds of the women you have in your student case load?
- Was there a better way to manage this situation so that it was culturally safe for the woman?

Elizabeth Grinter

- How do you think your attitudes and values will influence your practice as a midwife?
- What would you do if a woman and her family told you that they did not feel safe with you?

Knowledge

Knowledge in midwifery comes from a variety of sources. The theoretical knowledge may stem from ancient philosophers or more contemporary theorists. Practical knowledge comes from the sciences: physics, chemistry, psychology, sociology, biology, pharmacology and physiology. Your role as a midwife is to integrate theory and practical knowledge to ensure you are providing optimal care to women.

WORKING IN GROUPS

In your study group, list different knowledge sources and cite examples of how you can integrate this knowledge. For example, how would you integrate knowledge from pharmacology with knowledge from physiology?

Communication

Communication is perhaps the most important competency for you to develop, given that midwives must establish professional relationships with the women in their care and the woman's family. A productive and safe relationship is founded on effective communication. As you know, communication is the transmission of information between people.

An important aspect of communication is listening. Being able to listen to someone in a non-judgmental and supportive manner will enhance the care process. Listening involves not only *hearing* what the other person is saying but also *understanding* what is being said. It involves observing body language for any dissonance between what is being said and what the body language—posture, eye contact (or lack of it), tone of voice, and so on—reflect.

Point to ponder

Thinking about the case study above, what do you think the woman's body language was like?

Reconnaissance

A definition of the word **reconnaissance** is exploration. This chapter discussed briefly the qualities and competencies that describe the skilled midwife. These are the qualities and competencies you began to develop in your undergraduate program and will now have to continue developing as you begin practising as a registered midwife. This chapter should encourage you to do an intellectual stocktake of your own competencies and qualities to determine what you will require to be an excellent midwife. This intellectual stocktake will be ongoing and will require you to source evidence from research to inform your practice. You should also take advantage of experiential learning opportunities, as they present themselves, to inform your practice as a registered midwife.

Point to ponder

So what has your intellectual stocktake shown to you?

Elizabeth Grinter

SUMMARY

This chapter has discussed briefly some of the qualities and competencies you will need to practice as a registered midwife. You will have begun to develop these in your undergraduate program, but as you make the transition to registered midwife you will be expected to be able to demonstrate these qualities and competencies in your practice.

DISCUSSION QUESTIONS

1   What do you see as the three most important qualities for a midwife to have, and why?
2   How important is it for a midwife to be able to work collaboratively with other health professionals?
3   What are the key aspects of developing and maintaining effective professional relationships with women?

REFERENCES

Australian Nursing and Midwifery Council & Australian College of Midwives (2006) *National competency standards for the midwife*, Australian Nursing and Midwifery Council, Canberra, <www.anmc.org.au/userfiles/file/competency_standards/Competency%20standards%20for%20the%20Midwife.pdf>, accessed 1 October 2011.

Pairman, S & McAra-Couper, J (2010) 'Theoretical frameworks for midwifery practice' in S Pairman, S Tracy, C Thorogood & J Pincombe (eds), *Midwifery—preparation for practice*, Elsevier, Sydney, pp. 313–26.

Pelvin, B (2010) 'Life skills for midwifery practice' in S Pairman, S Tracy, C Thorogood & J Pincombe (eds), *Midwifery preparation for practice*, Elsevier, Sydney, pp. 298–309.

USEFUL WEBSITES

Australian College of Midwives: **www.midwives.org.au**

Australian College of Neonatal Nurses: **www.acnn.org.au**

Part 2

Contexts and competencies of clinical practice

Core competencies

As registered nurse or midwife, you will:

- demonstrate understanding of the Australian healthcare system
- practise within an evidence-based framework
- be able to conduct a comprehensive and systematic nursing assessment using relevant evidence-based information
- demonstrate cultural sensitivity and awareness when assessing, planning, delivering and evaluating nursing care
- promote a culture of safety and security in the workplace
- communicate and collaborate effectively with other members of the healthcare team and with patients.

Chapter 6

Australia's healthcare system

Maria Fedoruk

Learning objectives

After reading this chapter, you will be able to:
- describe Australia's healthcare system
- describe the healthcare workforce in Australia
- discuss the issues facing the nursing workforce in Australia
- describe the healthcare system you work in.

Key terms

Clinical nurse specialist
eHealth
National Health Agreement (NHA)
Nurse academic
Nurse entrepreneur
Nurse manager
Nurse practitioner
Nurse researcher
Professional skills escalation
Work—life balance

Australia's healthcare system

As a registered nurse, you should have an understanding of how Australia's healthcare system works. This is how Duckett and Willcox (2011, p. 1) summarise Australia's healthcare system:

- Health care is a system involving inputs (finance, workforce), processes, outputs and outcomes. It is situated in the broader socio-politcal environment which it both is affected by and affects.
- The outputs and outcomes of the health care system include individual or person-level outputs (patients treated), and outcomes (improved quality of life) and wider outputs/outcomes (research outputs, strong communities, changed environments). Health outputs and health outcomes are not always distributed evenly across all members of a society.
- The health care system can be evaluated in terms of its impact on equity, quality, acceptability and efficiency.
- The organisation and design of health systems must have regard to the differences between the need, demand and supply of health services. The 'need' for health services is not objective but is framed within a social and poliitical context.

A visual representation of Australia's healthcare system is provided in Figure 6.1. It shows you healthcare from a systems perspective. All organisations have inputs, processes and outputs or outcomes. Underpinning any set of inputs is the ability to pay for these inputs. Financing is critical to obtaining inputs such as workforce, capital, information and communication technologies, and supplies (Duckett & Willcox 2011). Thus, the availability of financial resources drives clinical and non-clinical decision-making in healthcare organisations.

Figure 6.1: Analysis framework of Australia's healthcare system

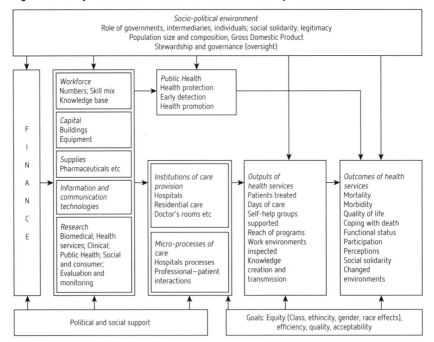

Source: S Duckett & S Willcox (2011) *The Australian health care system*, 4th edn,
Oxford University Press, Melbourne, p. 3.

Management of Australia's healthcare system is devolved to state and territory governments from the Federal Government's Department of Health and Ageing, which can be accessed at <www.health.gov.au>. This website will provide you with relevant resources that will help inform your practice. Resources include publications, research and statistical information. The resources may be accessed via drop-down menus or by typing in keywords. You should make use of this resource because it will help inform your practice by alerting you to new health policy initiatives that may result in new health treatments or models of service delivery.

The Department of Health and Ageing is responsible for ensuring that all Australians have access to high-quality health services and that well-educated health professionals provide these services in different locations, ranging from public and preventative health programs to technologically sophisticated tertiary-level teaching hospitals to community-based health programs. The department is also responsible for aged care service provision around the country. Having an awareness of what is happening at the national level of the healthcare system will improve your health literacy competencies; it will also raise your awareness of how national policy influences what happens, for example, in service delivery at the state and organisational levels. Improving your health literacy skills will ensure that in your interactions with the patient/consumer and their families or carers you will be able to either access relevant information for them or direct them to more appropriate service providers. This website will also alert you to health research programs that the Federal Government is funding, indicating which are the priority areas in health services for the government.

The Department of Health and Ageing's organisational chart is accessible from <www.health.gov.au/internet/main/publishing.nsf/Content/67596E6252 13CBCFCA25785B00105B24/$File/SES_org_chart_intranet_090911.pdf>. You can see from this chart how the department is organised into health and aged care programs. State departments of health have similar organisational charts that inform the public and health professionals of how the healthcare system is organised. As you can see from the chart, the Office of the Chief Nurse is located within the Health Workforce Division, indicating the significance to government of the healthcare workforce—especially the nursing workforce—in terms of policy and planning development.

WORKING IN GROUPS

In your study group, discuss the healthcare organisation as a system. What are the immediate connections you can see within your organisation? Use Figure 6.1, the framework for analysis of healthcare systems, as a starting point for your discussion.

Maria Fedoruk

Through fund allocation to the states and territories, the Federal Government controls the development and management of health services through the National Healthcare Agreement (NHA). The principal objective of this agreement is 'to improve the health outcomes for all Australians and the sustainability of the Australian health system (Council of Australian Governments 2009). This objective aligns with the Department of Health and Ageing's (2010) *Corporate Plan 2010–2013*. The NHA clearly articulates the scope of the agreement; objectives and outcomes; what the joint Commonwealth and state or territory responsibilities are; and what the responsibilities of the specific state or territory are. The NHA is very clear about expected health and organisational outcomes that government funding is used for. In summary, the NHA requires that state and territory governments make transparent the outcomes of their operational activities within their health services.

The corporate plan outlines the Department of Health and Ageing's key priorities for health and health services, and these priorities are focused on outcomes. It is important for you to be aware of these priorities because they indicate where the government will allocate resources over time in order to establish programs that will meet the ongoing health needs of Australian communities. These programs may be potential employment opportunities for you in the future.

Australia's healthcare system has undergone numerous reforms over the decades, with the aims of developing efficiencies and improving equity and access to healthcare services for all citizens. During your undergraduate program, no doubt there will have been some mention of reforms. The most recent reform document, from the Federal Government's National Health and Hospitals Reform Commission (NHHRC) is *A healthier future for all Australians* (NHHRC 2009). This document is the current Federal Government's blueprint for transforming Australia's fragmented healthcare system into an integrated system. The authors of the report note that Australia's healthcare system is under pressure because of changing demographic trends and associated healthcare needs; increasing concerns about the safety of healthcare services; and long waiting lists for services, reflecting access issues and ongoing equity issues (NHHRC 2009).

A key feature of the NHHRC's report is the proposal to move to primary healthcare and preventative health strategies, rather than the current interventionist mode of treatment we are all familiar with. The report recognises that the population of Australia is ageing: chronic diseases are on the increase and advances in medical technologies are driving healthcare costs upwards.

Point to ponder

While policy information may seem 'dry', it is worthwhile knowing.

FOR REFLECTION

Access the Australian Government's Department of Health and Ageing's website at <www.health.gov.au> and look at the information available to you. Select one or two items that are relevant to you in your practice and discuss these in your study groups.

Access the website of your state's or territory's department of health and look at the programs and initiatives that are occurring or are planned to occur. Which of these programs or initiatives are going to influence your future practice in the short term? Which will influence your future practice in the long term?

Australia's healthcare workforce

Duckett and Willcox (2011, pp. 76–7) provide the following summary of Australia's healthcare workforce:

- Almost a million people (956 143) or one in every 10 employed people in Australia (9.8%) work in the health and social assistance industries. Health and other professionals account for 41% of employment in the health industry. In 2009, there were 131 976 students enrolled in health-related courses in public universities in Australia, up 7.4% from 2008.
- Ten key professions are regulated through a national registration and accreditation scheme: chiropractors, dental practitioners, medical practitioners, nurses and midwives, optometrists, osteopaths, pharmacists, physiotherapists, podiatrists and psychologists.
- Nurses are fairly evenly distributed across metropolitan, regional and remote areas, with per capita provision in each area deviating less than 10% from the Australian average. In contrast, there is significant variation in the supply of medical practitioners, both those working in primary care and specialists.
- Improving workforce productivity is the key to addressing health workforce needs in the future. Productivity depends on a number of factors such as the proportion of paid hours given to patient care, how work is organised, and the contributions of other types of professionals.

Other factors which impact on addressing health workforce needs and which have particular relevance for registered nurses and midwives are professional skills escalation and expansion of the scope of practice (the nurse practitioner role).

As new registered nurses, you will be essential members of the healthcare workforce, and the skills and knowledge you bring to the health workplace are

Maria Fedoruk

central to the effective functioning of healthcare organisations in providing safe, high-quality care to healthcare consumers (Duckett & Willcox 2011).

Australia's healthcare workforce is multidisciplinary and comprises medicine, nursing and allied health staff, supported by management, administration and information technology personnel. Housekeeping services are now contracted out to private providers in the majority of hospitals as are catering services. Smaller hospitals, particularly in rural and remote parts of the country, may still employ their own housekeeping and catering staff. Professional healthcare workers are educated in the tertiary sector, as are some managers and other non-clinical staff.

The scope of the registered nurse's role has changed and continues to change rapidly to accommodate the evolving and increasing demands on the healthcare system due to:

* the burden of disease in the Australian population
* changes in service delivery
* community expectations
* workforce expectations
* workforce specialisation
* the unintended effects of workforce strategies (National Health Workforce Taskforce 2009, p. 4).

Point to ponder

What do you understand by 'scope of practice' and how does this influence your practice?

Below, we look at these issues in more detail.

Burden of disease

Australia's ageing population, lifestyle and environmental factors, together with increases in chronic diseases such as diabetes, cardiovascular diseases and the co-morbidities associated with the diseases of old age, are all driving the increased demand for health services. In Australia, almost four in five Australians have a chronic or long-term health condition, ranging from asthma to mental health conditions. More than 50 per cent of general practitioner consultations are for people presenting with a chronic health condition such as diabetes, cardiac disease or cancer (NHHRC 2009, p. 62). More than 70 per cent of health expenditure in Australia is on chronic disease management, and this will increase as the population ages in the future. From this, you can begin to see that the context of health services provision may change in the future.

Changes to service delivery

Changes to health services provision may result in significant changes to the way nurses practice, as well as changing where nurses practice. For instance, as you know from your undergraduate program, chronic disease management now occurs outside of healthcare facilities: in the community and/or patients' homes.

Table 6.1: Possible advances in health technologies

Rational drug design: computer search techniques could reduce the trial and error of random search for identifying likely drug candidates.

Pharmacogenomics: the use of molecular biology techniques to enable the creation of medicines that are personalised for an individual at a genetic level. This application has the potential to enhance effectiveness and tolerance of medicines and reduce adverse drug reactions.

Imaging and diagnostic advances: will likely expand the range of diseases that can be detected using imaging techniques (such as neuro-imaging as a biomarker of early Alzheimer's disease). Advances in miniaturisation of imaging devices could improve portability. There may be a reduced need for surgery to examine the structure and function of organs.

Telemedicine: allowing alternative 'remote' health care delivery options from health risk monitoring to intensivist supervision of emergency resuscitation or surgery.

Minimally invasive surgery, robotics, and virtual surgery: particularly for neurological and coronary procedures.

Genetic testing, gene therapy, and pharmacogenomics: testing could allow identification of genetic susceptibility to diseases and more effective targeted use of pharmaceuticals (pharmocogenetics); gene therapy could correct the genetic cause of disease rather than treating the symptoms.

New vaccines: could prevent cancers and may also offer less intrusive and costly ways to treat some cancers by stimulating patients' own immune systems.

Xenotransplantation and bioengineered organ, joint or tissue replacement: in theory xenotransplantation (from non-human species) could provide an increased supply of organs for transplantation; biomaterials have been used to improve artificial joints; and there has been progress in creating more complex organs, such as artificial pancreases and artificial hearts.

Stem cell therapies: could be based on adult or embryonic stem cells and possibly used to patch damaged hearts, restore pancreatic function in diabetes patients, and treat patients with Parkinson's Disease.

Nanotechnologies and nanomedicine: involve the production and application of materials at an atomic scale. Nanodevices could deliver medicines directly to the site of the body in need and reduce required dosages.

Source: National Health & Hospital Reform Commission (2009) *A healthier future for all Australians: final report June 2009*, AGPS Canberra, p. 66, <www.health.gov.au/internet/main/publishing.nsf/Content/nhhrc-report>, accessed 21 September 2011.

During your clinical placements you will have noticed the different models of service delivery in the various healthcare organisations you spent time in as a student nurse. Changes in service delivery are driven by policy directives; changes to medical technologies (such as pharmaceuticals and diagnostic technologies) and the impact of evidence-based research are all contributors to changes in service delivery. Another important element which determines the level and type of service delivery model is the availability of appropriately skilled and qualified health professionals, especially nurses.

Changes in technologies will also impact on the way health services are delivered. However, while health technologies are increasing life expectancies by improving diagnostic capacities, these technologies come at a cost. Advances in health technologies will require new skills and competencies and make changes to the way health services are managed and delivered. Web-based technologies used in treating health conditions will also change the way in which health services are delivered. Table 6.1, adapted from the NHHRC report (2009), shows the possible advances in health technologies.

Point to ponder

What impact, if any, will these changing technologies have on your future practice?

WORKING IN GROUPS

In your study group, reflect on the technologies you were introduced to as a student nurse in the clinical skills laboratories and clinical placement. What were your immediate reactions when you were asked to work with the piece of equipment or technology? Where was your attention focused: the patient or the technology?

Community expectations

The Australian community has had access to quality healthcare services for many years, and their expectations are that this will continue. However, escalating demand for health services, coupled with a diminishing health workforce, is currently making timely access for individuals problematic. The NHHRC (2009) reports that more than 75 per cent of Australians now have access to and use the internet to learn about their health conditions and the treatments available. This is increasing consumer knowledge and expectations for 'desired treatments and a particular health outcome' (NHHRC 2009, p. 64). So what does this increase in health consumer literacy mean for you as a new registered nurse? Your patients may be very well informed about their health condition, so your knowledge levels need to be equal to or better than that of your patients.

Web-based technology has also opened up opportunities for the provision of nursing and health services in different and innovative ways. These ways may potentially provide cost-effective and time-saving health and nursing services. Social networks such as Facebook, patient portals, YouTube, and electronic record platforms all have the potential to alter relationships between nurses and patients by moving control for healthcare from the provider to the patient. eHealth, the electronic management of health records, is slowly being implemented by the Australian Government, with draft legislation being sent out for review and consultation. Further information relating to eHealth can be accessed from <www.yourhealth.gov.au/internet/yourhealth/publishing. nsf/Content/theme-ehealth>. Communication technologies will be an integral part of your nursing practice in the future.

FOR REFLECTION

In your study group, reflect on the professional relationships you may have developed with patients during your clinical placements. These would have been one-on-one, face-to-face professional relationships. Now consider how you will manage these professional relationships using communication technologies. Some of you will be using Skype to connect with friends or relatives. How might you use Skype to deliver nursing care?

Web-based technologies are already being used to support people with mental health illnesses. They offer the possibility of more timely interactions between patient and providers, including nurses. Already there are telephone services managed by nurses to provide advice to the community on health-related issues (NHHRC 2009, p. 64). Some primary health services are using these technologies: <hellohealth.com> is an example of this.

You may wish to consider how, as a new registered nurse, you are going to manage increased patient expectations, patient knowledge and the technologies which are making all of this possible.

WORKING IN GROUPS

In your study group, discuss how you would manage the different technologies available to you and your colleagues. What are some things you would have to consider?

Workforce expectations

Australia's healthcare workforce is defined not only by different professional disciplines, but also by how individuals within the workforce choose to work. Individuals may vary in terms of the hours they can work or wish to work, and this then influences the supply of workers. Another factor that influences workforce expectations is the notion of **work–life balance**: the idea that workforce participation must be held in balance with an individual's personal and family commitments. Workforce expectations in the healthcare sector are also related to the generational aspects of the workforce (see Chapter 2). This is becoming particularly apparent with Generation Y becoming established in the health workforce. The National Health Workforce Taskforce (2009) notes that Generation Y has a 'stand alone workforce characteristic'. Generation Y is not as career-focused as Baby Boomers or Generation X, but instead expects work to accommodate their social lives (National Health Workforce Taskforce 2009, p. 38). Financial considerations are not as important as work–life balance to Generation Y, and they tend to look for work that has flexible hours and technology options that enable them to achieve this balance.

Point to ponder

Which generational cohort do you belong to? Are the assumptions made about your generation correct? Or is this a form of stereotyping?

Workforce specialisation

You will have noted from your clinical placement experiences the diversity and specialist nature of the healthcare workforce. Even non-clinical staff are becoming increasingly specialised, moving from general administrative services to more specialist human resources services, finance services, information technology services and consumer advocate personnel. Table 6.1 clearly indicates the potential for increased workforce specialisation in the future because of the new technologies being introduced into health services delivery. These new technologies have the potential to prolong life and to halt or slow down disease processes, which in turn has the potential to change the practice of nursing.

Nursing is becoming increasingly specialised, and this is evident in the clinical specialisations that nurses now work in. The more obvious clinical specialisations for nurses are: critical care nursing; emergency department nursing; renal nursing; cardiovascular nursing; aged care nursing; community nursing; and nurse practitioner in a clinical specialty. You may have already decided which nursing specialisation you wish to go into, or you may use the TPPP to help you make this decision. In making this decision, you will find out about the specific entry criteria required, what further studies you will be required to complete, and the registration and any other professional requirements you will need to meet. Because entry into these specific clinical specialisations is tightly controlled, you may find that the fluctuations in supply and demand seen elsewhere in the health workforce may not be as evident in them.

Unintended effects of workforce strategies

Historically, workforce strategies in health services included downsizing and re-engineering, resulting in reduction of staffing numbers, especially in nursing. It was especially common to reduce numbers of registered nurses, using workforce substitution: that is, replacing registered nurses with less skilled healthcare workers. This resulted in increased workloads, increased **hospital errors** and reduced staff morale. Consequently, organisations and governments have been forced to review the workforce strategies being used. More recently, healthcare organisations have introduced flexible working hours for nursing staff and many registered nurses have chosen to work part-time (Carryer et al. 2011; National Health Workforce Taskforce 2009).

Leach and Segal (2011) argue that current approaches to managing workforce shortages should be based on evidence, and not rely on previous workforce strategies that had short-term goals.

Australia's nursing workforce

A nurse labour force report released in 2009 by the Australian Institute of Health and Welfare (AIHW) reported that in 2007 there were 305 634 nurses in Australia, and of these 245 491 were registered nurses and 60 343 enrolled nurses (AIHW 2009 p. viii). The report also noted that nursing remained a female-dominated profession and a profession which continued to age. Between 2003 and 2007 the number of nurses aged 50 years and over rose from 28.2 to 33 per cent. This clearly has implications for employers as well as younger nurses in terms of the physical capacity of older nurses to cope with the physical demands of nursing work. Most nurses are clinicians providing direct care to patients, with other nurses working in administration, as educators or as researchers. More than 46 per cent of nurses work in hospitals or aged care facilities, so it is highly likely that you will be working in a hospital following graduation.

More recently, the Australian Government has established Health Workforce Australia (HWA), whose objective is to provide Australia with a health workforce that meets the health needs of the community (Leach & Segal 2011).

The *National Review of Nurse Education 2002* (Department of Education, Science and Training 2002) noted that within nursing there was a fragmentation of responsibilities for the different areas of nursing and nurse education 'combined with the different contexts in which nurses work' (Department of Education, Science and Training 2002, p. 91). As you can see, nursing workforce issues are long-standing. The national review (Department of Education, Science and Training 2002, p. 188) predicted a shortage of 40 000 nurses by 2010, which appears to have occurred (King & Ogle 2010).

Another issue facing the professional nurse is that clarification of the professional nursing role is needed to determine the number of nurses needed in the workforce (Duckett & Willcox 2011). Without this role clarification, educational institutions cannot design appropriate curricula or determine the numbers of students that need to be enrolled in nurse education programs (Duckett & Willcox 2011, p. 92). Currently, nurse education curricula are designed to prepare nurses to work in the acute hospitals (AIHW 2009), yet the NHHRC (2009) report recommends moving towards a primary healthcare model and using web-based technologies to develop virtual hospitals. These sorts of reforms to the healthcare services and treatment modalities will certainly change the way in which nurses are educated for the healthcare workforce of the future.

Nurses are able to take on the roles of other health professionals, and as nurses become better educated there is a risk that if they remain unchallenged at work this will lead to dissatisfaction and affect retention (Duckett & Willcox 2011). The broader educational preparation of nurses at the tertiary level has led to nurses developing capacity and capability to take on more complex functions within the healthcare sector. Some studies suggest that nurses could take up to 30 per cent of the work of doctors, but whether this labour substitution would be cost-effective is yet to be determined (Duckett & Willcox 2011).

From the latter part of the twentieth century onwards, expanded roles for nurses have emerged, providing non-traditional career pathways for registered nurses. These roles include:

- *Nurse practitioner:* is usually a Masters-prepared nurse and endorsed by state and territory regulators (Nurses Boards) to treat and prescribe for their own patients. These nurses work closely with other health service providers to provide patient-centred care. Nurse practitioners can be found in emergency departments, and mental health and aged care settings, as well as in rural and remote areas. There are also specialist nurse practitioners in wound care, in primary healthcare settings and in oncology and haematology settings. These nurses work independently and can accept referrals as well as refer to other health professionals.
- **Clinical nurse specialist:** this nurse has a postgraduate qualification in a clinical specialty and is considered to be an expert in a specialist area of practice. This nurse provides direct care to patients, educates other health professionals, acts as a consultant, and conducts research.

- *Midwife:* a midwife has graduated from a tertiary education program and is registered with a state or territory Nurse Board (from 1 July 2010 registration for all nurses and midwives is with the National Health Practitioners Regulation Authority). The midwife provides prenatal and postnatal care, and manages deliveries in normal pregnancies. Some hospitals have midwife-led clinics, providing services to women and babies. Midwives usually work in association with a hospital, giving them access to other service providers if complications arise.
- *Nurse researcher:* these nurses investigate nurse and patient care issues to improve patient care, as well as adding to nursing knowledge. They work in academic settings, teaching hospitals and research centres, and usually have doctoral and postdoctoral qualifications.
- **Nurse manager:** these nurses work in middle management positions and you would know them as nurse managers up to nurse executive level (director of nursing in the old terminology) to the chief nurse of states or territories. These nurses now have a qualification in nursing, as well as advanced degrees in management.
- **Nurse academic:** these nurses work in the university sector and have postgraduate qualifications in a specialty area; the majority of these nurses have doctoral qualifications and engage in research activities related to nursing practice and education.
- *Nurse entrepreneur:* a nurse who has an advanced degree and manages a health-related business.

(Adapted from Madsen 2009).

As you can see, the role and function of nurses has changed signifcantly, increasing the scope of nursing practice by providing nurses with opportunities to increase their knowledge, skills and competency base. While strategic nurse workforce planning seems a little slow, career development for nurses is much more apparent. While this may not seem immediately relevant to you during your TPPP year, this information may help you with career decision-making in the future.

FOR REFLECTION

Having read through this chapter, what do you think are the three most significant issues facing Australia's healthcare system? Have you accessed any of the websites mentioned in this chapter? Did you find the information helpful in developing your understanding of the issues being faced by health professionals?

Maria Fedoruk

SUMMARY

This chapter discusses how Australia's healthcare system is funded and managed at the national and state and territory levels. While this may seem like abstract or 'dry' information, you should at least have an awareness of how the healthcare system is organised and be familiar with the national and state and territory departments that manage it. You should keep up to date, through the media, with the Federal Government's proposed changes to the healthcare system. The recommendations in the most recent report, the National Health and Hospitals Reform Commission's *A healthier future for all Australians*, if implemented, may affect where you will work in the future.

This chapter also looks at health workforce issues, especially nurse shortages. Being aware of nurse workforce issues broadly will help you to understand the issues you will face in your own workplace and why staffing shifts in your workplace is a complex task. This chapter has been written to contextualise the healthcare workplace for you and to help you understand that the issues you are facing are being faced by other nurses in other parts of the country.

DISCUSSION QUESTIONS

1   How does Australia's healthcare system compare with other healthcare systems?
2   What are the key issues facing Australia's healthcare system?
3   How important is it for you to know about how the healthcare system operates?

REFERENCES

Australian Institute of Health & Welfare (2009) *Nursing and midwifery labour force 2007*, AGPS Canberra, cat. no. HWL 44, <www.aihw.gov.au/publications/index.cfm/title/10724>, accessed 14 June 2010.

Carryer, JB, Diers, AD, Mccloskey, B & Wilson, D (2011) 'Effects of health policy reforms on nursing resources and patient outcomes in New Zealand', *Policy, Politics and Nursing Practice*, vol. 11, no. 4, pp. 275–85.

Council of Australian Governments (2009) *National healthcare agreement*, Australian Government, Canberra.

Department of Education, Science and Training (2002) *National review of nursing education*, Nursing Education Review Secretariat, Canberra, DEST No. 6880 HERC02A.

Department of Health and Ageing (2010) *Corporate plan 2010–2013*, Performance Section, Portfolio Strategies Division, Canberra, <www.health.gov.au/internet/main/publishing.nsf/Content/9F083DC3BBA88FA2CA2577F900124CA2/$File/505-Corporate%20Plan%20H&A_concept04v9_12.1.11_Pages_150ppi.pdf>, accessed 6 October 2011.

Duckett, S & Willcox, S (2011) *The Australian health care system*, 4th edn, Oxford University Press, Melbourne.

King, S & Ogle, K(2010) 'Shaping an Australian nursing and midwifery framework for workforce regulation: Criteria development', *The International Journal of Health Planning and Management*, vol. 25, no. 4, pp. 330–40.

Leach, M & Segal, L (2011) 'New national health and hospitals network: Building Australia's health workforce—where is the evidence? *Economic Papers*, vol. 29, no. 4, pp. 483–9.

Madsen, W (2009), 'Historical and contemporary nursing practice' in B Kozier & G Erb (eds), *Fundamentals of nursing practice*, Pearson, Sydney, pp. 56–72.

National Health and Hospitals Reform Commission (2009) *A healthier future for all Australians*, final report June 2009, Commonwealth of Australia, Canberra, <www.health.gov.au/internet/main/publishing.nsf/Content/nhhrc-report>, accessed 21 September 2011.

National Health Workforce Taskforce (2009), *Health workforce in Australia*, KPMG, Melbourne.

USEFUL WEBSITES

Australian Government Department of Health & Ageing: **www.health.gov.au**

Australian Government Department of Health & Ageing's *Corporate plan 2011– 2013*: **www.health.gov.au/internet/main/publishing.nsf/Content/9F0 83DC3BBA88FA2CA2577F900124CA2/$File/505-Corporate%20Plan%20 H&A_concept04v9_12.1.11_Pages_150ppi.pdf**

Australian Government Department of Health and Ageing's organisational chart: **www.health.gov.au/internet/main/publishing.nsf/Content/67596E625213C BCFCA25785B00105B24/$File/SES_org_chart_intranet_090911.pdf**

Australian Capital Territory Health Directorate: **www.health.act.gov.au**

Department of Health and Ageing, South Australia (SA Health): **www.sahealth. sa.gov.au**

Department of Health and Human Services, Tasmania: **www.dhhs.tas.gov.au**

Department of Health, New South Wales: **www.health.nsw.gov.au**

Department of Health, Northern Territory: **www.health.nt.gov.au**

Department of Health, Victoria: **www.health.vic.gov.au**

Department of Health, Western Australia: **www.health.wa.gov.au**

eHealth information: **www.yourhealth.gov.au/internet/yourhealth/ publishing.nsf/Content/theme-ehealth**

National Healthcare Agreement (NHA): **www.coag.gov.au/ intergov_agreements/federal_financial_relations/index.cfm**

Maria Fedoruk

Chapter 7

Professional regulation

Di Wickett and Alice Wickett

Learning objectives

After reading this chapter, you will be able to:

- describe the history of nurse regulation in Australia
- discuss the benchmarks for competence to practice
- list the legislation relating to a nurse's practice
- determine your own continuing professional development needs
- show evidence of recency of practice.

Key terms

Regulation
Competence
Continuing professional development (CPD)
Fitness
Nurse Regulatory Authorities (NRAs)
Propriety

History of nurse regulation in Australia

The first nurses in Australia were reformed convicts, who were described as dirty, frowsy old women (Smith 1999; Russell & Schofield 1986). Henry Parkes, a colonial secretary, resolved that there was a need to improve the standard of nursing in Australia (Smith 1999). He sent to England for Nightingale-trained nurses who were to establish training programs for Australian nurses based on the British model of nursing, which was initiated by Florence Nightingale and was highly respected (Smith 1999; Minchin 1973). The Australasian Trained Nurses Association (ATNA) was established in New South Wales to coordinate the standard of nurse training. Branches were subsequently launched in other states, with a breakaway branch established in Victoria, called the Royal Victorian Trained Nurses Association (RVTNA) (Smith 1999; Minchin 1973). The ATNA developed curricula for hospital training courses, facilitated examinations and approved training institutions.

In an effort to improve the status of nurses, both the ATNA and the RVTNA sought registration for nurses. It was not until 1920 that the first Nurses Act was proclaimed in South Australia. Subsequently, other states followed, and by 1928 all states had a Nurses Act; statutory regulation had begun for nurses in Australia. This regulation was influenced by the British model of nursing practice and by medical practitioners, who were predominant members of nurse's boards.

There are two forms of regulation or control for nurses: statutory regulation and self-regulation. Statutory regulation for nurses is administered by a regulatory authority to protect the public from nurses practising either incompetently or unprofessionally (Caulfield, Gough & Osbourne 1998; Pickersgill 1998; Robinson 1995). Statutory regulation is derived from an Act of Parliament, and is enacted by an independent body, whereas self-regulation is overseen by the professional nursing organisation.

Point to ponder

Professional regulation is an important aspect of being a professional.

Statutory regulation is viewed as mandatory, as the title 'nurse' is protected and may only be used by persons who hold registration with the particular nurse regulatory authority. Statutory regulation determines educational standards and the standards for continuing registration. If a nurse breaches the determined standards, disciplinary action may be taken.

Professional regulation or self-regulation is 'the means by which order, consistency and control are brought to the profession and its practice' (Ralph 1993, p. 60). The International Council of Nurses (ICN) (1997, p. 3) notes that 'the goals of regulation relate to defining the profession and its members, determining the scope of practice, setting standards of education, ethical and competent practice plus establishing systems of accountability and credentialing processes'. The ICN acknowledges that the context for regulation is influenced by technological advances, consumer participation and expectations of healthcare, plus the formulation and application of various laws affecting nursing practice (ICN 1997).

Technological advances have been enormous in the past twenty years, and with the advent of the internet there is a greater focus on telecommunication and developments in biomedical research (Gaffney 1999). These developments have had a major influence on nursing practice and the regulation of that practice. An example of this is that rural nurses have the ability to link via telemedicine with a medical officer to assist with diagnoses and treatment of a patient (Bryant 2001). Telemedicine is an alternative system of health services delivery, where:

- there is geographical separation between provider and recipient of health related information
- information technology is used as a substitute for personal or face-to-face interaction
- there are staff to perform necessary functions
- there are clinical **protocols** for treating and triaging patients
- normative standards of professional behaviour are evident
- there are organisational structures suitable for system or network development (Bashur, Reardon & Shannon 2000, p. 614).

This poses an interesting dilemma about who is legally responsible for the patient's care, the nurse or the doctor, and so the debate continues among the profession as to what regulation is required to ensure public safety is maintained.

Recognition of a nurse's qualifications is part of the regulatory process, which assumes that holding a qualification in nursing from an accredited institution ensures competency and therefore protects the public. The main objective of statutory regulation for nurses is to protect the public by exercising a protective jurisdiction. This protective jurisdiction is part of administrative law, which is the branch of law that deals with the administrative processes of governments and quasi-judicial decision-making bodies such as nurse's boards (Staunton & Chiarella 2007). Each nurse regulatory authority in Australia, as part of administering the Nurses Act in their jurisdiction, has the delegated authority to establish and administer systems for accrediting various categories of nurses (Chiarella 2001).

The Australian Nursing and Midwifery Council was established in 1992 'to lead a national approach with State and Territory Nursing and Midwifery Regulatory Authorities in evolving standards for statutory nursing and midwifery regulation which are flexible, effective and responsive to healthcare requirements of the Australian population'. The ANMC is responsible for developing national standards of practice for nurses and midwives and codes of ethics for nurses and midwives, as well as managing the processing of migrant nurses. The ANMC works in partnership with the Australian Health

Practitioner Health Regulation Agency to protect the public and guide the profession.

Membership of the ANMC consisted of representatives from each state and territory Nursing and Midwifery Board, plus community representatives. While the ANMC had no legislative authority, there was a strong commitment by the state and territory Boards to work collaboratively through the ANMC to develop practice standards for nurses and midwives.

However, Australia has changed from state-based regulation to national regulation for nurses and other healthcare professionals. In July 2010, the *Health Practitioner Regulation National Law 2009* was enacted for ten groups of health professionals. This group of professionals are: nurses and midwives, physiotherapists, occupational therapists, dental care providers, medical practitioners, optometrists, osteopaths, pharmacists, podiatrists and chiropractors. Nurses will subsequently hold national registration, enabling nurses to practise anywhere in Australia. The Nursing and Midwifery Board of Australia (NMBA) was appointed on 31 August 2009 and consists of four community members and eight practitioner members from each state and territory in Australia.

The functions of the Board include overseeing:

- the registration of nursing and midwifery practitioners
- the development of nursing and midwifery profession standards
- the handling of notifications and complaints in relation to the profession
- the assessment of overseas-trained practitioners who wish to practise in Australia.

The Board also approves **accreditation** standards, lists accredited courses of study that meet the qualifications for registration, and conducts investigations and disciplinary hearings. The functions of the Board are supported by the AHPRA.

The NMBA is currently in the process of developing the benchmarks for practice for nurses and midwives, predominantly based on the ANMC national standards for nursing and midwifery practice.

Benchmarks of competency

There are many benchmarks a nurse must be able to practise to or within. These include providing evidence of **fitness** and propriety, English language proficiency, competence, continuing professional development, and **recency of practice**.

Fitness and propriety

All applicants for registration must provide evidence that they are a fit and proper person. This does not mean you are fit enough to run 200 metres: this is about your moral and legal fitness as a person. Moral and legal fitness refers to your capacity to work within the legislative frameworks and to act with honesty and integrity in your interactions with patients and their families and with your professional colleagues. In order to demonstrate this, the NMBA has produced a *Criminal history registration standard*, which requires all persons applying for registration to provide a criminal history (NMBA 2010b, p. 4). The criminal history relates to any convictions, findings of guilt, pending charges and no conviction charges. If an applicant has any of these recorded, the NMBA will determine whether these offences are relevant to the practice of their profession. Honesty is essential, as the NMBA will determine outcomes of their assessment on an individual basis.

English language skills

The ability to read, write, listen and speak English is considered an essential competency for all nurses, therefore the NMBA has determined in the *English language skills registration standard* (NMBA 2011) that all nurses should have had five years' full-time education in English. For nurses who do not have this, the standard continues:

4   An applicant for registration as an enrolled nurse who has not completed five (5) years (full-time equivalent) of education taught and assessed in English, in any of the recognised countries listed in this registration standard, will be required to demonstrate English language proficiency in accordance with Board approved English language tests.

5   The following tests for assessment of English language proficiency are approved by the Board:

a   International English Language Testing System (IELTS) examination (Academic) with a minimum score of 7 in each of the four components of listening, reading, writing and speaking; or

b   Occupational English Test (OET) with an overall pass, and with grades A or B only, in each of the four components of listening, reading, writing and speaking; or

c   other English language tests approved by the Board from time to time.

6   English language proficiency test results must have been obtained within two years before applying for registration. An IELTS or OET result (or approved equivalent) that is older than two years may be accepted as current, if accompanied by proof that an applicant:

a   has actively maintained continuous practice and/or employment as a registered nurse, enrolled nurse or midwife using English as the primary language of practice in any of the recognised countries listed in this registration standard; and/or

b   has been continuously enrolled in a program of study taught and assessed in English and approved by the recognised nursing and/or midwifery regulatory body in any of the countries listed in this registration standard.

Results from any of the above-mentioned English language proficiency tests must be obtained in one sitting.

7   The applicant is responsible for the cost of English language proficiency tests.

8   The applicant must make arrangements for test results to be provided to the Board for verification.

The NMBA may grant exceptions where an applicant may be provided with limited registration to demonstrate their ability to practise competently or to undertake research or postgraduate study (NMBA 2011).

Potential entrants into nursing programs need to provide evidence to the tertiary admissions centres in their state or territory that their secondary schooling results qualify them for admission to an undergraduate nursing program.

Competence to practise

All applicants must also demonstrate the determined Nursing and Midwifery Board of Australia's competency standards for either registered or enrolled nurses. These competency standards are the 'core competency standards by which your performance is assessed to obtain and retain your license to practice as a registered nurse in Australia' (ANMC 2006, p. 1).

These core competency standards are fundamental to your everyday practice and are the benchmark by which you must practise. Any deviation from this benchmark could lead to you being reported to the NMBA as either incompetent or unprofessional in your practice. While this may appear harsh, it is the very foundation on which you are able to call yourself a 'nurse'.

Point to ponder

The development of competencies in nursing and midwifery is paramount to continuing registration, and therefore practice, in this country.

Think of a patient scenario and document your understanding of each national competency standard for registered nurses. Remember that these are pivotal to your practice.

The competencies are overarching, however they are supported by a number of other documents, such as the code of ethics and the code of conduct. The code of ethics very clearly 'outlines the nursing profession's commitment to respect, promote, protect and uphold the fundamental rights of people who are both the recipients and providers of nursing and healthcare' (ANMC, RCNA & ANF 2008, p. 1). The code of conduct fundamentally 'sets the minimum standards for practice a professional person is expected to uphold both within and outside of professional domains in order to ensure the "good standing" of the nursing profession' (ANMC 2008, p. 1).

Case study: Inheritance

Mrs X is an elderly resident in an aged care facility with multiple co-morbidities and no living relatives. Mrs X considers you to be her friend as well as her nurse, as you have often shopped for her essentials such as toothpaste and hair shampoo. You have cared for Mrs X for five years and she considers you as her family. Mrs X suddenly deteriorates and dies on your day off. However, you receive a letter in the mail some months later informing you that you have inherited $50 000 in accordance with Mrs X's will. What should you do in this situation?

If you take the money, you would be in breach of the code of conduct. Why? You met Mrs X during your practice as a nurse and therefore had a therapeutic relationship. A therapeutic relationship means there is a power differential between you as the nurse and Mrs X as the patient. The code of conduct describes the professional boundaries within which all nurses must practise. Any breach of these professional boundaries may be viewed as unprofessional conduct if reported to the NMBA.

Professional boundaries are the limits which protect the space between the professional's power and the client's vulnerability: that is, they are the borders that mask the edges between a professional therapeutic relationship and a non-professional or personal relationship between a nurse and a person in their care. When a nurse crosses a boundary, they are generally behaving in an unprofessional manner and misusing the power the relationship (ANMC & Nursing Council of New Zealand 2010, p. 2).

Case study: Developing a personal relationship

Mr Y is the spouse of Mrs Y, whom you have been caring for in the community. Mrs Y has terminal cancer and is determined to stay at home to die. You have been caring for Mrs Y for some months and have developed a very close relationship with Mr Y, so much so that Mr Y has been asking you out for coffee. During these meetings you have become very attached to Mr Y who you believe feels the same way. What should you do?

Again, you met Mr Y while in a therapeutic relationship with Mrs Y, which means you must not engage with Mr Y under any circumstances other than in the care of his wife. This is a breach of the code of conduct and could be determined as unprofessional conduct.

Point to ponder

Nurses must understand the significance of professional boundaries to their practice.

FOR REFLECTION

While the code of conduct and code of ethics may seem harsh, these codes are there to protect the public. They also protect *you* indirectly, by ensuring the boundaries are clearly set as to how you should engage and practice with the people you care for and their significant others. Think about other situations you may have been exposed to and review the codes of conduct and ethics to guide you in your practice. Discuss these issues with your peers to determine their view on how the codes are interpreted.

The competencies and codes of conduct and ethics are just some of the benchmarks for practice. There are many others, such as legislation within each state and territory. This legislation relates to medicine prescribing and administration, mandatory reporting under Firearms Acts or Child and Elderly Protection Acts, and more. There is also legislation that affects you as an employee, such as the Occupational Health and Safety Acts and the Racial Discrimination Acts, to name just two. Ignorance of this legislation is no excuse: you are required to know and understand any legislation and standards that affect your ability to practise as a nurse.

Di Wickett and Alice Wickett

Take some time to access the different pieces of legislation which influence nursing practice. You will have been introduced to these during your undergraduate program. Good starting points are the Department of Health & Ageing website, <www.health. gov.au> and the website of the department of health in your state or territory.

Continuing professional development

In 2010, it was determined by the Nursing and Midwifery Board of Australia that each nurse must provide evidence of continuing competence annually. The means has been determined as providing evidence of completion of 20 hours of continuing professional development or CPD.

The NMBA has developed the *Continuing professional development registration standard* to assist nurses to provide such evidence. The requirements are as follows:

1   Nurses on the nurses' register will participate in at least 20 hours of continuing nursing professional development per year.

2   Midwives on the midwives' register will participate in at least 20 hours of continuing midwifery professional development per year.

3   Registered nurses and midwives who hold scheduled medicines endorsements or endorsements as nurse or midwife practitioners under the National Law must complete at least 10 hours per year in education related to their endorsement.

4   One hour of active learning will equal one hour of CPD. It is the nurse or midwife's responsibility to calculate how many hours of active learning have taken place. If CPD activities are relevant to both the nursing and midwifery professions, those activities may be counted in each portfolio of professional development.

5   The CPD must be relevant to the nurse or midwife's context of practice.

6   Nurses and midwives must keep written documentation of CPD that demonstrates evidence of 20 hours of CPD per year.

7   Documentation of self-directed CPD must include dates, a brief description of the outcomes, and the number of hours spent in each activity. All evidence should be verified. It must demonstrate that the nurse or midwife has:

   a   identified and prioritised their learning needs, based on an evaluation of their practice against the relevant competency or professional practice standards b developed a learning plan based on identified learning needs

c participated in effective learning activities relevant to their learning needs

d reflected on the value of the learning activities or the effect that participation will have on their practice.

8 Participation in mandatory skills acquisition may be counted as CPD.

9 The Board's role includes monitoring the competence of nurses and midwives; the Board will therefore conduct an annual audit of a number of nurses and midwives registered in Australia.

(NMBA 2010a, p. 10)

To date, there has not been any indication as to how the annual audits may be conducted. However, it appears there will be an emphasis on nurses maintaining a **professional portfolio**.

Many of the universities are providing portfolios for students which assist in electronically recording relevant information regarding your education and any other education attended outside your current study. However, you will need to keep hardcopy original documents such as academic transcripts and university parchments. Often these documents are required if you wish to pursue further academic study in the future.

Recency of practice

For many years, Nurse Regulatory Authorities (NRAs) have applied recency of practice criteria for all nurses. These criteria included nurses providing evidence to NRAs that they have practised nursing within a five-year time-frame. The NMBA has recently released their *Recency of practice registration standard* with the following requirements:

1 Nurses and midwives must demonstrate, to the satisfaction of the Board, that they have undertaken sufficient practice, as defined in (2) below, in their professions within the preceding five years to maintain competence.

2 Nurses and midwives will fulfil the requirements relating to recency of practice if they can demonstrate one, or more of the following:

a practice in their profession within the past five years for a period equivalent to a minimum of three months fulltime

b successful completion of a program or assessment approved by the Board, or

c successful completion of a supervised practice experience approved by the Board.

3   Practice hours are recognised if evidence is provided to demonstrate:

a   the nurse or midwife held a valid registration with a nursing or midwifery regulatory authority in the jurisdiction (either Australian or overseas) when the hours were worked; or

b   the role involved the application of nursing and/or midwifery knowledge and skills, or

c   the time was spent undertaking postgraduate education leading to an award or qualification that is relevant to the practice of nursing and/ or midwifery.

4   Extended time away from practice due to illness or any type of leave will not be counted as practice.

(NMBA 2010c, p. 12)

Professional portfolio

Given that you are required by the NMBA to produce evidence of continuing professional development and recency of practice to hold registration as a nurse, it is imperative that you maintain a professional portfolio of some description, whether it be hardcopy or an ePortfolio. To date, there has been no further information regarding penalties for not being able to produce such evidence. However, it could be assumed that if evidence is not provided this would constitute unprofessional conduct, as it is a breach of an NMBA standard. More information on the professional portfolio is provided in Chapter 13.

SUMMARY

The title 'nurse' is protected, hence it should be valued and cosseted. There is a regulatory framework that ensures nurses who care for the public of Australia are fit and proper persons and are competent in the area in which they practise. To maintain registration as a nurse you must understand all benchmarks of practice, which include both statutory legislation and professional standards. It is your responsibility to maintain your competence to practise, which includes lifelong learning. Both new graduates and experienced nurses are required to meet the same predetermined benchmarks for practice.

DISCUSSION QUESTIONS

1   The NMBA website provides mandatory and board-specific registration standards for nurses. Briefly discuss with peers your interpretation of each standard and the effect it has on your practice and on you as a person.

2 Identify the difference between the code of conduct and the code of ethics, and discuss why they are so important to the way a nurse practises.
3 Use a patient you have cared for as an example to discuss how you would meet the ANMC competencies as a registered nurse. Ensure you consider the information provided by the NMBA and the ANMC.

REFERENCES

Australian Nursing and Midwifery Council (2006) *National competency standards for the registered nurse*, 4th edn, January 2006, Australian Nursing and Midwifery Council, Canberra <www.anmc.org.au/userfiles/file/RN%20Competency%20Standards%20August%202008%20(new%20format).pdf>, accessed 13 September 2011.

Australian Nursing and Midwifery Council (2008) *Code of professional conduct for nurses in Australia*, <www.anmc.org.au/userfiles/file/research_and_policy/codes_project/New%20Code%20of%20Professional%20Conduct%20for%20Nurses%20August%202008.pdf>, accessed 13 September 2011.

Australian Nursing and Midwifery Council & Nursing Council of New Zealand (2010) *A nurse's guide to professional boundaries*, Australian Nursing and Midwifery Council, Canberra, <www.anmc.org.au/userfiles/file/PB%20for%20Nurses%20-%20Final%20for%20web%20+PPF%20Watermark%20-%20%20March%202010.pdf>, accessed 13 September 2011.

Australian Nursing and Midwifery Council, Royal College of Nursing, Australia & Australian Nursing Federation (2008) *Code of ethics for nurses in Australia*, Australian Nursing and Midwifery Council, ACT, <www.nrgpn.org.au/index.php?element=ANMC+Code+of+Ethics>, accessed 13 September 2011.

Bashur, RL, Reardon, TG & Shannon, GW (2000) 'Telemedicine—a new healthcare delivery system', *Annual Review of Public Health*, vol. 21, pp. 613–37.

Bryant, R (2001) 'The regulation of nursing in Australia: A comparative analysis', *Journal of Law and Medicine*, vol. 9, August, pp. 41–55.

Caulfield, H, Gough, P & Osbourne, R (1998) 'Putting you in the picture', *Nursing Standard*, vol. 12, no. 19, pp. 22–4.

Chiarella, M (2001) 'National review of nursing education: Selected review of nurse regulation', revised 2003, Commonwealth Department of Education, Science and Training, Canberra.

Gaffney, T (1999) *The regulatory dilemma surrounding interstate practice*, <www.nursingworld.org/ojin/topic9/topic91.htm>, accessed 29 January 2002.

International Council of Nurses (1997) *ICN on regulation: Towards 21st century models*, International Council of Nurses, Geneva.

Minchin, M (1973) *Revolutions and rosewater*, Hart Hamer, Melbourne.

Nursing and Midwifery Board of Australia (2010a) *Continuing professional development registration standard*, <www.nursingmidwiferyboard.gov.au/Registration-Standards.aspx>, accessed 19 October 2011.

Nursing and Midwifery Board of Australia (2010b) *Criminal history registration standard*, <www.nursingmidwiferyboard.gov.au/Registration-Standards.aspx>, accessed 19 October 2011.

Nursing and Midwifery Board of Australia (2010c) *Recency of practice registration standard*, <www.nursingmidwiferyboard.gov.au/Registration-Standards.aspx>, accessed 19 October 2011.

Nursing and Midwifery Board of Australia (2011) *English language skills registration standard*, revised September 2011, <www.nursingmidwiferyboard.gov.au/Registration-Standards.aspx>, accessed 19 October 2011.

Pickersgill, F (1998) 'Prioritise public protection', *Nursing Standard*, vol. 12, no. 18, pp. 12–13.

Ralph, C (1993) 'Regulation and the empowerment of nursing', *International Nursing Review*, vol. 40, no. 2, pp. 58–61.

Robinson, J (1995) 'The internationalization of professional regulation,' *International Nursing Review*, vol. 42, no. 6, pp. 183–6.

Russell, C & Schofield T (1986) *Where it hurts*, Allen & Unwin, Sydney.

Smith, S (1999) *In pursuit of nursing excellence: A history of the Royal College of Nursing, Australia, 1949–99*, Oxford University Press, Melbourne.

Staunton, P & Chiarella, M (2007) *Nursing and the law*, 6th edn, Elsevier Australia, Sydney.

USEFUL WEBSITES

Australian Health Practitioner Regulation Agency: **www.ahpra.gov.au**

Australian Nursing and Midwifery Accreditation Council Limited: **www.anmc.org.au**

Nursing and Midwifery Board of Australia: **www.nursingmidwiferyboard.gov.au**

Chapter 8

Essential competencies for the newly registered nurse

Maria Fedoruk

Learning objectives

After reading this chapter, you will be able to:
- differentiate between skills and competencies in nursing
- set priorities for your own competency development
- differentiate between management and leadership.

Key terms

Competencies
Clinical judgment
Clinical leadership
Critical thinking
Information management
Information systems
Information technology
Interprofessional conflict
Intraprofessional conflict
Management
Skills
Transcultural leadership

Essential competencies

This chapter uses the Australian Nursing and Midwifery Council's (2006) *National competency standards for the registered nurse* as a framework.

Chapter 7 discusses in more detail the relevance and significance of these standards to contemporary nursing practice in Australia. During your student nurse program you will have been introduced to the ANMC competency standards and their application to the practical aspects of nursing practice. This chapter discusses in broad terms what registered nurses do, while the following chapter discusses what nurses do in more detail. As you may be realising by now, becoming a safe, competent registered nurse is a lifelong learning pursuit and will continue throughout your nursing career. Safe, competent registered nurses are continually learning as their environments change; the technology they use changes; their patient populations change; patient expectations change; and service delivery models change.

Skills and competencies

The terms 'skills' and 'competencies' are often used interchangeably, but a skill is having the ability to do something well—the 'knowing how'—whereas a 'competency' is knowing how *and* knowing *why* you do something. So, a competent registered nurse not only knows how to do a procedure but also why it is necessary for the procedure to be done. In hospital-trained nursing programs, nurses focused on task completion but did not necessarily know or understand the rationales for procedures and how these would affect patient health outcomes. There was no critical thinking attached to the completion of tasks. In contrast, in tertiary nursing studies you are not only shown how to do procedures but are also taught to understand why you are doing them. Understanding why you are doing something helps you to explain procedures to your patients and the rationale behind them. Remember that your patients have the ability to check the information you give them with other health professionals, as well as using the internet to research information. So, as a professional nurse, you must give them the correct information in a timely manner. The ANMC (2006) National Competency Standards are the core competency standards by which you will be assessed to:

- become registered
- retain your registration so that you can continue to practise as a registered nurse in Australia.

Your university will have used these standards to develop the nursing curriculum (ANMC 2006, p. 1). So you have entered the healthcare workforce at the novice level of practitioner and your aim is to become an expert in your chosen area of nursing practice. How will you become an expert in your chosen clinical area of practice? What skills and competencies will you need to continue to develop further? This is where the SMARTTA framework may help you clarify your thinking (Dwyer & Hopwood 2010, p. 261). You were introduced to the SMARTTA framework in Chapter 1 (see page XX).

WORKING IN GROUPS

In your study group, use the SMARTTA framework to develop some learning objectives that will help you transition into the registered nurse role.

S What will your **specific** objectives look like? A good starting point is actually being very sure of what it is you want to achieve—the end-goal—and then working backwards to develop your plan.

M What will you use to **measure** the achievement of these objectives? What sort of criteria will you use? You could refer to the criteria of the ANMC national competencies, or your clinical unit will have clinical indicators that you can use.

A How **achievable** are these objectives? Do not set yourself unachievable objectives. It is always better to set objectives that are achievable (the 'baby steps' approach); otherwise you set yourself up for disappointment.

R How will the objectives be **relevant** to the clinical specialty?

T Remember **timeliness**—always set yourself timelines. This will help you maintain focus on achieving the objective, especially if one of your strategies is the completion of a professional development activity in your graduate year.

T You also need to be able to **track** your progress, evaluating each objective as you achieve it.

A There needs to be **agreement** with all parties involved in helping you achieve your objectives.

The following section deals with the essential skills and competencies you will need as a registered nurse to ensure your continuing registration with the Australian Health Practitioner Regulation Agency.

Point to ponder

These competencies are essential for all registered nurses. You will have to ensure that you have strategies in place to develop these. Using the SMARTTA framework may be a good starting point.

Maria Fedoruk

Beginning registered nurse competencies

During your student nurse program, emphasis will have been placed on competency development. Prospective employers expect you to provide evidence that you are a safe and competent registered nurse.

All new registered nurses must be able to demonstrate the following competencies:

- numeracy competencies
- literacy competencies
- information technology competencies
- biomedical technology competencies
- conflict management competencies
- management competencies
- leadership competencies
- interpersonal competencies.

Numeracy competencies

The most obvious nursing function where nurses and midwives must have good numeracy skills is drug calculations and medication administration. The most common critical incidents in Australian healthcare organisations are drug errors, and nurses are predominantly responsible and accountable for giving out medications to patients. There was a reason drug calculation tests featured prominently in your undergraduate program: to make you a safe, competent registered nurse when administering medications to patients. It is a fact of nursing life—nurses are expected to give the right drug, in the right dose, to the right patient at the right time. The nursing literature indicates that medication errors by nurses are a universal phenomenon (Peate 2006). The outcomes of medication errors can be clinically irreversible, and costly in terms of compensation and reputation for the healthcare organisation, and can result in deregistration for the nurse. So even though you are now a registered nurse, it is in your best interests to continue practising drug calculations. At 3 am in the morning during an emergency situation no one is going to give you a pen and paper or calculator to work out drug dosages. This is called 'the 3 am rule'.

Point to ponder

What are some of the strategies you have been taught around medication administration?

While accuracy in drug administration is important in adult nursing, it is particularly important in neonatal and paediatrics nursing, where drug dosages are calculated per gram or kilogram of the infant's body weight.

Another area of medication management where you will need good numeracy skills is managing intravenous therapies containing medications that need to be titrated against biochemical results or against body weight or even against changes in clinical symptoms. In these instances, you will also be monitoring insertion sites for the intravenous therapies for infections, inflammation dislodgement or clotting—all of which can affect the accuracy of the drug administration to a particular patient.

Point to ponder

Emergencies do not always occur between the hours of 9 am and 5 pm!

Drug administration is not the only area of nursing and clinical practice where numeracy skills are necessary. Numeracy skills are necessary when:

- working out blood results and noting any abnormality that has to be reported to medical staff because changes to treatment are indicated (other examples include when looking after respiratory-compromised patients where correct oxygen concentrations are essential, in cardiac patients where abnormal levels of potassium need treating, and so on)
- calculating body mass index
- counting patient's money on admission, especially where the patient's mental state is compromised
- calculating percentage of burns suffered by patients
- calculating the number of staff needed for safe practice on a shift
- calculating patient dependency levels
- reading and interpreting research results.

As a registered nurse, if you are unsure about a drug calculation or find that you cannot do it, then the best course of action is to ask for help. Remember the rule: if in doubt, don't give it!

This is particularly important when nursing babies and children, where you have to take extra care with medications to ensure the correct dose is administered.

WORKING IN GROUPS

In your study group, discuss the following scenario: You are checking the medication record of a patient and see that a new order for digoxin has been prescribed. The order is for 62.5 mgs. Would you give this dose?

- If yes, why? If no, why not? Where would you check for accuracy in this prescription?
- What are the potential outcomes of giving and not giving this mediction?

Maria Fedoruk

Your responsibility as a student and registered nurse is to ensure that no harm comes to your patients because of your actions. In Australia, the system of measurement in healthcare is the metric system. You will have used this system of measurement as a student nurse in the practice setting, as well as having your knowledge and comprehension tested in examinations.

Table 8.1: Metric measures used in healthcare

Weights	Volume	Length and depth
Kilograms	Litres	Kilometres
Grams	Millilitres	Metres
Milligrams		Centimetres

FOR REFLECTION

List the areas in clinical practice where you would use the following measures and why:

- weight measures
- volume measures
- length or depth measures.

See Appendix J for examples of medication calculations.

Literacy competencies

In the context of nursing practice, literacy skills are necessary for communication with patients, other health professionals and other workers in the healthcare organisation. Literacy skills include English language speaking skills and English language writing skills.

Point to ponder

Good language skills are the foundation of effective communication in healthcare. Would you agree?

To provide safe, competent care to your patients, good literacy and language skills are essential. Communications relating to patient care will have to be understood by diverse groups of people whose first language may not be English and who may not have a clinical background. Accurate, well-written, and easily understood patient records promote seamless care, especially if patients are moved on to other healthcare teams. Accurate record keeping is important for nurses following you on a shift, and becomes more important if the next shift of nurses are agency or relief nurses, unfamiliar with the patients and their care needs.

You should know by now that an important aspect of being a registered nurse is writing and maintaining accurate patient records. As a student nurse, you will have written academic papers as assignments and would have been marked down for poor use of language and grammatical inconsistencies.

All healthcare organisation and clinical units will have a standard format for entering information into the patient record. While in most organisations around the country the patient record is integrated, you may find yourself working in an organisation where the nursing information is kept separate from other health professionals. Logistically, this can be a problem, especially if you are trying to develop a plan of care or even change an existing plan of care from a number of information sources. The patient record is also a legal document, so it is imperative that the nursing entries are accurate, easily understood and relevant. Where healthcare organisations are working with electronic patient records, well-written, succinct and current information from nurses is required, particularly if the model of care is multidisciplinary.

The patient record is a record of the patient's period in a hospital or healthcare organisation. It must:

- specify the reason(s) the patient was in the care of the organisation
- record the treatments or interventions the patient received and from whom (with legible signatures)
- contain relevant and factual information
- be legible (this includes the signatures of the people making the entries).

Effective literacy skills include good language and writing competencies. This not only includes having a good vocabulary and the ability to spell correctly, but also knowledge of the language used in the clinical unit you are working in. As clinical practice becomes increasingly specialised, the language used in the units also begins to reflect the specialist clinical practices of units. Abbreviations should be used with caution, and you should only use the abbreviations that the healthcare organisation allows. While we may be living and working in a digital age, the use of text language is not appropriate for patient records. Effective literacy competencies are necessary irrespective of the way information is transmitted or relayed between health professionals.

Information technology competencies

Increasingly, the use of information technology by nurses and other health professionals is becoming more common in healthcare organisations. Information technology is used for managing nursing practice; for staffing;

for entering patient data; and, in some cases, for electronic patient records. Patient care is becoming more technologically sophisticated and your responsibility is to ensure that your information technology skills are at a level that ensures you are competent. Some of these competencies you will have been developing throughout your undergraduate program.

Information technology refers to the machines (computers) and applications (software) that provide the infrastructure support for information systems. *Information systems* are integrated, complex automated systems that are networked through computers and are used to support **information management**, data collection and decision-making. *Information management* is the collection, interpretation and storage of information for a particular purpose, which for nurses is patient care.

You may have been introduced to nursing clinical information systems during your clinical placements. These systems are used to support clinical decision-making, as well as measuring patient nursing needs. It is in your best interests to become very adept at using these information systems.

Information management competencies

Information management is an integral component of nursing work, because information is provided by nurses to the healthcare team involved in caring for patients. Information comes from a number of different sources, including the patient, and you will have been made aware of this during your clinical placement.

Point to ponder

Using information well is both an art and science—would you agree?

One important source of information used by nurses is the handover sheet or 'cheat sheet'. As a nurse, you will enter relevant information about your group of patients at handover prior to commencing your shift. Information technology enables 24-hour access to patient care information to clinicians, thus facilitating timely treatment and care delivery for patients. Nurses in some parts of Australia are trialling point-of-care devices such as handheld pilots and laptop computers to communicate with other health professionals and to record patient information, as well as to receive relevant information such as test results. Some state departments of health are trialling versions of the electronic patient record and you may be a part of these trials in your state or territory. Attending the training workshops for this will be important, not only for your skill development, but also for your professional development.

Attendance at these training sessions is another entry in your professional portfolio. The advent of the iPad and similar devices is adding another dimension to electronic information management.

In some aged care facilities, nurses use mobile phones and SMS texting to contact and communicate with other staff members. In the contemporary health and aged care sectors, the use of information technologies for communicating and transmitting information is an important element of a nurse's information management competency set.

WORKING IN GROUPS

In your study group, discuss the information systems you used while on clinical placement. Were they the same for all of you? Were they easy to use? Was the technology easy to access?

Biomedical technology competencies

You will have been exposed to patient care technologies during your student nurse program and will have noticed that these technologies are becoming increasingly sophisticated and are now an essential part of nursing practice. Developing skills in the use of biomedical technologies should be an integral part of your competency development and included in your professional portfolio. One thing you will have to know is what do to if the equipment fails or breaks down—who to call, what to do, how to keep the patient safe, and the procedures to implement while managing the patient during the time it takes to repair the equipment or change it over.

WORKING IN GROUPS

In your study group, discuss how you are using information management technologies and how this has influenced your nursing practice using the following questions as a starting point.

- What have been your experiences in using information technology? Were there any problems? What were the benefits?
- What are the differences between biomedical technologies and information technologies?
- What are some of the barriers to using technologies when delivering nursing care?

Maria Fedoruk

Conflict management competencies

Managing conflict in nursing is discussed in nursing management textbooks, but it is as a registered nurse that you will first be exposed to conflict situations during your work day. As a student nurse, you may have been exposed to or observed conflicts in the clinical area, but it will be as a registered nurse that you have to take positive action to minimise the negative outcomes of conflict.

Conflicts may arise:

- between nurses (**intraprofessional conflict**)
- between different groups of health professionals (**interprofessional conflict**)
- between nurses and patients (nurse–patient conflict).

Conflict is a fact of life where you have people from various backgrounds and with different value and belief systems working together in fast-paced, complex and high-stress environments. Conflict may be defined as 'real or perceived differences in goals, values, ideas, attitudes, beliefs or actions' (Sullivan & Garland 2010, p. 296). An area of conflict for the new graduate nurse may arise when you go to do a procedure as you were taught at university but a more experienced nurse comes along and tells you 'we don't do it that way; we do it this way'. So how do you manage this potential conflict situation? The main conflict responses (Sullivan & Garland 2010) are:

- *Competing*—an all-out effort to win, characterised by anger and aggression. Other competing behaviours include arguing, criticising, name calling and blaming others. This can be a form of bullying and intimidation.
- *Avoiding*—refusing to confront the situation and denying a conflict exists. Avoidance behaviours are characterised by doing nothing, fear of embarrassment, fear of consequences, fear of making things worse and a lack of assertiveness. Avoiding can be a part of bullying behaviours.
- *Accommodating*—yielding, giving up in favour of the other person. Sometimes this is the best option when a consequence can be advantageous in the future. The saying 'pick your battles' can apply here. Accommodating is often used with people who are more senior to you.
- *Compromising*—making a deal, meeting the other person midway—you give up something and they give up something. This strategy is sometimes held up as the best solution, but it can be unsatisfying because you can feel as if you have not really achieved an optimal outcome, and often the underlying reasons for the conflict are left unresolved.
- *Collaborating*—everyone involved in the conflict situation works together to achieve a mutually agreed upon solution, following discussion and sharing of insights, perspectives and available options, agreeing on the best option for all.

Conflict is context-dependent. The same strategy cannot be applied to every conflict situation. As individuals, we also develop our own responses to conflict situations. Research has shown that nurses tend to overuse avoidance and compromise strategies when dealing with conflict, and underuse the other three strategies (Sullivan & Garland 2010, p. 153).

Developing self-awareness of your conflict responses is an important aspect of your professional development as a registered nurse. Self-awareness will help you in managing your conflict responses in a rational and reasoned way. It is the difference between reacting to a situation and responding to a situation.

FOR REFLECTION

Reflect on how you approach and manage conflict situations. Consider a personal situation or a situation you encountered while on a clinical placement, as an example. What were your responses in this situation?

Read through the list above and decide which responses you think you often use at the present time. Then revisit this list at the completion of your TPPP and see if your repsonses have changed.

Point to ponder

Conflict situations are also extremely personal, making the resolution of conflicts personal—there is no 'one size fits all' solution to conflict situations.

WORKING IN GROUPS

In your study group, discuss your conflict management responses.

- Discuss a conflict situation where you avoided all the issues. Why do you think you engaged in avoiding behaviour? What were your feelings at the time? What was the outcome at the time?
- Think of a recent situation (personal or professional) where you gave in to the other party. Why did you give in? (You wanted to be well thought of; you were developing relationships, it was not a battle you felt you had to win, or you had no choice?) What was the outcome of this and what were your feelings?
- Recall a time when you stood up for yourself; when you truly believed that your opinion and solution was the right one. What were your feelings at the time and why were you so intent on standing your ground? What behaviours did you use and what was the impact of this? What was the outcome for you and for the conflict?

Maria Fedoruk

- Recall a time when the conflict situation was so bad all you wanted to do was leave and never return. What was the result of your leaving? Was the situation resolved? Did you return and why?

(Adapted from Sullivan & Garland 2010)

In the scenarios you discussed in your study group, thinking critically and reflectively, together with discussing the issues, may provide you with strategies to help you deal with conflict that perhaps you had not considered before.

Point to ponder

Conflicts occur wherever people work and if the workplace is a high-stress environment then the potential for conflict situations to arise increases.

Management competencies

You might throw up your hands in horror at the idea of management competencies. Surely you are a clinician, not a manager? Well, the truth is that even as a clinician you will use management skills and strategies to:

- manage your own workload—setting priorities, managing your time
- manage the workload on a shift
- organise patients for procedures, discharge and transfer to other units
- delegate functions to other staff
- make decisions
- communicate
- manage information.

All of the above activities are management functions that are a part of the clinician's role, and you will have engaged with some of these activities in your clinical placements. Next time you listen to a handover and fill out your handover sheet, think about what you are doing. You are setting priorities, determining your own workload needs, and developing time management skills. You develop time management skills so that you can deliver nursing care to patients in a timely and organised manner. You develop your communication skills so that you can pass on relevant information to other health professionals and, of course, to patients.

Another management competency you may not have considered is the ability to work in a team or with others. From your clinical placement experiences, you will have observed that in contemporary healthcare organisations, healthcare teams are multidisciplinary, working together to achieve positive health outcomes for patients and the organisation. Teamwork has been defined as 'cooperative efforts by members of a group or team to achieve a common goal' (Dwyer & Hopwood 2010, p. 223). Being an effective team member means that you are able to:

- work with others
- contribute to the goals of the team by demonstrating good clinical practice
- participate in team meetings by reporting and recording patients' clinical conditions and any changes that may occur, as well as any concerns patients may express
- act as an advocate for patients when necessary.

Point to ponder

Good teamwork, where all team members participate fully and cooperatively, improves team effectiveness.

As a team member you support other team members with workload management if this is necessary.

You should take the opportunity while on clinical placement to observe team leaders doing the following tasks:

- allocating team members to patients
- ensuring each team member is aware of what they need to do
- liaising with nurse managers if workload issues arise during the shift
- managing the administrative tasks that need to be completed.

All of these tasks underpin the effective and efficient management of a team of people on a shift, and the team leader has to have enough information to, for example, allocate team members to patients. It would not be very efficient to allocate the most inexperienced nurse to the sickest patient.

Point to ponder

Reread Chapter 2 on 'Belongingness' and see how it relates to teamwork.

Leadership competencies

Leadership is a combination of behavioural and functional processes, which include identifying what needs to be done, setting mutually agreed upon goals and targets, and motivating other people to achieve these goals or targets. There are many models of leadership and the most popular one at this point in time is transformational leadership. Transformational leadership is about developing and maintaining interpersonal relationships and being able to inspire belief in others that they can do exceptional things. Leadership is

Maria Fedoruk

about managing change, and in the clinical setting it is about changing clinical practice to achieve better health outcomes for patients. As a student nurse you may not be too comfortable about initiating change in clinical practice, but as a registered nurse on duty you may very well have to show clinical leadership, because more junior staff will expect you to. This may not apply in metropolitan healthcare organisations, but could apply in rural and remote organisations where you may be called upon to demonstrate clinical leadership in certain situations. There are community-based nursing organisations which offer TPPPs, and even though graduate registered nurses are mentored, there will be occasions when they are working by themselves and they will have to make clinical decisions that change current practices in the best interests of the patient and then provide the rationale for their decisions. Thus, the importance of leadership is something to consider as you near the completion of your student nurse program.

Clinical leadership

Point to ponder

Developing clinical leadership competencies and skills is something that should have occurred during your undergraduate program.

To become a clinical leader, you will need to develop expertise in clinical practice, be patient and focused, become innovative, dynamic, confident, assertive, resilient and able to work effectively in a collaborative way (Davidson et al. 2009). Your clinical leadership skills will begin to be evident in your nursing care outcomes and organisational efficiencies, perhaps in the form of workload management on a shift and your contributions to patient care discussions. A clinical leader has a good knowledge base that supports their clinical skills. It is your ability to transfer your knowledge to patient care that will identify you as a potential clinical leader. There is evidence that indicates that nursing practice influences patient care outcomes and contributes to organisational performance in a very positive way (Davidson et al. 2009). Many hospitals, usually in partnership with schools or faculties of nursing, have clinical leadership programs and you might consider enrolling in one of these following the successful completion of your TPPP. By that time, you may have decided upon the clinical area you wish to specialise in.

Point to ponder

Developing clinical leadership skills and competencies may be one learning objective for your TPPP.

WORKING IN GROUPS

In your study group, discuss examples of clinical leadership that you have observed during your clinical placements. What characteristics or attributes did clinical leaders demonstrate? What made you notice these clinical leaders?

Transcultural leadership

Transcultural leadership is a relatively new concept, and stems from developments such as globalisation; the emergence in Australia of a multicultural society; and, from a nursing perspective, the emergence of multicultural dimensions in nursing practice. Transcultural leadership is introduced here to make you aware that this is a concept which fits within the emerging culturally and linguistically diverse healthcare environment you are working in and will continue to work in. Transcultural leadership is another way of considering leadership. According to Derungs (2011), transcultural leadership is both innovative and transformative, and transcultural leaders:

- explore and understand the basic assumptions of a system (group or community)
- understand why people behave as they do within groups
- observe the interdependence and interaction between systems
- influence the processes of meaning and sense making
- support others with continual improvement
- create shared meanings.

FOR REFLECTION

How would having these transcultural competencies help you with delivering nursing care? How would you relate these transcultural competencies to nursing practice?

Interpersonal competencies

Interpersonal competencies relate to the ability to communicate with and understand other people and for them to understand you (Davidson et al. 2009, p. 20). All organisations are made up of people who communicate with each other to achieve organisational objectives. Nurses communicate with a diverse range of people during the course of their work. They develop professional relationships with their colleagues and with their patients. Having good communication competencies is fundamental to developing therapeutic relationships with patients and to developing professional relationships with colleagues. Effective communication skills include being a good listener. This is particularly important when you meet patients and/or their families for the first time. This may be in the emergency department or when they arrive in your clinical unit. Your initial approach to the patient and how you put them at ease, how you ask questions and how you listen and respond to their replies during the assessment phase will influence your patient's response to you and to the care he or she receives. Being a good listener and showing understanding and empathy to the patient are all elements of good interpersonal competencies.

Goleman (2005) described **emotional intelligence** (EI) as including the following elements:

- self-awareness
- self-management
- social awareness
- social skills.

So you can see that interpersonal competencies relate to emotional intelligence.

WORKING IN GROUPS

In your study group, discuss the concept of emotional intelligence, and reflect on your own levels of:

- self-awareness
- self-management
- social awareness
- social skills.

Rate these on a scale of 1 to 5, where 1 = least effective an 5 = most effective. This will give you a basis for further development of your interpersonal competencies.

Other nursing competencies

The ANMC national competencies are the core competencies for all registered nurses in Australia. While it is important to develop all competencies, there are some competencies which are a priority. These are:

- assessment competencies
- communication competencies

- critical thinking competencies
- cultural competencies.

Assessment competencies

In the nursing process framework, the first function is assessment, and rightly so. The first thing you do as a nurse is assess your patient or group of patients. Assessment is a process of observation, asking questions and making judgments that will lead to a care plan that meets a patient's care needs at the time of admission to your clinical unit. So how do you develop good assessment skills? Good assessment skills begin with:

- a good clinical knowledge base
- the ability to observe the patient and note the physical appearance and behaviour of the patient
- the ability to note any clinical symptoms and know what the symptoms indicate
- the ability to ask the patient the right questions and then to ask more probing questions should the initial responses indicate this
- the ability to note the non-verbal cues the patient may be exhibiting: i.e. body language may not reflect what the patient is saying
- the ability to document the assessment accurately.

Point to ponder

A good assessment is the foundation for all nursing care.

Assessment is an ongoing process and you are continually assessing patients' conditions during the course of your shift or work day. You are assessing patients when giving medication, attending to a patient's personal hygiene; beginning to mobilise patients; taking observations such as blood pressures, pulses or respirations; or monitoring patients following an emergency event or after a fall. Any activity that engages you with a patient is an opportunity for assessment, and any deviation from what is the norm for a patient is documented, reported and recorded in the patient record. Even an unconscious patient requires continual assessment. For example, while attending to the personal hygiene needs of the unconscious patient, you will be assessing:

- respiratory pattern and deteriorating gas exchange
- any airway impairment—need to clear secretions
- impact of immobility
- pressure ulcers, skin tears

Maria Fedoruk

- response to tactile stimuli
- nutritional and hydration status
- any deterioration in neurological status
- any alteration in cardiac status.

From this, you can see why assessment is a core competency for nurses. Nurses spend more time with patients than other health professionals, and so opportunities for continual assessment are always present. As you become more experienced, assessing patients becomes something you do unconsciously, and your ability to respond to even the smallest changes in the patient's clinical condition may start to seem intuitive.

WORKING IN GROUPS

In your study group, discuss the following scenario. You are working in a respiratory unit and are asked to assess a new patient. During the assessment you observe the following:

- The patient is drowsy, agitated and in considerable distress.
- The patient has difficulty in responding to your questions, because they have to take a breath every few words.
- You count the patient's respiratory rate and find it is more than 48 breaths per minute.
- You observe a central cyanosis.
- You observe that the patient has peripheral oedema.
- The patient is tachycardic — pulse rate of 132/minute.
- The patient is hypertensive: 210/100 mmHg.

What do these signs and symptoms indicate to you? What sort of clinical judgment will you make? Are there any tests that you believe should be done to validate your clinical judgment? Should you initiate any treatment? What would you document in the patient's record? What will the nursing care plan that you develop for this patient look like?

Communication competencies

Point to ponder

Communication is more than just talking.

Communication is one of the most fundamental human activities. It is a complex process used to pass on information, to influence, to teach and to show emotion (Sullivan & Garland 2010). Nurses need good communication skills to demonstrate knowledge and insights; to empathise; to manage conflict; to show trustworthiness and professional integrity; and to teach other nurses and patients. The purpose of communication is to arrive at a shared understanding of the message being sent and received. Communication is not just the sending of a message: it is also about careful listening and monitoring of responses. To be a good communicator, you not only have to have good language skills, but also good listening skills. You also need good assessment skills, because sometimes the real message is in the subtext that is observed through the other person's body language, tone, volume and inflection of voice. Observing body language is important when dealing with patients, because there are times when patients may be uncomfortable discussing issues they consider personal or intimate with virtual strangers. There are also times when patients minimise their levels of pain because of some underlying fears they may not have expressed to you. If you are astute and paying close attention to what the patient is *not* saying by observing the patient's body language and listening to their tone of voice, you will be able to make a more informed assessment and **clinical judgment** of the patient's clinical status and need for nursing interventions.

Effective communicators have a well-developed vocabulary and know the words to use in any situation. This means that when you are talking with patients you do not use medical or nurse language, but instead speak to the patient in language they can understand. You also avoid distorting communication by using abbreviations that others do not understand. Because of the nature of their work, nurses sometimes use humour to defuse situations or debrief following a critical event. It is important to know that not everyone may share your humour, and others may find it offensive, so you need to be mindful of this. Also, nurses from other cultures may find it difficult to understand the Australian slang that nurses commonly use: be mindful of this and use language that everyone can understand.

Point to ponder

Effective communication is context-specific and culturally dependent.

Nurses communicate using different methods. Communication is not only verbal; it is also non-verbal, written and electronic. What is common to all of these different modes of communication is that the sender has to ensure that the message being sent will be understood by the receiver. You should also remember that there is a form of etiquette (manners or courtesy) around effective communication.

In most organisations today, the most common form of communication is email. As a result, organisations now have guidelines for the proper use of email. You should become familiar with these guidelines. Good communication does not facilitate a conflict situation but instead ensures common understanding.

Maria Fedoruk

The Appendices include some advice to support your organisation's guidelines on using email. Appendix G contains tips for using email in the work context. As with written documentation, care needs to be taken that the information provided is precise, accurate and clear. Remember: emails are words that are interpreted without the reader having the benefit of observing non-verbal communication cues. Appendix H provides guidelines for using social media. Social media can be used as a form of communication between health professionals and the patient and family or carers, but care needs to be taken to ensure that patient confidentiality is not compromised.

Feedback is another aspect of good communication, so it is important that you give feedback to anyone you have delegated work to. Feedback is not criticism or negative comments but an objective assessment of the outcomes of an event or intervention. For example, you may have participated in the emergency resuscitation of a patient in your unit. There was a successful outcome for the patient, but if this was your first emergency resuscitation then you would like to receive feedback about your involvement in the procedure, noting the good points and the areas in which you could improve. The emergency resuscitation event is one area where if the communication is not clear, succinct and to the point, outcomes can be less than optimal. The majority of healthcare organisations now offer debriefing sessions for staff following critical incidents or emergencies.

FOR REFLECTION

As a student nurse, what forms of feedback have you received? What was the nature of the feedback? Was it negative and only focused on the deficits found in the paper or on what you failed to achieve during your clinical placement? What were your feelings? Did you feel inadequate? How was the feedback given to you? Was it written, verbal or both? What did you learn from the feedback?

Now think back to when you received positive feedback for the work you had done. What were your feelings? What did you learn from the feedback? Were you able to work out strategies that would help you to improve?

In both cases, was the feedback communicated to you in a reasoned way indicating that the reviewer had given some thought to the feedback and offered suggestions on how you could improve and/or enhance areas of your practice? Or was the feedback communicated to you in an offhand, 'care factor zero' manner?

What have you learnt from the way you received feedback? How might you give feedback to others based on your experiences?

Critical thinking competencies

This section discusses the concept of critical thinking in nursing and the relationship between critical thinking, nursing practice and patient outcomes. Critical thinking is an essential competency for you to develop if you are to become a safe, competent registered nurse. Critical thinking is a competency in the ANMC national competency standards for registered nurses (ANMC 2006). Critical thinking is 'purposeful and goal directed thinking' (Alfaro-Lefevre 2004, p. 4). The difference between critical thinking and thinking is that the former is purposeful, controlled and focused on achieving outcomes, while thinking can refer to any mental activity, including daydreaming or performing routine tasks (Alfaro-Lefevre 2004, p. 5).

Characteristics of a critical thinker

The characteristics of a critical thinker include:

- *being a lifelong learner*—for you, learning does not stop at graduation
- *being curious*—you continue to be curious about your work and your patients and ask why things occur
- *being confident*—you are confident in your ability to analyse questions or situations using inductive and deductive reasoning and to achieve the correct outcomes for patients
- *being courageous*—having the courage to challenge the status quo
- *being resilient*—not accepting setbacks, and persisting in finding the correct solutions
- *being self-aware*—having an awareness of your own limitations, knowing when to ask for help, and developing strategies to overcome these limitations.

WORKING IN GROUPS

In your study group, discuss the characteristics of a critical thinker, and reflect on your critical thinking abilities. Reflect on times when you used critical thinking skills to achieve an outcome. How successful were you?

- Would you have done anything differently?
- Is there some attribute you would like to develop further?
- Did the clinical leaders you observed demonstrate critical thinking competencies?

Maria Fedoruk

Problem solving

Problem solving is another cognitive activity, different from critical thinking. To arrive at a solution, in problem solving you do the following:

- Identify the problem or issue.
- Collect all the relevant information about the particular problem.
- Use the information to suggest several solutions.
- Make the best possible, safe decision based on the information you have at the time.

This last point is important, because to make the best possible decision you have to have knowledge of the context of the problem, knowledge of the patient and knowledge of the resources you have available to you. It is important to realise that a decision made for one patient may not necessarily be the best decision for another patient with a similar or the same problem or diagnosis. This is why it is important to have more than one solution, not discard any solutions, and to be able to apply a solution that meets the specific patient's needs. Problem solving is therefore context- and patient-dependent.

In nursing practice, the nursing process is a problem-solving process, made up of the following elements:

- assessment
- diagnosis
- planning
- implementation
- evaluation.

WORKING IN GROUPS

In your study group, compare the nursing process with the steps involved in problem solving, and with critical thinking. Are there any similarities or differences? Apply each of these processes to the following scenario. You have completed a physical assessment of a new patient, Mr W. You find that Mr W has pressure ulcers on his buttocks. The lesion on his left buttock is superficial and is located approximately 50 mm down the buttock next to the gluteal crease and measures 4 cm x 3 cm, with a depth of 0.2 cm. Mr W also has a sacral lesion with eschar present. You palpate the surrounding tissue and find that it is spongy to touch with a smelly, purulent discharge. You ask Mr W whether or not these lesions are causing him any discomfort, and he replies no. You report this to the team leader, who tells you to complete a care plan for Mr W and to take a swab from the wound.

- What do you do first? Why?
- Do you engage Mr W. in developing his care plan?

- When developing the care plan, what risk factors will you need to consider? How will you determine the outcomes of care?

Clinical judgment

Clinical judgment, often called clinical reasoning, is an important competency to develop. You will have developed some clinical reasoning ability from your study program, but ongoing development of this competency can be challenging. If we use Benner's (2001) 'novice to expert' paradigm, as a student nurse you were at the novice level but as a new registered nurse, you are at the advanced beginner level. So what do you need to do to move from the level of advanced beginner to the expert level? In Benner's model, you will proceed from advanced beginner level to the competence level, then to the proficient level, and finally to the expert level. Becoming an expert clinician takes time, but it is achievable if you continue to apply critical thinking skills to clinical problems as you come across them in the course of your work, work with more experienced clinician nurses and remain a lifelong learner, taking advantage of every opportunity to increase your knowledge. This is where using your portfolio and reflective thinking will assist you. If one of your career goals is 'To become an expert … (fill in your preferred clinical specialty) nurse' then make entries in your professional portfolio to monitor your progress in achieving this goal. Specify what you will need to do to get there, and develop a time-frame for doing so.

Developing and evaluating care plans for your patients is a good way of improving your critical thinking and clinical reasoning competencies. If we return to the care plan you developed for Mr W and you reflect on the cognitive processes you used to develop the plan:

- Were you forced to focus on the most important nursing intervention areas?
- Did you communicate with Mr W and with other members of the interprofessional team caring for Mr W?
- Did you ensure the information on the care plan and subsequent progress notes were able to be used by others—managers, other clinicians, and researchers?
- Did you identify specific patient outcomes to be achieved?
- Did you specify the interventions to be implemented during the care delivery process?
- Did you enable evaluation of the care plan and Mr W's progress?

Maria Fedoruk

Having developed the care plan for Mr W, how will his responses to the interventions be monitored? How will you measure progress and what will you do if Mr W does not respond to your interventions? How will you measure and manage any variances in care?

Cultural competencies

Australia in the twenty-first century is a multicultural country: it has been settled by people from more than '200 countries, practicing more than 116 religions and speaking more than 180 languages' and this does not include the cultural and language diversity of Australia's Indigenous peoples (Johnstone & Kanitsaki 2007, p. 247). Globalisation has made mass migration easier, and at the same time wars and other conflicts, natural disasters and oppressive politics have exposed millions of people to disease, illness and poverty (Papadopoulos 2006). For many people, including refugees, Australia is a preferred destination, resulting in cultural diversity within Australia's population.

Point to ponder

Multiculturalism is evident in Australia's healthcare system, not just in patient demographics but also in health professional demographics.

You will have been introduced to the concept of transcultural nursing in your undergraduate program. An early definition of transcultural nursing is:

> A formal area of study and practice focused on comparative holistic culture, care, health and illness patterns of people with respect to differences and similarities in their cultural values, beliefs and practices with the goal to provide culturally congruent, sensitive and competent nursing care to people of diverse cultures.

(Leininger 1995, p. 4)

The ANMC (2006, p. 12) standard 9.5 states that the registered nurse 'facilitates a physical, psychosocial, cultural, and spiritual environment that promotes individual/group safety and security'. The first three criteria under this standard are:

- demonstrates sensitivity, awareness, and respect for cultural identity as part of an individual's/group's perception of security
- demonstrates sensitivity, awareness and respect in regard to an individual's/group's spiritual needs

- involves family and others in ensuring that cultural and spiritual needs are met.

You will know from your studies that for many people from other countries their cultural identity and spiritual or religious beliefs are inextricably linked, and so your care planning needs to account for these. To help you with caring for patients from other cultural backgrounds there are now offices and agencies that you can call for assistance, should this be necessary when planning, implementing and evaluating care for patients.

Papadopoulos (2006) presents a model for developing **cultural competence**. Elements of this model are cultural awareness, cultural knowledge, **cultural sensitivity**, cultural competence and **cultural safety**.

Cultural awareness

To develop cultural awareness, you need to examine your own values and beliefs, because these are the principles which you use to live your life and make your decisions and judgments. You carry these principles into your working life, so from that perspective it is important that you understand and know your value and beliefs system, because it will influence your nursing practice. Cultural awareness means that you accept that people from different ethnic backgrounds will have different expectations of you as a registered nurse and the healthcare system based on their values and belief systems, including religious beliefs. You would use the nursing process to develop care plans that incorporated these different values and belief systems.

Cultural knowledge

Cultural knowledge comes from anthropology, the discipline which explores different cultures through their values, shared understandings, practices, habits, language and modes of communication, and through more visible expressions of culture such as clothing, art, music and etiquette (Papadopoulos 2006). Nursing has taken this knowledge and adapted it to nursing practice (Moss & Chittenden 2008; Leininger 1995). Nursing research informs nurses' knowledge of multiculturalism and its impact on the practice of nursing (Purnell 2000). A good reference for you to access is the *Journal of Transcultural Nursing*.

Cultural sensitivity

Cultural sensitivity is at the core of interpersonal relationships. As a registered nurse, you will develop interpersonal relationships with your patients and the people you work with. In culturally competent care, the patient is a true partner in the care process, but if this is to be achieved, then there has to be evidence of the values, beliefs and customs of the patient in the care plan. These may include dietary requirements or the religious needs of the patient, and when caring for children there should be evidence that the child's parents have been included in the care planning process.

An important aspects of cultural communicative competence is demonstrating knowledge of the patient's cultural values and, most importantly, their rules for interactions. In some cultures, male–female interactions are strictly prescribed: this can require some creativity to accommodate. Intercultural communication is the ability to recognise and deal with the challenges associated with communication across cultural boundaries (Papadopoulos 2006). Communication skills needed by you when caring for people from other ethnic backgrounds are both verbal and non-verbal; you should be sensitive to cues from body language and voice tone, volume and inflection, facial expressions, and eye contact. Also, be aware of what is considered to be appropriate personal space and know forms of greeting, as well as understanding of time (clock time versus social time): all of these may be specific to particular cultures (Papadopoulos 2006, p. 18).

Cultural competence

Cultural competence results from integrating the other three elements of this model (cultural awareness, cultural knowledge and cultural sensitivity). In addition to the skills already mentioned, assessment, clinical practice and critical thinking skills are also essential to developing cultural competence. Evidence of cultural competence from nursing personnel should be shown in the nursing documentation. The documentation should show that nurses have taken into account specific cultural issues relevant to the patient, such as diet, religious requirements or language support (interpreters). Most assessment forms have a section dealing with cultural details that you may have to address when assessing patients from multicultural backgrounds. The nursing care plan should be developed to address any specific cultural needs of a patient or groups of patients.

The following case study will help you to understand the elements of cultural competency. The case study also brings in the other skills and competencies discussed in this chapter.

Case study: Non-English-speaking patient

Mr T, a 52-year-old man from a non-English-speaking background was admitted to the coronary care unit with acute heart failure. He had experienced chest pain two days prior to the admission but did not seek medical help. His family had administered traditional medicines in accordance with their cultural beliefs. Mr T had otherwise been a fit and healthy man with no other known medical problems.

On examination, Mr T was found to have left-sided heart failure and pulmonary oedema. His blood pressure was low (90/50) and his pulse 110. He was sweaty with cool peripheries. These signs were suggestive of cardiogenic shock.

His electrocardiograph (ECG) showed that he had a completed anterior myocardial infarction. A subsequent echocardiogram showed that Mr T had an ejection fraction of 21 per cent (normal it is around 80 per cent), which meant that the left ventricle was severely impaired and could not maintain an adequate cardiac output, resulting in a backlog of fluid in the lungs and pulmonary oedema.

The normal treatment for acute myocardial infarction is reperfusion therapy (opening of the blocked coronary artery by thrombolytic 'clotbuster' drugs or balloon angioplasty). Unfortunately, Mr T had presented to the hospital too late for this treatment, which needs to be administered within six hours of onset of the infarct for best results. He had already completed his infarct, and therefore the muscle supplied by the blocked artery was dead: thus, there was nothing to be gained by opening the artery supplying this muscle.

Mr T was treated with IV medications to try and increase cardiac output and offload fluid to reduce the congestion on his lungs. However, in spite of best efforts, his blood pressure fell even further, his urine output decreased and his pulmonary oedema worsened.

Given these factors, the treating medical team decided that Mr T had a condition that was not reversible and that he should be given comfort care and not cardiopulmonary resuscitation (CPR) in the event of a cardiac arrest. However, all IV medication would be continued.

Mr T did not speak English, and nor did his wife and daughter, who were there with him. His son did speak English, however, and so the medical team explained the situation to the son and then left the son to explain the situation to the rest of his family and his father. The son agreed that all current efforts to help his father would continue, but in the event of cardiac arrest, he would not have CPR. The doctor wrote up IV Morphine 2.5–10 mg prn for comfort care.

In the setting of pulmonary oedema, morphine can reduce congestion in the pulmonary capillary beds, thus it may have an alleviating effect. It also reduces pain and anxiety in patients. However, it may also result in respiratory depression which can, in the extreme, be fatal.

Shortly after the doctor had discussed the situation with the son, Mr T became extremely distressed and short of breath. The nurse listened to his lungs and could hear that he had fluid up to the apices (the entire lung field). His family were distraught, and through the son, requested that the nurse give him something to help him. The nurse drew up morphine, and considering the size of Mr T and his distress decided to give him 10 mg. She checked it with another registered nurse, as was policy for drug administration.

As the nurse finished administering the morphine, Mr T went into asystole (absence of heartbeat). Mr T stopped breathing and the monitor alarmed for asystole. The family all looked accusingly at the nurse.

Questions

Discuss the following questions about this case study in your study group.

- Would you use problem solving or critical thinking skills to resolve the issues that emerged in the case of Mr T?
- Is there a potential for conflict between health professionals and the family? How would you prevent the conflict from escalating?

Cultural safety

Cultural safety is a concept that is embedded in the New Zealand nursing context and is culturally mandated in the Treaty of Waitangi, which has at its core the merging of indigenous peoples with those who colonised the country (Moss & Chittenden 2008, p. 174). The primary focus of cultural safety in the New Zealand context is the improvement of health for the indigenous people of New Zealand (Maoris). The concept of cultural safety recognises the various risks that face indigenous people from 'unsafe cultural practices' within the context of a caring environment (Johnstone & Kanitsaki 2007, p. 248). Unsafe cultural practices are defined as any actions which demean and diminish the cultural identity of people from minority ethnic groups (Johnstone & Kanitsaki 2007, p. 247). While cultural safety is embedded in the nursing curricula in New Zealand, there is little research-based evidence that it has improved cultural appropriateness and responsiveness in the delivery of health services to Maori people.

Moss and Chittenden (2008) point out that cultural safety and cultural sensitivity can be drawn from the broader social context of communities (indigenous peoples and culturally different groups) and from workplace culture. In Chapters 1 and 2 we discussed belongingness and that how, as a new employee, you achieve this is determined by workplace culture. A positive workplace culture will facilitate belongingness, whereas a negative workplace culture will not. During your clinical placements you will have come across negative and positive workplace cultures and this may have determined your choices of future employment.

You should be able to see and understand the relationships and connections between EI (good interpersonal competencies) and being able to work effectively in a culturally safe and sensitive workplace.

SUMMARY

This chapter is about the essential skills and competencies you will need to further develop as you move through your TPPP and beyond. The skills and competencies discussed in this chapter are fundamental for registered nurses working in contemporary healthcare environments. The twenty-first-century healthcare environment is technologically rich, with technologies changing at a fast pace. All the skills and competencies listed in this chapter are underpinned by critical thinking skills, and the registered nurse of the twenty-first century is first and foremost a critical thinker. Effective critical thinking skills enable you to manage and disseminate information; enhance your information literacy skills; enhance your cultural competencies; and certainly enhance your clinical judgment and decision-making skills. Critical thinking is at the core of safe, competent nursing practice.

DISCUSSION QUESTIONS

1   In your opinion, what are the core competencies for nurses and midwives? Give reasons for your responses.
2   What is the nursing process?
3   Why is cultural awareness necessary for nurses working in a contemporary healthcare system?
4   What are your responsibilities as a:
    – team member?
    – team leader?

REFERENCES

Alfaro-Lefevre, A (2004) *Critical thinking and clinical judgement*, 3rd edn, Elsevier Science, USA.

Australian Nursing and Midwifery Council (2006) *National competency standards for the registered nurse*, 4th edn, Australian Nursing and Midwifery Council, Canberra, <www.anmc.org.au/userfiles/file/competency_standards/Competency_standards_RN.pdf>, accessed 13 September 2011.

Benner, P (2001) *From novice to expert—excellence and power in clinical nursing practice*, Prentice-Hall, Upper Saddle River, NJ.

Davidson, P, Simon, A, Woods, P, Griffith, RW (2009) *Management*, 2nd Australasian edn, John Wiley & Sons, Australia.

Maria Fedoruk

Derungs, IMH (2011) *Trans-cultural leadership for transformation*, Palgrave Macmillan, UK.

Dwyer, J & Hopwood, N (2010) *Management strategies and skills*, McGraw-Hill, Australia.

Goleman, D (2005) *Emotional intelligence*, Bantam Books, New York.

Johnstone, M-J & Kanitsaki, O (2007) 'An exploration of the notion and nature of the construct of cultural safety and its applicability to the Australian healthcare context,' *Journal of Transcultural Nursing*, vol. 18, pp. 247–54.

Leininger, M (1995) *Transcultural nursing: Concepts, theories, research and practices*, McGraw-Hill and Greyden press, New York.

Moss, C & Chittenden, J (2008) 'Being culturally sensitive in development work' in K Manely, B Mc Cormack & V Wilson (eds) *International practice development in nursing*, Blackwell Publishing Ltd, UK, pp. 170–88.

Papadopoulos, I (2006) *Transcultural health and social care*, Churchill Livingstone Elsevier, Edinburgh.

Peate, I (2006) *Becoming a nurse in the 21st century*, John Wiley & Sons, UK.

Purnell, L (2000) 'A description of the Purnell model for cultural competence', *Journal of Transcultural Nursing*, vol. 11, no. 40, pp. 40–6.

Sullivan, E & Garland, G (2010) *Practical leadership and management in nursing*, Pearson Education, England.

Chapter 9

Applying competencies to registered nurse practice

Maria Fedoruk

Learning objectives

After reading this chapter, you will be able to:
- describe the role and function of the registered nurse
- describe the role of the registered nurse in quality management
- discuss the elements of nursing care organisation.

Key terms

Delegation
Evidence-based practice
Quality management

The role and function of the registered nurse

Defining the practice of nursing

Florence Nightingale described nursing as 'the act of utilizing the environment of the patient to assist him in his recovery' (Nightingale 1860). In 1966, Virginia Henderson (1966, p. 3) described nursing as follows:

> The unique function of the nurse is to assist the individual, sick or well, in the performance of those activities contributing to health or its recovery (or to peaceful death) that he would perform unaided if he had the necessary strength, will or knowledge and to do this in such a way as to help him gain independence as rapidly as possible.

In the twenty-first century, Walker (2009, p. 40) identified what we know as the meta-paradigm of nursing, composed of the following elements:

- person (patient)—the recipient of nursing care
- environment—the external and internal environments which make up the patient's world
- health—the degree of ill health or wellness experienced by the patient
- nursing—the act of nursing or the actions that make up nursing practice.

As you can see, the meta-paradigm of nursing contextualises nursing in the twenty-first century, but still draws on Nightingale's and Henderson's definitions. Nightingale and Henderson both identify health as an outcome of nursing interventions—in modern terms, they were evidence-based practitioners before it became the norm to be so.

As health is a key outcome of nursing practice, let's look at how health is defined in a twenty-first-century context. Blaxter (2010, p. 4) comments that of all the available definitions of health the most common is one of normality, with illness being a deviation away from the normal. However, normality must be considered in terms of the individual—what is normal health for a 20-year-old marathon runner will not be normal for a 70-year-old with diabetes and other chronic diseases. As a registered nurse, you have to be able to understand that 'normal' health is specific to an individual.

Central to the practice of nursing is the concept of caring. Nurses care by:

- showing respect and consideration for the patients they look after
- demonstrating professional behaviours
- being safe practitioners
- demonstrating competencies in technical tasks, including being effective during emergencies
- demonstrating 'soft' skills—i.e. good communication skills; good interpersonal skills; good intraprofessional and interprofessional skills
- demonstrating effective good information management skills and competencies

- applying knowledge to practice
- demonstrating good clinical judgment and decision-making.

You can probably add to this list from your own experiences and observations.

In your study group, reflect on your definition of caring and/or the definitions of caring given to you in your undergraduate program. Are these reflected in the list above? Do you agree with the notion that caring in nursing is an action? That is: to care in nursing is to *do*?

What do nurses do?

To answer this question critically we could analyse a day in your life as a registered nurse at work. For example, let's examine in detail what you would do when you work an early shift. In most hospitals or healthcare agencies, an early shift begins at 7 am. You arrive at work just before 7 am, having awoken some time after 5 am, depending on your home life responsibilities (getting yourself ready for work; getting children ready for school or child care; making breakfast; making sure children have lunches; organising the pick-up and delivery of children to their various destinations and then your transport to work. If you take public transport, you need to get the bus, tram or train that will get you to work as close as possible to 7 am. If you use your own car, you may need to leave enough time to find a car park close to work, or you may be fortunate enough to have an allocated parking place. Having dealt with all of these things before you get to work, you finally arrive at your clinical unit just before 7 am. The night staff are glad to see you and the rest of the team, and when everyone is present you listen to the handover, paying particular attention to the group of patients you will be responsible for.

Having listened to the handover, you go to your patients and see if they are ready for breakfast. Or do you? You might also:

- plan the day's activities—who needs medications; intravenous therapies checked; who is going to theatre; who is going to be discharged
- set priorities—which nursing activities need to be attended to first
- allocate patients to other members of your team (if you have an enrolled nurse or assistant in nursing with you)
- check the care plans of patients allocated to you.

All nursing activities are time-based. A simple example is the administration of medications. Medications are given at a set time. So time management is an important competency for you develop. Some rules for effective time management are:

- Know what has to be done, by whom and when.
- Set priorities—what needs to done first?
- Plan for potential problems and have strategies for dealing with these.
- Do not make work for yourself and others through poor documentation, poor communication and general sloppiness.
- Recognise your own time-wasting strategies and manage these.
- Recognise time-wasting strategies in others and deal with these.
- Try and plan ahead—plan for the unexpected.
- Try and avoid becoming stressed—when you are stressed you tend not to think clearly and therefore impair your decision-making ability.

Looking at the sample nurse checklist, you know that in addition to the normal activities for these patients—hygiene care, meals, checking wounds— the nurse has to contact the medical staff to review pain medications for at least two patients, make appointments, and notify an aged care facility of the return of a resident following treatment for a fractured elbow. Inherent in all of these are a series of sub-activities that will need to be performed if positive

Table 9.1: Sample nurse checklist

Patient name and age	Consultant	Problem/ diagnosis	Nursing activity	Notes
A, 72 years	Green	Fractured humerus	Pain management	Need to change pain medication
B, 99 years	Brown	Fractured neck of femur	Begin mobilisation	Make physio appointment
C, 80 years	White	Fractured elbow	Prepare for discharge	Make OPD` appointments. Book transport. Notify aged care facility
D, 56 years	Grey	Total hip replacement	Monitor diabetes	Check BSL
E, 63 years	Black	Knee replacement	Check level of pain relief needed	Note effectiveness of analgesic

Adapted from Siviter (2008)

health outcomes are to be achieved and patient expectations for quality care met. So, you can see that what nurses do is complex, requiring the transfer of knowledge to clinical practice and to others.

You will have your own style of checklist, but it is important for you to have something that you can refer to and jog your memory. Given the fast pace of nursing practice today, relying on your memory is not a good idea.

FOR REFLECTION

To find out how effective your time management skills are, keep a log of your own activities at work.

This is a sample time activity log and you can use this or compile one of your own. Keep the log for 7–14 days and then check through it. Critically analyse your entries, paying particular attention to the identified time wasters, and then develop strategies to better manage time wasters or even remove them from your 'to do' lists. Where you spent more time on an activity than was allocated, analyse why this occurred. Were there activities you could have delegated to others? You do need to remember you cannot do everything, and asking for help is not a sign of not coping or being helpless but an indicator of being patient-focused. It indicates that you have assessed your workload and

Table 9.2: Sample nurse activity log

Activity	Start time	Finish time	Allocated time	Time actually spent	Your own feelings at the time	Identify and list your time wasters	Areas for improvement
Handover							
Check allocated patients							
Patient-related activities, e.g. medications							
Break							
Professional development activities							

Adapted from Siviter (2008)

Maria Fedoruk

found that there are things you cannot do in the best interests of the patients. The belief that some nurses carry that they actually *do* have to do everything is a myth perpetuated by those who appear to have some sort of martyr complex. Do not accept this belief as truth!

Point to ponder

Accepting that you cannot do everything is a sign of professional maturity—would you agree?

Talking with patients or with other staff may be considered time wasting, but there are times when these conversations may provide you with information that will help you with care planning for individual patients. So you make decisions about what is necessary for you to deliver care to patients and what is necessary to maintain contact with other health professionals working with you. While time management is an important aspect of nursing practice, it is also important to maintain social contact through 'chatting' with colleagues and patients, because these informal chats often identify issues that need to be managed in the best interests of the patients. Nursing practice has social as well as clinical dimensions and it is important for you to maintain balance between your clinical responsibilities and social needs. Human beings are social beings, requiring social contact with others.

Point to ponder

The social dimensions of nursing practice are important for your professional life.

FOR REFLECTION

Reflect on a time at work when you had planned your work, set your priorities for managing your workload and then an emergency occurred—a patient had a respiratory arrest. How did you respond? How did you manage the emergency? On reflection is there anything you would have done differently? And why?

What nurses do in the clinical environment

This section explains what nurses do in the clinical environment and how nurses manage care. The framework that underpins nursing care or practice is the nursing process. You will have been introduced to the nursing process in your undergraduate program. The nursing process is a five-step analytical or problem solving process:

- assessment
- diagnosis
- planning
- implementation
- evaluation.

The nursing process is used continuously by nurses for the duration of a patient's stay in hospital, reflecting the changes in the patient's clinical condition. For example, consider a patient returning to your clinical unit following surgery. How would you use the nursing process to monitor the patient's recovery?

Decision-making in nursing

As nurses working with patients you will in the course of your work make clinically based decisions while caring for patients. So how do you make these decisions? What information do you need? What is the process for making decisions? Reaching a decision is part of a problem-solving process. Patients do not always respond to treatments and interventions as described in your textbooks. Therefore, having good observation and assessment skills and competencies will assist you in making good clinical decisions for your patients. Remember that your patients rely on you to make the correct decisions on their behalf. This includes relying on you to observe changes that may herald a more serious event, to contact medical staff if needed, and to interpret observations and making professional judgments that ensure patient health outcomes are positive and safe.

Clinical decision-making is something a registered nurse does every day. The Australian Nursing and Midwifery Council (2007) has developed the following decision-making tool for nurses.

Take the time to look at this decision-making tool closely, because it clearly identifies the steps in the decision-making process. For each step in the process, you are prompted with questions that enable you to choose from options that will lead you to make the best decision for the patient at the time. Decision-making in nursing is not always straightforward unless it is an emergency situation, in which case there are very clear procedures to follow.

Point to ponder

Clinical decision-making is a core function of nursing.

Maria Fedoruk

Figure 9.1: Nursing practice decisions summary guide

 NURSING PRACTICE DECISIONS
SUMMARY GUIDE

AUSTRALIAN NURSING &
MIDWIFERY COUNCIL

[NOTE: the order in which these issues are considered may vary according to context]

Identify client need/benefit
- Has there been a comprehensive assessment by a registered nurse to establish the client's needs/or their need for improved access to care?
- Has there been appropriate consultation with the client/their family/significant others?
- Is the activity in the client's best interests?

Yes to all / No to any

Reflect on scope of practice and nursing practice standards
- Is this activity within the current, contemporary scope of nursing practice?
- Have legislative requirements (eg specific qualification needed) been met?
- If authorisation by a regulatory authority is needed to perform the activity, does the person have it or can it be obtained before the activity is performed?
- Will performance comply with nursing practice standards / evidence?
- If other health professionals should assist, supervise or perform the activity, are they available?

Yes to all / No to any

Consider context of practice/organisational support
- Is this activity/practice supported by the organisation?
- If organisational authorisation is needed, does the person have it or can it be obtained before performing the activity?
- Is the skill mix in the organisation adequate for the level of support / supervision needed to safely perform the activity?
- Have potential risks been identified and strategies to avoid or minimise them been identified and implemented?
- Is there a system for ongoing education and maintenance of competence in place?
- If this is a new practice:
  – Are there processes in place for maintaining performance into the future?
  – Have relevant parties been involved in planning for implementation?

Yes to all / No to any

Select appropriate, competent person to perform the activity
- Have the roles and responsibilities of registered and enrolled nurses and non-nurses been considered?
- Does the person who is to perform the activity have the knowledge, skill, authority and ability (capacity) to do so either autonomously or with education, support and supervision?
- Is the required level of education, supervision / support available?
- Have all factors associated with delegation been considered?
- Is the person confident and do they understand their accountability and reporting responsibilities in performing the activity?

Yes to all / No to any

YES TO ALL	NO TO ANY
ACTION	**ACTION**
Proceed to: • perform the activity *OR* • delegate to a competent person • document the decision and the actions	• Consult/seek advice (eg NUM, DON other health professional) *OR* • Refer/collaborate *OR* • plan to enable integration / practice change if appropriate (including developing/implementing policies, gaining qualifications as needed)
EVALUATE	Document and evaluate and, if change still desired, commence process again

CONTEXT

AUSTRALIAN NURSING & MIDWIFERY COUNCIL
NATIONAL FRAMEWORK FOR THE DEVELOPMENT OF DECISION-MAKING TOOLS 2007

Effective clinical decision-making emerges from high-level assessment skills that focus on a patient's need for care. Once the assessment has been made, you move on to determining whether the proposed nursing intervention falls within your current scope of practice and is based on nursing practice standards. You then have to consider whether the proposed intervention is supported by the organisation and can be done within the current organisational context. Finally, you select the most competent person to perform the intervention. In the majority of instances, that person will be you.

FOR REFLECTION

Reflect on your decision-making ability. List the steps you take when making a decision at work. Are they very different to the steps listed above? Are you comfortable making decisions to do with patient care? Is this an area that could be improved, and what would you need to achieve this outcome?

Delegation

As a registered nurse, you will soon discover that you cannot do everything and that trying to do so only leads to stress and burnout, which then compromises your ability and capacity to work as a competent registered nurse. Therefore to get through all the things that need to be done—say, for instance, on your early shift—you will have to delegate some tasks or functions to other staff. Delegation may be defined as 'the act of transferring to a competent professional the authority to perform a selected nursing task in a selected situation and the process of doing the work' (National Council of State Boards of Nursing in ANMC 2007, p. 17). Delegation is not the same as allocating staff to patients for a shift, which is about the assigning of workload. There are six steps to delegation:

1 deciding what to delegate
2 selecting the delegatee
3 assigning the tasks—the delegated task has to be explained in detail; you have to be sure the individual understands what needs to be done and the responsibilities that are inherent in the tasks are explained and understood
4 ensuring the delegatee is competent and has the capacity to complete the task—do not set people up to fail (this is what a bully would do)
5 supervising the task(s) being done, as well as maintaining good communication with the individual

6   ensuring successful completion of the task, evaluating the outcomes and congratulating the delegatee for doing it well.

(Adapted from Curtis & Nicholls in ANMC 2007, p. 17)

As you can see, delegation is a complex process that requires good clinical knowledge and judgment, and the final accountability for the delegation lies with the delegator. Effective delegators in nursing possess high-order critical thinking skills, a solid and comprehensive knowledge base, and most importantly are excellent communicators with exceptional interpersonal skills. All delegated functions must be evaluated according to indicators such as:

• Was the task performed correctly in relation to safe practice and expected outcomes?
• Was the communication timely and relevant between delegator and delegate?
• Were any problems identified? How were they managed? Did this influence the outcomes?
• Was there a better way to do this?
• Did the patient's plan of care have to be adapted?
• Did the delegatee receive feedback?
• Was the delegated function within the scope of practice of the delegatee?
• Was the delegated function specific to one patient?

(ANMC 2007)

Using these indicators to evaluate a delegated function supports clinical practice, because it identifies areas for improvement and it also supports professional and competency development in individuals. However, a word of caution: if you are going to delegate a function you need to be very sure that the person you intend to delegate to does have the skills, knowledge and confidence to carry out the task. As a first-year registered nurse, do not agree to do anything that is outside your scope of practice. Building and developing experience is integral to your professional development but it can also be detrimental if things go wrong. There will be times when you will be asked to do something and while the challenge to do something new and/or different may be enticing, you may hear a little inner voice telling you not to take this on at this point in time. This is your intuition talking and you should listen to it.

The ANMC has produced guidelines for *Delegation and supervision for nurses and midwives*. These guidelines are a national approach for nurses and midwives to make good and appropriate decisions when delivering care to patients (ANMC 2008).

Intuition

You will probably have noted during your clinical placements that some nurses seem to make decisions seamlessly and effortlessly. The role of intuition in clinical decision-making by nurses is beginning to be discussed in nursing literature (Benner 2001). Intuition may be defined as 'a defining characteristic of professional expertise and is gaining acceptance as a legitimate way of knowing in clinical nursing' (Pretz & Folse 2011, p. 2878). Do these nurses have special psychic abilities or are they drawing on their experiences and knowledge and responding unconsciously to cues in front of them? It would seem that clinical experience enables nurses to recognise changes in clinical symptoms, patient responses to clinical changes and treatments, and the nurse then draws on experiences and knowledge to make the correct decision. If these nurses are asked why they made the decision they made, a common response is 'I just knew' or 'I had a feeling'. As you become more experienced and are exposed to different clinical situations, you will develop this inner voice that will guide your decision-making at different times. Some key aspects of intuition in clinical nursing have been described by Dreyfus and Dreyfus in Benner (2001) as:

- drawing on clinical experiences and knowledge to identify similarities and links with past experience
- using commonsense—understanding the context of the clinical situation
- expert clinical knowledge—using clinical expertise to inform clinical decision-making
- recognising similarities with other patients
- an ability to prioritise events in terms of clinical signs and symptoms
- emotional intelligence—the ability to prioritise clinical signs and symptoms from different perspectives.

Point to ponder

What factors must registered nurses or midwives consider when engaging with the processes of clinical decision-making?

As you can see, all of these indicators are based on expert clinical knowledge relating to the clinical condition, as well as the context or setting where this is occurring.

Evidence-based practice

Evidence-based nursing practice stems from the evidence-based medicine paradigm. Evidence-based medicine has been defined as the application of relevant, valid, research-based evidence in nurse decision-making (Cullum et al. 2008, p. 2). This definition can be applied to all aspects of clinical and non-clinical nursing practice. Research-based evidence does not determine what nursing practice is, but should be used alongside existing nursing knowledge that includes:

- the patient's symptoms
- the patient's diagnoses
- the patient's preferences
- the context in which this clinical practice is occurring
- the availability of resources (Cullum et al. 2008, p. 2).

If you apply this definition to nursing practice, you can begin to see how and why nursing research can be used to inform clinical nursing practice. You will have heard terms such as 'best practice' and 'clinical guidelines' as you moved through your undergraduate program, and these terms relate to aspects of evidence-based practice. Funding bodies and patients and other key stakeholders, including patients, expect that the care being delivered in healthcare facilities is of the highest standard possible and that the health professionals are able to deliver this care in a safe and competent manner.

Evidence-based nursing practice focuses on clinical decision-making using the best available evidence from research together with clinical expertise and knowledge and taking into account patient preferences and available resources (DiCenso, Cullum & Ciliska in Ellis & Hartley 2009). The focus in this description of evidence-based nursing practice is clinical decision-making. As a registered nurse you are accountable and responsible for the decisions you make. These decisions are made using your clinical knowledge and expertise for patients and therefore it is important that you use the best available evidence to make these decisions. Now that you are a registered nurse, it is important that you continue to learn and develop your clinical knowledge base so that your practice is current and appropriate. While you may have completed your degree, you will have to continue learning, because changes occur in clinical practice continuously and if you are to be a safe and competent registered nurse you will need to continually 'upskill' in using evidence to support your clinical practice. The use of research-based evidence to support your clinical practice is an integral component of quality improvement processes and practices in healthcare organisations.

Measuring performance

You have entered an environment that is complex and where everything is measured, from the number of paperclips used by office staff to the number of medications given to patients in a clinical unit. This emphasis on measurement is driven by reporting requirements from governments and other funding bodies. As you aware, maintaining health is costly and in a country that has a government-funded healthcare system, an ageing population and an increasingly culturally diverse population, the demands on the healthcare system are increasing, thereby increasing costs. Measuring performance requires evidence from good-quality research, including nursing research.

Reporting on a healthcare agency's performance is a part of the quality improvement program and it is clear from the literature that nurses are integral to the success of quality improvement (Needleman & Hassmiller 2009). So, the work you do links directly to the organisation's quality improvement program. An example of nurses reporting data is the organisational management and reporting of critical incidents, which is a function of the **quality management** program. This is discussed in more detail in Chapter 10.

Safety in healthcare agencies is of paramount importance and is the responsibility of everyone working there. It is directly related to the quality improvement program. Because of their intimate work with patients, nurses have specific responsibilities in relation to safety. These responsibilities range from all aspects of nursing care delivery to delegation of duties to other health professionals (such as enrolled nurses or assistants in nursing).

In August 2008, Australian health ministers endorsed the Australian Charter of Healthcare Rights. This charter summarises the basic rights of patients and consumers in relation to accessing and receiving healthcare services across Australia. The principles underpinning this charter are:

- access
- safety
- respect
- communication
- participation
- privacy
- comment.

(Commonwealth of Australia 2008)

These principles are now embedded in healthcare organisations' quality improvement programs and can be converted into **key performance indicators** (KPIs), which are measurable indicators of organisational performance.

Quality improvement

Quality improvement is embedded in all aspects of a healthcare organisation's activities, including management and clinical practice processes. Quality improvement in healthcare organisations may be described as a series of processes designed to systematically evaluate the care and services delivered to patients and residents, in order to identify and rectify problem areas. Quality improvement is the process of measuring, monitoring, evaluating and controlling clinical and management processes to provide funders and the public with evidence that the services provided are safe and standards-based.

From a nursing perspective, registered nurses need to know the basics of quality improvement: that is, how to collect and analyse data and then what to do with this information. You should be able to evaluate the outcomes of your nursing care and compare this to standards of practice. The ANMC standards of nursing practice will be supplemented by clinical standards of practice based on research-based evidence in your clinical unit.

Quality improvement is closely linked to **risk management** processes in healthcare services, and registered nurses have a very significant role in quality improvement and risk management activities. Central to quality improvement is the process of evaluation. All aspects of service delivery are evaluated to ensure that service delivery is of a consistently high standard. At the clinical level, you will be evaluating the outcomes of your care interventions and reporting these outcomes in the patient's record. Below are some key terms used in quality improvement that you should become familiar with.

BOX 9.1: QUALITY IMPROVEMENT TERMS

Benchmarking—continuous measurement of a process, product or service compared to those of competitors, industry leaders, or similar units in your facility.

Clinical indicator—a measure of clinical management or an outcome of care.

Evaluation—judging the value of something by collecting valid information about it in a systematic way and by making a comparison.

Outcome measures—actual results of care delivery.

Performance indicators—criteria that measure the extent to which outcomes of care meet standards or which evaluate the quality of processes leading to that outcome.

Quality indicators—specific, measurable elements of care delivery.

Research—diligent and systematic enquiry or investigation into an area of interest in order to discover facts, principles or new knowledge.

Adapted from Ellis & Hartley 2009; Zwerkeh & Claborn 2009; ACHS 2006.

Barriers to quality improvement

A significant barrier to quality improvement is cost. As you are aware, the cost of health services is increasing. It has probably increased even during the time you took to complete your undergraduate nursing program. The increases in costs are due to several factors, including:

- the introduction of new biomedical technologies
- increases in the salaries and wages of healthcare professionals
- increased demand for health services
- increased costs of education for the healthcare workforce
- costs associated with providing a safe, secure working environment for staff and patients
- increases in infrastructure costs for healthcare facilities—building renovations; information systems; maintaining a clean and hazard-free environment; reporting demands of key stakeholders and funders; human resource management functions
- increases in costs of resources used to deliver health and nursing care services
- external events such as the recent global financial crisis
- increases in private health insurance costs for individuals and families
- increased costs associated with the increase in chronic diseases and an ageing population.

You may be able to add to the list from your own knowledge and experience as you move through your first year and beyond as a registered nurse.

This list also provides a rationale for why quality improvement programs are important to healthcare organisations. An effective quality improvement program is evidence-based and focused on the outcomes of all organisational activities and processes. Analysis of outcomes indicates how well an organisation uses its resources. It shows areas of deficit and areas where there is need for improvement, as well as areas of excellence. The outcomes are used by funding bodies to make decisions about levels and types of services to be provided. This is explained in more detail in Chapter 6.

Another barrier to quality improvement is resistance to change. Some staff may be reluctant to change their practice even when research evidence indicates that the proposed changes will result in improved outcomes for patients and staff. Thus these staff create barriers to effective quality improvement.

WORKING IN GROUPS

In your study group, discuss the following situation. You are working in a surgical unit and over a period of one month there is a noticeable increase in surgical wound infections resulting in increased lengths of stay and subsequently increased costs to the unit. The Clinical Nurse Manager, the Infection Control Nurse and the Quality Improvement Manager meet to review the infection control data relating to these infections and make recommendations. This group identified that the surgical wound infections occurred in patients having the same surgical procedure who were then located in the same unit area. The only common factors were the surgical procedure and postoperative location of the patients. The wound cultures done revealed that the infecting agent was *Staphylococcus aureas*. The group of senior registered nurses implemented measures to reduce the infection rate. These measures included the introduction of the **hand hygiene** project, developed by the Australian Commission of Safety & Quality in Healthcare (ACSQHC) (2009).

- What might these measures be?
- What determined the group's decision to implement these measures?
- What influenced their decision-making?
- What would the implications be for nursing practice in the surgical unit?
- Were nursing staff informed of the changes to nursing practice?
- Was there an evaluation process to measure the effectiveness of the hand hygiene project?
- What were the indicators used to evaluate the change in practice?
- Was this a quality improvement initiative? Why or why not?
- Would you have done anything differently? Why or why not?
- Should other health professionals working in the surgical unit be informed of the changes to practices?
- Should the patients be informed?
- Are there ethical issues associated with not informing patients?

Accreditation

In Australia and in other countries, compliance with quality improvement and risk management standards is monitored and measured through an accreditation process. Accreditation is a formal process that ensures the delivery of high-quality care based on standards and processes developed by healthcare professionals (Australian Council on Healthcare Standards 2006). Accreditation is a public acknowledgment that a healthcare or aged care facility has achieved the requirements of national health and aged care standards.

In Australia, the Australian Council on Healthcare Standards (ACHS) is the principal agency that carries out accreditation of healthcare facilities. The Aged Care Standards Agency reviews aged care facilities. Aged care accreditation is tied to Federal Government funding of aged care facilities, and every now and again failure to meet standards may be reported in the media. Other agencies that accredit health and aged care organisations include the Quality Improvement Council and the International Organization for Standardization (ISO).

Accreditation as a process has five elements:

- a **governance** or stewardship function
- a standards-setting process
- a process of external evaluation that measures compliance against standards
- suggestions for remediation following a review
- promotion of **continuous quality improvement** (ACHS 2006).

All accreditation programs used in Australia are standards-based, use key performance indicators (KPIs) to measure performance and outcomes, and focus on risk and best-practice management. As registered nurses, you will be involved in preparing for accreditation, as it involves all categories and levels of health professionals. Your involvement could include collecting data and checking documentation. Accreditation is one reason you need to ensure accuracy in nursing documentation and compliance with organisational policy across all areas of practice.

Risk management in health services

Managing risk in the healthcare workplace is perhaps the most important aspect of all healthcare organisational practices. Risk management has clinical and non-clinical dimensions and registered nurses are essential to this process. International nursing research clearly shows that the presence of registered nurses makes a difference to patient safety and that there is an inverse relationship between registered nurses and **adverse events** (Fedoruk 2012). The most common kinds of error in healthcare facilities are:

- medication errors
- errors in patient identification
- patient falls
- decubitus ulcers
- hospital-acquired infections
- poor communication.

Errors may occur because nurses and others are dealing with:

- multiple complex issues simultaneously
- staff shortages
- patient demands
- inadequate communication between members of the multidisciplinary team and the patient
- misunderstandings and misinterpretation of information
- members of the team racing to complete tasks

- members of the team taking shortcuts
- poor record keeping
- reliance on human memory.

In Australia, the Australian Commission on Safety and Quality in Healthcare (ACSQHC) has been established to oversee the risk management processes in the healthcare system. Contributing factors to errors are human and systemic, and that is why so much time and resources are spent on developing strategies for minimising risk and harm to patients and staff. The ACSQHC has a centre for research excellence in patient safety available at <www.crepatientsafety. org.au> where you can access research information relating to patient safety.

One of the most problematic areas for nurses and patient safety is medication errors. State and territory departments of health have policies and guidelines relating to the safe administration of medications, and you should know these well. Check for the latest federal updates at <www.safetyandquality. gov.au>.

The ACSQHC publishes information on safe medication management. The information from the ACSQHC can inform and support your nursing practice. For instance, they provide a national inpatient medication chart, which is helpful in medication management—there is a chart developed for adult acute inpatient care and one for paediatric inpatient care. Both are available from<www.safetyandquality.gov.au/internet/safety/publishing.nsf/content/NIMC_001>.

Strategies to minimise the incidence of medication errors include:

- standardising terminology and abbreviations used when prescribing and communicating information about medicine
- avoiding distractions when administering medications
- always checking when in doubt.

Registered nurses also have a significant role in preventing falls, correctly identifying patients and preventing decubitus ulcers by ensuring that individual patient care plans identify nursing care strategies that minimise harm to patients.

Occupational Health, Safety and Welfare (OHS&W) issues are also important for you to be aware of, especially those relating to manual handling and moving patients. You should know how to report work-related incidents and other factors contributing to workplace injury.

An integral component of workplace safety is the security of staff and patients. Security refers not only to security of belongings but also to the physical security of staff and patients. In the majority of healthcare facilities there are security staff employed to protect staff and patients from harm.

You will be introduced to the organisation's safety and security policies during your initial orientation period. Safety and security for staff and patients are discussed in more detail in Chapter 11.

The Australian Institute of Health & Welfare manages data and information relating to adverse and **sentinel events** from hospitals and other healthcare organisations across Australia. Safety in healthcare organisations is also closely monitored by federal, state and territory governments. The Federal Government monitors this aspect of healthcare through its various agencies, and data are available through agency websites. You should access the Department of Health websites in your state or territory to check how this is managed in your state or territory.

The Australian Commission on Safety and Quality in Healthcare is the federal agency which reports on risk management practices and outcomes in all Australian hospitals and aged care facilities (ACSQHC 2010). The ACSQHC publishes reports, available online, about medication management, **clinical handover** and hospital-acquired infections and other matters that relate to nursing practice.

Reporting critical incidents and sentinel events

In all healthcare organisations there are mechanisms and processes for reporting critical incidents and sentinel events, and you have to be familiar with these. A critical incident involves some harm occurring to patients and/or staff. A sentinel event has resulted in very serious consequences for patients. For example:

- cardiac arrest from medication errors
- fractured femurs or other bones as a result of falls
- surgical removal of the wrong limb because of incorrect identification checks.

While these examples may seem extreme, they occur regularly because of staff working outside the policies and procedures that frame safe systems of work. Unfortunately, these types of incidents continue to occur in hospitals despite education programs and reviews of mandatory competencies.

Healthcare organisations are required to report critical incidents and sentinel events to their respective departments of health, which then report back to the Commonwealth Department of Health. As a priority, you need to know what the reporting mechanisms are in your organisation and the requirements of the department of health in your state or territory.

What should you do when you make a mistake?

Because you are working in a fast-paced environment, often with competing demands on your time and skills, you may at some time in your career make a mistake. All healthcare agencies have policies and procedures for reporting incidents and you should be aware of these. In Australia, there is the Advanced Incident Management System (AIMS) reporting system linked to departments of health, and the data collected is reported to government. The **AIMS reporting** system requires that health professionals report incidents, usually by telephone, to a department within the state health department. The call is logged, and details of the location, type and nature of the incident are recorded. The caller may remain anonymous. The details of the incident are then relayed back to the organisation, usually to the quality improvement coordinator or another designated employee, who then investigates the incident.

Mistakes made by nurses usually occur because:

- The nurse is overconfident and careless.
- The nurse does not listen to others.
- The nurse does not pay attention to detail.
- The nurse does not pay attention to cues in front of her.
- The nurse is distracted.

Managing your mistakes

Here are suggestions for how best to manage the situation when you have made a mistake:

- Own up to the mistake.
- Complete the required incident form(s).
- Reflect on what happened and the circumstances that resulted in the error occurring.
- Learn from the experience.
- Do not dwell on the incident—you cannot undo it.
- Remember that patients always come first.

FOR REFLECTION

Think back to your clinical experiences as an undergraduate student nurse. Think of a particular event that has remained with you because:

- it exemplified safe nursing practice
- it was an example of unsafe nursing practice.

In the first case, what made this event a good example of safe nursing practice? List at least ten factors.

In the second case, what made you think this was unsafe nursing practice? List at least ten factors.

For both instances, did the nurses involved offer any explanations for the way in which they carried out their nursing activities?

Mandatory reporting

Countries such as Australia, Canada and the United States have developed 'child abuse reporting laws' as a part of a centralised government strategy to protect children, in particular, from abuse and neglect (Matthews & Kenny 2008, p. 50). In Australia, as registered nurses you are mandated, therefore, to report any suspected cases of abuse or neglect to the relevant government authority in your state and territory. In some states and territories, registered nurses are also required to report suspected elder abuse (abuse of the older person). Abuse is defined as sexual abuse, physical abuse (violence to the individual) and neglect.

Mandatory reporting requirements for the registered nurse are complex and cover professional practice and professional conduct. It is worth considering how you would deal with situations that come under the banner of mandatory reporting. Areas covered by mandatory reporting include child abuse cases, elder abuse cases, and unprofessional conduct. Child abuse and elder abuse cases should be reported through organisational channels or directly to health departments or police in your state or territory. Unprofessional conduct should be reported to AHPRA. It is your responsibility to find out the organisational policies and processes for reporting cases to the appropriate authorities in your state or territory.

Child abuse and neglect

As a registered nurse you are required by law to report any instances of child abuse and neglect or suspected child abuse and neglect. All states and territories except Western Australia have mandatory reporting laws which impose on selected professions such as nursing 'a statutory duty to report a reasonable suspicion' that a child has been abused or neglected—a suspicion that arises during the course of your professional work (Matthews, Walsh & Fraser 2006, p. 505). A child is considered to have been abused or neglected if he or she has 'suffered physical, psychological, emotional, sexual abuse or neglect' (Matthews, Walsh & Fraser 2006, p. 505). Failure to report such cases will result in penalties. These differ in the various states and territories. The legislation offers notifiers the protection of confidentiality.

Elder abuse

To address the issues of elder abuse, the Australian Government has enacted amendments to the *Aged Care Act 1997* (Cwlth) which apply to aged care providers receiving subsidies from the Commonwealth Government (Forrester 2008). These amendments are directed at protecting the older person through mandatory reporting of sexual and serious assault in the aged care sector (Forrester 2008, p. 216). Older persons living by themselves may also be subject to forms of abuse such as social isolation and physical assault. It may be more difficult to detect abuse of those living alone than for those who receive professional care services from community health agencies. If you happen to be in a TPPP with a community-based agency you may come across cases of elder abuse that you will have to report through organisational channels.

Professional misconduct

Professional misconduct includes:

* conduct that is substantially below the standard reasonably expected of a registered health practitioner of an equivalent level of training or experience
* more than one instance of unprofessional conduct
* conduct that is not consistent with being a fit and proper person to hold registration in the profession.

Notifiable conduct

Practitioners, employers and education providers are all mandated by law to report certain notifiable conduct by a practitioner or student. Registered practitioners who fail to report notifiable conduct may face disciplinary action by their National Board.

Such conduct includes:

* intoxication by alcohol or drugs while practising or training in the profession
* engagement in sexual misconduct in connection with the practice or training of the profession
* an impairment that places the public at risk of substantial harm
* a significant departure from accepted professional standards that places the public at risk of harm (AHPRA 2010).

SUMMARY

This chapter has looked at the work of the registered nurse. The role of the registered nurse is complex, requires intellectual capacity and encompasses far more than the physical aspects of nursing care.

The responsibilities for assuring safety in the healthcare workplace are organisational (policies, procedures, protocols, safe systems of work) and operational (nursing practices, supervision, reporting). The major causes of harm to patients are all nursing-related—errors related to medication administration, infection control management, falls management, pressure ulcer management and the administration of blood and blood products. Safety and quality improvement are inextricably linked and nurses play a major role in ensuring safety and quality in the workplace. As a registered nurse you will be collecting data on aspects of clinical practice as well as interpreting information that will support your practice.

Reporting errors in these areas of practice is done through well-established reporting processes within the organisation. You have been given a number of websites related to patient safety which you may find useful.

This chapter also introduced you to your legal responsibilities in regards to mandatory reporting. It is important to understand your legal responsibilities and obligations as you engage in professional nursing practice.

DISCUSSION QUESTIONS

1   What is the role and function of the registered nurse?
2   What are the key responsibilities of the registered nurse?
3   How can you use the information in this chapter to begin developing your role as a registered nurse?

REFERENCES

Australian Commission on Safety and Quality in Healthcare (2009) *National hand hygiene program aims to halve hospital superbug infections*, media release 5 May, <www.safetyandquality.gov.au/internet/safety/publishing.nsf/Content/E523D A01FF0E5A51CA2575AC007E5A69/$File/NatHHInitLaunch-2009-05-05. pdf>, accessed 6 October 2011.

Australian Commission on Safety and Quality in Healthcare (2010) *Medication safety*, Issue 4, August, <www.safetyandquality.gov.au/internet/safety/publishing.nsf/ Content/com-pubs_NIMC-34210-MedSafetyUpdateAug2010>, accessed 26 September 2011.

Australian Council on Healthcare Standards (2006) *EQuIP standards*, 4th edn, <www.achs.org.au/EQUIP4/>, accessed 13 September 2011.

Australian Health Practitioner Regulation Agency (2010) <www.ahpra.gov.au/Complaints-and-Outcomes/Conduct-Health-and-Performance/Conduct.aspx>, accessed 31 October 2011.

Australian Nursing and Midwifery Council (2007) *Midwifery practice decisions summary guide*, <www.anmc.org.au/userfiles/file/DMF%20A4%20Midwifery%20Summary%20Guide%20Final%20%202010.pdf>, accessed 13 September 2011.

Australian Nursing and Midwifery Council (2008) *Delegation and supervision for nurses and midwives*, <www.anmc.org.au/userfiles/file/guidelines_and_position_statements/Delegation%20and%20Supervision%20for%20Nurses%20and%20Midwives.pdf>, accessed 9 September 2011.

Benner, P (2001) *From novice to expert: Excellence and power in clinical nursing practice*, Prentice-Hall, Upper Saddle River, NJ.

Blaxter, M (2010) *Health*, 2nd edn, Polity Press, UK.

Commonwealth of Australia (2008) *Australian Charter of Healthcare Rights*, Australian Government, Canberra, <www.safetyandquality.gov.au/internet/safety/publishing.nsf/Content/PriorityProgram-01>, accessed 9 September 2011.

Cullum, N, Ciliska, D, Marks, S & Haynes, B (2008) 'An introduction to evidence based nursing' in N Cullum, D Ciliska, RB Haynes & S Marks (eds) *Evidence-based nursing: An introduction*, Blackwell Publishing; BMJ Publishing Group, RCN Publishing Company, and American College of Physicians ('ACP') Journal Club, UK.

Ellis, JR & Hartley, CL (2009) *Nursing in today's world*, 9th edn, Wolters Kluwer/Lippincott Williams & Wilkins, Philadelphia.

Fedoruk, M (2012) 'Safety' in *B Kozier & G Erb Fundamentals of Nursing*, 2nd edn, Pearson, Australia, pp. 744–79.

Forrester, K (2008) 'Nursing in the aged care sector: Resident abuse and the reporting obligations,' *Journal of Law and Medicine*, vol. 16, pp. 216–19.

Henderson, V (1966) *The nature of nursing: A definition and its implications for practice, research and education*, Macmillan, New York.

Matthews, B, Walsh, K & Fraser, JA (2006) *Mandatory reporting of child abuse and neglect*, 13 JLM Lawbook Co. pp. 505–17.

Matthews, B, Kenny, MC (2008) Mandatory legislation in the United States, Canada and Australia: A cross-jurisdictional review of key features, differences and issues, *Child Maltreatment*, vol. 13, no. 1, pp. 50–63.

Nightingale, F (1860) *Notes on nursing: What it is and what it is not*, D. Appleton & Company, New York.

Needleman, J & Hassmiller, S (2009) 'The role of nurses in improving hopsital quality and effciency: Real world results, *Health Affairs*, vol. 28, no. 4, pp. w6250–w633, <http://content.healthaffairs.org/content/28/4/w625.full.html>, accessed 12 June 2009.

Pretz, JE & Folse, VN (2011) 'Nursing experience and preference for intuition in decision making', *Journal of Clinical Nursing*, vol. 20, pp. 2878–89.

Siviter, B (2008) *The newly qualified nurse's handbook*, Baillere Tindall Elsevier, Edinburgh.

Walker, S (2009) 'Nursing themes and conceptual frameworks' in B Kozier & G Erb (eds) *Fundamentals of Nursing*, vol.1, Pearson, Sydney, pp. 23–40.

Zerwekh, J & Claborn JC (2009) *Nursing today. Transitions and trends*, 6th edn, Saunders Elsevier, St Louis, MI.

USEFUL WEBSITES

Aged Care Standards and Accreditation Agency, Ltd: **www.accreditation.org.au**

ANMC *Delegation and supervision for nurses and midwives*: **www.anmc.org.au/userfiles/file/guidelines_and_position_statements/Delegation%20and%20Supervision%20for%20Nurses%20and%20Midwives.pdf**

Australian Commission on Safety and Quality in Healthcare's Centre For Research Excellence In Patient Safety: **www.crepatientsafety.org.au**

Australian Council on Healthcare Standards: **www.achs.org.au**

International Organization for Standardization: **www.iso.org**

Quality Improvement Council: **www.qic.org.au**

Part 3

The working environments of registered nurses

Core competencies

As a registered nurse or midwife, you will:

- practise within an ethical and professional framework
- identify and respond appropriately to observed unsafe practices
- deliver safe, effective and comprehensive nursing to a patient or groups of patients
- use research-based evidence to inform your clinical practice
- evaluate the outcomes of health and nursing care, and make changes to care when indicated
- be able to respond quickly and effectively to episodes of clinical deterioration
- develop, maintain and conclude therapeutic relationships with patients and/or their families, significant others or carers
- engage in professional development programs to maintain competence and meet registration requirements.

Chapter 10

Quality improvement and contemporary nursing practice

Marion Eckhart

Learning objectives

After reading this chapter, you will be able to:
- describe the role of the nurse in quality management
- describe key performance indicators within the clinical setting
- describe the role of the nurse in maintaining a safe practice environment
- discuss the multicultural dimensions of nursing care
- describe the challenges of multicultural nursing care
- describe how research can inform and support nursing practice.

Key terms

Continuous quality improvement
Critical incidents
Evidence-based practice
Key performance indicators (KPIs)
Quality management
Risk analysis
Risk assessment

Quality management

It is important to understand the role of the nurse in relation to patient safety within the context of the entire healthcare system, and particularly important to appreciate the systemic factors that have an impact on quality management and critical incident reform. Patient safety is the reduction or elimination of adverse events that are caused by healthcare professionals' errors (O'Byrne 2008). Historically, detecting and preventing errors has been the responsibility of the individual clinician, often the registered nurse (Wakefield et al. 2001). However, in the 1990s, investigators and administrators recognised that the system surrounding the individual played an important role in the occurence of errors (Throckmorton & Etchegaray 2007). Current thinking about patient safety no longer supports blaming the individual practitioner, but rather emphasises the need to review the entire healthcare system to better appreciate the factors that result in harm (Canadian Patient Safety Institute 2011). Errors are seen not as the result of only one person's actions, but rather as a chain of small errors leading to a mistake that affects the patient. Examining these work chains and focusing on the systems and environments surrounding them is increasingly the means used to develop better preventative strategies and improve quality management. However, to learn how errors occur, the errors and near misses must be reported. Nurses play a significant role in creating an environment focused on reporting and examining the systems and changes needed to prevent errors and improve quality care delivery. Nurses provide 24/7 surveillence for risk assessment and quality improvement strategies. However, if reporting is not encouraged through positive leadership from more senior clinicians, then improvement in safety and quality healthcare provision will not occur (Ferguson et al. 2007).

Point to ponder

Nurses play a pivotal role in quality care and safe practice.

Healthcare costs have been a driving force in the focus on patient safety by government (National Steering Committee on Patient Safety 2006), healthcare management and health professionals (Baker et al. 2004). The concept of patient safety is now embedded and operationalised within the risk management frameworks of healthcare organisations.

The political, personal and industrial drivers for patient safety have been reviewed, and patient safety is now considered a component of risk management for many healthcare agendas. For nurses, this involves formalising the previously informal risk analysis of patient care within the context of delivery. Risk assessment and management is now an integral component of a registered nurse's or midwife's role when delivering care to patients. Managing risk in the healthcare workplace is achieved through surveillance, discipline and regulation of populations. Surveillance is achieved through constant monitoring (assessment) of the environment, patients and other professional staff and visitors. Discipline refers to working within professional standards, and regulation refers to the policies, protocols and guidelines which underpin professional practice (Rogers 2008).

While the overarching organisational goals are patient safety and quality management, it is the role of the clinical nursing leader that is under the spotlight when errors or near misses occur. Pressures of workload, inadequate staffing and resources, multiple tasks and responsibilities, poor teamwork and communications systems and a lack of focus at the clinical level on safety and quality of care delivery are often cited as factors that threaten patient safety (Laschinger & Leiter 2006). The individual contribution to risk assessment and quality improvement is the responsibility of all nurses, governed through the legislative act and a national competency framework. Not understanding quality management and risk assessment can result in adverse professional outcomes, as all nurses are accountable for their actions.

Quality management can be considered to reflect evaluative processes of service(s) provided and the results achieved compared to accepted standards. Traditionally, measurements have been linked to considerations such as pressure-area care outcomes, falls rates and adverse events such as infection rates and mortality. All of these outcome measurements form part of the national framework of data collected and reported through the National Health Roundtable reviews. There is little evidence to suggest that the established safety and quality model implemented has made the healthcare system any safer in Australia than it was in the 1990s (Rubin & Leeder 2005; Van Der Weyden 2005; Wilson & Van Der Weyden 2005). A focus on systems improvement using broad tools such as clinical audits and feedback, accreditation of organisations, professional development and credentialling is no longer considered adequate or sufficient in terms of improving the safety and quality of care. Much broader approaches, involving both top-down and bottom-up methods of changing practice, are vital. These broad approaches include but are not limited to total quality management, risk management and error prevention, evidence-based practice, organisational and leadership development and consumer involvement in the redesign of healthcare delivery (Ferguson et al. 2007).

Ferguson and others (2007) descibe how a cohort of clinical leaders who were undertaking a leadership development program used a relatively simple, patient-focused intervention called the 'observation of care' to help focus the clinical team's attention on areas for improvement within the clinical setting. Observation of care is a simple tool that is based on the premise that 'seeing' and 'observing' are not the same, and that observing care as it is delivered and then learning from what has been observed is the basis for quality improvement (Royal College of Nursing 2004). Taking time out from a hectic program of work to systematically observe the practice environment can help clinicians see what is often taken for granted, to see the difference between what is believed to be happening and what is really happening (Ferguson et al. 2007).

The primary quality and safety themes resulting from the observations that were undertaken by the clinical leaders in the study by Ferguson and others were related to the environment, occupational health and safety, communication and team function, clinical practice and patient care. The observation of care intervention is a relatively simple tool that could be adopted within most clinical settings as a means of engaging clinicians in structure observation, critical questioning, discussion and action planning for service improvement. It encourages the clinicians to focus on patient care and the environment in which that care is delivered, and it puts the responsibility for practice review and change back on the staff that provides the patient with care.

For the newly graduated nurse, this model of 'observation of care' encompasses critical questioning and enquiry, which is a component of the undergraduate curriculum. Therefore, this strategy should not be foreign to you. However, your ability to put the necessary skills into practice is now a significant factor in your ability to measure, assess, quantify risk and enact quality improvement for each of your individual patients. It is particularly helpful for new graduates to be able to review practice in order to focus on patient care and the environment. To enable this, key performance indicators are often themed and linked to particular cohorts of patients. On a local level, the establishment of quality care measures are often discussed and agreed through team discussion with the clinical leader and, when required, involving the multidisciplinary healthcare team. This understanding can allow new graduates to plan their care delivery in a structured, meaningful way and target successful outcomes; it also provides more defined measurement parameters with which to gauge clinical practice improvement.

Understanding the link between key performance indicators and clinical practice improvement is important for graduates and all healthcare providers. KPIs help ensure that your practice is contemporary and consistent with evidence-based standards and clinical practice improvement measures. Key performance indicators are measurable units of care and can be clinical or non-clinical. Clinical KPIs relate to the clinical aspects of nursing care delivery, such as responses to interventions, while non-clinical indicators reflect patient activity data, such as admission and discharge rates. KPIs indicate compliance with policies, protocols and guidelines related to clinical practice and are used to monitor and evaluate clinical practice.

Key performance indicators

On a large scale, key performance indicators are generated through broad consultation and developed into a conceptual framework through agreed measures, and then this data can be benchmarked across sites, services and broader stakeholders. There are significant risks associated with this process, as not all sites have established and agreed tools to acquit the data through a standardised process. Therefore, although the data is being collated, the recording abilities may not always be consistent. There are strategic agendas established at many levels and these can be based on significant local, state-wide initiatives and the National Health Performance Framework.

The Australian Council on Healthcare Standards continues to develop key performance indicators that inform accreditation standards, and these are available in healthcare organisations. More recently the Australian Commission on Safety and Quality in Healthcare developed the National Safety and Quality Health Service Standards, which will be used in healthcare organisations' accreditation processes.

Evidence-based practice drives many of these policy frameworks. The established indicators act as monitoring, evaluation and information tools. They can be used to inform decision-making, quality improvement initiatives and interventions. These guiding efforts form continuous quality improvement.

For registered nurses and midwives, KPIs are part of the everyday standards of practice. There are a myriad of potential indicators available in healthcare. For example, operational KPIs may be average lengths of stay, waiting times in emergency departments, and infection rates. Human resource KPIs may be retention rates, staff satisfaction rates and consumer complaints. KPIs should be used to identify or flag any issues or areas where a positive change can be made using quality improvement processes.

KPIs can be useful in benchmarking and comparative analysis with other organisations. Knowing targeted KPIs within the working environment is essential to ensure that all nursing and midwifery staff have a clear understanding of the common goal(s) as they relate to the organisation, strategic resource allocation or human resources.

At an individual professional level, KPIs can be part of the performance review and organisational development (PR&OD) process, in regards to the individual's progress on goals, related to the context in which the work is provided, competency status, and overall performance rating. Agreed, achievable goals can be established at the individual level that impact on the nurse/midwife, the clinical unit, the department or the organisation as a whole. These established metrics linked to an individual's PR&OD measure the individual's ability to act according to one's knowledge and clinical judgment—the development in **autonomy** and the ability to be able to articulate care delivered and practice linked to these outcomes builds professional accountability and the individual nurses' participation in the agreed goals and KPIs. Research has indicated that patient outcomes can be improved when nurses actively participate in decision-making, strengthening the impact nurses have on clinical practice. This active participation in clinical management and relevance to the individual nurse's accountability aids risk minimalisation, suggesting an important link between ability or skill and patient outcomes (Manojlovich 2007).

Maintaining safe practice

New graduates begin with a somewhat prescriptive and linear approach to both their thinking and their practice, which then changes over time as they become more experienced (Duchscher 2009). As new graduates advance through the stages of transition, their learning and professional development needs change. During the second stage of transition, the graduate nurse has advanced through what Benner (2001) refers to as the 'novice' level of competence and into the stage of 'advanced beginner'. In general, newly graduated nurses understand the routines of their unit; their familiarity with roles and responsibilities have been established by the experiences gained during the initial months of their transition and these serve as a foundation from which they can draw to both predict and respond to presenting situations (Duchscher 2009). The pressure they are under is the constant requirement to maintain safe practice and ensure the patient is receiving the best care the graduate can deliver while understanding the routines and the culture of the unit in which he or she works. This pressure can influence the satisfaction of the graduate and many suffer from what has been termed 'reality shock' (Kramer 1974). Reality shock occurs with the transition from the educational to the service setting, where there are different priorities and pressures. The graduate nurse must learn to balance the need of the individual patient with the needs of the setting (the system). However, ensuring a clinically safe environment and optimal care delivery for the patient competes with priorities such as time pressures and patient turnover, which in most clinical settings poses additional risk and pressure for the graduate to grapple with.

Patient safety and quality of care do not sit in isolation with one person, though the care delivered can be directly influenced by one person. Patient safety should be an overarching organisational goal, with active involvement and support from the highest levels of governance.

Point to ponder

As a registered nurse, you have a responsibility to know how adverse events and critical incidents are managed in the workplace

Reporting of adverse events and near misses are more often undertaken by the nurses who work the closest with the patients (Throckmorton & Etchegaray 2007). Medication errors are one of the most common types of adverse events reported in hospital systems. It is estimated that around 2–3 per cent of admissions to hospital have an adverse medical event; in some populations it is estimated to be as high as 30 per cent. This makes medical errors the eighth leading cause of death in Australia. Approximately 7000 people per year are estimated to die from medication errors alone (Agency for Healthcare Research and Quality 2000) and the National Health and Medical Research Centre—Centre of Research Excellence in Patient Safety (2009). It has been identified that investment is needed in assessing gaps in care; improving product safety; and developing medication management systems and education and competency assessment, in an effort to reduce medication errors and improve patient safety at the system level. New graduates administer medications as a large part of their role. The following case study outlines a problem-based learning example, outlining strategies to improve efficiencies without compromising safe practice.

Case study: Graduate nurse on medical ward

This case study relates to a graduate nurse working in a general medical ward for four weeks as his first placement.

The Clinical Nurse Support (CNS) receives a complaint from ward staff that the graduate nurse is too slow with the medication round. It is taking him up to an hour to complete a round for four to six patients. The CNS attends and reviews the situation with the graduate nurse — the graduate feels that he is just being 'safe' and checking all drugs carefully.

The CNS decides to 'buddy' with the graduate and directly observe his practice. This leads to the discovery that the graduate nurse is indeed checking all medications carefully, but that he is even looking up medications that he is quite familiar with each time he administers them, and that he is often being distracted by patient enquiries and requests during his drug round.

The issues identified for the graduate nurse are:

- knowledge deficit regarding some of the medications used
- clinical confidence deficit in continuing to look up medications even when he was familiar with the drug, actions, precautions, etc.
- clinical competence deficit in prioritising care needs and remaining focused on medication round.

Marion Eckhart

As a result, the graduate nurse commences a performance development plan in the area of medication administration. As part of this, he is encouraged to compile a list of commonly used medications on the ward—their uses, actions, adverse reactions, usual doses, side effects, and so on—in a notebook for his own use. Repetition, writing and reading back, helps to consolidates knowledge.

A four-week timeline is set for improved practice, and feedback is sought from permanent staff weekly. The CNS visits the registered nurse weekly to accompany him as a 'buddy' on the medication round and reinforce procedures and prioritisation. The graduate uses 'Medication administration and knowledge' as one of his three personal learning goals for his placement.

The following outcomes are noted:

- The graduate nurse's performance improvement is noted by clinical staff (within one week).
- His medication rounds improve to 20 minutes within four weeks.
- The graduate nurse is able to verbally explain to the CNS the uses, actions, adverse reactions, usual doses and side effects of ten commonly used medications on the medical ward.
- The CNS audit at the four-week mark notes that the graduate nurse's practice had improved markedly: he remained focused, checked medications when unfamiliar, but was able to safely administer medications more efficiently and with minimal interruption.
- The graduate nurse's practice continues to improve throughout placement.

This case study demonstrates that even if a nurse initially struggles with a particular aspect of the role, safe practice can still be achieved through review of efficient processes adopted by the graduate. Reflecting on strategies to improve clinical practice throughout the first year as a registered nurse is key to improving delivery of care and timing without compromising safe practice.

Point to ponder

Healthcare performance is usually measured in six areas: safety, effectiveness, 'patient centredness', timeliness, efficiency, and equity.

Although healthcare performance is usually measured in the six areas of safety, effectiveness, 'patient centredness', timeliness, efficiency, and equity, there is a significant focus now on patient-centred care, in hospitals and healthcare centres. Berwick (2009), argues that this is a dimension of healthcare quality in its own right, and not just because of its connection with other desired aims, such as safety and effectiveness. There is growing evidence that **patient-centred care** has a positive effect on health status outcomes. The correlation between patient safety and care delivered results from the individual approach taken to the needs of each patient. However, to adopt this approach universally there would need to be some radical shifts in healthcare design. The health systems would need to be redesigned to include patient centredness as a quality dimension in its own right. It would require effective clinical leadership to monitor and adopt this model of care and it would need to be part of the undergraduate curriculum, so that new graduate nurses understood the need for change. This would ensure that new graduates understood their accountability for the care provided, in relation to patient safety and the focus on patient care and the environment in which that care is delivered. In the undergraduate nursing curriculum, priority needs to be given to ensuring that graduate nurses can define and articulate the concepts of outcomes and risks as these relate to each patient in their direct clinical care. Importantly, the graduate nurse needs to be clear about the consequences of risk decisions and quality of care provided (French 2005).

Point to ponder

Decision-making is an important nursing competency. Reflect on your own decision-making competencies.

The complexities of the clinical environment and the adaptiveness that new graduates require extend across many facets of healthcare delivery, as part of patient-focused care, quality and safety, risk stratification and the area of multicultural nursing. The context in which the new graduate practises requires astute perception skills and willingness to understand diversity in a rapidly changing environment.

Multicultural dimension of nursing care

The culture of a healthcare organisation can powerfully influence its ability to manage human resources and care for the multifaceted cultural needs of patients.

There are many and varied definitions of culture. Hunt and Colander (1984) point out that culture includes the totality of a group's behaviours, values and behaviours shared by a group, taught across generations, relatively stable but capable of change across time. Culture is more than a 'way of life'. Culture tells us what is good, bad, right and wrong. Culture influences our preferred way of thinking, behaving and decision-making (Eckermann et al. 2010).

Marion Eckhart

Recruiting and retaining a culturally diverse workforce can be a successful strategy for providing culturally competent care and maintaining patient safety. Working towards mirroring the population served, by providing a health workforce reflective of the community, can be an effective strategy for meeting the needs of the increasingly diverse population (Nease 2009). A diverse workforce enables the healthcare providers to reflect and respond to community diversity. There is evidence that patients from minority cultural groups and language backgrounds are disproportionately at risk of experiencing preventable adverse events while in hospital compared to the mainstream patient groups (Johnstone & Kanitsaki 2006). Although there have been significant improvement strategies in the area of patient safety and understanding, and in the multifaceted processes contributing to preventable adverse events, it could be argued that an area of patient safety that is yet to be addressed formally and systematically is that of culture and language and its links to patient safety outcomes in patient groups of diverse minority cultural and language backgrounds. Even less well recognised is the impact that a culturally diverse workforce could have on the incidence and reporting of preventable adverse events (Smedley, Stith & Nelson 2003). Reducing the vulnerability of patients from minority cultural and language groups is critical, but there is a significant gap in the nursing literature that highlights the correlation between these cultural issues and patient safety. There is a relationship between culture, language and patient safety and the particular risks that patients from minority racial, ethno-cultural and language backgrounds encounter when being cared for by healthcare professionals who are culturally unaware (Johnstone & Kanitsaki 2006).

There are a significant number of cases of a lack of understanding of an individual's culture and language that have resulted in formal legal proceedings. For many, this could have been avoided if appropriate cultural competence processes had been applied. An example of cultural miscommunication resulting in legal action was that of a 28-year-old Muslim woman who was awarded damages after her obstetrician and gynaecologist negligently sterilised her without her consent. In 1998, the woman had consulted with her doctor regarding a gynaecological infection that required a draining procedure. The woman did not speak, write or read English. The doctor subsequently performed a permanent sterilisation procedure (tubal ligation) on the woman, which she had thought was a procedure to remedy her infection. In reaching a decision, the court made explicit comment on the duty of a doctor to be 'sensitive to cultural issues' (Johnstone & Kanitsaki 2006). Health professionals cannot make assumptions and impose their own values—namely that this woman, who already had four children, would not want more.

Care needs to be taken in the multicultural environment of health that individuals' values and norms are not imposed on those who do not subscribe to them. The balance between culture, language and patient safety outcomes cannot be understated. Providing formal interpreting services allows for the patient to express their views, and for the health practitioner to ask questions and gather understanding through the translation of not just the words spoken but also the shared meaning behind them. This highlights that a diverse workforce can articulate cultural knowledge and skills in an intercultural transaction to assist communication (Clyne 1994).

The International Council of Nurses (ICN 2001) believes that establishing a multicultural healthcare workforce supports culture-sensitive healthcare. Nurses are a mobile workforce, and one consequence of the global nursing shortage is that there is increased diversity of nurses across the globe. These changes are reflective of community cultural changes and therefore the support of many culturally diverse healthcare practitioners can provide benefits to the healthcare environment.

The importance of identifying the vulnerabilities of patients from minority cultural and language backgrounds cannot be underestimated, and all healthcare providers need to actively address the potential barriers by developing systems and processes to reduce errors, and make it harder for people to do the wrong thing and easier for people to do the right thing. This work needs to be developed through an evidence-based approach to ensure accuracy and robust research aimed at exploring the links between culture, language and patient safety outcomes.

Research informing and supporting nursing practice

The past twenty years have seen a rapid expansion in health information. Increasingly, the challenge nurses, midwives and all healthcare professionals face is how to keep abreast of the research related to clinical practice. However, evidence-based practice is more than practising with an awareness of research evidence. An accepted definition of evidence-based medicine is that it 'conscientious, explicit and judicious use of current best evidence in making decisions about individual patients' (Sackett et al. 1996). The concept of incorporating research evidence into decisions could be considered a simple approach to clinical practice improvement, resulting in increased knowledge by the clinician and more effective practice. However, in light of the above definition, we need to ask:

- what is 'current' and what is 'best'?
- how do nurses find this evidence?
- what sort of judgments need to be applied in using it 'judiciously'?

Marion Eckhart

This is the key to starting to consider changing practice and aiming for improved knowledge and clinical practice improvement.

Even nurses who keep up to date, regularly read professional journals and current textbooks, in addition to attending conferences and postgraduate presentations, will still see only a fraction of the available literature. To put this into perspective, the volume of available literature can be quantified. For example, the database MEDLINE has 'indexed over 12 million citations in more than 4800 journals since 1966' (Cullum 2008, p. 101). Because it is impossible to review this volume of research, you will have been taught how to critcally appraise literature in your undergraduate program. This ability to critically appraise the literature will enable you to use and apply relevant research findings to your practice (Cullum 2008).

Evidence can be characterised into a hierarchy and researchers in Australia refer to the National Health and Medical Research Council (NHMRC) evidence hierarchy as shown in Table 10.1 (NHMRC 2009).

All nurses need to have grounding in the ability to review research for quality in order to articulate if it can be used to change or improve clinical practice. Sometimes a new treatment is so obviously effective that there is no difficulty in making that decision, and no need to undertake a rigorous review of the literature. However, understanding how to critically appraise literature when required is a key professional skill that all graduates should develop and undertake throughout their professional nursing career. Nursing graduates should consider if the treatment currently offered is effective. A step-by-step approach would then reflect details about the disease and the patient. When reviewing the evidence in answering the question, the nurse would then need to identify and review (appraise) the evidence and then consider how this would translate into current practice.

Point to ponder

All nurses need to develop the ability and competency to read and interpret research findings in order to inform their practice.

Once the evidence in favour of modifying or changing practice has been reviewed and reflected in their current working context, influencing and articulating the need for change is the challenge for the graduate. Bringing about effective change in healthcare practice is not straightforward. However, nurses need to build these change management skills in tandem with critical appraisal skills, as knowledge alone will not influence effective clinical outcomes.

Table 10.1: NHMRC evidence hierarchy: designations of 'levels of evidence' according to type of research question

Level	Intervention	Diagnostic accuracy	Prognosis	Aetiology	Screening Intervention
I	A systematic review of level II studies	A systematic review of level II studies	A systematic review of level II studies	A systematic review of level II studies	A systematic review of level II studies
II	A randomised controlled trial	A study of test accuracy with: an independent, blinded comparison with a valid reference standard, among consecutive persons with a defined clinical presentation	A prospective cohort study	A prospective cohort study	A randomised controlled trial
III-1	A pseudorandomised controlled trial (i.e. alternate allocation or some other method)	A study of test accuracy with: an independent, blinded comparison with a valid reference standard, among non-consecutive persons with a defined clinical presentation	All or none	All or none	A pseudorandomised controlled trial (i.e. alternate allocation or some other method)
III-2	A comparative study with concurrent controls: • Non-randomised, experimental trial • Cohort study • Case-control study • Interrupted time series with a control group	A comparison with reference standard that does not meet the criteria required for? Level II and III-1 evidence	Analysis of prognostic factors amongst persons in a single arm of a randomised controlled trial	A retrospective cohort study	A comparative study with concurrent controls: • Non-randomised, experimental trial • Cohort study • Case-control study
III-3	A comparative study without concurrent controls: • Historical control study • Two or more single arm study • Interrupted time series without a parallel control group	Diagnostic case-control study	A retrospective cohort study	A case-control study	A comparative study without concurrent controls: • Historical control study • Two or more single arm study
IV	Case series with either post-test or pre-test/post-test outcomes	Study of diagnostic yield (no reference standard)	Case series, or cohort study of persons at different stages of disease	A cross-sectional study or case series	Case series

NHMRC levels of evidence and grades for recommendations
December 2009

Marion Eckhart

SUMMARY

This chapter discussed the role of the registered nurse in quality improvement within healthcare organisations. The case study in the chapter takes you through an event in the day of a graduate nurse. It takes you through the steps in the process, which is one of teaching and supporting the graduate nurse through this particular event. The chapter links quality improvement and safety in the workplace and the role of the registered nurse.

Take home messages from this chapter should include the central role registered nurses have in managing safety in the healthcare workplace and in quality improvement.

The chapter discusses using research outcomes to support clinical practice. You are introduced to the concept of evidence-based research and there is a brief introduction to the NH&MRC evidence hierarchy used by researchers in Australia.

DISCUSSION QUESTIONS

1   What is the role of the registered nurse or midwife in managing safety in the workplace?
2   What is the role of the registered nurse or midwife in quality improvement?
3   What are the links between risk management and quality improvement?
4   How does the application of research outcomes to clinical practice improve patient outcomes?

REFERENCES

Baker, GR, Norton, PG, Flintoft, V, Blais, R, Brown, A, Cox, J, Etchells, E, Ghali, W, Hebert, P, Majudar, S, O'Beirne, M, Palacios-Derflingher, L, Reid, R, Sheps, S & Tamblyn, R (2004) 'The Canadian adverse events study: The incidence of adverse events among hospital patients in Canada', *Canadian Medical Association Journal*, vol. 170, pp. 1678–86.

Benner, P (2001) *From novice to expert: Excellence and power in clinical nursing practice*, Prentice-Hall, Upper Saddle River, NJ.

Berwick, D (2009) 'What "patient-centred" should mean: Confessions from an extremist', *Health Affairs*, vol. 28, no. 11. pp. w555–65.

Canadian Patient Safety Institute (2011), *About patient safety*, <www.patient-safetyinstitute.ca>, accessed 9 October 2011.

Clyne, M (1994) *Inter-cultural communication at work; Cultural values in discourse*, Cambridge University Press, Cambridge.

Cullum, N (2008) 'Users' guide to the nursing literature: An introduction' in N Cullum, D Ciliska, RB Haynes & S Marks (eds) *Evidence-based nursing*, Blackwell Publishing, BMJ Journals, RCN Publishing Company, UK, p. 101–3.

Duchscher, JEB (2009) 'Transition shock: The initial stage of role adaptiation for newly graduated registered nurses', *Journal of Advanced Nursing*, vol. 65, no. 5, pp. 1103–13.

Eckermann, AK, Dowd, T, Chong, E, Nixon, L, Gray, R & Johnson, S (2010) *Binan Goonj: Bridging cultures in Aboriginal health*, Elsevier, Australia

Ferguson, L, Calvert, J, Davie, M, Fred, N, Gerbach, V & Sinclair, L (2007) 'Clinical leadership: Using observations of care to focus risk management and quality improvement activitities in the clinical setting', *Contemporary Nurse*, vol. 24, no. 2, pp. 212–24.

French, B (2005) 'Evidence-based practice and the management of risk in nursing', *Health, Risk & Society*, vol. 7, no. 2, pp. 177–92.

Hunt, EF & Colander, DC (1984) *Social science: An introduction to the study of society*, Macmillan, New York

Kramer, M. (1974) *Reality shock: Why nurses leave nursing*, CV Mosby Company, St Louis.

International Council of Nurses (2001) *Position statement: Ethical nurse recruitment*, International Council of Nurses, Geneva.

Johnstone, M-J & Kanitsaki, O (2006) 'Culture, language, and patient safety: Making the link', *International Journal for Quality in Healthcare*, vol. 18, no. 5, pp. 383–8.

Laschinger, HKS & Leiter, MP (2006) 'The impact of nursing work environments on patient safety outcomes', *The Journal of Nursing Administration*, vol. 36, no. 5, pp. 259–67.

Manojlovich, M (2007) 'Power and empowerment in nursing: Looking backward to inform the future,' *Online Journal Issues Nursing*, vol. 27, no. 1.

National Health and Medical Research Council (2009) *NHMRC levels of evidence and grades for recommendations for developers of guidelines*, Australian Government, National Health and Medical Research Council, <www.nhmrc. gov.au/_files_nhmrc/file/guidelines/evidence_statement_form.pdf>, accessed 11 October 2011.

National Steering Committee on Patient Safety (2006), *Building a safer system: A national integrated strategy for improving patient safety in Canadian healthcare*, <www.patientsafetyinstitute.ca>, accessed 11 October 2011.

Nease, B. (2009) 'Creating a successful transcultural on-boarding program', *Journal for Nurses in Staff Development*, vol. 25 no. 5, pp. 222–6.

O'Byrne, P (2008) 'The dissection of risk: A conceptual analysis', *Nursing Inquiry*, vol. 15, no. 1, pp. 30–9.

Rogers, AE (2008) 'Role of registered nurses in error prevention, discovery and correction' *BMJ Quality & Safety*, vol. 17, pp. 117–21.

Royal College of Nursing (2004) *Clinical leadership toolkit*, Royal College of Nursing, London.

Rubin, GL & Leeder, SR (2005) 'Healthcare safety: What needs to be done?' *Medical Journal of Australia*, vol. 183, no. 10, pp. 529–31.

Sackett, DL, Rosenberg, WM, Gray, JM, Haynes, RB & Richardson, WS (1996) 'Evidence-based medicine: What it is and what it isn't', *British Medical Journal*, vol. 312, pp. 71–2.

Smedley B, Stith A & Nelson, A (eds) (2003) *Unequal treatment: Confronting racial and ethnic disparities in healthcare*, Institute of Medicine, National Academics Press, Washington, DC.

Throckmorton, C & Etchegaray, J (2007) 'Factors affecting incident reporting by registered nurses: The relationship of perceptions of the environment for reporting errors, knowledge of *Nursing Practice Act* and demographics on intent to report errors', *Journal of PerAnaesthesia nursing*, vol. 22, no. 6, pp. 400–12.

Van Der Weyden, MB (2005) 'The Bundaberg hospital scandal: The need to reform in Queensland and beyond', editorial in *Medical Journal of Australia*, vol. 183, pp. 284–5.

Wakefield, B, Blegen, M, Uden-Holman, T, Vaughn, T, Chrischilles, E & Wakefield, D (2001) 'Organisational culture, continuous quality improvement and medication administration error reporting', *American Journal of Medical Quality*, vol. 27, no. 4, pp. 49–55.

Wilson, RM &Van Der Weyden, MB (2005) 'The safety of Australian healthcare: 10 years after QAHCS', *Medical Journal of Australia*, vol. 182, pp. 260–1.

USEFUL WEBSITES

Australian Patient Safety Foundation: **https://raer.aimslive.com/Help/View. aspx?Page=AustralianPatientSafetyFoundation**

Department of Health and Ageing's guiding principles for medication management: **www.health.gov.au/internet/main/publishing.nsf/Content/ nmp-guide-medmgt-jul06-contents~nmp-guide-medmgt-jul06-guidepr12**

Patient safety reports: **www.patientsafetyinstitute.ca/English/research/ cpsiResearchCompetitions/2005/Documents/Weisbaum/Reports/Full Report.pdf and www.patientsafetyinstitute.ca/english/search/pages/ default.aspx?k=%20national%20%20steeringcommittee%20on%20 patient%20safety**

Chapter 11

Safety and the registered nurse

Maria Fedoruk

Learning objectives

After reading this chapter, you will be able to:

- discuss the role and responsibilities of the registered nurse in relation to risk management in the workplace
- discuss the role and responsibilities of the registered nurse in relation to occupational health, safety and welfare in your state or territory
- develop plans and strategies to ensure safety of patients
- discuss the processes for managing critical incidents in the workplace
- discuss the factors affecting safety in the healthcare workplace
- discuss clinical governance and the role of the registered nurse.

Key terms

AIMS reporting system
Clinical governance
Critical incident
Employee assistance programs (EAPs)
Occupational health, safety and welfare (OHS&W)
Risk management
Root cause analysis
Sentinel event

Managing workplace safety

A fundamental responsibility of the registered nurse in Australia is ensuring safe work practices and environments for patients and staff. The management of risk and the promotion of safety in the healthcare workplace are core functions and responsibilities of the registered nurse, irrespective of their practice context. Managing safety in the healthcare workplace is what is known as a mandatory competency, which is reviewed annually as a part of your performance review process. All nurses need to be aware of the risk factors in their healthcare environments, including patients' homes. Safe nursing practice is mandated in the ANMC competency standards, as well as by AHPRA.

Point to ponder

Managing safety in the workplace is everyone's responsibility. As a student nurse, you have a responsibility to report hazards or anything that has the potential to harm patients, staff or visitors.

When people become patients in healthcare or aged care facilities, they may be unable to protect themselves from harm or injury because of altered health (physical or psychological) status. The role of the nurse is to ensure that risk of harm to patients is minimised and, as a part of the assessment process, identify potential risk factors for individuals and then develop appropriate care plans. The ability of people to protect themselves from harm is affected by such factors as age and development, lifestyle, mobility and health status, sensory-perceptual alterations, cognitive awareness, ability to communicate, safety awareness and environmental factors. Nurses need to assess each of these factors when they plan care or teach clients how to protect themselves.

BOX 11.1: WORKPLACE SAFETY TERMS

- *Risk management* is a series of processes developed to minimise harm to patients and staff working in healthcare organisations. Risk management also applies to staff — providing staff with safe systems of work.
- *Critical incidents* are unintended consequences of an action or actions that may result in harm to recipients of care or staff involved in care delivery. Critical incidents can also involve staff being exposed to violence in the workplace or to activities that result in needlestick injuries.
- *Sentinel events* are the unintended consequences of health professional activities that can result in serious or even fatal injury to recipients

of care. Sentinel events may also involve staff in incidents that result in psychological injury or physical injury.

- **Root cause analysis** is a process used for investigating and categorising unintended consequences of healthcare professional actions during the course of their work.
- **AIMS (advanced incident management system) reporting system** is a voluntary reporting system of incidents that have occurred in the healthcare workplace.

The department of health in your state or territory will provide information about the AIMS reporting system.

An example of the national approach to managing risk in the healthcare workplace is the National Hand Hygiene Initiative (NHHI), organised by Hand Hygiene Australia. The purpose of the National Hand Hygiene Initiative is 'to develop a national approach to improving HH [hand hygiene] and monitor its effectiveness. This initiative is based on the World Health Organization (WHO) World Alliance for Patient Safety campaign' (Hand Hygiene Australia 2011).

Other examples of national approaches to managing risk in healthcare include those noted by ACSQHC:

- national inpatient medication chart
- Australian safety and quality goals for healthcare
- national recommendations for user-applied labelling of injectable medicines, fluids and lines.

Risk management

Minimising risk in the healthcare workplace is the responsibility of all health professionals—clinicians and non-clinicians. The organisation has a responsibility to provide workers with a safe working environment that includes:

- sufficient space to deliver patient care
- a hazard-free environment that will prevent injury to patients, staff and visitors
- equipment that is fully functional and well maintained
- a risk management program that is supported by policies, procedures and protocols
- education for staff relating to safety in the workplace, including emergency procedures (clinical and non-clinical)
- safe systems of work for all staff

Maria Fedoruk

- a system for reporting faults: for example, faulty equipment, environmental hazards, clinical errors
- a system for monitoring and evaluating the effectiveness of risk management strategies.

You as a health professional also have responsibilities in relation to risk management. These include:

- working within your scope of practice (check the ANMC competencies for registered nurses and midwives)
- having the knowledge and competencies to work in the healthcare environment
- being able to respond appropriately in emergency situations
- knowing how to report faults in the workplace
- understanding your statutory obligations in relation to delivering safe patient care.

Sources of error in the healthcare workplace

In healthcare organisations in developed countries, there are five main sources of harm to patients:

- medication errors
- hospital-acquired infections for patients
- hospital-acquired infections for staff (for instance, needlestick injuries)
- falls
- pressure ulcers
- errors in the management of blood products
- patient identification errors (Fedoruk 2012).

All of these errors fall within the scope of nursing practice. Nurses administer medications, manage infection control processes, monitor patients' mobility, check bedridden patients for pressure ulcers, and administer blood and blood products. The registered nurse is responsible for ensuring that organisational policies and procedures are followed where checking is required. Accuracy in patient identification, especially when administering blood, blood products or medications, is an important nursing function.

Such stringent checking procedures must be used when you are administering or checking other staff administering medications and blood or blood products to patients, or any procedures requiring accuracy in patient identification. In some instances you as the registered nurse will be signing off that patient identification was accurate. For example, when administering medications and blood or blood products, the following process may be used. The 'eight rights':

- right time
- right patient
- right medication
- right dose
- right route
- right effect
- right documentation
- right education.

The 'right' framework is used in most healthcare facilities and you would probably have been introduced to a framework like this in your undergraduate program.

The WHO has developed a surgical safety checklist which has been adopted and adapted by healthcare organisations in this country. As you are aware, surgical care has been an integral component of healthcare worldwide for more than a century century. As the incidences of traumatic injuries, cancers and cardiovascular disease continue to rise, there will be an increase in surgical interventions with a potential for increase in adverse events occurring in the operating room. You will find that most hospitals have implemented this surgical checklist as part of the risk management and quality improvement framework.

The WHO safe surgery checklist identifies three phases of a surgical procedure, each corresponding to a specific period in the normal flow of work:

1 before the induction of anaesthesia ('sign in')
2 before the incision of the skin ('time out')
3 before the patient leaves the operating room ('sign out').

In each phase, a checklist coordinator must confirm that the surgery team has completed the listed tasks before it proceeds with the operation (WHO 2009).

FOR REFLECTION

- How would you rate your work environment in terms of safety on a scale of 1 to 5, with 1 = most unsafe and 5 = most safe?
- How confident are you in administering medications and/or blood and blood products?
- How important is the registered nurse's role in ensuring safety in the workplace?
- Reflect on your orientation to the organisation—was there an emphasis on the registered nurse's role in ensuring safety in the workplace?
- Did your orientation to the clinical unit focus on safe practice in that unit?

Maria Fedoruk

Table 11.1: WHO surgical safety checklist

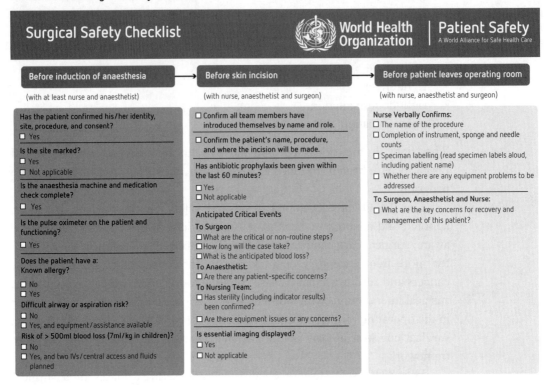

The healthcare environment

Registered nurses have a pivotal role in managing safety in the healthcare environment, which includes ensuring a safe physical environment; ensuring compliance with established safe systems of work; and reporting any risks identified when at work.

The healthcare environment for beginning registered nurses, and indeed all nurses and healthcare workers, is both complex and dynamic. It can range from a clinical unit in a tertiary-level teaching hospital to a country hospital providing secondary health services and/or community services or a stand-alone community service, providing community nursing and other health services. In the community-based setting, a nurse's work environment may include the car and the patient's home. A safe working environment for nurses can vary and be dependent on the location for nursing practice.

Because nurses work in diverse environments, ensuring a safe working environment can be problematic, especially in circumstances where the employer and the employee have no control over the site of nursing care. Nurses need to be aware of the policies and procedures relating to safe practice in their organisations, including the responsibilities of their employer, as well as their responsibilities as an employee under the OHS&W legislation in their state or territory. Inherent in the notion of safe nursing practice is that nurses are accountable for ensuring that their work practices comply with the legislation.

Point to ponder

All nurses need to understand their workplace environment and the legislative and policy framework that supports safe, competent practice. 'Cutting corners' while delivering nursing care can be costly, not only in financial terms.

It should also be noted that work practices may legitimately vary because of differences in work environments and the availability of resources. For example, workplace safety in a tertiary-level teaching hospital may be defined differently to workplace safety for those working in the community. The core principles and the spirit of the legislation remain the same but the application of these principles is context-dependent.

Safety in the healthcare workplace covers all clinical processes and procedures, as well as the physical aspects of safety, such as manual handling, transporting patients, managing technology and chemicals, and the physical environment. There should be safe operating procedures for all mechanical and electronic devices, which should be clearly labelled and tagged as being safe to use. When new equipment is introduced into clinical practice, all nurses and users of this equipment should receive instruction in its safe operation prior to using it, and these safe operating procedures should be written down and easily accessible to staff.

Point to ponder

Workplace safety is everyone's responsibility.

Occupational health, safety and welfare

Occupational health, safety and welfare is enshrined in legislation which applies to all workplaces in Australia. The OHS&W legislation is state- and territory-specific. For example, South Australia has the *Occupational Health*

Maria Fedoruk

Safety & Welfare Act 1984; Victoria has the *Occupational Health & Safety Act 2004*; New South Wales has the *Occupational Health & Safety Act 2000*. You should become familiar with the relevant legislation in your state and territory. This legislation has been developed to protect workers in their respective workplaces, ensuring a safe working environment, free of hazards that could cause harm to workers and, in healthcare organisations, to patients. Nurses, because of the very nature of their work, which is complex, physically and intellectually demanding, need the assurance of a safe working environment, as well as properly functioning equipment in order to deliver safe care to patients.

While you may have been taught manual handling techniques in your undergraduate program, performing these in the clinical skills laboratory at the university or in the virtual classroom is very different from performing them in the clinical workplace. Patients come in all shapes and sizes, and have varying levels of comprehension, mobility and consciousness: this adds to the complexity of providing nursing care to them. Most healthcare agencies now have 'no lift' policies, meaning that mechanical devices are used to move and lift patients. Safe manual handling practices are an integral aspect of risk management processes in healthcare organisations. Manual handling is a mandatory competency for nurses and is reviewed annually as part of the performance review, which links to the organisational quality and accreditation processes. There should be clear instructions on how to use these lifting devices provided to you—you should also be shown how to use these devices, because these can vary from unit to unit, healthcare agency to healthcare agency. It is advisable that you check the regulations that will govern your practice under the Australian Health Practitioner Regulation Agency, available at <www. ahpra.gov.au>.

These devices and all equipment used by nurses when delivering care to patients should be checked on a regular basis to ensure that they are safe to use by staff members in your organisation. In most organisations this is the responsibility of the nurse manager or the person in the equivalent position (nursing titles, roles and functions can vary from agency to agency and state to state across the country), but it is your responsibility to report equipment that is need of repair

Manual handling injuries can also occur during the bending and stretching activities that form part of what nurses do in delivering care to patients: for example, bending over patients while making a bed; doing wound dressings and checking wound drains, such as chest wound drains or abdominal wound drains.

Despite safe practices, the potential for accidents to occur in the healthcare workplace persists. As a responsible employee you should know how work-related injuries are managed by your employer.

All states and territories have agencies that collect data about work-related injuries. These are listed at the end of this chapter. The national peak body is Safe Work Australia.

Reported unsafe work practices that result in injury to workers can result in heavy fines and in extreme circumstances to closure of facilities. There can be negative outcomes for specific nursing staff as well, where they are involved in unsafe practices in the workplace.

Violence in the workplace

Unfortunately the environments in which nurses work are becoming increasingly hostile and violence is becoming a commonplace event. This violence may be either physical or non-physical. Nurses, being in the front line of health service provision, are often the target of hostility. While the sources of workplace violence are varied, the major sources are 'clients/patients; visitors/relatives; other nurses, nursing management; medical practitioners' (Hegney et al. 2006, p. 220). Physical violence is most often from alcohol- or substance-abuse patients, patients with a mental illness or patients reacting to medical interventions such as drug therapy.

Point to ponder

Violence in the workplace is increasing, and 'hospital rage' is now being reported in the literature.

A recent study from Queensland (Hegney et al. 2006), which involved a random sample of 3000 nurses and compared that with an earlier 2001 study, showed that workplace violence had increased in all three major healthcare sectors (public, private and aged care). This study also found a relationship between workplace violence and age, gender and classification of nurses, with younger, more inexperienced nurses being the most vulnerable to workplace violence. There is a growing discussion about workplace violence in hospital emergency departments, where nurses, as frontline workers, are the targets of violence that manifests as verbal and physical abuse. Think carefully before committing to spending time in your TPPP year in an emergency department: you may prefer to apply to go there when you are more experienced and have developed competencies and the confidence to deal with the complex and difficult people you will come across in this clinical area.

Maria Fedoruk

In Australia, the majority of healthcare agencies hold aggression management workshops for all staff and it would be in your best interests to attend these workshops, especially if you are going to work in designated high-risk areas, such as emergency departments.

All healthcare agencies have safety and risk management policies and procedures, linked to the quality improvement program. You should familiarise yourself with these—especially the emergency telephone numbers, which are usually printed on the back of your staff ID badge next to the type of emergency (colour coded). All clinical areas will also have their own local procedures and again you should become familiar with these as a priority.

Violence in the workplace becomes even more troublesome for nurses working alone, either in remote and rural areas, or in the community. For these nurses, there must be well-established safety procedures and they should be supplied with appropriate communication and location technology that allows immediate access to a responsible authority (such as the police) to ensure their safety at all times.

Ensuring the safety of staff is an organisational responsibility under the OHS&W legislation in each state and territory, but you must also accept responsibility for your own safety: for example, by being aware of your environment and heeding patient cues, especially if they are restless, appear to be responding inappropriately to questions you are asking, or if you feel the home environment is unsafe. This applies in both hospital environments and community-based healthcare organisations. High-risk areas in the community include homes with known violent occupants and suburbs with reported and documented high crime rates. The level of risk to healthcare professionals working in these areas must be identified and documented (it is part of the environmental assessment) and appropriate strategies implemented to ensure their safety.

Horizontal/lateral violence

Horizontal or lateral **violence** refers to hostile and aggressive behaviour within a particular group of people (such as a team of healthcare workers). The phenomenon of horizontal or lateral violence is well documented in nursing literature and has been acknowledged as a 'critical global issue for healthcare organisations' (Hutchinson et al. 2010, p. E60).

Bullying

Non-physical violence in the healthcare workplace is often the result of bullying. Bullying is antisocial behaviours expressed as intimidation, verbal abuse, rudeness, threatening another, embarrassing others, and so on. The result of these antisocial behaviours on the staff member being bullied is psychological distress. If you are the target of bullying, this must be reported under the OHS&W legislation in your state or territory. Sustained bullying can cause severe psychological distress, which can manifest as physical and mental illnesses. All healthcare organisations, as part of their human resource management strategies, should give staff the opportunity to access **employee assistance programs** (EAPs) using external service providers.

Bullying in nursing appears to be becoming more prevalent (Hutchinson et al. 2010). New graduate nurses are particularly vulnerable to bullying and harassment in the workplace (Duchscher & Myrick 2008). Bullying is violence that has social and emotional elements. It manifests as antisocial and aggressive behaviour, which can escalate into physical violence, but usually bullies favour humiliating, denigrating, criticising, and telling lies about the person or persons that are their targets. Bullies usually operate through weaving an intricate web of lies and denial. Because they are charming when doing this, it can take some time before this behaviour is recognised for what it truly is.

The sole aim of bullies is to make their targets feel inadequate and compliant to their wishes through threats and intimidation. Bullies are threatened by competent, strong people. They use power and control to achieve their goals, and if they are very good at manipulating situations and others, their behaviours may go unchecked. Bullies are people who are weak and less than competent but because they have been unchecked are still in the workplace. Bullies do not care about their victims and so it is pointless to try and reason with them—they have an agenda to humiliate others, from which they will not be turned.

As a new registered nurse you are a prime candidate for bullying, especially if you are competent and knowledgeable—all the things the bullies probably are not. You will need to recognise bullying behaviours in order to defend yourself. Because these are covert, usually one-on-one between the bully and the victim, others may find it difficult to accept that bullying is occurring. Victims of bullying often develop physical and psychological symptoms that can result in ill health requiring medical treatment. Once this happens, you lose your confidence and self-esteem, and your work performance slips, which may be reflected in errors or poor decision-making. A good rule of thumb for recognising bullying behaviour when it is directed at you is: if you believe you are being bullied, you most probably are.

Strategies to deal with bullying and to stop being a victim include:

- Recognise the bullying behaviour for what it is—unacceptable behaviour from an inadequate person.
- Understand that it is not your fault—you are not responsible for the bully's behaviour.
- Understand that bullies are weak, vindictive people who can only feel good about themselves by diminishing others.

Maria Fedoruk

- Your hospital or agency will have human resource policies that deal with bullying—find out what these are and use them.
- Keep a written record of instances (date, time, context, nature) of bullying so that you have evidence when reporting.
- Be courageous and just refuse to play the bully's game—this can be difficult to do, but once it is, your confidence returns.
- Report the bullying behaviour to senior management under the OHS&W legislation in your state.
- If you feel intimidated because the bully is your immediate manager, then you can go to the nurses union (in most states it will be the Australian Nursing Federation) for advice and support.
- In the most extreme cases you should seek legal advice.

It is important for you to recognise that bullying is unacceptable behaviour. You do not have to accept this sort of behaviour, and there are legislative and administrative processes that are in place to protect you. Remarks such as 'Don't worry, so and so always does this to new staff—it's part of your unofficial orientation' are wrong, inappropriate and only serve to support the bully.

Harassment in the workplace

Closely aligned to bullying is harassment. Harassment, too, is becoming more prevalent. It may be based on gender, age, race or religion. Harassment can be as insidious as bullying, but the more overt forms are:

- sexual harrassment, such as inappropriate touching
- inappropriate comments
- 'jokey' emails that you might find offensive
- smutty jokes that others find offensive
- lies told about you
- being told off in front of others
- being insulted in front of others.

The more covert forms of harassment include:

- having your performance as a registered nurse continually criticised
- always being rostered onto the 'unsocial' shifts
- always being allocated the most difficult patients with little or no support
- being denied the opportunity to act in a more senior position, even though you have the competency and knowledge to do so
- being told that you are on probation and that your employment is contingent on favourable reports from other staff.

Just as bullying is unacceptable behaviour, so is harassment. The way to deal with harassment is by standing up for yourself. If you ask why you have been rostered on for the past five weekends or you have had a disproportionate number of late shifts compared to others then the person doing the rostering needs to be able to provide you with a rationale for this, a rationale that is focused on patient care and is not about others' social needs/wants.

WORKING IN GROUPS

In your study group, discuss your responses to unsociable behaviours from others. Are you able to stand up for yourself, or do you give in to other people all the time? Role play may be useful to identify unsociable behaviours as well as strategies to manage these situations

- Have you ever felt unsafe at work? How did you manage the situation?
- What policies and support are available to you to deal with these situations?

Everyone's responsibility

Bullying and harassment are not twenty-first-century phenomena, and we have all experienced bullying or harassment at some point in our lives. Which of these can be described as harassment?

- having someone make inappropriate comments to you—comments that make you feel uncomfortable
- being questioned about your personal life in an open forum
- being criticised in front of others
- being rostered unfairly so that others can meet their social obligations
- being sent a smutty email.

There are elements of bullying and harassment in all of the above points.

Unfortunately, workplace violence is a fact of life for nurses and for all health professionals (Mercer 2007). We seem to live and work in an increasingly fast-paced society where violence is a byproduct. Healthcare organisations have systems, policies and procedures to support safe practice. However, you too have a responsibility to ensure your own safety and the safety of the patients in your care. If you find yourself in a potentially dangerous situation, try and remove yourself from it. If you are unsure about carrying out a procedure, say so. Do not put yourself or your patients at risk.

Maria Fedoruk

Clinical governance

Managing risk in the healthcare workplace has both personal and professional dimensions, as you will have observed from clinical placement or work experiences. These dimensions are now being integrated under clinical governance. This section provides you with a brief overview of clinical governance and how the role of registered nurse relates to it. **Clinical governance** is defined as

> the system by which the governing body, managers, clinicians and staff share responsibility and are held accountable for patient care, minimising risks to consumers and for continuously monitoring the quality of career and services. (Balding & Maddock 2006, p. 13)

Clinical governance therefore integrates the clinical and corporate functions in a healthcare organisation and is a shared responsibility. As a beginning registered nurse the care and services you deliver to patients fits into the clinical governance framework. Clinical governance is the organisational approach to harm minimisation in healthcare organisations and while the principles of clinical governance are universal the application of these principles is context-dependent. (Sivitier 2008)

Clinical governance has a relatively new history in health services dating from the late 1990s, when it was introduced in the National Health Service in the United Kingdom as a framework for minimising clinical risk following the Bristol Inquiry. The Bristol Inquiry examined episodes of unethical and substandard clinical practice and identified that there were no systems of accountability for health practitioners.

Clinical governance provides frameworks of accountability and responsibility for health professionals reflected in organisational policies, procedures, clinical protocols, scope of practice and safe systems of work. So you can see the significance of your registration requirements and the ANMC competencies for registered nurses and midwives and why these were emphasised in your undergraduate programs.

SUMMARY

The core of nursing practice is the ability and capacity of individual nurses to be safe and competent practitioners. As a registered nurse you will be expected to act within the bounds of legislation and the ANMC competencies. The organisation you work for will have policies and procedures that support safe systems of work and you must know what these are. Safe systems of work apply equally to direct care delivery to patients and to staff. Incidents occur because of system breakdowns such as workload stress or interruptions while carrying out nursing functions. When these incidents occur, you need to know how and to whom to report them so that they are managed effectively and so that strategies are implemented to minimise reoccurrences.

Despite legislation, policies and procedures, antisocial behaviours such as bullying and harassment are prevalent in healthcare organisations. This chapter gives you some strategies to help you deal with these behaviours. The most important thing to remember is that you *do not have to put up with these behaviours*, which are reportable under OHS&W legislation.

The community expects safe, competent practitioners when they enter the healthcare system. Your responsibility is to ensure that these community expectations are met. Failure to do so can have negative consequences for you and for the patients in your care. Safe practice is an integral element of nursing in the twenty-first century.

Clinical governance, while relatively new, is linked to quality management that monitors safe practice. As a student nurse or midwife you may not think that clinical governance is something you need to concern yourself with, but if you are delivering care to patients then you are engaging with the requirements of clinical governance.

DISCUSSION QUESTIONS

1   What do you understand safe nursing practice to be?
2   What are some sources of errors in the healthcare workplace?
3   How would you ensure safe nursing or midwifery practice?
4   How does clinical governance apply to you as a student nurse or midwife? How will it apply to you as a registered nurse or midwife?
5   What are some of the consequences of bullying in the workplace?
6   Do you think you will be able to recognise the signs of bullying?

Maria Fedoruk

200   **Part 3**   The working environments of registered nurses

REFERENCES

Balding, C & Maddock, A (2006). *South Australian Safety and quality framework & strategy 2007–2011*, project report and supporting documents, Government of South Australia, Department of Health.

Duchscher, JEB & Myrick, F (2008) 'The prevailing winds of oppression: Understanding the new graduate experience in acute care', *Nursing Forum*, vol. 43, no. 4, pp. 191–206.

Fedoruk, M (2012) 'Safety' in *Kozier & Erb's fundamentals of nursing*, 1st Australasian edn, Pearson Publishing Australia.

Hand Hygiene Australia (2011) *The National Hand Hygiene Initiative*, <www.hha.org.au>, accessed 11 October 2011.

Hegney, D, Eley, R, Plank, A, Buikstra, E & Parker, V (2006) 'Workplace violence in Queensland, Australia: The results of a comparative study,' *International Journal of Nursing Practice*, vol. 12, pp. 220–31.

Hutchinson, M, Jackson, D, Wilkes, L & Vickers, M (2010) 'A new model of bullying in the nursing workplace', *Advances in Nursing Science*, vol. 32, no. 2, pp. E60–71.

Mercer, M (2007) 'The dark side of the job: Violence in the emergency department', *Journal of Emergency Nursing*, vol. 33, pp. 257–61.

Sivitier, B (2008) *The newly qualified nurse's handbook*, Bailliere Tindall Elsevier, Edinburgh.

World Health Organization (2009), *Safe surgery saves lives*, <www.who.int/patientsafety/safesurgery/en/>, accessed 11 October 2011.

USEFUL WEBSITES

Australian Commission on Quality and Safety in Healthcare (ACSQHC): www.safetyandquality.gov.au

ACSQHC Clinical handover: www.safetyandquality.gov.au/internet/safety/publishing.nsf/content/PriorityProgram-05#Tools

ACSQHC Knowledge portal: www.safetyandquality.gov.au/internet/safety/publishing.nsf/content/inforx-lp

ACSQHC National inpatient medication chart: www.safetyandquality.gov.au/internet/safety/publishing.nsf/content/NIMC_001

ACSQHC patient identification advice: www.health.gov.au/internet/safety/publishing.nsf/Content/PriorityProgram-04

ACSQHC medication safety advice: www.safetyandquality.gov.au/internet/safety/ publishing.nsf/Content/PriorityProgram-06

ACSQHC windows into safety and quality in healthcare: www.safetyandquality. gov.au/internet/safety/publishing.nsf/Content/windows-into-safety-and-quality-in-health-care-2008

Hand Hygiene Australia: www.hha.org.au

Nursing Australia Stafffing Solutions FAQ: http://www.nursingaustralia.com/ohs-faq.htm

SA Health Advanced Incident Management Systems (AIMS): www. safetyandquality.sa.gov.au/Default.aspx?PageContentMode=1&tabid=67 (See 'Incident management' link on the left-hand toolbar)

Safe Work Australia: http://safeworkaustralia.gov.au/Pages/default.aspx

Safework SA: www.safework.sa.gov.au/

Chapter 12

Legal responsibilities and ethics

Maria Fedoruk

Learning objectives

By the end of this chapter you will be able to:

- differentiate between law and ethics
- discuss the relationship between law and ethics
- apply ethical principles to your practice
- analyse personal values that may influence your decision-making
- understand your role as a registered nurse in ethical healthcare issues.

Key terms

Autonomy
Beneficence
Bioethics
Consent to treatment
Fidelity
Justice
Non-maleficence
Veracity

Ethics

As an undergraduate nurse, you will have been introduced to the ethical dimensions of nursing practice. It is the intent of this chapter to raise your awareness and understanding of the significance of ethics to nursing practice and provide you with some case studies to illustrate this. There are a number of texts available which discuss the ethical and legal responsibilities of the registered nurse in more detail: if you are interested, you may wish to investigate the titles included in the 'Further reading' section at the end of this chapter. As a beginning registered nurse you will be expected to apply the principles and concepts of ethical nursing practice to real-life, real-world and real-time situations. To do this in a competent manner you will need to become familiar with the definitions and terminology relating to ethical nursing practice.

The Australian Nursing and Midwifery Council has produced the following codes of ethics and professional conduct:

- *Code of ethics for midwives in Australia* (ANMC, Australian College of Midwives & ANF 2008a)
- *Code of ethics for nurses in Australia* (ANMC, Royal College of Nursing & ANF 2008b)
- *Code of professional conduct for midwives in Australia* (ANMC 2008a)
- *Code of professional conduct for nurses in Australia* (ANMC 2008b)

Appendices A–D present the purpose and core statements of each of these codes.

There are similar codes and standards in other countries, with many countries using the ICN *Code of ethics for nurses* (2006) as a framework.

BOX 12.1: ETHICS TERMS

You will find it useful to be familiar with the following terms.

- **Ethics**—Rules or principles that differentiate between right and wrong human activities.
- **Bioethics**—A multidisciplinary approach for critically examining ethical nursing and healthcare issues from different moral and theoretical perspectives or ethics concerning life.
- *Bioethical issues*—issues of right and wrong as they apply to human life concerns such as euthanasia and abortion, stem cell research, human cloning
- *Ethical dilemma*—a situation involving competing principles that appears not to have a satisfactory outcome for those involved or where choices have to be made between two or more undesirable alternatives
- *Moral or ethical principles*—the core values and principles that determine how patients should be treated. These also apply to your everyday life activities,

---

Maria Fedoruk

- *Moral reasoning*—used to consider different approaches to resolve ethical issues—an ethical decision-making process
- *Moral uncertainty*—occurs when an individual is unsure which moral principles or values apply in a certain context
- *Values*—the beliefs that influence an individual's behaviour
- *Values clarification*—this strategy requires you to examine your own personal value system.

Adapted from Pappas (2009, p. 397)

FOR REFLECTION

Your value system is unique to you and is a product of your upbringing, schooling, attitudes, relationships, and so on. Your personal value system may influence how you react and respond to situations at work. It is important to remember that others may hold different opinions and points of view from you. Critically examining your personal value system can give you greater insight into your behaviours and interactions with others. It will give you some insights into why you make the decisions you do; the choices you make; what you believe to be important in your life and work.

List up to ten personal values and write down why these are important to you.

As a registered nurse, you will be faced with ethical dilemmas in the course of your working day. Remember that patients and other members of the community do not know that you are a new graduate—all they see is a registered nurse—and they will expect you to be able to deal with their queries in an objective and proper manner. In some situations, you may not have a ready solution for someone's problem, but you should be able to refer them on to an appropriate health professional.

Point to ponder

Some issues are specific and require specialist help, so your role (and the correct ethical behaviour) is to refer patients to the staff who can help.

Ethical principles

There are four main ethical principles (Staunton & Chiarella 2007):

- **Autonomy**—the right to self-determination and, from a patient perspective, the right of individuals to make choices about treatment without interference from external parties, including healthcare teams, even when those choices differ from that of health professionals

- **Non-maleficence**—the principle of doing no harm. Nurses have a professional responsibility to avoid harming patients and to practise competently.

Point to ponder

In the case study below, which nurses demonstrated competent practice?

- **Beneficence**—the principle of doing good or acting for the benefit of others. All nursing practice is directed at achieving positive benefits for others.
- **Justice**—this has two meanings in the field of ethics: 'fairness' and the equal distribution of burdens and benefits. This principle is about treating all patients fairly, especially in relation to access to scarce resources in the healthcare system.

Case study: A tragic outcome

Mr B, an 80-year-old man, is admitted to a clinical unit with chronic hypertension and mild left ventricular failure. He is admitted for elective surgery—trans-urethral resection of the prostate. He is accompanied by his 74-year-old sister, Ms W, who informs the nursing staff that they live together in the country, approximately 250 kilometres away from the hospital. To get to the hospital, they had to catch a bus at 7 am in their town. They have no living relatives or close friends they can call on for help following Mr B's discharge from hospital.

While completing Mr B's assessment, both brother and sister tell the nursing staff that they enjoy good health apart from the usual 'getting old' things. Both say they are active when at home and enjoy gardening and bowls at their local club.

Mr B has his surgery on a Tuesday and is discharged on the following Saturday, with an indwelling catheter. Prior to discharge, his sister is shown how to manage the catheter, how to change the catheter bag and how to attach the night-time bag. Ms W does not want to appear to be 'difficult' so she does not ask the nurse any questions about care of the catheter.

They travel home on the bus, and when they arrive home Mr B remembers he gave his antihypertensive tablets to a nurse on admission and forgot to get them back. His sister rings the hospital and the ward and explains the situation, but is told by the registered nurse that she cannot do anything about it because the drugs have been returned to the pharmacy, as per hospital policy, and the pharmacy is now closed.

Maria Fedoruk

Because they have returned to the country, there is no way she can get the medication to them. Ms W begins to get upset and panic, but the registered nurse assures her that the community nursing service have been advised of Mr B's discharge and will contact them later in the evening.

Ms W contacts the community nursing service and is told someone will be there shortly once they find the faxed referral. After this, Ms W notices that her brother seems drowsy, his movements are slow and his speech is slurred. She contacts the community nursing service again, explaining her brother's clinical condition. The nurse explains that there is no referral from the hospital, but tells her a nurse will come within thirty minutes.

However, the community nurses are particularly busy and it is more than an hour before a registered nurse arrives. During this time, Ms W tries to rouse her brother but he seems to be increasingly drowsy. Thinking that there might be some antihypertensive tablets in the medication cupboard, Ms W climbs onto a chair to look for them. The chair wobbles, and Ms W falls and fractures the neck of her right femur. When the community nurse arrives at their home, she finds Ms W on the floor in pain and Mr B unconscious in his chair.

The community nurse rings for an ambulance to take brother and sister to the local hospital for initial treatment, but Mr B passes away in the ambulance. He had had a cerebrovascular accident and the case is referred to the coroner. Ms W has a total hip replacement, but is not told of her brother's death for at least two days following her surgery.

Questions

Referring to the ethical principles above:

- Identify the ethical principles in this case study
- If you were the hospital nurse, would you have done anything differently?
- Would you have told Ms W her brother had passed away sooner?
- Were there any legal issues in this case study?
- Which ethical principle is the most important in this case?

Two other ethical principles which you may wish to consider are:

- **Fidelity**—the duty to be faithful to commitments and involves maintaining confidentiality, privacy and trust. To whom did the nurse owe fidelity in the case study above—the patient, the patient's family or the hospital?
- **Veracity**—the duty to tell the truth. Two situations in which this principle may become an issue are:

  – when a patient asks for their diagnosis and the medical staff have not yet discussed it with them

– when you witness a critical incident (such as a medication error) by a colleague which results in a negative outcome for a patient and you are asked by the nurse manager to give an accurate report of the incident. Do you tell the truth?

Patient rights

In Australia, in 2009 the Council of Australian Governments (COAG) released the Australian *Charter of healthcare rights*.

The charter is underpinned by three principles:

- Everyone has the right to be able to access healthcare and this right is essential for the Charter to be meaningful.
- The Australian Government commits to international agreements about human rights which recognise everyone's right to have the highest possible standard of physical and mental health.
- Australia is a society made up of people from different cultures and ways of life and the Charter recognises and respects these differences.

(ACSQH 2010)

Under the charter, all citizens have:

- a right to access healthcare
- a right to receive safe and high-quality care
- a right to be shown respect, dignity and consideration
- a right to be informed about services, treatment options and costs in a clear and open way
- a right to be included in decisions and choices about their care
- a right to privacy and confidentiality of their personal information
- a right to comment on their care and to have their concerns addressed.

(Adapted from ACSQH 2010)

FOR REFLECTION

As you go about your work as a registered nurse, observe whether or not these principles and patient rights are evident in the care being delivered to patients in your clinical unit. Where would you expect to see this evidence?

So what does all of this mean for you as a registered nurse? It means that you need to take into account the ethical dimensions of nursing practice when planning, implementing and evaluating nursing care and interventions.

Maria Fedoruk

It means that your decision-making relating to nursing care must not result in harm to the patient(s) in your care. It means that clinical nursing practice is multifaceted, culturally appropriate and complex, and you as the registered nurse must be able to manage these complexities in order to achieve positive outcomes for the patient(s).

Consent to treatment

At this point, it is timely to revisit the concept of 'consent to treatment'. Consent to treatment is a broad concept that also includes the patient's rights to refuse treatment or to refuse to be resuscitated, and also the practitioner's right to detain and restrain patients without their consent (Staunton & Chiarella 2007). There are, of course, ethical dimensions to these rights, and you should be able to relate these to the *Charter of healthcare rights* discussed above.

Consent to treatment means that a patient has agreed to treatment by a health professional. Conversely, a patient may also refuse to have treatment, and there is legislation in the states and territories to support this. While you do not need to know the details of the relevant legislation at this point in your career, you do need to be aware that such legislation exists. For example, South Australia has the *Consent to Medical Treatment and Palliative Care Act, 1995*. You should know of the equivalent legislation in your state or territory.

What is a valid consent?

A valid consent must satisfy the following criteria:

- The consent has been freely and voluntarily given.
- The consent given is properly informed.
- The person giving the consent has the legal capacity to do so (Staunton & Chiarella 2007, p. 118).
- *Consent freely given*—means that the person giving the consent has not been coerced or misled in terms of the information given to give the consent
- *Consent is properly informed*—means that the person has been given sufficient information, which includes the risks involved in the procedure to be performed, to make an informed decision
- *Person giving consent has the legal capacity to do so*—means that the person giving the consent has the intellectual capacity to understand the nature, purpose and effects of the proposed treatment. The person needs to be competent to:

  - receive, understand and recall relevant information
  - integrate the information being presented and relate it to one's own situation

- evaluate the benefits and risks in terms of personal values and beliefs
- rationally work through the information presented in order to select the best option and be able to support the choice
- communicate the choice to others
- stand by the choice until action is taken.

(Staunton & Chiarella 2007, pp. 125–6)

For adults who lack the capacity to give consent to treatment there are statutory bodies in the states and territories which can act on their behalf within a guardianship board framework. Again, you do not know about this in detail at this point in your career, but it is something you should be aware of.

Advance directives

Advance directives or 'living wills' are a recent phenomenon. They ensure that patient rights are honoured when the patient no longer has the capacity to refuse treatment. In Australia, some states and territories have legislated for advance directives: South Australia has the *Consent to Treatment and Palliative Care Act 1995*; Victoria has the *Medical Treatment Act 1988*, the *Medical Treatment (Enduring Power of Attorney) Act 1990* and the *Medical Treatment (Agents Act 1992)* and the Northern Territory has the *Natural Death Act 1988*.

It is also worth noting that in Australia you may come across patients who have given their relatives an 'Enduring medical power of attorney' which grants the relatives the legal right to make decisions on behalf of the patient in all medical matters.

At some point you may be asked to witness legal documents for patients— it is advisable to be cautious, and not do this. While, as an adult, you are legally entitled to be a witness, it is more prudent to refer these sorts of matters to managers in the health organisation who will make appropriate arrangements for this to be done. The organisation should have policies relating to this, which you can refer to.

Non-clinical ethical issues

The section above considered ethical principles from a clinical perspective, but as a registered nurse you will be faced with ethical dilemmas that for the purposes of this section may be considered non-clinical or administrative. Some examples include instances of:

- perceived unsafe staffing levels in terms of skill levels and knowledge, rather than numbers of staff

- poor nursing practice
- unprofessional behaviours from other nurses or other health professionals
- covering up of nurse-initiated mistakes or errors
- errors or poor practice from other health professionals

What would you do as a registered nurse if you observed another health professional engaging in unsafe practices? Would you:

- report this using the organisational processes for reporting these sorts of incidents?
- speak to the other health professional outlining your concerns?
- do nothing?

FOR REFLECTION

Think back to your student nurse days when you were on clinical placement. Did you observe other nurses 'cutting corners' in order to finish their work on time—not having medications checked when they should? Does this fall under the banner of ethical misconduct? Which ethical principle is breached? Now fast-forward to the present and you are the registered nurse—do you believe it is all right to cut corners when you are on a busy shift because usually nothing bad happens—patients really don't know anything and they are OK. Or if you do question unsafe practices the response is 'Oh we always do it this way, nothing bad ever happens'. Another reason for cutting corners: 'if we do not finish our work on time we get into trouble.' From what you now know are any of these reasons justifiable?

Whistleblowing

Whistleblowing in the healthcare sector is achieving prominence in the media, with cases of unsafe and incompetent practices by health professionals being reported. Your registration as a registered nurse is dependent on you being able to show evidence of safe, competent and ethical practice (your professional portfolio) to the national registering authority, the Australian Health Practitioner Regulation Agency. These professional portfolios will be subject to random audits in the coming years, as a quality management strategy. Inherent in your legal and ethical responsibility to be a safe, competent nurse is your duty to report areas of unsafe, incompetent practice from other health professionals, including nurse colleagues.

Whistleblowing is not specific to healthcare. In the corporate world, whistleblowing usually occurs around financial fraud, and it can result in companies collapsing and managers being jailed.

In healthcare, apart from whistleblowing about unsafe practices, there have also been cases of faulty medical devices and drugs used having negative outcomes for patients. These are usually reported in the media in the context of litigation, with victims seeking legal reparation for pain and suffering.

It should be noted that whistleblowing does not always result in sensationalised media attention: it can be managed appropriately and sensitively by organisations and regulatory agencies.

Point to ponder

Always remember the criteria for registration and continuing registration.

Nurse whistleblowers have been defined as nurses 'who identify incompetent, unethical or illegal situations in the workplace and report it to someone who has the power to stop the wrong' (McDonald & Ahern in Firtko & Jackson 2005, p. 52). A more generic definition of whistleblowing, provided by Firtko and Jackson (2005, p. 52), is 'the reporting of information to an individual, group or body that is not part of an organisation's usual problem-solving strategy'. As a registered nurse, you have a duty of care not to harm patients either directly or indirectly. All healthcare organisations in Australia are mandated to provide safe and competent health services. This is reflected in standards, clinical protocols, policies and procedures, and you are expected to work within these frameworks. However, reporting others for wrongdoing poses ethical dilemmas for nurses, and you have to make a decision in relation to your values, belief systems and regulatory obligations.

To be a whistleblower or not presents you with an ethical dilemma that challenges your core personal and professional values. It may make you question the level of responsibilities you have to patients, the community, your profession and your employer (Firtko & Jackson 2005). These are all issues you will have to grapple with in coming to a decision on the best way to act in the circumstances. There may be risks to you in reporting incidents. You may be labelled as a troublemaker and this may have an impact on your future employment prospects. In extreme cases, this may result in your being dismissed from the organisation. There may also be risks to the organisation from legal actions taken by patients and/or their relatives. Another thing to remember is that whistleblowing does not often result in an immediate positive outcome, especially if legal proceedings are initiated. It is important to be aware of the risks of whistleblowing. This is not intended to discourage or scare you, but instead to remind you of your professional responsibilities to ensure safe practice and ensure patients and other staff members come to no harm.

Maria Fedoruk

Therefore, before proceeding down the whistleblower path you should:

- use all the processes available in the organisation to report potential incidents that can cause harm to staff or patients
- discuss your concerns with a mentor or someone who may be able to intervene to stop the poor behaviour
- collect evidence relating to the incidents and be very certain of your facts. You will need objectivity not subjectivity when collating your evidence
- be very sure of organisational policies and procedures, and the laws governing practice
- seek advice from an external party such as an industrial organisation or even a lawyer.

Most states and territories have legislation to protect whistleblowers. For example in South Australia there is the *Whistleblowers Protection Act 1993*. It is wise to check your legal status under the relevant legislation if you find yourself in a whistleblowing situation.

SUMMARY

This chapter has given you a brief overview of the connection between nursing practice and the ethics of nursing practice. As an individual, you come to the workplace with a set of values and beliefs that influence your behaviours and attitudes, which may be very different from those of the people you work with and the patients you care for. There are also connections between ethics and the legal dimensions of nursing practice. This chapter has provided an overview, and there are resources available to you that deal with these issues in a much more comprehensive way. The message that you should take away after reading this chapter is that the ethics and the legal dimensions of nursing practice are integral to the practice of nursing and your responsibility is to be aware of these dimensions.

DISCUSSION QUESTIONS

1   Have you given any consideration to how you might manage unethical behaviours in the workplace?
2   Have you witnessed any unethical behaviour in the workplace? How was it managed? Was it reported? How were the individuals involved in these matters managed?
3   Why is it important for nurses and for all health professionals to comply with ethical codes of conduct?

REFERENCES

Australian Commission on Safety and Quality in Healthcare (2010) *Australian charter of healthcare rights*, Australian Government, Canberra, <www.safetyandquality.gov.au/internet/safety/publishing.nsf/Content/com-pubs_ACHR-pdf-01-con/$File/17537-charter.pdf>, accessed 1 October 2011.

Australian Nursing & Midwifery Council (2008a) *Code of professional conduct for midwives in Australia*, Australian Nursing and Midwifery Council, Canberra, <www.anmac.org.au/userfiles/file/New%20Code%20of%20Professional%20Conduct%20for%20Midwives%20August%202008(2).pdf>, accessed 26 September 2011.

Australian Nursing & Midwifery Council (2008b) *Code of professional conduct for nurses in Australia*, Australian Nursing and Midwifery Council, Canberra, <www.anmac.org.au/userfiles/file/New%20Code%20of%20Professional%20Conduct%20for%20Nurses%20August%202008(1).pdf>, accessed 26 September 2011.

Maria Fedoruk

Australian Nursing & Midwifery Council, Australian College of Midwives & Australian Nursing Federation (2008), *Code of ethics for midwives in Australia*, Australian Nursing and Midwifery Council, ACT, <www.anmac. org.au/userfiles/file/New%20Code%20of%20Ethics%20fo%20rMidwives%20 August%202008.pdf >, accessed 26 September 2011.

Australian Nursing & Midwifery Council, Royal College of Nursing & Australian Nursing Federation (2008), *Code of ethics for nurses in Australia*, Australian Nursing and Midwifery Council, ACT, <www.anmac.org.au/userfiles/file/ New%20Code%20of%20Ethics%20for%20Nurses%20August%202008. pdf>, accessed 26 September 2011.

Firtko, A & Jackson, D (2005) 'Do the ends justify the means? Nursing and the dilemma of whistleblowing,' *Australian Journal of Advanced Nursing*, vol. 23, no. 1, pp. 51–6.

International Council of Nurses (2006) *The ICN code of ethics for nurses*, International Council of Nurses, Geneva, <www.icn.ch/images/stories/documents/about/ icncode_english.pdf>, accessed 26 September 2011.

Pappas, AB (2009) 'Ethical issues' in JA Zwerkeh & JC Claborn, *Nursing today, transition and trends*, 6th edn, Saunders Elsevier, St Louis, MI.

Staunton, P & Chiarella, M (2007) *Nursing & the law*, 6th edn, Elsevier Australia, Sydney.

USEFUL WEBSITES

Australian Health Practitioner Regulation Agency, legislation: **www.ahpra.gov. au/Legislation-and-Publications/Legislation.aspx**

FURTHER READING

Berglund, CA (2007) *Ethics for health care*, 3rd edn, Oxford University Press, Melbourne.

Edwards, SD (2009) *Nursing ethics: A principle based approach*, Palgrave Macmillan, Basingstoke, United Kingdom.

MacIlwraith, J & Madden, B (2010) *Health care and the law*, 5th edn, Thomson Reuters (Professional) Australia Limited, Sydney.

Part 4

Being ready for practice

Core competencies

As a registered nurse or midwife, you will:

- understand the legislative and administrative frameworks governing nursing and healthcare
- understand your responsibilities as a registered nurse or midwife
- engage in lifelong learning in your new role
- begin the transition process into the new role of registered nurse or midwife
- work within your own scope of practice.

Chapter 13

Professional development for registered nurses

Maria Fedoruk

Learning objectives

After reading this chapter, you will be able to:
- discuss the principles underpinning professional nursing practice
- demonstrate evidence of professional nursing practice
- develop a professional portfolio
- develop short-term and long-term career plans.

Key terms

Curriculum vitae (CV)
Emotional intelligence (EI)
Professional portfolio
SWOT analysis

A career in nursing

Congratulations! You have just graduated, landed your first job and—lucky you—this job is in your preferred healthcare agency. You worked here as an enrolled nurse (EN) or an assistant in nursing while completing your undergraduate program, so you are familiar with the organisation. Your luck continues: your first clinical placement is also your first preference.

So why do you need to think about a career in nursing at this point? Why do you need to plan your career? You have achieved your goals. Well, yes, you have, and becoming a registered nurse is a worthy achievement, but the TPPP is only for twelve months—you have a long working life ahead of you unless you are even luckier and win the lottery (which mathematicians have calculated is a 1 in 8 000 000 chance). If you are from Generation Y, you are at the beginning of a very long working life, because:

- Australia's population is ageing and living longer and healthier
- the environment is becoming degraded, which is having an impact on the health of populations, leading to pressure for nurses to stay in the workforce for longer
- the current tax base which supports the nation may be severely depleted, meaning that in the future the retirement age may be later.

Given this situation, wouldn't you rather plan a career that you want, one which will give you satisfaction and financial security? A career that will stretch you intellectually and professionally? And a career that you have designed, developed and made happen? Whether you are a Generation Y graduate, a mature-age graduate who has achieved a lifelong ambition, or a graduate with family commitments, you do need to plan your career. If you view nursing as just a job instead of a career, you will limit your professional opportunities for career advancement and personal and professional growth (Marquis & Huston 2012).

Each one of you is different and so your approach to career planning will be different. Some of you may have begun to think about your career in nursing during your undergraduate program, especially during your clinical placements. Most universities have websites devoted to career planning; there are career advisers whom you can contact. It may be appropriate for you to do this perhaps in your final year of study. It is definitely something you should consider, perhaps not at the beginning of the TPPP but halfway through the program, once you have had time and opportunities to settle into the registered nurse role.

In Chapter 2, you were introduced to professional nursing organisations. These can be a good source of information as you begin planning your career in nursing.

Universities have career advisory services and you should check your teaching institution's website for links to career planning advice. Some teaching institutions also organise career expos and/or invite speakers from industry to talk to students about future career options. Take every opportunity to get as much information as you can.

Whatever your circumstances are, you should plan your career in nursing. The career choices and decisions you make will impact not only on you but also on those around you (family, friends and colleagues) and on your nursing practice. It is wise to make the decision that is right for you, because your career is such an important part of your life. You should feel happy and satisfied with your choice of career.

However, you should also allow yourself some flexibility. Career opportunities for nurses may change as technology and demands for health services change, so your career pathway should be developmental. Career opportunities for nurses are expanding and you need to keep your career goals up to date, because this will enable you to develop and plan your career strategies. Some of you may use the knowledge and competencies you develop as a nurse to move in other career directions at some time in the future. Futurists predict that in the twenty-first century the average person will need to engage in career construction, because careers will be organised differently and job transitions will become more frequent and complex. You will be a worker in the Information Age, a lifelong learner using more 'sophisticated technologies, having to embrace flexibility and maintain your employability' (Savickas et al. 2009, p. 240).

Point to ponder

It is never too early to begin thinking about career development and career goals.

SWOT analysis

A useful way of beginning to plan your career is to do a **SWOT analysis**. A SWOT analysis is a simple framework used in project management but which can also be used to assess career opportunities. SWOT stands for strengths, weaknesses, opportunities and threats.

Table 13.1: SWOT analysis

Strengths	Weaknesses
Opportunities	Threats

This analytic framework can be very helpful in planning your career in nursing, but first you must have a specific career goal in mind. For example, if your goal is to be a nurse practitioner, then by using a SWOT analysis you will be able to identify:

- *your strengths*—competencies and knowledge that you already have but which will have to be further developed to expert status
- *your weaknesses*—areas of your practice which need serious work if you are to achieve your goal. This may include specific courses in the Masters of

Maria Fedoruk

Nurse Practitioner program and working in clinical areas which will enable you to further develop the skills and competencies you will need to achieve your career goal

- *your opportunities*—be alert to opportunities in your workplace that may support your career goals; conferences that are in your clinical area of interest that will not only enhance your knowledge but also introduce you to nurse experts already working in the area you are interested in
- *your threats*—an obvious threat may be competition from other registered nurses with the same career goals and aspirations as you, or a hostile environment that does not support professional development.

The structure of nursing in organisations

From your clinical and work experiences you will have observed that nursing in healthcare organisations operates within a hierarchical structure. This reflects the historical organisation of nursing based on the military structures familiar to Florence Nightingale. The hierarchical structure also reflects the bureaucratic nature of healthcare organisations. Bureaucracies are systems characterised by division of labour, a clearly defined hierarchy and detailed rules and regulations (Dwyer & Hopwood 2010, p. 14).

Point to ponder

Hierarchies exist in nursing—think about the senior and junior nurse titles, and consider the rules and regulations that govern nursing practice.

The structure of organisations clearly shows how the work processes are organised, the reporting lines and the responsibilities of different staff members. While your specific position may not appear on the organisational chart (a formal document describing the role and function of the organisation), you are indicated in the nursing division, with an executive director of nursing assuming responsibility for all nursing-related activities in the organisation.

Closely aligned to organisational structure is organisational culture. Organisational culture is defined as a system of shared meanings and values held by members of a particular organisation that distinguish it from other organisations (Dwyer & Hopwood 2010, p. 583). Organisational cultures can be supportive (that is, staff are valued and supported) or they can be non-supportive (staff are not valued nor supported). A negative organisational culture is characterised by high staff turnover; an increase in error rate; and a high absenteeism rate. These are all objective indicators that measure the culture of an organisation. A rule of thumb for you may be to ask yourself: How happy are you in your current workplace? Do you feel supported and valued?

Do you enjoy coming to work? If you can answer 'yes' to these questions, then you are working in a supportive organisational culture.

Point to ponder

Organisational culture influences nursing practice and behaviours, and therefore patient outcomes.

However, in the twenty-first century, because of the emphasis on collaborative practice and a relaxation in rules and social norms, communication channels are more open, giving you opportunities to discuss patient-related issues with a team of health professionals. This means that you are now expected to participate fully in planning and delivering care to patients and not wait to be told what to do. The hierarchy and bureaucracy give form and structure to the organisation, but it is how people act and behave within these structures that determine the organisational culture.

Hierarchy also means an imbalance in power, and some staff members may use a hierarchy to intimidate and bully others. Abuse of power in a workplace creates a negative organisational culture, which makes working there extremely stressful and difficult.

Point to ponder

It is how people act and behave inside organisational structures that determines how an organisational culture develops and in what form.

As you are aware, there are continual changes being made to healthcare organisations to improve the delivery of health services to communities. Often these changes result in changes to staffing models, usually reflected as reductions in staff numbers. This creates uncertainty and increases stress levels among staff. Where this occurs, workloads increase, again increasing stress levels, and a culture of negativity may develop in the workplace, with accompanying negative behaviours from staff.

Refer back to Chapter 11 and the sections on bullying and harassment: two prime examples of a power imbalance and the hierarchical structures in nursing that can facilitate such an imbalance.

WORKING IN GROUPS

In your study group, discuss the hierarchical structures in nursing and how they influence peoples' behaviours.

- Have you observed instances of power imbalances? How did you feel?
- Were the behaviours resulting from this acceptable in your opinion?
- What was the effect on patient care?

Maria Fedoruk

The power imbalance will also be present between you and your patients, especially in cases where a patient may be dependent on you for helping them manage activities of daily living (ADLs). If we are honest, patients can be exposed to some indignities related to treatments during their stay in hospitals or other healthcare agencies and residential care facilities. Being aware of the patient–nurse power imbalance should help you plan care for individual patients in ways that support a return to health and that demonstrate a respect for the individual and maintain their dignity as much as possible.

The ANMC has developed *A national framework for decision making by nurses and midwives on scopes of practice* (ANMC 2007). This framework provides you with a guide to clinical decision-making. You may find decision-making daunting in the early days of working as a registered nurse or midwife. Professional nursing practice in the twenty-first century is fast-paced and complex and so being able to make effective and correct decisions is a competency you will need to begin to develop and demonstrate in your new role.

National competency standards

The *National competency standards for the registered nurse* (ANMC 2006) are outlined in Appendix E. They are the blueprint for your professional practice. Your performance reviews will use the ANMC standards as indicators to measure your performance as a registered nurse or midwife, as well as to define your scope of practice. You can also use these standards to plan your professional development and to make decisions about your capacity to accept delegated functions from others. In relation to accepting delegated functions, the best rule is, 'if in doubt don't accept'. Delegation is dealt with in more detail in Chapter 9, but it is worth noting here that if you are unsure about performing a task or function then in the best interests of patient safety and your safety the best course of action is to say 'no'. All delegated functions require supervision but there are times when the level of supervision may be minimal because of competing priorities for nurses.

These competency standards for registered nurses are organised into four domains: professional nursing practice, critical thinking and analysis, provision and coordination of care, and collaborative and therapeutic practice.

Professional nursing practice

This domain refers to the professional, legal, ethical responsibilities that underpin your practice as a registered nurse. As a registered nurse you will have to demonstrate a satisfactory knowledge base, accountability for your practice and that you are practising within legislation affecting nursing and healthcare and the protection of human rights (ANMC 2006, p. 3) Use the following reflection exercises for discussion in your study group, and try and relate them to areas of nursing practice discussed in preceding chapters. You could also discuss case studies from your clinical placements.

FOR REFLECTION

A competency within the domain of professional nursing practice is: 'recognises and responds appropriately to unsafe or unprofessional practice'. You witness an incident where you encounter another nurse engaging in unsafe and unprofessional practice. This clearly has a number of issues—ethical, legal and professional—that you may have to deal with. What would be your immediate response?

Critical thinking and analysis

This domain relates to self-appraisal, professional development and the use of quality, research-generated evidence to inform your practice. During your undergraduate program you were often asked to reflect on different aspects of your course and perhaps for some of you this seemed far removed from the actual practice of 'hands on' nursing—well, now you know that the ability to reflect on your practice is linked to the ANMC competency standards. Your ability to think and analyse critically is described as an 'important professional benchmark' (ANMC 2006, p. 3), so it is a competency that needs continual development.

FOR REFLECTION

Referring to the incident above, how would being able to critically reflect on the incident help you in determining a course of action? What would be a priority in the course of action?

Provision and coordination of care

This domain relates to the registered nurse's competency to coordinate, organise and deliver nursing care. This competency includes assessment, implementation and evaluation of care, which of course is the nursing process.

Maria Fedoruk

FOR REFLECTION

The incident is now close to resolution, and you are asked to develop a new plan of care for the patient or group of patients who were central to the incident (that is, they were on the receiving end of the unsafe behaviour). How would you go about this? Describe the process or processes you would employ.

Collaborative and therapeutic practice

This domain relates to how you develop and maintain professional relationships with individuals and groups. As a registered nurse, you will develop, maintain and end professional relationships with diverse groups of people, including fellow professionals and people requiring nursing care. The competencies contained within this domain also relate to the contributions you will make to the multidisciplinary healthcare team.

FOR REFLECTION

In developing a new plan of care, would you collaborate with other health professionals? How would you determine that this was necessary?

Professional boundaries

Implicit in the learning activities in the previous section is the notion of professional relationships and professional boundaries. Historically, professional boundaries in nursing and healthcare were clearly defined and as a nurse your boundaries were very clear and prescribed by the rigid hierarchical structures that organised the healthcare workforce. In the twenty-first century, a diminishing healthcare workforce and an increasingly expanded scope of practice for registered nurses have meant that these boundaries are becoming increasingly blurred—hence the ANMC competency guidelines and frameworks underpinning nursing practice.

The ANMC and the Nursing Council of New Zealand have published a guide to professional boundaries: *A nurse's guide to professional boundaries* (2010). The ANMC has published an equivalent guide for midwives: *A midwife's guide to professional boundaries* (ANMC 2010). These guides are part of the ANMC professional practice framework and a supporting document to the ANMC *Code of professional conduct for nurses* (Appendix C) and *Code of ethics for nurses in Australia* (Appendix A). There are therefore no excuses for not knowing what is expected of you as a registered nurse or midwife. Professional boundaries in nursing are defined as 'limits which protect the space between the professional's power and the client's vulnerability' (ANMC and the Nursing Council of New Zealand 2010, p. 2). Professional boundaries delineate the edge between 'professional therapeutic relationships and the non-professional or personal relationship between a nurse and the patient in their care' (ANMC and the Nursing Council of New Zealand 2010, p. 2). Moving outside of these boundaries constitutes a boundary violation and is unprofessional practice. As a registered nurse, you establish a therapeutic relationship with your patients because of your specialist knowledge and skills. The fact that you possess personal information places you in a position of power and your patients in a position of vulnerability—this is a power imbalance. Patients and the community in general place a great deal of trust in nurses, and you have a responsibility to ensure that this trust is not abused either by you or by other nurses.

Case study: The 'bad' patient

During the course of your undergraduate program, you will probably have encountered the stereotypes 'good patient' and 'bad patient'. The 'good patient' is compliant, obeys the nurse's directives, and does not use the call bell often, if at all. The 'bad patient' is always asking for assistance and always ringing the call bell.

You observe an instance of a nurse ignoring a persistent call bell ringing. When you ask the nurse allocated to the patient why she does not respond to the patient, you are told 'they're always ringing for something and I'm getting sick of it. If you are so worried, *you* go and see what they want!'

So you do go and see the patient, who tells you that he is experiencing chest pain and asks for pain relief. You return to your colleague and suggest that it might be appropriate to assess the patient's chest pain and any other symptoms and perhaps call for a medical review. The nurse comments that this patient is a 'wuss', always complaining about something, and she continues to ignore the patient. While you are still discussing the patient, he has a cardiac arrest. He is successfully resuscitated.

Questions

- Would you have done anything differently?
- Was the other nurse's behaviour professional?
- What could you learn from this experience?

Maria Fedoruk

The ANMC (ANMC and the Nursing Council of New Zealand 2010) has developed a continuum of professional behaviour for nurses and midwives. The continuum consists of three distinct 'zones':

- underinvolvement (in which the nurse or midwife is uninterested and neglectful)
- zone of helpfulness (the therapeutic relationship)
- overinvolvement (where boundary violations occur).

FOR REFLECTION

- Where on the continuum was the nurse discussed in the case study?
- Where on the continuum were you?
- Where should you have been?

Professional portfolio

As you are aware, nurses live and work in a world that is based on evidence. There is evidence-based medicine (EBM), evidence-based practice (EBP), evidence-based management (EBMgt) and evidence-based nursing (EBN). The use of evidence to support nursing practice is discussed in more detail in Chapter 9. This section focuses on you and the evidence that you will need to support your continuing registration and professional development.

You will need to have a professional portfolio that provides evidence of your competency to practise as a registered nurse or midwife. Since 1 July 2010, the national registration requirements for registered nurses and midwives are for evidence of continuing professional development through 20 hours of engagement in professional development activities annually and recency of practice, as described in the ANMC (2009) *Continuing competence framework.*

The aims of the framework are to:

- provide a national, standardised process for nurses and midwives to demonstrate their continued competence
- set standards for participation in continuing professional development
- guide nurses and midwives in developing and maintaining a record of their participation in the ANMC Continuing Competence Framework through the use of a professional portfolio.

(ANMC 2009, p. 3)

Before the new requirement of a professional portfolio came into place on 1 July 2010, nurses used to develop a curriculum vitae (CV), which listed employment history and emphasised strengths. The CV was a marketing document and the same is true for the professional portfolio—you are marketing yourself to potential employers as a registered nurse or midwife they need on their staff. A professional portfolio includes a CV. When applying for a position, you may be asked to submit a CV separately, but you would take your professional portfolio to the interview. CVs are separate documents that you can submit electronically.

There are different forms of portfolios and while you were an undergraduate student you would have kept an educational portfolio that contained evidence of your learning—think about the reflective pieces you wrote. All those reflective pieces you wrote as assessment pieces during your student nurse program were practice for developing and maintaining your own professional portfolio. You may have even begun your professional portfolio during your undergraduate program and even used it when you went for your interview for your position as a graduate registered nurse.

Your professional portfolio can be kept electronically or in hard copy but an electronic portfolio is easier to update and maintain.

A professional portfolio 'is a structured collection of different types of evidence' (Andre & Heartfield 2007, p. 2) that details your professional goals, achievements and participation in and completion of professional development activities. Items to include in a professional portfolio include:

- an employment record
- educational and professional qualifications
- evidence of successful completion of professional development activities (including the mandatory competencies required by employers)
- evidence of competence in your area of practice, based on critical analysis of your knowledge, experiences and skills
- career aspirations and professional goals, and strategies to achieve these
- reflective pieces about your experiences and knowledge and competency development (Andre & Heartfield 2007).

A professional portfolio, as described in the ANMC (2009) *Continuing competence framework*, has the following elements:

- portfolio standards—all nurses and midwives will have a comprehensive portfolio containing evidence that demonstrates their competence to continue practising in their context of practice
- measurement criteria—this includes an annual self-assessment of practice against relevant ANMC competency standards and a professional review using the self-assessment

- evidence of participation in professional development activities—these should be aligned with your area of practice and/or support your professional career aspirations
- evidence of recency of practice
- a signed self-declaration of competence—this is a legal document and penalties may apply for false self-declarations

While your professional portfolio does not have to be submitted annually, it may be audited at any time by the AHPRA.

Andre and Heartfield (2007, p. 18) provide the following suggestions for what your professional portfolio should include:

- table of contents
- personal details—demographic data
- a list of competency statements or standards that you wish to develop further
- appendices that provide summaries and evidence of your employment history
- academic transcripts
- referee reports and testimonials
- completed clinical skills assessments
- completed professional practice assessments
- medication assessment calculations, as a part of mandatory competency testing by healthcare organisations.

You may find that there are other items relevant to you and to your area of practice which you will need to add. For example, if you are working in a specialty clinical unit then the competency and professional development activities you participate in will be included in your professional portfolio.

Portfolios can be paper-based or electronic. It is up to you how you want to develop and maintain your professional portfolio, as long as you have documented evidence that you are eligible for ongoing registration.

FOR REFLECTION

Reflect on the information provided above, and begin to plan and develop your own professional portfolio. What will it look like? What might be a starting point for you? What sort of evidence will you include? Where will you go to get the evidence? How will your professional portfolio support your career planning?

Applying for a job

When you first decide to apply for a job, it is useful to do a SWOT (strengths, weaknesses, opportunities and threats) analysis on yourself. Reflecting on your current performance as a registered nurse:

- What are your strengths?
- Which areas of your nursing practice do you believe need further development?
- What are the opportunities available to you in terms of career development? Are these in the area you are currently employed in? Or do you see yourself moving into other areas of nursing practice or even other organisations?
- What are potential threats to you when applying for new positions?

FOR REFLECTION

Use the SWOT analysis framework to begin planning your career. Reflect on your

- strengths
- weaknesses
- opportunities
- threats.

When completing your SWOT analysis, be objective and honest with yourself. On your clinical placements you will have received evaluations which highlighted your strengths and weaknesses—use these to help you. Most of us tend to focus on our weaknesses, but it is also important to focus on our strengths. For example, if in one of your clinical placements your evaluation indicated that one of your strengths was that you were a good communicator, how could you build on this to enhance your communication competencies? A weakness may have been something to do with time management—you had a tendency to be late in completing functions. Reflect on this, and consider what support you would require to improve your time management skills.

Having completed the SWOT analysis on yourself, then consider where you want to work and why. Some of you may be offered employment in the hospitals or healthcare agencies where you spent time on clinical placement or where you have worked as an EN or AIN.

Pick your referees carefully. Referees' comments should enhance and support your CV and the evidence in your professional portfolio.

Maria Fedoruk

Where to look for a position

The internet has made job seeking a lot easier: you can search for jobs online and send in your job applications electronically. If you are looking to move to a new healthcare organisation, check their website—the majority of healthcare organisations now list available positions on their websites. Alternatively, go to the Department of Health and Ageing website and see what positions are available within the public health sector in your state or territory or in other places around the country. The major papers, especially the weekend papers, list vacancies and these papers have dedicated employment websites. State and territory departments of health may also list vacancies. Professional nursing journals, career expos and the career advisory service of your university are also good sources for employment opportunities.

There is also the 'cold call' approach in which you contact the human resource department or the nursing department of the hospital or healthcare agency where you want to work and make enquiries about potential positions. The 'cold call' approach demonstrates initiative, which can be very appealing to employers. You may then be invited to submit a letter of application and your CV and professional portfolio.

The application letter

Your letter of application and professional portfolio are critical, because the decision to interview you will be made on the basis of the information in these documents. The application letter should introduce you to the prospective employer, stating your reasons for applying for a position, and outlining why you should be considered for it. It should therefore contain a brief summary of your competencies and knowledge. Try and be succinct with your information: your potential employer and their staff are busy people and do not have the time to read two or three pages. You will expand on your strengths during the interview. The purpose of the application letter is to get you to the interview stage.

The interview

Whatever the format of the interview, you need to be prepared with the correct documentation and evidence of your suitability for the position for which you have applied For the TPPP, the interview may be with nurse managers or managed centrally by the Department of Health. For more senior positions, it may be a panel interview. If you are being interviewed for a nursing position interstate or overseas, it may be a telephone interview.

Now that you have reached the interview stage, you do not want to compromise your chances of being successful by interviewing badly. Once you know that you are to be interviewed, you should research the organisation by accessing their website—find out what the organisational philosophy is, what the philosophy of the nursing service is and which clinical services are offered. Plan any questions you may want to ask at the interview, because it is not one-sided—you will have the opportunity to ask questions of your prospective employer.

For the interview itself:

- Dress appropriately—T-shirts, shorts, thongs, excessive jewellery and heavy makeup are not appropriate. Clothes should be neat, clean and pressed and should fit you comfortably. If your clothes make you uncomfortable, it will be hard to make a good impression with the interview panel.
- Arrive early—this will give you time to check your appearance and tidy up if necessary. It also gives you time to mentally prepare by doing some relaxation techniques such as deep breathing and going over any documentation you may have brought with you.
- Always try and make eye contact with the person asking the question and then be inclusive of others on the interview panel when responding to questions.
- If your mind suddenly goes blank during a question, ask if you can return to the question later in the interview.
- Try and relax during the interview, although this can be difficult—remember you are at the interview because the organisation wants you.

Taking care of yourself

Believe it or not, taking care of yourself is also an important part of your professional development. If you are not fit, healthy and mentally alert, you will not be able to care for your patients in a safe and competent way. As a new registered nurse, change becomes a constant in your life. As a registered nurse, your colleagues and patients hold certain expectations of you, and you may well also place certain expectations on yourself. These factors are coupled with demanding workloads in hospitals and other healthcare facilities resulting from the implementation of efficiency measures and changes to service delivery systems that 'have replaced length of stay with increased patient acuity' (Duchscher & Myrick 2008, p. 191).

Point to ponder

Nurses must always remember to take care of themselves. This means *not* volunteering for extra work when you are tired, coming to work when you sick or assuming the workplace cannot do without you.

Maria Fedoruk

Nursing is a stressful occupation, and stress can have an impact on levels of job satisfaction as well, causing psychological and physical ill health (Chang et al. 2006). Some stressors identified by graduate nurses include:

- lacking confidence in your abilities to work as a registered nurse
- a fear of making mistakes because of increased workloads and responsibilities
- having to negotiate new environments and social structures
- learning to work with new staff
- working in a unit that is continually understaffed
- working with unhappy nurses
- not knowing who to go to for help
- being marginalised from other nurses in the clinical unit
- having to demonstrate and apply new knowledge and skills.

WORKING IN GROUPS

In your study group, discuss your career development plans. You could look at where you hope to be in three years' time.

- What will you need to do to achieve your career goals?
- Where will you go to access resources to support your career development?
- How will understanding the transition process help you achieve your career goals?

As a registered nurse, you have a responsibility to look after yourself in order to be effective as a nurse caring for patients. As a student nurse and as a registered nurse, you should make taking care of yourself a priority, or you may find yourself burning out (Zerwekh & Claborn 2009). Signs of burnout include:

- depression
- feelings of helplessness
- frequent headaches and gastrointestinal disturbances
- insomnia
- being continually negative—a 'glass half empty' person
- cynicism
- always being tired
- weight fluctuations
- self-criticism—the 'I'm no good/can't do anything right' syndrome (Zerwekh & Claborn 2009, p. 35).

Do any of these signs apply to you? If they do, then you should take action immediately, using the strategies listed below.

Learning to care for yourself means developing self-awareness of your feelings and knowing how to deal with them. Nurses who have good emotional health are able to deal with their emotions appropriately without embarrassing themselves or others. You need to express your feelings, especially negative feelings, to avoid them becoming internalised to such an extent that you begin to develop some of the symptoms listed above.

Self-care strategies

Here are some strategies to help you avoid or deal with stress in the life of a registered nurse or midwife.

- Manage your physical environment—ensure that it is hazard-free, safe and tidy.
- Manage your time effectively. Plan and prioritise. Do not buy into the myth of the perfect nurse.
- Deal with procrastination. Think about the potential consequences of not doing something compared to doing something.
- Learn to delegate. You are not 'super nurse'.
- Manage your personal and professional goals through a professional portfolio.
- Engage in physical exercise. Many healthcare organisations now have gyms on site that offer subsidised membership to staff.
- Walk for at least 20 minutes a day.
- Take stretch breaks while at work.
- Learn to laugh, and laugh frequently.
- Remember to have fun. Take up a relaxing hobby such as doing puzzles or Sudoku.

There is a great deal of information available for you to discover what sort of activities help you keep healthy.

You may feel that between your home and work commitments you do not have time to do all this. You need to *make* the time unless you want to become a statistic. To paraphrase Henry Thoreau: 'we are all busy but what are we busy about?' How can you deliver good health messages to patients when you are obviously not heeding your own advice?

Maria Fedoruk

SUMMARY

This chapter has focused on professional development in nursing and how this is determined by the ANMC competence framework. The requirements for continuing registration as a registered nurse and midwife include using an evidence-based professional portfolio. Nurse and midwives are expected to take a strategic approach to managing their careers and assume responsibility for their professional development. Even though there is a nursing workforce shortage, healthcare organisations are still looking for nurses who are safe, competent, professional practitioners and who will fit in and work with their organisational philosophy and mission statements.

An integral part of your professional development is maintaining your own physical and mental well-being. Nursing is a stressful occupation, with competing demands on nurses wherever nurses work. Nursing literature is now discussing the adverse effects on new graduates of workload stress at the national and international levels. The factors that contribute to workload stress in nurses are universal—you are not alone in experiencing the workload stress phenomenon.

As a graduate nurse you have the added stressors of entering a new work environment in a new role that brings with it different expectations and responsibilities. The section on taking care of yourself in this chapter outlines the risks and also provides strategies for minimising the effects of workload stress. There are many strategies available to you: the most important thing is to use the one that works for you.

DISCUSSION QUESTIONS

1   What are three 'take home' messages for you from this chapter?
2   How important is organisational culture to effective nursing practice?

REFERENCES

Andre, K & Heartfield, M (2007) *Professional portfolios: Evidence of competency for nurses and midwives*, Elsevier, Australia.

Australian Nursing & Midwifery Council (2006) *National competency standards for the registered nurse*, 4th edn, January 2006, Australian Nursing and Midwifery Council, Canberra, <www.anmc.org.au/userfiles/file/RN%20Competency%20Standards%20August%202008%20(new%20format).pdf>, accessed 13 September 2011.

Australian Nursing and Midwifery Council (2007) *A national framework for decision making by nurses and midwives on scopes of practice* (National DMF), Australian Government Department of Health and Ageing, Canberra,

<www.acnc.net.au/upload/File/DMF%20-Newsletter%20article%20V3.1%20 with%20backgroundpdf.pdf>.

Australian Nursing and Midwifery Council (2009) *Continuing competence framework*, Australian Nursing and Midwifery Council, Canberra, <www. anmc.org.au/userfiles/file/research_and_policy/continuing_competencies/ Continuing%20Competence%20Framework%20-%20Jan%202009%20 Final%20Doc%20for%20web.pdf>, accessed 26 September 2011.

Australian Nursing and Midwifery Council (2010) *A midwife's guide to professional boundaries*, Australian Nursing and Midwifery Council, Canberra, <www.nursingmidwiferyboard.gov.au/Search.aspx?q=guide%20to%20 professional%20relationships>, accessed 12 October 2011.

Australian Nursing and Midwifery Council & Nursing Council of New Zealand (2010) *A nurse's guide to professional boundaries*, Australian Nursing and Midwifery Council, Canberra, <www.anmc.org.au/userfiles/file/PB%20for%20 Nurses%20-%20Final%20for%20web%20+PPF%20Watermark%20-%20% 20March%202010.pdf>, accessed 13 September 2011.

Chang, E, Daly, J, Hancock, K, Bidewell, JW, Johnson, A, Lambert, VA & Lambert, CE (2006). 'The relationships among workplace stressors, coping methods, demographic characteristics, and health in Australian nurses', *Journal of Professional Nursing*, vol. 22, no. 1, pp. 30–8.

Duchscher, JEB & Myrick, F (2008) 'The prevailing winds of oppression: Understanding the new graduate experience in acute care,' *Nursing Forum*, vol. 43, no. 4, pp. 191–8.

Dwyer, J & Hopwood, N 2010, *Management strategies and skills*, McGraw-Hill, Australia.

Goleman, D (2005) *Emotional intelligence*, Bantam Books, New York.

Marquis, BL & Huston, CJ (2012) *Leadership roles and management functions in nursing*, 7th edn, Wolters Kluwer/Lippincott Williams & Wilkins, Philadelphia.

Savickas, ML, Nota, L, Rossier, J, Dauwalder, J-P, Duarte, ME, Guichard, J, Soresi, S, Van Esbroack, R, van Vianen, AEM (2009) 'Life designing: A paradigm for career construction in the 21st century', *Journal of Vocational Behaviour*, vol. 75, pp. 239–50.

Zerwekh, J & Claborn JC (2009) *Nursing today: Transitions and trends*, 6th edn, Saunders Elsevier, St Louis, MI.

USEFUL WEBSITES

Australian Nursing and Midwifery Council: **www.anmc.org.au**

Department of Health and Ageing: **www.health.gov.au**

Chapter 14

Joining the dots

Maria Fedoruk

Congratulations! You have now reached the final chapter of the book. We hope that that you have found it to be an interesting read. Just like you, we too experienced a journey to become registered nurses, so we understand what it means to be a student nurse and face the complexities of nursing practice. While nursing practice is continually evolving to meet the demands of a changing healthcare system and increasingly informed health consumers or patients, the need for competent nurses and midwives who know the 'whys and hows' of their practice has not changed. You are entering a dynamic environment which is economically driven, where healthcare technologies are used by nurses and multidisciplinary teams of health professionals to deliver specific episodes of care to diverse patient populations.

In this chapter, we briefly look back over the content of this book and 'join the dots' to show you how the various aspects of nursing practice connect with each other. Nurses are continually joining the dots when delivering nursing care to patients. The nursing process is a series of connected processes, beginning with assessment, that result in a plan of nursing care. Nurses implement this plan and then evaluate the health outcomes for patients. Continuous quality improvement is a series of processes designed and implemented to measure the quality of care being delivered to patients. The nursing process connects with the continuous quality improvement processes, both having the same objective of achieving positive health outcomes for patients. The preceding chapters discuss these processes in detail.

Part 1, Becoming a Health Professional, covered the theory of transition and belongingness—processes that you will experience as you move into the registered nurse or registered midwife role. The chapters in this section also provided practical applications of the theoretical constructs that underpin transition and belongingness. Chapter 2 also introduced you to professional nursing organisations you may consider joining. Belonging to professional nursing organisations is part of your continuing professional development.

Part 2, Contexts and Competencies of Clinical Practice, covered nursing contexts and competencies in Australia. Chapter 6, Australia's Healthcare System, provided the context for your individual clinical practice setting. It gave an overview of the healthcare system and the various sites of healthcare where registered nurses and midwives practise. Having an understanding of how the healthcare system is managed gives you an insight into government policy-making. One current example of this is the establishment of national healthcare workforce committees to deal with the healthcare workforce shortage in this and other countries.

Chapter 7, Professional Regulation, provided information on the requirements for initial and continuing registration in Australia. These are clearly described by the Australian Health Practitioner Regulation Agency. You should familiarise yourself with the AHPRA requirements so that you understand what it means to be a registered nurse or midwife.

Chapter 8, Essential Competencies for the Registered Nurse, dealt with competency development for registered nurses and midwives, and specifically the Australian Nursing and Midwifery Council competency frameworks for nurses and midwives. This also links back to the AHPRA registration requirements for registered nurses and midwives.

Chapter 9, Applying Competencies to Registered Nurse Practice, discussed and described the practice side of nursing, using the competency framework. It provided useful tools and exercises, and may have also given you ideas on how to develop your own 'tools of the trade'. As a registered nurse or midwife, you will work in teams with health professionals from different disciplines. As you become more experienced, you may be expected to lead teams of health professionals. So it is appropriate that you begin to think about how you might manage a multidisciplinary team of health professionals.

Chapter 9 also covered evidence-based practice, a key feature of clinical practice, not only here but also around the world. Ensuring that your practice is evidence-based and current means using evidence-based practice principles to source the best available evidence, and specific competencies are required to do this.

Part 3, The Working Environments of Registered Nurses, contained chapters on quality management, safety and clinical governance. These areas are underpinned by policies and are integral to nursing practice. All healthcare organisations have a mandate to ensure safe care to patients, and this is reflected in the clinical governance frameworks. As a health professional, you

Maria Fedoruk

have a mandate to provide safe nursing care to patients, and this is enshrined in legislation and policy.

Chapter 11, Safety and the Registered Nurse, discussed the role of the registered nurse in relation to safety. Safety in practice means ensuring safe systems of work and maintaining a safe environment for staff, patients and visitors. Registered nurses also have a responsibility under the OHS&W legislation to ensure a safe, hazard-free work environment. Part of your induction as a registered nurse will include information about OHS&W legislation, which covers not only physical injury but also psychological injury. This chapter included sections on bullying (horizontal violence), harassment, and the mandated reporting responsibilities of the registered nurse or midwife. These responsibilities are outlined in the legislation governing nursing and midwifery practice, in the ANMC competency standards for registered nurses and midwives and in organisation policy.

Chapter 12, Legal Responsibilities and Ethics, reinforced that nursing practice has ethical dimensions. The ANMC codes of ethics for registered nurses and midwives are provided as Appendix A and Appendix B. Closely aligned with ethics are the legal responsibilities of the registered nurse. Legally and ethically you are required to work within your scope of practice, and any breaches may result in adverse outcomes for you and for patients in your care.

Chapter 13, Professional Development for Registered Nurses, provided information on how to develop your career in nursing and the options and opportunities that will be available to you. This chapter also gave you information about preparing for interviews and the use of the professional portfolio.

Finally, a number of useful appendices have been included, as reminders of key areas of responsibility and accountability for the registered nurse or midwife. Appendix F provides guidelines for accuracy in documentation, which is necessary for maintaining care continuity; it is a form of communication between health professionals. Appendices G and H provide advice on the use of electronic communication: email and social media sites, in the work context. Finally, Appendices I and J provide a medical calculation test for your use. Accuracy in drug calculations is a competency all registered nurses and midwives have to have, and once in the workplace drug calculations are a mandatory competency monitored annually in most healthcare organisations.

All of these aspects, you will find, are an integral part of what the registered nurse or midwife in the twenty-first century has to know in order to manage well and competently.

The authors trust you will find the book helpful and useful in your nursing career.

Appendices

A   Code of Ethics for Nurses in Australia

Purpose

The purpose of the *Code of ethics for nurses in Australia* is to:

*   identify the fundamental ethical standards and values to which the nursing profession is committed, and that are incorporated in other endorsed professional nursing guidelines and standards of conduct
*   provide nurses with a reference point from which to reflect on the conduct of themselves and others
*   guide ethical decision-making and practice
*   indicate to the community the human rights standards and ethical values it can expect nurses to uphold.

Code of ethics for nurses

1   Nurses value quality nursing care for all people.
2   Nurses value respect and kindness for self and others.
3   Nurses value the diversity of people.
4   Nurses value access to quality nursing and healthcare for all people.
5   Nurses value informed decision-making.
6   Nurses value a culture of safety in nursing and healthcare.
7   Nurses value ethical management of information.
8   Nurses value a socially, economically and ecologically sustainable environment promoting health and well-being.

Source: ANMC, Royal College of Nursing & ANF 2008.

B   Code of Ethics for Midwives in Australia

Purpose

The purpose of the Code of ethics for midwives in Australia is to:

- identify the fundamental ethical standards and values to which the midwifery profession is committed, and that are incorporated in other professional midwifery codes and standards for woman-centred midwifery practice
- provide midwives with a reference point from which to reflect on the conduct of themselves and others
- indicate to each woman receiving midwifery care and her family, colleagues from other professions, and the Australian community generally the human rights standards and ethical values they can expect midwives to uphold
- guide ethical decision-making and midwifery practice.

Code of ethics for midwives

1   Midwives value quality midwifery care for each woman and her infant(s).
2   Midwives value respect and kindness for self and others.
3   Midwives value the diversity of people.
4   Midwives value access to quality midwifery care for each woman and her infant(s).
5   Midwives value informed decision-making.
6   Midwives value a culture of safety in midwifery care.
7   Midwives value ethical management of information.
8   Midwives value a socially, economically and ecologically sustainable environment promoting health and well-being.

Source: ANMC, Australian College of Midwives & ANF 2008, ANMC.

C Code of Professional Conduct for Nurses in Australia

1   Nurses practise in a safe and competent manner.
2   Nurse practise in accordance with the standards of the profession and broader health system.
3   Nurses practise and conduct themselves in accordance with laws relevant to the profession and practice of nursing.
4   Nurses respect the dignity, culture, ethnicity values and beliefs of people receiving care and treatment, and of their colleagues.
5   Nurses treat personal information obtained in a professional capacity as private and confidential.
6   Nurses provide impartial, honest and accurate information in relation to nursing care and health care products.
7   Nurses support the health, well-being and informed decision-making of people requiring or receiving care.
8   Nurses promote and preserve the trust and privilege inherent in the relationship between nurses and people receiving care.
9   Nurses maintain and build on the community's trust and confidence in the nursing profession.
10 Nurses practise nursing reflectively and ethically.

Source: ANMC 2008b.

D   Code of Professional Conduct for Midwives in Australia

Purpose

The purpose of the *Code of professional conduct for midwives in Australia* is to:

- outline a set of minimum national standards of conduct for midwives
- inform the community of the standards of professional conduct it can expect midwives in Australia to uphold (as supported by the Australian Nursing and Midwifery Council National competency standards for the midwife, and stated in the International Confederation of Midwives Definition of the midwife)
- provide each woman, their families, and regulatory, employing and professional bodies, with a basis for evaluating the professional conduct of midwives.

The Code is not intended to give detailed professional advice on specific issues and areas of practice. Rather, it identifies the minimum requirements for conduct in the midwifery profession. In keeping with national competency standards, midwives have a responsibility to ensure their knowledge and understanding of professional conduct issues is up to date. While mandatory language such as 'must', 'shall' and 'will' is not used throughout this Code, it is important for midwives to understand that there is a presumption that the conduct discussed is mandatory and therefore not discretionary for midwives practising midwifery.

A breach of the Code may constitute either professional misconduct or unprofessional conduct. For the purposes of this Code these terms are defined similarly to those for nurses. Professional misconduct refers to 'the wrong, bad or erroneous conduct of a (midwife) outside of the domain of his or her practice; conduct unbefitting a (midwife)'[1] (e.g. sexual assault, theft or drunk and disorderly conduct in a public place). Unprofessional conduct refers to 'conduct that is contrary to the accepted and agreed practice standards of the profession'[2] (e.g. violating confidentiality in the woman–midwife relationship).

The midwifery profession expects midwives will conduct themselves personally and professionally in a way that maintains public trust and confidence in the profession. Midwives have a responsibility to the individual woman, her infant(s) and family, colleagues, society and the profession, to provide safe and competent midwifery care responsive to individual, group and community needs and the profession.

---

1 M Johnstone & O Kanitsaki 2001.

2 ibid.

Code of conduct

Midwives practise competently in accordance with legislation, standards and professional practice

1 Midwives practise in a safe and competent manner.
2 Midwives practise in accordance with the standards of the profession and broader health system.
3 Midwives practise and conduct themselves in accordance with laws relevant to the profession and practice of midwifery.
4 Midwives respect the dignity, culture, values and beliefs of each woman and her infant(s) in their care and the woman's partner and family, and of colleagues.
5 Midwives treat personal information obtained in a professional capacity as private and confidential.
6 Midwives provide impartial, honest and accurate information in relation to midwifery care and health care products. Midwives practise within a woman-centred framework.
7 Midwives focus on a woman's health needs, her expectations and aspirations, supporting the informed decision-making of each woman.
8 Midwives promote and preserve the trust and privilege inherent in the relationship between midwives and each woman and her infant(s).
9 Midwives maintain and build on the community's trust and confidence in the midwifery profession. Midwives practise midwifery reflectively and ethically.
10 Midwives practise midwifery reflectively and ethically.

Source: ANMC 2008a.

E   National Competency Standards for the Registered Nurse

The competencies which make up the ANMC *National competency standards for the registered nurse* are organised into domains:

- professional practice
- critical thinking and analysis
- provision and coordination of care
- collaborative and therapeutic practice.

Professional practice

This relates to the professional, legal and ethical responsibilities which require demonstration of a satisfactory knowledge base, accountability for practice, functioning in accordance with legislation affecting nursing and health care, and the protection of individual and group rights.

1.   Practises in accordance with legislation affecting nursing practice and health care

1.1   Complies with relevant legislation and common law
- Identifies legislation governing nursing practice
- Describes nursing practice within the requirements of common law
- Describes and adheres to legal requirements for medications
- Identifies legal implications of nursing interventions
- Actions demonstrate awareness of legal implications of nursing practice
- Identifies and explains effects of legislation on the care of individuals/ groups
- Identifies and explains effects of legislation in the area of health
- Identifies unprofessional practice as it relates to confidentiality and privacy legislation

1.2   Fulfils the duty of care
- Performs nursing interventions in accordance with recognised standards of practice
- Clarifies responsibility for aspects of care with other members of the health team
- Recognises the responsibility to prevent harm
- Performs nursing interventions following comprehensive and accurate assessments

1.3 Recognises and responds appropriately to unsafe or unprofessional practice
• Identifies interventions which prevent care being compromised and/or law contravened
• Identifies appropriate action to be taken in specified circumstances
• Identifies and explains alternative strategies for intervention and their likely outcomes
• Identifies behaviour that is detrimental to achieving optimal care
• Follows up incidents of unsafe practice to prevent re-occurrence

2. Practises within a professional and ethical nursing framework

2.1 Practises in accordance with the nursing profession's codes of ethics and conduct
• Accepts individuals/groups regardless of race, culture, religion, age, gender, sexual preferences, physical or mental state
• Ensures that personal values and attitudes are not imposed on others
• Conducts assessments that are sensitive to the needs of individuals/groups
• Recognises and accepts the rights of others
• Maintains an effective process of care when confronted by differing values, beliefs and biases
• Seeks assistance to resolve situations involving moral conflict
• Identifies and attempts to overcome factors which may constrain ethical decisions in consultation with the health team

2.2 Integrates organisational policies and guidelines with professional standards
• Maintains current knowledge of and incorporates relevant professional standards into practice
• Maintains and incorporates organisational policies and guidelines into practice
• Reviews and provides feedback on the relevance of organisational policies and professional standards procedures to practice
• Demonstrates awareness and understanding of developments in nursing that have an impact on the individual's capacity to practice nursing
• Considers individual health and wellbeing in relation to being fit for practice

2.3 Practises in a way that acknowledges the dignity, culture, values, beliefs and rights of individuals/groups
• Demonstrates respect for individual/group common and legal rights in relation to health care
• Identifies and adheres to strategies to promote and protect individual/ group rights

- Considers individual/group preferences when providing care
- Clarifies individual/group requests to change and/or refuse care with relevant members of the health care team
- Advocates for individuals/groups when rights are overlooked and/or compromised
- Accepts individuals/groups to whom care is provided regardless of race, religion, culture, age, gender, sexual preferences, physical or mental state
- Undertakes assessments that are sensitive to the needs of individuals/ groups
- Recognises and accepts the rights of others
- Maintains an effective process of care when confronted by differing values, beliefs and biases
- Provides appropriate information within the nurse's scope of practice to individuals/groups
- Questions and/or clarifies orders and decisions that are unclear, not understood or questionable
- Questions and/or clarifies interventions that appear inappropriate with relevant members of the health care team

2.4   Advocates for individuals/groups and their rights for nursing and health care within organisational and management structures

- Identifies when resources are insufficient to meet care needs of individuals/ groups
- Communicates skill mix requirements to meet care needs of individuals/ groups to management
- Protects the rights of individuals and groups and facilitates informed decisions
- Identifies and explains policies/practices which infringe on the rights of individuals or groups
- Clarifies policies, procedures, and guidelines when rights of individuals or groups are compromised
- Recommends changes to policies, procedures and guidelines when rights are compromised

2.5   Understands and practises within own scope of practice

- Seeks clarification when questions, directions and decisions are unclear or not understood
- Undertakes decisions about care that are within scope of competence without consulting senior staff
- Raises concerns about inappropriate delegation with the appropriate registered nurse
- Demonstrates accountability and responsibility for own actions within nursing practice

- Assesses consequences of various outcomes of decision making
- Consults relevant members of the health care team when required
- Questions and/or clarifies interventions which appear inappropriate with relevant members of the health care team

2.6 Integrates nursing and health care knowledge, skills and attitudes to provide safe and effective nursing care
- Maintains a current knowledge base
- Considers ethical responsibilities in all aspects of practice
- Ensures privacy and confidentiality when providing care
- Questions and/or clarifies interventions which appear inappropriate with relevant members of the health care team

2.7 Recognises the differences in accountability and responsibility between Registered Nurses, Enrolled Nurses and unlicensed care workers
- Understands requirements of statutory and professionally regulated practice
- Understands requirements for delegation and supervision of practice
- Raises concerns about inappropriate delegation with relevant organisational or regulatory personnel

Critical thinking and analysis

This relates to self-appraisal, professional development and the value of evidence and research for practice. Reflecting on practice feelings and beliefs and the consequences of these for individuals/groups is an important professional benchmark.

3. Practises within an evidence-based framework

3.1 Identifies the relevance of research to improving individual/group health outcomes
- Identifies problems/issues in nursing practice which may be investigated through research
- Considers potential for improvement in reviewing the outcomes of nursing activities and individual/group care
- Discusses implications of research with colleagues
- Participates in research
- Demonstrates awareness of research in own field of practice

3.2 Uses best available evidence, nursing expertise and respect for the values and beliefs of individuals/groups in the provision of nursing care
- Uses relevant literature and research findings to improve current practice
- Participates in review of policies, procedures and guidelines based on relevant research

- Identifies and disseminates relevant changes in practice or new information to colleagues
- Recognises that judgements and decisions are aspects of nursing care
- Recognises that nursing expertise varies with education, experience and context of practice

3.3 Demonstrates analytical skills in accessing and evaluating health information and research evidence
- Demonstrates understanding of the registered nurse role in contributing to nursing research
- Undertakes critical analysis of research findings in considering their application to practice
- Maintains accurate documentation of information which could be used in nursing research
- Clarifies when resources are not understood or their application questionable

3.4 Supports and contributes to nursing and health care research
- Participates in research
- Identifies problems suitable for research

3.5 Participates in quality improvement activities
- Recognises that quality improvement involves ongoing consideration, use and review of practice in relation to practical outcomes, standards and guidelines and new developments
- Seeks feedback from a wide range of sources to improve the quality of care
- Participates in case review studies
- Participates in clinical audits

4. Participates in ongoing professional development of self and others

4.1 Uses best available evidence, standards and guidelines to evaluate nursing performance
- Undertakes regular self-evaluation of own nursing practice
- Seeks and considers feedback from colleagues about, and critically reflects on, own nursing practice
- Participates actively in performance review processes

4.2 Participates in professional development to enhance nursing practice
- Reflects on own practice to identify professional development needs
- Seeks additional knowledge and/or information when presented with unfamiliar situations

- Seeks support from colleagues in identifying learning needs
- Participates actively in ongoing professional development
- Maintains records of involvement in professional development which includes both formal and informal activities

4.3 Contributes to the professional development of others
- Demonstrates an increasing responsibility to share knowledge with colleagues
- Supports health care students to meet their learning objectives in cooperation with other members of the health care team
- Facilitates mutual sharing of knowledge and experience with colleagues relating to individual/group/unit problems
- Contributes to orientation and ongoing education programs
- Acts as a role model to other members of the health care team
- Participates where possible in preceptorship, coaching and mentoring to assist and develop colleagues
- Participates where appropriate in teaching others including students of nursing and other health disciplines, and inexperienced nurses
- Contributes to formal and informal development

4.4 Uses appropriate strategies to manage own responses to the professional work environment
- Identifies and uses support networks
- Shares experiences related to professional issues mutually with colleagues
- Uses reflective practice to identify personal needs and seek appropriate support
- Provision and coordination of care
- This relates to the coordination, organisation and provision of nursing care that includes the assessment of individuals/groups, planning, implementation and evaluation of care.

5. Conducts a comprehensive and systematic nursing assessment

5.1 Uses a relevant evidence-based assessment framework to collect data about the physical, socio-cultural and mental health of the individual/group
- Approaches and organises assessment in a structured way
- Uses all available evidence sources, including individuals/groups/ significant others, health care teams, records, reports, and own knowledge and experience
- Collects data that relates to physiological, psychological, spiritual, socio-economic and cultural variables on an ongoing basis
- Understands the role of research-based, and other forms of evidence

- Confirms data with the individual/group and members of the health care team
- Frames questions in ways that indicate the use of a theoretical framework/ structured approach
- Ensures practice is sensitive and supportive to cultural issues

5.2   Uses a range of assessment techniques to collect relevant and accurate data
- Uses a range of data gathering techniques including observation, interview, physical examination and measurement in obtaining a nursing history and assessment
- Collaboratively identifies actual and potential health problems through accurate interpretation of data
- Accurately uses health care technologies in accordance with manufacturer's specifications and organisational policy
- Identifies deviations from normal or improvements in the individual's/ group's health status
- Identifies and incorporates the needs and preferences of individuals/ groups into a plan of care

5.3   Analyses and interprets assessment data accurately
- Recognises that clinical judgements involve consideration of conflicting information and evidence
- Identifies types and sources of supplementary information for nursing assessment
- Describes the role of supplementary information in nursing assessment
- Demonstrates knowledge of quantitative and qualitative data to assess individual/group needs

6. Plans nursing care in consultation with individuals / groups, significant others and the interdisciplinary health care team

6.1   Determines agreed priorities for resolving health needs of individuals/ groups
- Determines priorities for care based on nursing assessment of an individual's/group's needs for intervention, current nursing knowledge and research
- Considers individual/group performances when determining priorities of care

6.2   Identifies expected and agreed individual/group health outcomes including a timeframe for achievement
- Establishes realistic short- and long-term goals that identify individual/ group health outcomes and specify conditions for achievement

- Identifies goals that are measurable and achievable, and congruent with values and beliefs of the individual/group and/or significant other
- Uses resources to support the achievement of outcomes
- Identifies criteria for evaluation of expected outcomes

6.3   Documents a plan of care to achieve expected outcomes
- Ensures that plans of care are based on an ongoing analysis of assessment data
- Plans care that is consistent with current nursing knowledge and research
- Documents plans of care clearly

6.4   Plans for continuity of care to achieve expected outcomes
- Collaboratively supports the therapeutic interventions of other health care team members
- Information necessary for continuity of the plan of care is maintained and documented
- Responds to individual/group or carer's educational needs
- Provides or facilitates an individual/group or carer's resources and aids as required
- Identifies and recommends appropriate agency, government and community resources to ensure continuity of care
- Initiates necessary contacts and referrals to external agencies
- Forwards all information needed for continuity of care when an individual/ group is transferred to another facility or discharged

7. Provides comprehensive, safe and effective evidence-based nursing care to achieve identified individual/group health outcomes

7.1   Effectively manages the nursing care of individuals/groups
- Uses resources effectively and efficiently in providing care
- Performs actions in a manner consistent with relevant nursing principles
- Performs procedures confidently and safely
- Monitors responses of individuals/groups throughout each intervention and adjusts care accordingly
- Provides education and support to assist development and maintenance of independent living skills

7.2   Provides nursing care according to the documented care or treatment plan
- Acts consistently with the predetermined plan of care
- Uses a range of approved strategies to facilitate the individual/group's achievement of short and long term expected goals

7.3   Prioritises workload based on the individual's/group's needs, acuity and optimal time for intervention
- Determines priorities for care, based on nursing assessment of an individual's/group's needs for intervention, current nursing knowledge and research
- Considers the individual's/group's priorities for care

7.4   Responds effectively to unexpected or rapidly changing situations
- Responds effectively to emergencies
- Maintains self-control in the clinical setting and under stress conditions
- Implements crisis interventions and emergency routines as necessary
- Maintains current knowledge of emergency plans and procedures to maximise effectiveness in crisis situations
- Participates in emergency management practices and drills according to agency policy

7.5   Delegates aspects of care to others according to their competence and scope of practice
- Delegates aspects of care according to role, functions, capabilities and learning needs
- Monitors aspects of care delegated to others and provides clarification/ assistance as required
- Recognises own accountabilities and responsibilities when delegating aspects of care to others
- Delegates to and supervises others consistent with legislation and organisational policy

7.6   Provides effective and timely direction and supervision to ensure that delegated care is provided safely and accurately
- Supervises and evaluates nursing care provided by others
- Uses a range of direct and indirect techniques such as instructing, coaching, mentoring and collaborating in the supervision and support of others
- Provides support with documentation to nurses being supervised or to whom care has been delegated
- Delegates activities consistent with scope of practice/competence

7.7   Educates individuals/groups to promote independence and control their health
- Identifies and documents specific educational requirements and requests of individuals/groups
- Undertakes formal and informal education sessions with individuals/ groups as necessary
- Identifies appropriate educational resources, including other health professionals

8. **Evaluates progress towards expected individual/group health outcomes in consultation with individuals/groups, significant others and interdisciplinary health care team**

8.1 Determines progress of individuals/groups toward planned outcomes
- Recognises when individual's/group's progress and expected progress differ and modifies plans and actions accordingly
- Discusses progress with individual/group
- Evaluates individual/group responses to interventions
- Assesses the effectiveness of the plan in achieving planned outcomes

8.2 Revises the plan of care and determines further outcomes in accordance with evaluation data
- Revises expected outcomes, nursing interventions and priorities with any change in an individual's/group's condition, needs or situational variations
- Communicates new information and revisions to members of the health care team as required

Collaborative and therapeutic practice

This relates to establishing, sustaining and concluding professional relationships with individuals/groups. This also contains those competencies that relate to the nurse understanding their contribution to the interdisciplinary healthcare.

9. **Establishes, maintains and appropriately concludes therapeutic relationships**

9.1 Establishes therapeutic relationships that are goal directed and recognises professional boundaries
- Demonstrates empathy, trust and respect for the dignity and potential of the individual/group
- Interacts with individuals/groups in a supportive manner
- Effectively initiates, maintains and concludes interpersonal interactions
- Establishes rapport with individuals/groups that enhances their ability to express feelings and fosters an appropriate context for expression of feeling
- Understands the potential benefits of partnership approaches on nurse individual/group relationships
- Demonstrates an understanding of standards and practices of professional boundaries and therapeutic relationships

9.2 Communicates effectively with individuals/groups to facilitate provision of care
- Uses a range of effective communication techniques
- Uses language appropriate to context

- Uses written and spoken communication skills appropriate to the needs of individuals/groups
- Uses an interpreter where appropriate
- Provides adequate time for discussion
- Establishes where possible, alternative communication methods for individuals/groups who are unable to verbalise
- Uses open/closed questions appropriately

9.3 Uses appropriate strategies to promote an individual's/group's self-esteem, dignity, integrity and comfort
- Identifies and uses strategies which encourage independence
- Identifies and uses strategies which affirm individuality
- Uses strategies which involve the family/significant others in care
- Identifies and recommends appropriate support networks to individuals/groups
- Identifies situations which may threaten the dignity/integrity of an individual/group
- Implements measures to maintain dignity of individuals/groups during periods of self-care deficit
- Implements measures to support individuals/groups experiencing emotional distress
- Information is provided to individuals/groups to enhance their control over their own health care

9.4 Assists and supports individuals/groups to make informed health care decisions
- Facilitates and encourages individual/group decision-making
- Maintains and supports respect for an individual/group's decision through communication with other members of the interdisciplinary health care team
- Arranged consultation to support individuals/groups to make informed decisions regarding health care

9.5 Facilitates a physical, psychosocial, cultural and spiritual environment that promotes individual/group safety and security
- Demonstrates sensitivity, awareness and respect for cultural identity as part of an individual's/group's perceptions for security
- Demonstrates sensitivity, awareness and respect in regard to an individual's/group's spiritual needs
- Involves family and others in ensuring that cultural and spiritual needs are met
- Identifies, eliminates or prevents environmental hazards where possible
- Applies relevant principles to ensure the safe administration of therapeutic substances

- Maintains standards for infection control
- Applies ergonomic principles to prevent injury to individual/group and self
- Prioritises safety problems
- Adheres to occupational health and safety legislation
- Modifies environmental factors to meet an individual's/group's comfort needs where possible
- Promotes individual/group comfort throughout interventions
- Uses ergonomic principles and appropriate aids to promote the individual/group's comfort

10. Collaborates with interdisciplinary health care team to provide comprehensive nursing care

10.1 Recognises that the membership and roles of health care teams and service providers will vary depending on an individual's/group's needs and the health care setting

- Recognises the impact and role of population, primary health and partnership health care models
- Recognises when to negotiate with or refer to other health care or service providers
- Establishes positive and productive working relationships with colleagues
- Recognises and understands the separate and interdependent roles and functions of health care team members

10.2 Communicates nursing assessments and decisions to the interdisciplinary health care team and other relevant service providers

- Explains the nursing role to the interdisciplinary team and service providers
- Maintains confidentiality in discussions about an individual/group's needs and progress
- Discusses individual/group care requirements with relevant members of the health care team
- Collaborates with members of the health care team in decision making about care of individuals/groups
- Demonstrates skills in written, verbal and electronic communication
- Documents, as soon [as] possible, forms of communication, nursing interventions and individual/group responses

10.3 Facilitates coordination of care to achieve agreed health outcomes

- Adopts and implements a collaborative approach to practice
- Participates in health care team activities
- Demonstrates the necessary communication skills to manage avoidance, confusion and confrontation
- Demonstrates the necessary communication skills to enable negotiation

- Demonstrates an understanding of how collaboration has an impact on the safe and effective provision of comprehensive care
- Establishes and maintains effective and collaborative working relationships with other members of the health care team
- Consults with relevant health care professionals and service providers to facilitate continuity of care
- Recognises the contribution of, and liaises with, relevant community and support services
- Records information systematically in an accessible and retrievable form
- Ensures that written communication is comprehensive, logical, clear and concise, spelling is accurate and only acceptable abbreviations are used
- Establishes and maintains documentation according to organisational guidelines and procedures

10.4 Collaborates with the health care team to inform policy and guideline development
- Regularly consults policies and guidelines
- Demonstrates awareness of changes to policies and guidelines
- Attends meetings and participates in practice reviews and audits
- Demonstrates understanding of the implications of national health strategies for nursing and health care practice

Source: ANMC 2006.

F   Guidelines for Effective Documentation

- All entries should be accurate and factual.
- Make corrections as required under hospital policies—information should not be deleted.
- All information should be timely and relevant.
- All nursing actions need to be evaluated and outcomes documented.
- All identified patient problems, nursing actions taken and patient outcomes need to be noted.
- Do not describe patient problems without including the nursing actions taken and the patient responses.
- Be objective with charting. Document within the specific clinical and/or psycho-social parameters.
- It is important to chart non-actions, but do so within the context of the patient's clinical condition.
- All entries from health professionals should have their full name and designation clearly written.
- Follow through with pertinent details of who saw the patient and what interventions were initiated. Be especially mindful to note if you had to call the doctor; any interventions ordered; any nursing actions as a result of these orders; and what the patient response was.
- Notes need to be legible and clearly reflect the clinical condition of the patient.

G   Guidelines for Using Social Media

The government of South Australia (2010) has released guidelines and principles of engagement for using social media. While these guidelines and principles have been developed for government they can be applied to the healthcare sector and its employees. You should check with your state and territory government for similar guidelines.

As you know, information technology has changed the way we communicate and share information. However, the main point about the technologies described as 'social media' is that they can connect with large numbers of people easily (SA Government 2011).

There are risks associated with using social media and, in the context of healthcare, breaching patient confidentiality is a significant risk. As students and as future registered nurses and midwives you have a professional responsibility to maintain patient confidentiality, and breaches of this may result in disciplinary action by healthcare organisations and universities.

CAUTION WHEN USING SOCIAL MEDIA

- If it is online — it can be found.
- If you delete it — it still can be found
- Even if you secure it — it can still be accessed

(Tim Scully, Head of Cyber Security Operations Centre, Department of Defence, Commonwealth of Australia)

Guidelines for using social media

- Could what you are doing or posting harm the reputation of your organisation, other employees or your patients?
- Are you disclosing information you are not authorised to disclose?
- Have you made it clear your contribution is as a private citizen and not as an employee of the organisation?
- Are you willing to defend what you post to your manager and other key stakeholders? Would you be comfortable saying it to a stranger at a bus stop or posting it in a public place?
- Are you behaving with integrity, respect and accountability?
- Are you behaving within the framework of the ANMC code of ethics and conduct for registered nurses and midwives?

Source: Adapted from South Australian Government 2011.

H   Tips on Using Email Effectively at Work

Stop and think about what you want say, then write your email. Never write an email when you are angry, upset or in a negative frame of mind.

Include a descriptive subject line—let the reader know what the email is about. Make sure your email is easy to read—short paragraphs of no more than five sentences, and get to the point quickly.

Be precise, concise and clear.

Demonstrate 'netiquette': be professional and maintain appropriate online tone. Do not type in capitals, as this denotes yelling. Do not type in all lower case—instead observe the standard rules of English grammar and usage.

Be careful with attachments—open attachments only if you trust the source. Attachments can contain files with viruses that can contaminate your IT network.

Watch humour—use taste and discretion before sending any humorous emails.

Include a signature—your signature is the last thing the receiver will read.

Review your message before sending—remember emails are not confidential; do not send personal or sensitive emails. Always review and proof read your email before pressing the 'send' button.

Respond to email—make an effort to respond to emails within twenty-four hours or use the auto-reply function to let people know when you will respond.

Adapted from Zerwekh & Claborn 2009, pp. 250–1.

I Medical Calculation Test

Drug calculations

1   Digoxin **125 mcg** is ordered. Tablets available are **0.25 mg**. How many tablets should be given?

2   A patient is ordered Frusemide (Lasix) **60 mg,** orally. In the ward are **40 mg** tablets. How many tablets should be given?

3   A patient is ordered **750 mg of Erythromycin,** orally. Calculate the volume required if the suspension on hand has strength of **250 mg/5 ml.**

4   An injection of **Morphine 8 mg** is required. Ampoules on hand contain **10 mg in 1 ml.** What volume is drawn up for injection?

5   A patient is to receive an IV dose of **Gentamicin 160 mg.** Stock ampoules contain **100 mg in 2 ml.** Calculate the volume that is needed for the injection.

6   Heparin is available at strength of **5000 units/5 ml.** What volume is needed to **give 800 units?**

Intravenous infusions

Note: Giving set: 20 drops per ml.

Calculate mls per hour and drops per minute for the following:

1   A patient is to receive **one litre** of normal saline **over 8 hours.**

2   An anaemic patient must be given one unit of packed cells **over 4 hours.** The unit of packed cells **holds 250 mls.**

3   Vancromycin **500 mg** is ordered. Stock on hand contains **1 g in 10 ml,** once diluted. What volume is required? The required dose is added to **100 ml** normal saline in the burette and is to be infused **over one hour** as per protocol.

4   A postoperative patient has a patient controlled analgesia (PCA) running via a syringe pump. The syringe contains **600 mcg of Fentanly in 60 ml of Normal Saline.** The PCA has been programmed as per doctor's order, so that when the button is pressed the patient receives a **bolus dose of 1 ml.** What is the concentration **(mcg/ml)** of the solution in the syringe? How much Fentanly is in **each bolus dose?** If the patient has **6 × bolus doses** within an **hour,** how much fentanly has the patient received in **that hour?**

Source: Australian Registered Nurse Training Program, University of South Australia

J Medical Calculation Test Answers

The following pages show how medical calculations have been worked out using specific formulae. These formulae are from the School of Nursing and Midwifery at Flinders University, South Australia, and can be accessed at: **<http://nursing.flinders.edu.au/students/studyaids/drugcalculations/page.php?id=6>**.

You may also find it useful to purchase the following applications (apps) for iPads or iPhones

- Adult Drug Calculations: **<http://itunes.apple.com/us/app/adult-drug-calculations/id426915918?mt=8>**
- Epocrates:**<http://itunes.apple.com/app/epocrates/id281935788?mt=8**
- MedCalc: **<http://itunes.apple.com/app/medcalc-medical-calculator/id299470331?mt=8>**

MEDICATION ORDER	WARD STOCK	CALCULATE DOSE TO BE ADMINISTERED

MEDICATION ORDER

Start Date 18/06/13	Medication (use Generic Name) Print TOBRAMYCIN	
	Dose 120 mg	Frequency BD
Prescriber Signature David Dimer	Print Name D. DIMER	Pager No. 73293

WARD STOCK: 80 mg in 2 ml

CALCULATE DOSE TO BE ADMINISTERED

$$\frac{\text{Dose to be given} \times \text{Stock volume}}{\text{Stock Strength} \times 1}$$

= Amount of solution given

$$\frac{120 \times 2}{80 \times 1} = 3 \text{ mls}$$

Start Date 18/06/13	Medication (use Generic Name) Print PREDNISOLONE	
Route PO	Dose 30 mg	Frequency MANE
Prescriber Signature David Dimer	Print Name D. DIMER	Pager No. 73293

WARD STOCK: 10 mg tablets

CALCULATE DOSE TO BE ADMINISTERED

$$\frac{\text{Dose to be given}}{\text{Stock strength}} = \text{no. of tablets to be given}$$

$$\frac{30 \text{ mg}}{10 \text{ mg}} = 3 \text{ tablets}$$

Start Date 18/06/13	Medication (use Generic Name) Print GLIBLENCLAMIDE	
Route PO	Dose 7.5 mg	Frequency MANE
Prescriber Signature David Dimer	Print Name D. DIMER	Pager No. 73293

WARD STOCK: 5 mg tablets

CALCULATE DOSE TO BE ADMINISTERED

$$\frac{\text{Dose to be given}}{\text{Stock strength}} = \text{Number of tablets to be given}$$

$$\frac{7.5 \text{ mg}}{5 \text{ mg}} = 1.5 \text{ tablets}$$

| | MEDICATION ORDER | WARD STOCK | CALCULATE DOSE TO BE ADMINISTERED |

MEDICATION ORDER

Start Date 18/06/13	Medication (use Generic Name) Print ADRENALINE HCl		
Route IV	Dose 500 mcg	Frequency PRN	
Prescriber Signature David Dimer	Print Name D. DIMER	Pager No. 73293	

WARD STOCK

1 mg/ml ampoules

CALCULATE DOSE TO BE ADMINISTERED

$$\frac{\text{Dose to be given} \times 1}{\text{Stock Strength} \times 1} = \frac{\text{Amount of solution}}{\text{to be given}}$$

$$\frac{500 \text{ mcg} \times 1}{1000 \text{ mcg} \times 1} = 0.5 \text{ mls}$$

Start Date 18/06/13	Medication (use Generic Name) Print ATROPINE SULPHATE		
Route IM	Dose 300 mcg	Frequency PRN	
Prescriber Signature David Dimer	Print Name D. DIMER	Pager No. 73293	

0.4 mg/ml ampoules

$$\frac{\text{Dose to be given} \times 1}{\text{Stock Strength} \times 1} = \frac{\text{Amount to be}}{\text{given}}$$

$$\frac{300 \text{ mcg} \times 1}{400 \text{ mcgs} \times 1} = 0.75 \text{ mls}$$

Start Date 18/06/13	Medication (use Generic Name) Print DIGOXIN		
Route Oral	Dose 125 mcg	Frequency MANE	
Prescriber Signature David Dimer	Print Name D. DIMER	Pager No. 73293	

62.5 mcg tablets

250 mcg tablets

$$\frac{\text{Dose to be given}}{\text{Stock strength}} = \frac{\text{Number of tablets}}{\text{to be given}}$$

$$\frac{125 \text{ mcg}}{62.5 \text{ mcgs}} = 2 \text{ tablets (should use this)}$$

$$\frac{125 \text{ mcgs}}{62.5 \text{ mcgs}} = \frac{1}{2} \text{ tablet}$$

DATE	FLUID TYPE	VOLUME	DURATION	ADDITIVES	PRESCRIBER	CALCULATE MLS/HR & DROPS/MINUTE
	One fluid/pack per line — maximum order 24 hours	Total volume and time or mls/hour		Drugs to be added to flask before commencement	Signature, Printed Name, Pager No.	Giving set administers 20 drops/ml
18/06/13	0.9% NaCl	1000 mls	8/24		David Dimer D. DIMER 73293	$\dfrac{\text{Total volume to be given}}{\text{Time in hours}}$ $\dfrac{1000 \text{ mls}}{8 \text{ hours}} =$ $\dfrac{\text{Total volume (mls)} \times \text{drop factor}}{\text{Time in minutes} \times 1}$ $\dfrac{1000 \times 20}{480 \text{ minutes} \times 1}$ Answers: 125____ mls/hr 41___ dpm
18/06/13	5% Dextrose	500 mls	6/24		David Dimer D. DIMER 73293	$\dfrac{\text{Total volume to be given}}{\text{Time in Hours}}$ $\dfrac{500 \text{ mls}}{6 \text{ hours}}$ $\dfrac{\text{Total volume to be given} \times \text{drop factor}}{\text{Time in minutes}}$ $\dfrac{500 \times 20}{360 \text{ minutes}}$ Answers: 83____ mls/hr 28___ dpm

| 18/06/13 | 0.9% N/Saline | 1 L | 10/24 | 2 gms KCl stock = 1 g/10 ml | David Dimer D. DIMER 73293 | |
| 18/06/13 | RBC | 1 unit | 3/24 | | David Dimer D. DIMER 73293 | |

$$\frac{\text{Total volume to be given}}{\text{Time in hours}}$$

$$\frac{1000 \text{ mls}}{10 \text{ hours}}$$

$$\frac{\text{Total volume to be given} \times \text{drop factor}}{\text{Time (minutes)}}$$

$$\frac{1000 \times 20}{600 \text{ minutes}}$$

Answers: 100 _____ mls/hr
33 _____ dpm

$$\frac{\text{Total volume to be given}}{\text{Time}}$$

$$\frac{395 \text{ mls}}{3}$$

$$\frac{\text{Total volume to be given} \times \text{drop factor}}{\text{Time (minutes)}}$$

$$\frac{395 \times 20}{180 \text{ minutes}}$$

Answers: 132 _____ mls/hr
44 _____ dpm

RED BLOOD CELLS

395 mls

Exp: SEP 13

0.9% SODIUM CHLORIDE +
2 gms POTASSIUM CHLORIDE

1000 mls

Exp: SEP 13

5% DEXTROSE

500 mls

Exp: SEP 13

0.9% SODIUM CHLORIDE

1000 mls

Exp: SEP 13

Glossary

Accountability

being answerable/accounting for one's actions.

Accreditation

status conferred on a healthcare organisation when they have been assessed as meeting specific clinical and non-clinical standards.

Adaptation

modifying or altering one's physical/psychological state to accommodate changing conditions.

Advance directives

instructions that consent to or refuse medical interventions in the future.

Advanced life support

the preservation or restoration of life by establishing and maintaining airway breathing and circulation using defibrillation, advanced airway management, intravenous access and drug therapy.

Adverse event

an incident in which harm has occurred to a person either a staff member, member of the public or patient.

AIMS reporting

Advanced Incident Management reporting system is a voluntary reporting of incidents that have occurred in the workplace.

Autonomy

the right to self-determination and, from the patient perspective, the right of individuals to make choices about treatment without interference from external parties, including healthcare teams, even when those choices differ from that of health professionals.

Basic life support

the preservation of life by the initial establishment and maintenance of airway, circulation and related emergency care including the use of an automated external defibrillator.

Belongingness

the socialisation process an individual goes through to become a member of a new group.

Beneficence

the principle of doing good. Nurses work for the benefit of others.

Bioethics

a multidisciplinary approach for critically examining ethical nursing and healthcare issues from different moral or theoretical perspectives concerning life.

Bullying

antisocial behaviours expressed as intimidation, verbal abuse, rudeness, threatening and embarrassing others.

Clinician

a healthcare provider, educated as a health professional and registered with the Australian Health Practitioners Regulatory Agency providing direct clinical care.

Clinical governance

a system of accountability by which healthcare organisations demonstrate accountability for the provision of safe, quality care and services.

Clinical handover

the transfer of professional responsibility and accountability for some or all aspects of care for a patient or group of patients.

Clinical judgment

the use of expert clinical knowledge to make clinical decisions for patients.

Clinical leadership

demonstrating continued clinical competence in the practice setting.

Clinical nurse specialist

an experienced registered nurse working in a specialised clinical role.

Clinical placement

a place for students to work under supervision during their undergraduate program.

Clinical reasoning

the process used by nurses to collect cues from patients and use this information to develop and implement a plan a of care that addresses the current clinical problem(s) or situation and then evaluate the outcomes of a particular intervention or interventions.

Communities of practice

groups of people such as nurses and colleagues from other professions who share a concern for something they all do, and a desire to learn how to do it better as they interact with others.

Competence

the combination of knowledge, skills, abilities, attitudes and values used by professional nurses to provide quality care to patients.

Continuing professional development

> refers to how members of a profession improve and broaden their knowledge, expertise and competence to maintain continuing professional registration.

Continuous quality improvement

> a systematic method for continually improving care and services.

Critical incidents

> unintended actions by health professionals, including nurses, that may result in harm to patients, staff, volunteers or visitors.

Critical thinking

> complex thinking patterns that examine situations in terms of context and content. Critical thinkers also anticipate the consequences of decision-making.

Cultural competence

> integrates cultural sensitivity, cultural knowledge and cultural awareness.

Cultural sensitivity

> the affective aspects of being respectful towards other persons' cultures.

Cultural safety

> includes the principles of participation, partnership and protection to provide culturally sensitive health/nursing care.

Curriculum vitae

> a document that details employment history.

Decision-making

> the process of considering several options and choosing the best one.

Delegation

> the transfer of authority to another individual to perform a task or procedure.

Employee Assistance Program

> an outside counselling service retained by the healthcare service to provide confidential counselling services to staff.

Emotional intelligence

> has the following elements: self-awareness, empathy, social awareness, developing relationships with others.

Ethics

> rules or principles that determine which human actions are right or wrong.

Evidence-based nursing

> the application of relevant, valid research-derived outcomes to clinical decision-making.

Experiential learning

> acquiring knowledge from experiences, e.g. the knowledge acquired during clinical placement.

Fidelity

keeping information patient information confidential and acting to maintain patient privacy and trust.

Fitness

moral and legal fitness to work as a registered nurse.

Governance

the set of relationships developed and maintained by a healthcare organisation between its executive, workforce and consumers. Governance specified the mechanisms for monitoring, evaluating and correcting (where necessary) all aspects of organisational performance.

Guidelines

clinical practice guidelines; evidence-based statements developed to support clinical decision-making.

Hand hygiene

a term referring to any action relating to hand cleansing.

Harassment

pestering, annoying, disturbing nuisance behaviours that are usually gender-related.

Healthcare workforce

the nursing, medical and allied health staff who provide healthcare to patients and students who provide care under supervision.

Horizontal violence

antisocial behaviours between members of the same profession where one member(s) bullies another.

Hospital error

errors that occur to a patient during an episode of care while in hospital.

Information management

the collection, analysis of patient-related information by health professionals to plan and provide care and services to patients.

Infection control

actions taken to prevent the spread of pathogens between people in a healthcare setting.

Information systems

the software and hardware used by a healthcare organisation to communicate and record details of activities related to patient care.

Interprofessional conflict

conflicts which occur between members of different health professions.

Intraprofessional conflict

conflicts which occur between members of the same profession.

Justice

justice in healthcare has two meanings. The first is related to fairness and the second is about the equitable distribution of resources. The principle of justice is about treating all patients fairly in relation to access to scarce resources.

Key Performance Indicators

specific measures used in healthcare organisations to measure clinical and non-clinical performance.

Lifelong learning

continual learning in pursuit of personal development and excellence in professional practice.

Multigenerational workforce

a workforce comprising personnel of different years of experience and different values and attitudes.

Non-maleficence

the principle of doing no harm. Nurses have a professional responsibility to do no harm to patients.

Nurse academic

a registered nurse who chooses to work in a university or other such institution.

Nurse manager

an experienced registered nurse who manages the delivery of patient care services.

Orientation

a formal process for training and informing a new staff member entering an organisation. The orientation process covers all processes, procedures and policies of the organisation.

Patient

a person receiving healthcare.

Patient-centred care

the health/nursing care provided to patients that is responsive to the needs and preferences of individual patients.

Policy

a set of principles that reflect the healthcare organisation's mission and strategic direction.

Protocol

an established set of rules used to inform clinical and non-clinical practice.

Preceptorship

the pairing of a new registered nurse with a more experienced nurse for a specific period of time focusing on policies, procedures and competency development within a clinical area. Preceptors act as role models for the new registered nurse.

Professional boundaries

in nursing and healthcare these were clearly defined by profession. Professional boundaries also define the relationship between health professional (nurse) and patient.

Professional portfolio

a record of evidence detailing your competency to practise as a registered nurse/midwife. The professional portfolio can be commenced during the undergraduate program.

Quality management

a program implemented in a healthcare organisation to monitor the effectiveness of activities from the patient perspective.

Recency of practice

the length of time away from nursing practice.

Reconnaissance

self-appraisal of knowledge, skills and competencies.

Regulation

nurses and midwives must be registered with the Nursing and Midwifery Board Australia and meet the Board's registration standards before they can practise.

Risk

the chance or possibility of an event occurring that will have a negative outcome.

Risk management

a program developed to identify, minimise and/or avoid risks to patients, staff, volunteers, visitors and the organisation.

Root cause analysis

the process used for investigating unintended consequences of healthcare professionals actions while providing care to patients.

Sentinel events

the unintended consequence of health professional activities that can result in serious or fatal injury to patient(s).

SMARTTA

an acronym that describes the specific, measurable, achievable, relevant, time framed, trackable and agreed objectives.

SWOT analysis

an acronym (strengths, weaknesses, opportunities & threats) that describes a management tool that can be used for considering the pros and cons of a situation.

Therapeutic relationship

the relationship that is established between a health professional (nurse) and patient during an episode of care.

Time management

organising and prioritising workloads within the time available.

Transition

the changes that occur over a period of time as individuals change from one state to another.

Veracity

the duty to tell the truth.

Whistleblowing

in healthcare the disclosure of unprofessional, unsafe and corrupt practices by health professionals to a more senior staff member and/or the media.

Work–life balance

the balance between work and personal life.

Bibliography

Alfaro-Lefevre, A (2004) *Critical thinking and clinical judgement*, 3rd edn, Elsevier Science, USA.

Alsup, S, Emerson, L, Lindell, A, Bechtle, M, & Whitmer, K, (2006) Nursing Cooperative Partnership: A recruitment benefit, *Journal of Nursing Administration*, vol. 36, no. 4, pp. 163–6.

Andre, K & Heartfield, M (2007) *Professional portfolios: Evidence of competency for nurses and midwives*, Elsevier, Australia.

ANMC *see* Australian Nursing and Midwifery Council.

Australian Commission on Safety and Quality in Healthcare (2009) *National hand hygiene program aims to halve hospital superbug infections*, media release 5 May, <www.safetyandquality.gov.au/internet/safety/publishing.nsf/Content/E523D A01FF0E5A51CA2575AC007E5A69/$File/NatHHInitLaunch-2009-05-05. pdf>, accessed 6 October 2011.

Australian Commission on Safety and Quality in Healthcare (2010) *Medication safety*, Issue 4, August, <www.safetyandquality.gov.au/internet/safety/publishing.nsf/ Content/com-pubs_NIMC-34210-MedSafetyUpdateAug2010>, accessed 26 September 2011.

Australian Council on Healthcare Standards (2006) *EQuIP standards*, 4th edn, <www.achs.org.au/EQUIP4/>, accessed 13 September 2011.

Australian Health Practitioner Regulation Agency (2010) <www.ahpra.gov.au/ Complaints-and-Outcomes/Conduct-Health-and-Performance/Conduct. aspx>.

Australian Institute of Health & Welfare (2009) *Nursing and midwifery labour force 2007*, AGPS Canberra, cat. no. HWL 44, <www.aihw.gov.au/publications/ index.cfm/title/10724>, accessed 14 June 2010.

Australian Nursing and Midwifery Council (2006) *National competency standards for the registered nurse*, 4th edn, Australian Nursing and Midwifery Council, Canberra, <www.anmc.org.au/userfiles/file/competency_standards/ Competency_standards_RN.pdf >, accessed 13 September 2011.

Australian Nursing and Midwifery Council (2007) *Midwifery practice decisions summary guide*, <www.anmc.org.au/userfiles/file/DMF%20A4%20 Midwifery%20Summary%20Guide%20Final%20%202010.pdf>, accessed 13 September 2011.

Australian Nursing and Midwifery Council (2007) *A national framework for decision making by nurses and midwives on scopes of practice (National DMF)*, Australian Government Department of Health and Ageing, Canberra, <www. acnc.net.au/upload/File/DMF%20-Newsletter%20article%20V3.1%20 with%20backgroundpdf.pdf>.

Australian Nursing and Midwifery Council (2008a) *Code of professional conduct for midwives in Australia*, Australian Nursing and Midwifery Council, Canberra, <www.nursingmidwiferyboard.gov.au/Codes-Guidelines-Statements/Codes-Guidelines.aspx#codesofprofessionalconduct>, accessed 26 September 2011.

Australian Nursing and Midwifery Council (2008b) *Code of professional conduct for nurses in Australia*, Australian Nursing and Midwifery Council, Canberra, <www.nursingmidwiferyboard.gov.au/Codes-Guidelines-Statements/Codes-Guidelines.aspx#codesofprofessionalconduct>, accessed 26 September 2011.

Australian Nursing and Midwifery Council (2009) *Continuing competence framework*, Australian Nursing and Midwifery Council, Canberra, <www. anmc.org.au/userfiles/file/research_and_policy/continuing_competencies/ Continuing%20Competence%20Framework%20-%20Jan%202009%20 Final%20Doc%20for%20web.pdf>, accessed 26 September 2011.

Australian Nursing and Midwifery Council (2010) *A midwife's guide to professional boundaries*, Australian Nursing and Midwifery Council, Canberra, <www.nursingmidwiferyboard.gov.au/Search.aspx?q=guide%20to%20 professional%20relationships>, accessed 12 October 2011.

Australian Nursing and Midwifery Council & Australian College of Midwives (2006) *National competency standards for the midwife*, January 2006, Australian Nursing and Midwifery Council, Canberra, <www.anmc.org.au/userfiles/ file/competency_standards/Competency%20standards%20for%20the%20 Midwife.pdf>, accessed 1 October 2011.

Australian Nursing & Midwifery Council, Australian College of Midwives & Australian Nursing Federation (2008), *Code of ethics for midwives in Australia*, Australian Nursing and Midwifery Council, Canberra, <www.anmac.org. au/userfiles/file/New%20Code%20of%20Ethics%20fo%20rMidwives%20 August%202008.pdf >, accessed 26 September 2011.

Australian Nursing and Midwifery Council & Nursing Council of New Zealand (2010) *A nurse's guide to professional boundaries*, February 2010, Australian Nursing and Midwifery Council, Canberra, <www.anmc.org.au/userfiles/ file/PB%20for%20Nurses%20-%20Final%20for%20web%20+PPF%20 Watermark%20-%20%20March%202010.pdf>, accessed 13 September 2011.

Australian Nursing and Midwifery Council, Royal College of Nursing, Australia & Australian Nursing Federation (2008) *Code of ethics for nurses in Australia*, Australian Nursing and Midwifery Council, Canberra, <www. nursingmidwiferyboard.gov.au/Codes-Guidelines-Statements/Codes-Guidelines.aspx#codeofethics>, accessed 26 September 2011.

Baker, GR, Norton, PG, Flintoft, V, Blais, R, Brown, A, Cox, J, Etchells, E, Ghali, W, Hebert, P, Majudar, S, O'Beirne, M, Palacios-Derflingher, L, Reid, R, Sheps, S & Tamblyn, R (2004) 'The Canadian adverse events study: The incidence of adverse events among hospital patients in Canada', *Canadian Medical Association Journal*, vol. 170, pp. 1678–86.

Balding, C & Maddock, A (2006). *South Australian Safety and quality framework & strategy 2007–2011*, project report and supporting documents, Government of South Australia, Department of Health.

Barr, H (1998) 'Competent to collaborate: Towards a competency based model for interprofessional education', *Journal of Interprofessional Care*, vol. 12, no. 2, pp. 181–7.

Bashur, RL, Reardon, TG & Shannon, GW (2000) 'Telemedicine—a new healthcare delivery system', *Annual Review of Public Health*, vol. 21, pp. 613–37.

Becker, G (1997) *Disrupted lives: How people create meaning in a chaotic world*, University of California Press, Berkeley.

Benner, P (2001) *From novice to expert: Excellence and power in clinical nursing practice*, Prentice-Hall, Upper Saddle River, NJ.

Berger, AM & Hobbs, BB (2005) 'Impact of shift work on the health and safety of nurses and patients', *Clinical Journal of Oncology Nursing*, vol. 10, no. 4, pp. 465–71.

Berglund, CA (2007) *Ethics for health care*, 3rd edn, Oxford University Press, Melbourne.

Berwick, D (2009) 'What "patient-centred" should mean: Confessions from an extremist' *Health Affairs*, vol. 28, no. 11. pp. w555–65.

Black, B P. (2011) Critical thinking, the nursing process and clinical judgement. In Chitty, KK, Black, BP. *Professional nursing, concepts and challenges*. Saunders Elsevier, MI, Chapter 8.

Blaxter, M (2010) *Health*, 2nd edn, Polity Press, UK.

Boyce RA, Moran MC, Nissen, LM, Chenery, HJ & Brooks, PM (2009) 'Interprofessional education in health sciences, University of Queensland Healthcare Team Challenge' *Medical Journal of* Australia, vol. 190, no. 8, pp. 433–6.

Boychuk, JE & Cowin, LS (2004a) 'The experience of marginalization in new nursing graduates', *Nursing Outlook*, vol. 52, pp. 289–96.

Boychuk, JE & Cowin, LS (2004b) 'Multigenerational nurses in the workplace', *Journal of Nursing Administration*, vol. 34, pp. 403–501.

Bradbury-Jones, C, Hughes, SM, Murphy, W, Parry, L, & Sutton, J (2009) A new way of reflecting in nursing: The Peshkin approach *Journal of Advanced Nursing*, vol. 65, no. 11, pp. 2485–2493.

Bridges, W (2004) *Transitions: Making sense of life's changes*, Da Capo Press, Cambridge, MA.

Bryant, R (2001) 'The regulation of nursing in Australia: A comparative analysis', *Journal of Law and Medicine*, vol. 9, August, pp. 41–55.

Burt, RS (1999) 'The social capital of opinion leaders', *The Annals*, American Academy of Political and *Social Science*, vol. 566, pp. 37–54.

Canadian Patient Safety Institute (2011) *About patient safety*, <www.patient-safetyinstitute.ca/patientsafety/about.html>.

Carryer, JB, Diers, AD, Mccloskey, B & Wilson, D (2011) 'Effects of health policy reforms on nursing resources and patient outcomes in New Zealand', *Policy, politics and nursing practice*, vol. 11, no. 4, pp. 275–85.

Carver, L & Candela, L (2008) 'Attaining organizational commitment across different generations of nurses', *Journal of Nursing Management*, vol. 16, pp. 984–91.

Caulfield, H, Gough, P & Osbourne. R (1998) 'Putting you in the picture', *Nursing Standard*, vol. 12, no. 19, pp. 22–4.

Chang, E, Daly, J, Hancock, K, Bidewell, JW, Johnson, A, Lambert, VA & Lambert, CE (2006). 'The relationships among workplace stressors, coping methods, demographic characteristics, and health in Australian nurses', *Journal of Professional Nursing*, vol. 22, no. 1, pp. 30–8.

Chiarella, M (2001) 'National review of nursing education: Selected review of nurse regulation', revised 2003, Commonwealth Department of Education, Science and Training, Canberra.

Clyne, M (1994) *Inter-cultural communication at work; Cultural values in discourse*, Cambridge University Press, Cambridge, UK.

Commonwealth of Australia (2008) *Australian Charter of Healthcare Rights*, Australian Government, Canberra, <www.safetyandquality.gov.au/internet/safety/publishing.nsf/Content/com-pubs_ACHR-pdf-01-con/$File/17537-charter.pdf>, accessed 1 October 2011.

Council of Australian Governments (2009) *National healthcare agreement*, Australian Government, Canberra.

Cullum, N (2008) 'Users' guide to the nursing literature: An introduction' in N Cullum, D Ciliska, RB Haynes & S Marks (eds) *Evidence- based nursing*, Blackwell Publishing, BMJ Journals, RCN Publishing Company, UK, pp. 101–3.

Cullum, N, Ciliska, D, Marks, S & Haynes, B (2008) 'An introduction to evidence based nursing' in N Cullum, D Cliliska, RB Haynes & S Marks (eds) *Evidence-based nursing: An introduction*, Blackwell Publishing; BMJ Publishing Group, RCN Publishing Company, and American College of Physicians ('ACP') Journal Club, UK.

Cutcliffe, JR & Weick, KL (2008) 'Salvation of damnation: Deconstructing nursing's aspirations to professional status', *Journal of Nursing Management*. vol. 16, no. 5, pp. 499–507.

Davidson, P, Simon, A, Woods, P, Griffith, RW (2009) *Management*, 2nd Australasian edn, John Wiley & Sons, Australia.

Department of Education, Science and Training (2002) *National review of nursing education,* Nursing Education Review Secretariat, Canberra, DEST No. 6880 HERC02A.

Department of Health and Ageing (2010), *Corporate plan 2010–2013,* Performance Section, Portfolio Strategies Division, Canberra, <www.health.gov.au/internet/main/publishing.nsf/Content/9F083DC3BBA88FA2CA2577F900124CA2/$File/505-Corporate%20Plan%20H&A_concept04v9_12.1.11_Pages_150ppi.pdf>, accessed 6 October 2011.

Department of Health and Ageing & National Health and Medical Research Council (2008) *Australian immunisation handbook,* ninth edition, Australian Government, Canberra, <www.health.gov.au/internet/immunise/publishing.nsf/content/handbook-home>, accessed 1 October 2011.

Derungs, IMH (2011) *Trans-cultural leadership for transformation.* Palgrave Macmillan, UK.

Duchscher, JEB (2008) 'A process of becoming: The stages of new nursing graduate professional role transition', *The Journal of Continuing Education in Nursing,* vol. 39, no. 10, pp. 441–51.

Duchscher, JEB (2009) 'Transition shock: The initial stage of role adaptation for newly graduated registered nurses', *Journal of Advanced Nursing,* vol. 65, pp. 1103–13.

Duchscher, JEB & Cowin, L (2004) 'Multigenerational nurses in the workplace', *Journal of Nursing Administration,* vol. 34, no. 11, pp. 493–501.

Duchscher, JEB & Myrick, F (2008), 'The prevailing winds of oppression: Understanding the new graduate experience in acute care, *Nursing Forum,* vol. 43, no.4, pp. 191–206.

Duckett, S & Willcox, S (2011) *The Australian health care system,* 4th edn, Oxford University Press, Melbourne.

Dwyer, J & Hopwood, N (2010), *Management strategies and skills,* McGraw-Hill, Australia.

Eckermann, AK, Dowd, T, Chong, E, Nixon, L, Gray, R & Johnson, S (2010) *Binan Goonj: Bridging cultures in Aboriginal health,* Elsevier, Australia.

Edwards, SD (2009) *Nursing ethics: a principle based approach,* Palgrave Macmillan, Basingstoke, UK.

Elliott M (2002) 'The clinical environment: A source of stress for undergraduate nurses', *Australian Journal of Advanced Nursing,* vol. 20, no. 1, pp. 34–8.

Ellis, JR & Hartley, CL (2009) *Nursing in today's world,* 9th edn, Wolters Kluwer/ Lippincott Williams & Wilkins, Philadelphia.

Ernstmann, N, Ommen, O, Driller, E, Kowalski C, Neumann, N & Bartholomeyczik, S (2009). 'Social capital and risk management in nursing', *Journal of Nursing Care Quality,* vol. 24, no. 4, pp. 340–7.

Etheridge, SA (2007) 'Learning to think like a nurse: Stories from new nurse graduates'. *The Journal of Continuing Education,* vol. 38, no. 1, pp. 24–30.

Fedoruk, M (2012) 'Safety' in *Kozier & Erb's Fundamentals of nursing*, 1st Australasian edn, Pearson Publishing Australia.

Ferguson, L, Calvert, J, Davie, M, Fred, N, Gerbach, V & Sinclair, L (2007) 'Clinical leadership: using observations of care to focus risk management and quality improvement activities in the clinical setting', *Contemporary Nurse*, vol. 24, no. 2, pp. 212–24.

Firtko, A & Jackson, D (2005) 'Do the ends justify the means? Nursing and the dilemma of whistleblowing,' *Australian Journal of Advanced Nursing*, vol. 23, no. 1, pp. 51–6.

Forrester, K (2008) 'Nursing in the aged care sector: Resident abuse and the reporting obligations,' *Journal of Law and Medicine*, vol. 16, pp. 216–19.

French, B (2005) 'Evidence-based practice and the management of risk in nursing', *Health, Risk & Society*, vol. 7, no. 2, pp. 177–92.

Gaffney, T (1999) *The regulatory dilemma surrounding interstate practice*, <www.nursingworld.org/ojin/topic9/topic91.htm>, accessed 29 January 2002.

Goleman, D (2005) *Emotional intelligence*, Bantam Books, New York.

Gorton, M (2010) Mandatory Reporting client bulletin. Russell Kennedy, Kennedy Strang, Legal Group, Melbourne.

Greenwood, J (2000) 'Critique of the graduate nurse: an international perspective', *Nurse Education Today*, vol. 20, pp. 17–23.

Grootaert, C, Narayan, D, Nyhan Jones, V & Woolcock, M (2004) *Measuring social capital: An integrated questionnaire*, World Bank working paper no. 18. Washington, DC.

Hand Hygiene Australia (2011) *The National Hand Hygiene Initiative*, <www.hha.org.au>, accessed 11 October 2011.

Hegney, D, Eley, R, Plank, A, Buikstra, E & Parker, V (2006) 'Workplace violence in Queensland, Australia: The results of a comparative study,' *International Journal of Nursing Practice*, vol. 12, pp. 220–31.

Henderson, V (1966) *The nature of nursing: A definition and its implications for practice, research and education*, Macmillan, New York.

Hofmeyer, A & Marck, PB (2008) 'Building social capital in healthcare organizations: Thinking ecologically for safer care,' *Nursing Outlook*, vol. 56, pp. 145–51.

Homer, C. S. E., Griffiths, M., Ellwood, D., Kildea, S., Brodie, P. M., Curtin, A. (2010). *Core competencies and educational framework for primary maternity services in Australia. Final report.* Centre for Midwifery, Child and Family Health, University of Technology, Sydney.

Hu, J, Herrick, C & Hodgin, K (2004). 'Managing the multigenerational nursing team', *The Healthcare Manager*, vol. 23, no. 4, pp. 334–40.

Hunt, EF & Colander, DC (1984) *Social science: An introduction to the study of society*, Macmillan, New York.

Hutchinson, M, Jackson, D, Wilkes, L & Vickers, M (2010), 'A new model of bullying in the nursing workplace', *Advances in Nursing Science*, vol. 32, no. 2, pp. E60–71.

International Council of Nurses (1997) *ICN on regulation: Towards 21st century models*, International Council of Nurses, Geneva.

International Council of Nurses (2001) *Position statement: Ethical nurse recruitment.*

International Council of Nurses (2006) *The ICN code of ethics for nurses*, International Council of Nurses, Geneva, <www.icn.ch/images/stories/documents/about/icncode_english.pdf>, accessed 26 September 2011.

Jacobson GA (2002) 'Maintaining professional boundaries: Preparing student nurses for the challenge', *Journal of Nursing Education*, vol. 41, no. 6, pp. 279–82.

Johnson, SL (2009) 'International perspectives on workplace bullying among nurses: A review. *International Nursing Review*, vol. 56, no. 4, pp. 34–40.

Johnstone, M-J & Kanitsaki, O (2006) 'Culture, language, and patient safety: Making the link', *International Journal for Quality in Healthcare*, vol. 18, no. 5, pp. 383–8.

Johnstone, M-J & Kanitsaki, O (2007) 'An exploration of the notion and nature of the construct of cultural safety and its applicability to the Australian healthcare context,' *Journal of Transcultural Nursing*, vol. 18, pp. 247–54.

Kane, R L, Shamliyan, T, Mueller, C, Duval, S & Wilt, T J (2007) The Association of Registered Nurse Staffing Levels and Partient Outcomes. *Medical Care.* vol. 45, no. 12, pp. 1195–204.

King, S & Ogle, K (2010) 'Shaping an Australian nursing and midwifery framework for workforce regulation: Criteria development', *The International Journal of Health Planning and Management*, vol. 25, no. 4, pp. 330–40.

Kralik, D & van Loon, A (2008) 'Community nurses facilitating transition' in D Kralik & A van Loon (eds) *Community nursing in Australia*, Blackwell Publishing, Melbourne, pp. 109–21.

Kralik, D, Visenttin, K & van Loon, A (2006) 'Transition: A literature review', *Journal of Advanced Nursing*, vol. 55, no. 3, pp. 320–9.

Kramer, M. (1974) *Reality shock: Why nurses leave nursing*, CV Mosby Company, St Louis.

Laschinger, HKS & Leiter, MP (2006) 'The impact of nursing work environments on patient safety outcomes', *The Journal of Nursing Administration*, vol. 36, no. 5, pp. 259–67.

Leach, M & Segal, L (2011) 'New national health and hospitals network: Building Australia's health workforce: Where is the evidence?' *Economic Papers*, vol. 29, no. 4, pp. 483–9.

Leininger, M (1995) Transcultural nursing: Concepts, theories, research and practices, McGraw-Hill and Greyden Press, New York.

Leiter, MP, Jackson, NJ & Shaughnessy, K (2009) 'Contrasting burnout, turnover intention, control, value congruence and knowledge sharing between Baby Boomers and Generation X', *Journal of Nursing Management*, vol. 17, pp. 100–9.

Levett-Jones, T & Fitzgerald, M (2005) A review of graduate nurse transition programs in Australia. *Australian Journal of Advanced Nursing*, vol. 23, no. 2, pp. 40–5.

Levett-Jones, T & Lathlean, J (2006) 'Belongingness: A montage of nursing students' stories of their clinical placement experiences, *Contemporary Nurse*, 24, pp. 162–74.

Levett-Jones, T & Lathlean, J (2008) 'Belongingness: A prerequisite for nursing students' clinical learning', *Nurse Education in Practice*, vol. 8, pp. 103–11.

Levett-Jones, T & Lathlean, J (2009) '"Don't rock the boat": Nursing students' experiences of conformity and compliance', *Nurse Education Today*, vol. 29, pp. 342–9.

Levett-Jones, T, Lathlean, J, Maguire, J & Mcmillan, M (2007) 'Belongingness: A critique of the concept and implications for nursing education', *Nurse Education Today*, 27, pp. 210–18.

Li, LC, Grimshaw, JM, Nielsen, C, Judd, M, Coyte, PC & Graham, ID (2009) 'Evolution of Wenger's concept of community of practice', *Implementation Science*, vol. 4, p. 11.

Maben, J, Latter, S & Macleod Clark, J (2006) 'The theory-practice gap: Impact of professional-bureaucratic work conflict on newly qualified nurses', *Journal of Advanced Nursing*, vol. 55, pp. 465–77.

MacIlwraith, J & Madden, B (2010) *Health care and the law*, 5th edn, Thomson Reuters (Professional) Australia Limited, Sydney.

Madsen, W (2009), 'Historical and contemporary nursing practice' in B Kozier & G Erb, *Fundamentals of nursing practice*, Pearson, *New Forest, New South Wales*, pp. 56–72.

Manojlovich, M (2007) 'Power and empowerment in nursing: Looking backward to inform the future,' *Online Journal Issues Nursing*, vol. 27, no. 1.

Marquis, BL & Huston, CJ (2012) *Leadership roles and management functions in nursing*, 7th edn, Wolters Kluwer/Lippincott Williams & Wilkins, Philadelphia.

Matthews, B, Walsh, K & Fraser, JA (2006) *Mandatory reporting of child abuse and neglect*, 13 JLM Lawbook Co., pp. 505–517.

Matthews, B, Kenny, MC (2008) Mandatory Legislation in the United States, Canada and Australia: A cross-jurisdictional review of key features, differences and issues, *Child Maltreatment*, vol. 13, no. 1, pp. 50–63.

Mayer, RM & Mayer, C (2000) 'Utilization-focused evaluation: Evaluating the effectiveness of a hospital nursing orientation program', *Journal for Nurses in Staff Development*, vol. 16, no. 5, pp. 205–8.

Meleis, AI & Trangenstein, PA (1994) 'Facilitating transitions: Redefining of the nursing mission, *Nursing Outlook*, vol. 42, pp. 255–9.

Mercer, M (2007) 'The dark side of the job: Violence in the emergency department,' *Journal of Emergency Nursing*, vol. 33, pp. 257–61.

Minchin, M (1973) *Revolutions and rosewater*, Hart Hamer, Melbourne.

Moltram, A (2009) 'Therapeutic relationships in day surgery: A grounded theory study'. *Journal of Clinical Nursing*, vol. 18, no. 20, pp. 2830–7.

Mooney, M (2007), 'Facing registration: The expectations and the unexpected', *Nurse Education Today*, vol. 27, pp. 840–7.

Morrow, S (2009) 'New graduate transitions: leaving the nest, joining the flight', *Journal of Nursing Management*, 17, pp. 278–87.

Moss, C & Chittenden, J (2008) 'Being culturally sensitive in development work' in K Manely, B Mc Cormack & V Wilson (eds) *International practice development in nursing*, Blackwell Publishing Ltd, UK, pp. 170–88.

Nash, R, Lemcke, P & Sacre, S (2009) 'Enhancing transition: An enhanced model of clinical placements for final year nursing students', *Nurse Education Today*, vol. 29, pp. 48–56.

National Health and Hospitals Commission (2009) *Health for all Australians*, Australian Government, Canberra.

National Health and Hospitals Reform Commission (2009) *A healthier future for all Australians*, final report June 2009, Commonwealth of Australia, Canberra, <www.health.gov.au/internet/main/publishing.nsf/Content/nhhrc-report>, accessed 21 September 2011.

National Health and Medical Research Council (2009) *NHMRC levels of evidence and grades for recommendations for developers of guidelines*, Australian Government, National Health and Medical Research Council, <www.nhmrc.gov.au/_files_nhmrc/file/guidelines/evidence_statement_form.pdf>, accessed 11 October 2011.

National Health Workforce Taskforce (2009) *Health workforce in Australia*, KPMG.

National Steering Committee on Patient Safety (2006), *Building a safer system: A national integrated strategy for improving patient safety in Canadian healthcare*, <www.patientsafetyinstitute.ca/patientsafety/about.html>.

Nease, B. (2009) 'Creating a successful transcultural on-boarding program', *Journal for Nurses in Staff Development*, vol. 25 no. 5, pp. 222–6.

Needleman, J & Hassmiller, S (2009) 'The role of nurses in improving hopsital quality and effciency: Real world results, *Health Affairs*, vol. 28, no. 4, pp. w6250–w633, <http://content.healthaffairs.org/content/28/4/w625.full.html>, accessed 12 June 2009.

Newman, MA (1994) *Health as expanding consciousness*, 2nd edn, National League for Nursing, publication no. 14-2626, New York.

Newton, JM & McKenna, L (2007) 'The transitional journey through the graduate tear: A focus group study', *International Journal of Nursing Studies*, 44, pp. 1231–7.

Newton, MS, Hofmeyer, A, Scott, CS, Angus, D & Harstall, C (2009a) 'More than mingling: The potential of networks in facilitating knowledge translation in healthcare', *Journal of Continuing Education in the Health Professions*, vol. 29, pp. 192–3.

Newton, JM, Kelly, CM, Kremser, AK, Jolly, B & Billett, S (2009b) 'The motivations to nurse: and exploration of factors amongst undergraduate students, registered nurses and nurse managers', *Journal of Nursing Management*, vol. 17, pp. 392–400.

Nightingale, F (1860), *Notes on nursing:What it is and what it is not*, D. Appleton & Company, New York.

Nyhan Jones, V & Woolcock, M (2009) 'Measuring the dimensions of social capital in developing countries' in E Tucker, M Viswanathan & G Walford (eds) *The Handbook of Measurement*, Sage Publications, Thousand Oaks, CA.

Nursing and Midwifery Board of Australia (2010a) *Continuing professional development registration standard*, <www.nursingmidwiferyboard.gov.au/Registration-Standards.aspx>, accessed 19 October 2011.

Nursing and Midwifery Board of Australia (2010b) *Criminal history registration standard*, <www.nursingmidwiferyboard.gov.au/Registration-Standards.aspx>, accessed 19 October 2011.

Nursing and Midwifery Board of Australia (2010c) *Recency of practice registration standard*, <www.nursingmidwiferyboard.gov.au/Registration-Standards.aspx>, accessed 19 October 2011.

Nursing and Midwifery Board of Australia (2011) *English language skills registration standard*, revised September 2011, <www.nursingmidwiferyboard.gov.au/Registration-Standards.aspx>, accessed 19 October 2011.

O'Byrne, P (2008) 'The dissection of risk: A conceptual analysis', *Nursing Inquiry*, vol. 15, no. 1, pp. 30–9.

Pairman, S & McAra-Couper, J (2010) 'Theoretical frameworks for midwifery practice' in S Pairman, S Tracy, C Thorogood & J Pincombe, *Midwifery-preparation for practice*, Elsevier, Sydney, pp. 313–26.

Papadopoulos, I (2006) *Transcultural health and social care*, Churchill Livingstone Elsevier, Edinburgh.

Pappas, AB (2009) 'Ethical issues' in JA Zwerkeh & JC Claborn, *Nursing today, transition and trends*, 6th edn, Saunders Elsevier, St Louis, Missouri.

Pelvin, B (2010) 'Life skills for midwifery practice' in S Pairman, S Tracy, C Thorogood & J Pincombe (eds) *Midwifery preparation for practice*, Elsevier, Sydney, pp. 298–309.

Pearson, H (2009) 'Transition from nursing student to staff nurse: A personal reflection', *Paediatric Nursing*, vol. 21, pp. 30–2.

Peate, I (2006) *Becoming a nurse in the 21st century*, John Wiley & Sons, UK.

Pew Health Professions Commission (1998) 'Twenty one competencies for the twenty first century', Chapter IV of *Recreating Health Professional Practice for the New Century*, the fourth report of the Pew Health Professions Commission.

Pittet, D (2005) 'Infection control and quality health care in the new millennium', *Journal of Infection Control*, vol. 33, pp. 258–67.

Pickersgill, F (1998) 'Prioritise public protection', *Nursing Standard*, vol. 12, no. 18, pp. 12–13.

Pretz, JE & Folse, VN (2011) 'Nursing experience and preference for intuition in decision making', *Journal of Clinical Nursing*, vol. 20, pp. 2878–89.

Purnell, L (2000) 'A description of the Purnell model for cultural competence', *Journal of Transcultural Nursing*, vol. 11, no. 40, pp. 40–6.

Rafferty, AM & Clarke, SP (2009) 'Editorial, Nursing workforce: A special issue', *International Journal of Nursing Studies*, vol. 46, pp. 875–8.

Ralph, C (1993) 'Regulation and the empowerment of nursing', *International Nursing Review*, vol. 40, no. 2, pp. 58–61.

Robinson, J (1995) 'The internationalization of professional regulation,' *International Nursing Review*, vol. 42, no. 6, pp. 183–6.

Roberts, D & Johnson, M (2009) 'Newly qualified nurses: Competence or confidence?' *Nurse Education Today*, vol. 29, pp. 467–8.

Rogers, AE (2008) 'Role of registered nurses in error prevention, discovery and correction' *BMJ Quality & Safety*, vol. 17, pp. 117–21.

Rogers, EM (2003) *Diffusion of innovations*, 5th edn, Free Press, New York.

Royal College of Nursing (2004) *Clinical leadership toolkit*, Royal College of Nursing, London.

Rubin, GL & Leeder, SR (2005) 'Healthcare safety: What needs to be done?' *Medical Journal of Australia*, vol. 183, no. 10, pp. 529–31.

Russell, C & Schofield T (1986) *Where it hurts*, Allen & Unwin, Sydney.

Sackett, DL, Rosenberg, WM, Gray, JM, Haynes, RB & Richardson, WS (1996) 'Evidence-based medicine: What it is and what it isn't', *British Medical Journal*, vol. 312, pp. 71–2.

Safework Australia, <www.safeworkaustralia.gov.au/swa/NewsEvents/MediaReleases>

Santuci, J (2004) 'Facilitating the transition into nursing practice', *Journal for Nurses in Staff Development*, vol. 20, no. 6, pp. 274–84.

Savickas, ML, Nota, L, Rossier, J, Dauwalder, J-P, Duarte, ME, Guichard, J, Soresi, S, Van Esbroack, R, van Vianen, AEM (2009) 'Life designing: A paradigm for career construction in the 21st century' *Journal of Vocational Behaviour*, vol. 75, pp. 239–50.

Schumacher, KL & Meleis, AI (1994) 'Transitions: A central concept in nursing,' *IMAGE: Journal of Nursing Scholarship*, vol. 26, no. 2, pp. 119–27.

Scott, C & Hofmeyer, A (2007) *Networks and social capital: A relational approach to primary healthcare reform*, Health Research Policy and Systems, <www.health-policy-systems.com/articles/browse.asp?date=&sort=&page=3>, accessed 4 January 2010.

Sheingold, BH (2009) *Measuring the extent, distribution and outcomes of social capital in the nursing community*, ProQuest Dissertation and Theses Database.

Sherman, R (2006) 'Leading a multigenerational nursing workforce: Issues, challenges and strategies' *Online J Issues Nurs*, vol. 11 no. 2, <www.medscape.com/viewarticle/536480_print>, accessed 22 May 2009.

Siviter, B (2008) *The newly qualified nurse's handbook*, Baillere Tindall Elsevier, Edinburgh.

Smedley B, Stith A & Nelson, A (eds) (2003) *Unequal treatment: Confronting racial and ethnic disparities in healthcare*, Institute of Medicine, National Academics Press, Washington, DC.

Smith, S (1999). *In pursuit of nursing excellence: A history of the Royal College of Nursing, Australia, 1949–99*, Oxford University Press, Melbourne.

South Australian Government (2011) *Social media guidance for agencies and staff*, Government of South Australia, <www.espi.sa.gov.au/files/socialmedia_guidelines.pdf>, accessed 4 October 2011.

Staunton, P & Chiarella, M (2007) *Nursing and the law*, 6th edn, Elsevier Australia, Sydney.

Stuenkely, D, Cohen, J & de la Cuesta, K (2005) 'The multigenerational workforce: Essential differences in perceptions of work environments', *Journal of Nursing Administration*, vol. 35, no. 6, pp. 283–5.

Sullivan, E & Garland, G (2010) *Practical leadership and management in nursing*, Pearson Education, England.

Thompson, GN, Estabrooks, CA & Degner, LF (2006) 'Clarifying the concepts in knowledge transfer: A literature review', *Journal of Advanced Nursing*, vol. 53, no. 6, pp. 691–701.

Throckmorton, C & Etchegaray, J (2007) 'Factors affecting incident reporting by registered nurses: the relationship of perceptions of the environment for reporting errors, knowledge of *Nursing Practice Act* and demographics on intent to report errors', *Journal of PerAnaesthesia nursing*, vol. 22, no. 6, pp. 400–12.

Tourangeau, AE & Cranley, LA (2006) 'Nurse intention to remain employed: Understanding and strengthening determinants,' *Journal of Advanced Nursing*, vol. 55, no. 4, pp. 497–509.

Tourangeau, AE, Cummings, G, Cranley, LA, Ferrone, M & Harvey, S (2010) 'Determinants of hospital nurse intention to remain employed: Broadening our understanding', *Journal of Advanced Nursing*, vol. 66, no. 1, pp. 22–32.

Van Der Weyden, MB (2005) 'The Bundaberg hospital scandal: The need to reform in Queensland and beyond' editorial in *Medical Journal of Australia*, vol. 183, pp. 284–5.

Wakefield, B, Blegen, M, Uden-Holman, T, Vaughn, T, Chrischilles, E & Wakefield, D (2001) 'Organisational culture, continuous quality improvement and medication administration error reporting', *American Journal of Medical Quality*, vol. 27, no. 4, pp. 49–55.

Wenger, E, McDermott, RA & Snyder, W (2002) *Cultivating communities of practice*, Harvard Business School Press, Boston, MA.

White, D, Suter, E, Parboosingh, J & Taylor, E (2008) 'Communities of practice: Creating opportunities to enhance quality of care and safe practices', *Healthcare Quarterly*, vol. 11, pp. 80–4.

Wilson, RM & Van Der Weyden, MB (2005) 'The safety of Australian healthcare: 10 years after QAHCS', *Medical Journal of Australia*, vol. 182, pp. 260–1.

Woolcock, M & Narayan, D (2000) 'Social capital: Implications for development theory, research, and policy,' *World Bank Research Observer*, vol. 15, pp. 225–50.

World Health Organization (2009) *Safe surgery saves lives*, <www.who.int/patientsafety/safesurgery/en/>, accessed 11 October 2011.

World Health Organization (2010) The Framework for action on inter professional education and collaborative practice. WHO Department of Human Resources for Health, Geneva.

Wray, J, Aspland, J, Gibson, H, Stimpson, A & Watson, R (2009) 'A wealth of knowledge: A survey of the employment experiences of older nurses and midwives in the NHS.' *International Journal of Nursing Studies*, vol. 46, pp. 977–85.

Yonge, O, Myrick, F & Haase, M (2002) Student nurse stress in the preceptorship experience,' *Nurse Educator*, vol. 27, no. 2, pp. 84–8.

Zetler, J (2010) 'Legal aspects of nursing' in B Kozier & G Erb, *Kozier & Erb's Fundamentals of nursing*, 1st Australasian edn, Pearson Publishing, Sydney, pp. 55–85.

Zwerekh, J & Claborn J (2009) Nursing today. Transitions and Trends. 6th edn. Saunders Elsevier, St Louis, MI.

WEBSITES

Aged Care Standards and Accreditation Agency, Ltd: **www.accreditation.org.au**

Australian Capital Territory Health Directorate: **www.health.act.gov.au**

Australian College of Midwives: **www.midwives.org.au**

Australian College of Neonatal Nurses: **www.acnn.org.au**

Australian Commission on Quality and Safety in Healthcare (ACSQHC): **www.safetyandquality.gov.au**

ACSQHC Clinical handover: **www.safetyandquality.gov.au/internet/safety/publishing.nsf/content/PriorityProgram-05#Tools**

ACSQHC Knowledge portal: **www.safetyandquality.gov.au/internet/safety/publishing.nsf/content/inforx-lp**

ACSQHC National inpatient medication chart: **www.safetyandquality.gov.au/internet/safety/publishing.nsf/content/NIMC_001**

ACSQHC patient identification advice: **www.health.gov.au/internet/safety/publishing.nsf/Content/PriorityProgram-04**

ACSQHC medication safety advice: **www.safetyandquality.gov.au/internet/safety/publishing.nsf/Content/PriorityProgram-06**

ACSQHC windows into safety and quality in healthcare: **www.safetyandquality. gov.au/internet/safety/publishing.nsf/Content/windows-into-safety-and-quality-in-health-care-2008**

Australian Commission on Safety and Quality in Healthcare's Centre for Research Excellence in Patient Safety: **www.crepatientsafety.org.au**

Australian Council on Healthcare Standards: **www.achs.org.au**

Australian Government Department of Health & Ageing: **www.health.gov.au**

Australian Government's OHS &W (Workplace Health and Safety) advice: **http:// australia.gov.au/topics/employment-and-workplace/ohs-workplace-health-and-safety**

Australian Health Practitioner Regulation Agency (AHPRA): **www.ahpra.gov.au**

Australian Health Practitioner Regulation Agency, legislation: **www.ahpra.gov. au/Legislation-and-Publications/Legislation.aspx**

Australian Nursing and Midwifery Accreditation Council Limited (ANMAC): **www.anmc.org.au**

Australian Nursing and Midwifery Council (ANMC): **http://studentweb.usq. edu.au/home/w0031419/Site2/web%20links/ANMC.htm**

Australian Nursing and Midwifery Council *Delegation and supervision for nurses and midwives*: **www.anmc.org.au/userfiles/file/guidelines_and_position_ statements/Delegation%20and%20Supervision%20for%20Nurses%20 and%20Midwives.pdf**

Australian Nursing Federation: **www.anf.org.au**

Australian Patient Safety Foundation: **https://raer.aimslive.com/Help/ View.aspx?Page=AustralianPatientSafetyFoundation**

Department of Health and Ageing *Australian immunisation handbook*: **www. health.gov.au/internet/immunise/publishing.nsf/content/handbook-home**

Department of Health & Ageing's *Corporate plan 2011–2013*: **www.health.gov. au/internet/main/publishing.nsf/Content/9F083DC3BBA88FA2CA2577F 900124CA2/$File/505-Corporate%20Plan%20H&A_concept04v9_12.1.11_ Pages_150ppi.pdf**

Department of Health and Ageing's guiding principles for medication management: **www.health.gov.au/internet/main/publishing.nsf/Content/ nmp-guide-medmgt-jul06-contents~nmp-guide-medmgt-jul06-guidepr12**

Department of Health and Ageing *Infection control guidelines*: **www.health.gov.au/ internet/main/publishing.nsf/content/icg-guidelines-index.htm**

Department of Health and Ageing's organisational chart: **www.health.gov.au/ internet/main/publishing.nsf/Content/67596E625213CBCFCA25785B0010 5B24/$File/SES_org_chart_intranet_090911.pdf**

Department of Health and Ageing, South Australia (SA Health): **www.sahealth. sa.gov.au**

Department of Health and Human Services, Tasmania: **www.dhhs.tas.gov.au**

Department of Health, New South Wales: **www.health.nsw.gov.au**

Department of Health, Northern Territory: **www.health.nt.gov.au**

Department of Health, Victoria: **www.health.vic.gov.au**

Department of Health, Western Australia: **www.health.wa.gov.au**

eHealth information: **www.yourhealth.gov.au/internet/yourhealth/publishing. nsf/Content/theme-ehealth**

Hand Hygiene Australia: **www.hha.org.au**

International Organization for Standardization (ISO): **www.iso.org**

National Healthcare Agreement (NHA): **www.coag.gov.au/intergov_ agreements/federal_financial_relations/index.cfm**

National Health and Medical Research Council's information on the regulation of health privacy in Australia: **www.nhmrc.gov.au/guidelines/publications/nh53**

Nursing Australia Stafffing Solutions FAQ: **www.nursingaustralia.com/ohs-faq.htm**

Patient safety reports: **www.patientsafetyinstitute.ca/English/research/ cpsiResearchCompetitions/2005/Documents/Weisbaum/Reports/Full Report.pdf** and **www.patientsafetyinstitute.ca/english/search/pages/default. aspx?k=%20national%20%20steeringcommittee%20on%20patient%20 safety**

Quality Improvement Council: **www.qic.org.au**

Royal College of Nursing, Australia: **www.rcna.org.au**

SA Health Advanced Incident Management Systems (AIMS): **www. safetyandquality.sa.gov.au/Default.aspx?PageContentMode=1&tabid=67** (See 'Incident management' link on the left-hand toolbar)

Safe Work Australia: **http://safeworkaustralia.gov.au/Pages/default.aspx**

Safework SA: **www.safework.sa.gov.au/**

Workers Health Centre fact sheet on sleep and shift work: **www.workershealth. com.au/facts043.html**

Index
